# Manipulation 101

# *Manipulation 101: Code of Ethics*

**Annie Mick**

# Copyright



Cover design by Josh with Pro-design-X

# Table of Contents

# Prologue

Opening the front door to uniformed men with papers in hand is a nightmare all of us wives dread. Peeking through the sidelight every time I hear car doors close out front is a habit of mine; a bad one at that. He's only injured, right? It's why we chose to live in military housing – so I would be close if I were needed. He probably broke his leg on a dive. He's waiting at the hospital for me to come get him; bring him home so I can nurse him back to health. I'll massage his shoulders, hear him moan as he rolls his neck – feel the tension release with every caress of my fingers. Hear him moan with a little more than just the caress of my fingers on his shoulders as soon as he's able. It will be good to have him home with me for more than a few days at a time.

Closing my eyes, I slip into my happy place where I picture his face; the boyish smile enhanced by dimples. The bright green eyes that soften with admiration, light with mischief, and flare with heated moments. The short blonde hair I love to run my fingers through. The voice that lights up my insides and makes my skin tingle. That first kiss every time he comes home from a long mission. The arms wrapped so tightly around me at night, as if he'll never let go. The words whispered in my ear, telling me how good it feels as he moves within me. If I stay in my happy place –

pretend – then none of this is happening.

The doorbell rings for the umpteenth time as I wrap my arms tighter around myself. My butt remains frozen to the spot on the floor where I've sunk; my body rocking as I hug myself in fear, as if I don't get up, this moment in time is a blip, a mistake. Maybe if I don't answer, they'll go away and everything will be all right.

"Mrs. Arkelpaine," the voice from the other side of the door echoes in my ears. "We know you're home. Please open the door."

If you were to ask me what they look like, I couldn't tell you. They're like any other uniformed officers with a note in their hand; nameless, faceless voices laced with pity.

The chaplain sits with me on the sofa, his voice droning on in an effort to give comfort. I was always taught to be polite, mind my manners. Lucky for him, I guess, because all I want to do is scream bloody murder. Order him and his cohorts out of my house, let me die on the inside in peace.

A helicopter crash. Exploded before it hit the ground because it was shot down and the gas tank blew up. Does it get any worse than this? Well, yeah, I guess it does. Not only have I lost my husband, but I have no remains to bury. I can't even tell him goodbye. I'll never hold him again, I'll never be able to touch him. There were six men on the chopper. God only knows if the ashes – should they be able to collect any – will be his.

I barely make it to the toilet before the contents of my stomach are emptied into it. I'd like to think I cleaned up after myself, but I can't say that, because the last thing I remember is heaving over the bowl and the next thing I know, I'm waking up with two of the other military wives from the base sitting around me on the edge of my bed.

"Your family is on their way," Tessa says softly, holding one hand.

"They'll be here soon, Sasha," Maddie adds, holding the other.

Don't get me wrong. I love my family. But they're not what I need right now. I need my husband to come home, make this all go away – tell me it was only a nightmare. I need to feel his arms around me and hear him whisper, *"It was only a dream, Sassy. I'm right here."*

# ANNIE MICK

# Chapter 1

## Sasha

My mom and dad, sister Jolie, brother Trent, and my three best friends have all helped me get the house packed up. The moving truck is on its way out and my SUV sits waiting in the drive.

"The sooner we get you out of here," Trent reassures me as he places his arm over my shoulder, "the sooner we can put your pieces back together."

My eyes fill with tears once more as I swallow hard and hold back another sob. "What are you going to fill the hole in my heart with?"

He squeezes tighter and breathes a sad sigh. "It's a puzzle, Sash. One day, one step, one piece at a time. We gotcha."

Jolie steps between us and takes me in a hug. "You know you're more than welcome to come and stay with us. The kids would love it. Bart has already said he's more than happy to have you with us. We have plenty of room. You can write all you want. The kids won't bother you during the day, I promise. Sasha, come back with me."

The thought of three kids – no matter how much I love them – running through the house, shouting at the top of their lungs, makes me want to reach for the nearest bottle and pour. And I'm not even a drinker! Those plans were years down the road for Ben and me – at least a couple. And our plans were to have them one at a time.

Going back home to Tennessee with any of my family is not an option. They know it, I know it. Going back home at all isn't an option. Everyone there knows who I am. The controversy surrounding the crash and the lack of anonymity for me makes it a no-brainer. To the literary world, I'm Sara Paine. To all of our friends and family, I'm Sasha Arkelpaine. But as of next week, I will become Sasha Taylor . . . again. To my Big Ben, I was his Little Sassy. It warms my heart as it echoes in my mind and *breaks* my heart knowing I will never hear it again.

"Tennessee isn't big enough, Jo."

"But South Carolina?" she nearly howls. "It's so far, Sash. Why?"

"It's where the girls are. They're my team, Jo. We may as well stay together. The only reason we weren't before is because I was on the base. You know that."

"We're your team too!" she cries.

"You know what I mean." I reach for her stiff shoulders and hold them firmly. "They're my work team. You're my family. And unfortunately, you still live in a town that's going to be up in my business from sunup to sundown. I can't take that."

She sniffles and swipes her nose with the back of her hand. "They're more than your work team. They're your best friends."

"You're still my best friend too," I whisper.

"But not your bestest best," she whines, then waves a hand toward the girls where they stand waiting for me. "And they're so . . . so single."

I ignore the sharp pain that strikes in my chest at her comment – I rejoined their rank two weeks ago. "It's not my fault you married Brat."

She slaps my arm lightly and scowls. "It's Bart!"

"If you say so, sis." I chuckle and pull her into a tight hug. "Come visit. Leave the kids with Brat. You can be single for a while and we'll drink Mai Tais all day long."

She won't visit. We both know it, and that's okay. It's how we roll. The only reason she's standing here with me right now is because Trent would have kicked *Brat's* ass to kingdom come had he hesitated for one moment to kiss her goodbye, reassure her he would keep everything under control at home, and make sure the kids were well cared for while she was gone. He's not a bad guy, per se. He's like a shot of espresso when your preference is cappuccino. Too bold, a tad bitter, and a whole lot obnoxious. I'm sure she precooked the meals before she left and his mommy will heat them every night for him and the kids. Cold cereal for breakfast and cold meat sandwiches for lunch will suffice. Carryout pizza if his mom has bingo night. He loves her, loves his kids, treats them well, holds a job. Not exactly Prince Charming but he could hold a candle to Archie Bunker, sans the bigotry of course.

"You'll check in tonight as soon as you get to the hotel?" Dad wraps his arm around my shoulders and kisses the top of my head. It's not really a question, though it is stated with love. He insisted we stay at a hotel tonight instead of making the trip in one nine-hour drive. We could easily alternate drivers, but he made the hotel reservations himself and, like all good girls do, we are abiding by the rules set down by my father.

"I will," I reassure him as I squeeze his middle a little tighter.

"If your mom and I could take this pain away, we'd do it in a heartbeat, sweetheart," he murmurs.

"I know, dad." I nod against his chest, leaving more damp spots on his shirt as my eyes leak salty tears. "Thanks for being here."

My mom cries as hard or harder than I do as she pulls me in for one last heartfelt hug. "This is just so wrong. He loved you so much." She takes my face in her palms and holds my gaze. "You are going to be okay. You hear me?"

I nod shakily. "Yeah, mom. I hear you."

She arches a brow the way only a mother can. "But do you believe me?"

Another tear falls and I sniffle. "I'm trying."

"You lived a great love story, Sasha – albeit a short one." She squeezes my cheeks a little firmer. "Now, write about it when you're ready. I look forward to reading it when you're done."

A low dramatic groan from my brother sounds from behind us before Trent says, "You can spare us the sex scenes in that one."

Leaving on a high note. This is my family. It's how we say goodbye . . . until we meet again.

*Myrtle Beach, South Carolina: Here I Come.*

# Chapter 2

## Sasha

"You want to take the coastal highway for a bit or jump on the interstate right away?" Sky asks me as we leave Fort Pierce. The coastal highway is the scenic route. The interstate is inland and looks pretty much like any other in the country. She's giving me the choice. I'll be looking out at the ocean everyday where we're going if I choose to do so. She's simply making conversation.

I stare out the window on the passenger's side, taking in the last views I plan to see in the state of Florida. I can't imagine ever wanting to come back here. There's a group of sailors jogging on the beach; navy shorts, gray T-shirts emblazoned with the four letters of the branch of service they proudly represent. It's mid-morning and the sticky humidity leaves their shirts nothing more than wet rags covering even wetter skin.

Rhea's wistful sigh rings from the backseat. "My God, if I had lived down here, I'd have never gotten any work done. Who needs an ocean view when you can . . . Holy shit!" she shrieks suddenly. "I don't think that one is wearing a jock strap! Talk about letting it all hang out."

The sound of the slap on her arm snaps through the air.

"Stop it," Shae scolds her with a low whisper. "Too soon."

Rhea huffs loudly, "You're just pissed because you're sitting on the wrong side of the car."

Sky groans next to me as she presses the gas pedal harder. "I-95 it is."

I roll my eyes and shoot her a wry look. "Because of me or because of the wet spot you're afraid Rhea might leave on the seat?"

After an uncomfortable interval of dead silence, Shae finally chirps, "Was that a quip from our own beloved Sasha?"

Holding my hand up and tilting it back and forth, I scrunch my nose, fighting the burn behind my eyes. "I'm getting there. If I were a true friend, I'd offer to have Sky pull over and let you get your fill before we leave."

"Could we?" Rhea bounces behind me enthusiastically and grabs the back of my seat. "I haven't been filled in . . ."

"Sit back and shut up or I'm going to make you sit on a towel!" Shae grouses, though she does lean back and take advantage of the open spot for viewing while she has the chance.
These are my best friends:

*Skylar Morell.* My editor and agent. Deadpanner extraordinaire. One-line wonder. Severe, all business when necessary, but one of the most compassionate people you could ever meet. Legs that go on for miles – tall – a butt that proves squats really do pay off, a face that can actually draw men's eyes away from her chest – at least for a little while – blue eyes reminiscent of the Mediterranean sea, chestnut hair that wig companies would pay a fortune for, and a heart that's been broken more times than I can count, but only because she gives it so freely.

*Shae Purcell.* My public relations manager. Brilliant, bulldog, straight-man – well, woman. You know what I mean. She's bold, works like she's on a 24-hour caffeine buzz, and cracks a whip like a dominatrix – I haven't asked her, and quite frankly, I don't want to know. She's beautiful, legs that go on for yards – average height – soulful heather eyes with gold flecks, and red hair that makes one question if her personality comes from the fiery tresses that flow down her back.

*Rhea Daniels*. My street team manager. Methodically ditzy. She's a genius. The easy target of blonde jokes until she squares you with a look searing enough to shrink a man like a cold shower or humiliate a woman caught in the salon with her hair in foils. She can reel off equations that would have made Albert Einstein squirm. Legs that go on for only a few feet – she's petite. Eyes as blue as sapphires and lips that men stare at when she speaks, because all it takes is one "Eyes up here, dickhead!" when they're homed in on her ample chest. If she really wants to humiliate them, it's "The cleavage is nothing. My nipples are awesome. But since you're not going to see them, look at my face!"

Our friendships didn't develop through our business relationships. No, our friendships developed in grade school. We're all from the blink-and-you'll-miss-it town of Shockemall, Tennessee. Our plan when we left for college was to do just that; shock 'em all. We haven't put too much emphasis on it in the last ten years though. We've been too busy working. The past is the past, and our present and future have been too bright to look back.

We spent years retraining our voices to shake the heavy southern accents; refining our girly giggles into sophisticated, charmed chuckles. Unless of course we're alone or with close friends. Public drinking is limited to one or two glasses of wine. We are professionals first. And let me tell you, there is nothing like a southern belle with too many spirits *in* her to cause her spirits to rise and bubble *out* of her. There is no corralling the horse once the gate is open. Those girls at the rodeos down south are not screaming "Ride 'em cowboy!" They're screaming "Let me ride you, cowboy!"

*Shameless.*

One snack run, a stop for gas – though I don't know why – three bouts of tears, and numerous conversations, we pull into the hotel parking lot in St. Augustine. It's four o'clock in the afternoon. We could have easily made the entire trip in one day.

"Why are we doing this?" I run my hands through my hair as I drop my head back onto the seat. "It would have been so much easier to drive all the way and get it over with."

Shae reaches over from the driver's seat and places her hand on my leg, dipping her chin. "Because we promised your dad. He wants us well rested in order to drive safely."

I don't care about rest. I haven't slept in weeks. I pass out due to physical need and wake up in sweats. When I close my eyes, all I can picture is a helicopter exploding or the face I will never see again. I get sick when I imagine the terror in my husband's eyes. I hear the voice I know will fade with time. I've listened to his messages on my phone so many times over the last two weeks, I have them memorized word for word. I've pulled my phone out so many times so I can see his picture on the screen, I might just as well not set it down.

"I'll rest when I'm dead," I mutter without thinking.

"Good to know," Sky grumbles, throwing her door open behind me. She opens my door on the front passenger side and extends her hand. "Because we've got a shitload of work ahead of us and you're a long way from dying. Ben may have loved your company, but I'm sure he wasn't looking forward to sharing it in the afterlife until you were both in your nineties." She prods with a wave of her fingers. "Come on. He'll be waiting for you, sweetie. You've got a lot of life yet to live here."

"I want him here!" I bellow, my body rocking against the shoulder belt still holding me in my seat. "I don't care about an afterlife. I want the now life. The one those bastards took from us!"

She leans in and takes me in a hug. "Oh, Sash. I don't have the words to fix this. There aren't any. We can't fix it, we can only be here. Let us be here for you."

My other two besties join us and they gently pull me from the vehicle and we make our way into the hotel. The key cards are ready at the front desk and Sky and Shae check us in. Adjoining rooms, two queens in each, a sofa, table and chairs, and a big screen TV. My dad and his accommodations.

A bouquet of flowers and an envelope with my name on it sits on the table.

*My dear daughter Sasha,*

*I cannot say this is a new beginning for you. It doesn't seem right to say begin again. You don't begin again with experience like yours. You move forward. It's the only way to go, sweetheart. You are so strong. I know you relied on Ben for a lot; moral support, comfort, love. But he relied on you, too. He told me once you were his greatest gift. It may be hard to believe today, but the pain will lessen over time. Be his gift still. Don't let this crush your spirit. Ben would hate that for you. Don't let it temper your sass. It's what he loved most. Listen to your old man, he's been around the block a time or two. Call whenever you need me.*
*All my love,*
*Dad*

Tears spill from my eyes freely, and I let them. This is the last time, I tell myself. Though I know it's a lie. I've cried oceans over the last two weeks. I've never hated before in my life. The men that shot that ground rocket in the air, aiming for the helicopter that carried my husband and his fellow SEALs will pay. As soon as the SEALs find them. It's not my job. I doubt they'll ever tell me when it happens. But it will happen. Their allegiance to each other is unbreakable and has no limits. One day when they least expect it . . .

"Dinner in?" I look to the other three as I set the note back down on the table.

Sky slides her arm in mine. "Not a chance. There's a restaurant downstairs with a reservation in our name. Surf and turf awaits. Choose your own critter. Huge tank. Peaches and cream cake. Your favorite."

Rhea gasps. "I gotta pick my own lobster? You know I hate that. Those beady little eyes staring at me!" She shudders dramatically. "Ewwww!"

Sky smirks. "Would you rather try to catch crabs?"

Rhea taps her chin and narrow her eyes before grinning impishly. "They have fast remedies these days. Do I get to choose the critter that gives them to me?"

"Oh my God," Shae groans, snatching Rhea's elbow and dragging her toward the door. "Shut up or we'll throw you out into the water and make you ride a dolphin to South Carolina."

"Awesome!" Rhea shrieks. "Did you know some of them have nine-foot dongs?"

"Put a gag on her!" Sky shouts before they're out the door. "And don't let them give her any liquor!"

We head for the door behind them. "It's gonna be okay, Sash."

"It's never going to be okay, Sky." I cross the threshold and step out into the hall. "But it will be bearable with you guys around."

The door closes behind her and she double checks to assure it is locked before she wraps her arm around my shoulder. "You'll always have us around."

Two bodies come up behind us unexpectedly, one on each side, and hook elbows with ours – literally taking up the entire width of the hallway.

"Ready?" Rhea asks as she takes a long forward sidestep to the left, pushing Sky towards me, and Shae takes a sidestep to the left, pulling me away from Sky. Had we not done this a thousand and one times before, we'd likely be on our asses by now. But as is the routine, they all follow by taking the next lengthy forward sidestep to the right, pulling me with them, and start skipping and singing, "We're off to the see the wizard" as we make our way down the hall toward the elevator.

We did it when Shae lost her mom, when Rhea lost her granddad, when Sky lost her brother, etc. We never have found the wizard, nor have we ever found Oz. I'll never look at a rainbow again with any ray of hope. They're reflections of light, that's all. There is no pot of gold at the end.

Tonight, we're a group of women in our late twenties, going on thirteen.

And by midnight, I'm sure my pillow will be soaked with tears I thought I'd run out of. Funny thing about tears; the well never runs dry.

# *Fort Pierce*
## *Earlier that same day*

"She's already gone, Cap. The other wives said she and her family left this morning."

"Find her and get the dog delivered. It's bad enough the whole unit wasn't there for his service. We owe it to Commander Arkelpaine."

"Sir, I'm not sure where to start."

"Call Ben's parents. You've got their information. They'll know how to find her. You've got 48 hours. Show me what you're made of."

"I'll do my best, Cap."

"Failure is not an option, Lieutenant. Get that dog to Mrs. Arkelpaine. Don't come back to the base until you do." Cap sighs. "And Berkel?"

"Yes, sir?"

"Thank you."

# Chapter 3

## Sasha

The phone on the nightstand buzzes before the sun shines through the window. We left the curtain cracked before we went to bed so we wouldn't sleep too late this morning. My goal was to get an early start and get this trip out of the way. The sooner I find a place to land, the sooner I can start rebuilding my life.

Glancing at the screen, I see my dad's face. Sky groans from the bed on the other side of the room. "Everything okay?"

"Dad?" I answer with a swipe of the screen.

"Hey, sweetheart. Tell me you're still in St. Augustine."

"Uh." I shake my head in an effort to collect a morning thought and blink fast to shed some sleep from my eyes. "Yeah?"

"You sure about that, Sasha?" He chuckles.

I glance around the hotel room and eye Sky who is now sitting on the edge of her bed, head in her hands, looking a bit worse for wear. "We're in St. Augustine, right?"

She narrows one eye and scowls. "Unless we rode that dolphin Rhea was so dead set on, yes."

Aha. I remember now. Sex on the beach – the drinks – not the act. Note to self: never let Rhea drink sexually suggestive alcohol.

"Yes, dad. We're in St. Augustine."

"Good. Stay put. There will be a delivery to you in about an hour. I'm not quite sure what to make of it myself, but instructions are to meet the man in front of the hotel."

I hop out of bed, nearly tripping over the sheet rolled around my feet. "What?! A man? An hour? What delivery?"

"Sasha," he explains in his very *dad* voice. "I would never put you in a precarious situation. You call me after everything and let me know what you want to do, okay?"

"Dad, what is . . ."

"Call me. I love you." He disconnects, leaving me stunned and staring at the phone in my hand.

"What was that about?" Sky asks.

I turn to look at her, my face screwed into fifty shades of doubt and unsurety. "Gotta grab a shower. Then I'm going to meet a man out front."

She jumps off the bed, nearly face planting as her feet get caught on the blanket hanging off the edge. "You're what? What man?"

"If you want to join me, hurry up and call down for coffee and bagels." I turn and grimace, shaking my head. "I meant to meet the man, not the shower. You're not really my type. I'll be out in ten."

As I close the door to the bathroom, I hear her yell, "Shae, Rhea! Get up! As usual, nothing can be normal. We gotta roll."

* * *

Four showers, coffee, bagels, and an hour later we all walk out of the hotel and see a camouflage Hummer parked curbside at the guest check-in lane. The girls and I exchange puzzled glances before a soldier in fatigues exits the vehicle and rounds the back where he opens it and extracts a dog. Not just any dog though. A beautiful Belgian Malinois. He's black faced, large pointy ears on full alert, nearly adult but a little clumsy still, not quite fully grown into his huge paws.

"Hot damn," Skylar whispers next to me, though I know she's not talking about the dog. She's eyeing the tank of a man holding onto it. "Why do I suddenly want to get sweaty right after a shower?"

"Sweet Jesus," Shae mutters. "Forgive me for the indecent thoughts I am having about that man right now. I want to climb that wall and stay perched on the top for a while before I descend the backside slowly. I'll bet he has a butt like granite."

Rhea doesn't miss a beat as she walks toward him, swaying her hips in time with a song that isn't playing at the current time. She marches to the beat of a different drum. We call it the music of lust and lunacy. No notes needed, just the rhythm.

The dog takes a defensive stance and growls. "Ma'am, I need you to stay back," the soldier warns.

"Oh, please." She laughs, pressing a hand to her chest. "He's not going to bite me any harder than I'll bite you."

The dog barks loudly and pulls at the leash. "Heel," the soldier orders as he tugs back on the leash. The dog immediately obeys and sits by his side. "Ma'am," the disciplined, unblinking, concrete-jawed soldier says. "I'm looking for Mrs. Benjamin Arkelpaine."

The pang in my chest is sharp as I know today is the last day I will hear that reference to me. After today I am Sasha Taylor. The controversy cannot follow me. I love my name, but the constant badgering would be unbearable. Let the press get ahold of this and my brand will forever be connected to the helicopter crash. The pain will be mine and my loved ones' to carry. That's enough. Daily reminders aren't necessary.

I step closer, Sky and Shae close behind me. "I'm her. What can I help you with?" The dog doesn't seem agitated with my closeness. In fact, his nose tips up and he sniffs the air as if my presence has triggered something. He whines softly and rises to all four legs, looking to the soldier as if asking permission.

The man grins proudly, drops the leash, gives a hand signal to the dog, waving him toward me and praises and orders at the same time, "Good boy. Guard Sassy."

My breath is literally sucked from my lungs; the crushing emotions overwhelming every sense in my body. My knees buckle and Sky and Shae try to prevent my fall, but it's the dog who breaks it as he leaps forward and slides his body beneath mine – like a baseball player trying to hit home before the catcher can tag him. He's warm, fuzzy, gentle. I study his face for a long moment as the shape of a contrasting light brown heart against the black bridge of his nose captures my attention, and I bury my face in his coat. A beating heart beneath my hands.

*Oh God, Ben, what have you done?*

They leave us be for who knows how long, my new companion and me. My nose buried in his coat, him patiently waiting for me to get through a new crying jag. I slowly rise to my feet and brush a few dog hairs from my clothes. "Okay," I say with feigned resolve. "I'm done. What now?"

"Commander Arkelpaine left all information from his prior training and instructions for any further training in this packet, ma'am. His vaccination records and AKC registration are in there as well." He hands over a large manilla envelope after we've made our way to the Hummer. "I'll load his food and kennel into your vehicle for you. The kennel folds down so it should fit."

"Did you know him? My husband?" I ask on a sniffle.

He nods and lowers his head. "He was one of the best men I've ever known." He raises his eyes and speaks softly. "We all felt it when we lost him. He always said he loved his job, but he adored his wife. You were his favorite subject, ma'am. I am very sorry for your loss, Mrs. Arkelpaine."

"Thank you."

"There's a letter in that packet for you. Ben wrote it a long time ago when he started training the dog. He never did anything without a purpose."

"What's his name? The dog?"

He smiles sheepishly. "It's all in the packet, Mrs. Arkelpaine."

"What if I have questions? What if I have problems?"

He reassures me once more as he extends his hand to shake mine, "Lieutenant Berkel. It's all in the packet, ma'am. You'll do fine. It was an honor to serve with Ben. Take care."

Rhea calls out as he turns to leave, "Lieutenant, would you walk a little slower? I don't often get a view like this. Mm, mm, mm. So fine."

I swear I see the man blush before he smirks and shakes his head. "Have a safe trip, ladies." He swings up and into the driver's seat like it's second nature and starts the vehicle. It roars to life and his shadowed face lights with a smile showing perfectly straight pearly white teeth as he slides his aviators on.

I turn to see three jaws gaping as they watch him drive away. I roll my eyes and grasp Rhea's elbow. "One animal drooling at a time is enough. Let's go."

## *Fort Pierce*
### *One hour later*

"Delivered to his charge, Cap."

"Did the dog respond as expected?"

"Commander Arkelpaine would be serving that dog a porterhouse, sir."

Cap sighs heavily. "You were one of only a few he trusted, Lieutenant."

"Just doing my job, sir."

"You did it well, Berkel. The Commander would be proud. Get back to base."

# ANNIE MICK

# Chapter 4

## Sasha

"So who's gonna ride in the back with Mr. Chompers?" Rhea asks as we load our luggage into the SUV.

I have no idea what the dog's name is; I haven't opened the packet yet. I truly doubt it's Mr. Chompers, though. My intention is to open the packet in private. There is more than instructions and registration papers in there.

We were able to sneak him into the hotel by way of the back doors and up the stairs with two lookouts in front and one in the back while I took him up. He really is well behaved. He hasn't left my side since being dropped off. It's like he's waiting for me to tell him what to do. If I had any ideas I would oblige him, but as it is, I'm lost.

"He's not riding in the back," Shae answers Rhea indignantly. "He's hung. You're simply hungover. He's in the front passenger seat all the way home." She turns to me and scrunches her nose. "Unless you think he can drive. He does seem to be pretty smart."

Walking the dog to the grassy area next to the parking lot, I look over my shoulder. "I'll ride in the back with him." I jiggle his leash and raise my brows as I look to the dog and point my free finger. "You need to pee before we hit the road." He looks at me, questioning as he tilts his head. "Pee," I order my new furry friend. Imagining a command a sailor might use, I chance, "Squat, lift, piss?" Spotting a palm tree approximately thirty feet away, we walk to it. He circles the edge as he sniffs for a few seconds, lifts his hind leg and empties his bladder.

I squeal with glee and pat him on the head. "Good boy!"

"What did he do?" Sky inquires, tossing her overnight bag in the back.

"He peed!" I exclaim proudly as we walk back to the SUV.

"Uh, uh, uh," she says, holding a finger up. "Not so fast, proud mama. Did he pass the real test?"

"What test?"

"Did he put the seat back down?"

I shoot her a wry grin. "Baby steps, Sky. Baby steps."

* * *

Four hours later we pull into the drive of my temporary residence – Sky's home. Shae's and Rhea's cars are lined up in the driveway, awaiting their arrival.

"Are you sure you're okay with having a four-legged guest? It's not exactly how we planned it."

Sky shrugs casually before opening the door to my car. "What have we always said about the best laid plans, Sasha? Besides, I kinda like the big guy."

"I do too," Shae adds from where she sits on the other side of the dog in the backseat. "I thought he might slobber, but I've had boyfriends who drooled more than he does. He smells better too and isn't as hairy as some of them were. Man, if we could teach him to cook and clean house, we'd have the perfect boyfriend. Vibrators could take care of the rest."

Rhea sighs from the front passenger seat. "I'll bet Lieutenant Berkel cooks and cleans house. Damn, the things I could do with a Navy SEAL."

Shae scoffs and clicks her tongue. "Fodder for your dreams,

Rhea. Just keep a fresh supply of batteries."

We unload our belongings and Shae and Rhea toss their suitcases into their cars. The movers have already been here and gone. Sky's parents met them to instruct what to leave here and what to move to the storage garage. They reassured us via text that the move went smoothly and they were at both places to oversee everything.

We make tentative plans to meet later this week and say our goodbyes in the driveway. Sky unlocks and opens the front door, but before she can get to the alarm to turn it off, the dog runs in ahead of us, charging through as if he owns the place.

"Hey!" she yells. "Wait a minute, mutt! This is my house."

"Hang on," I shush her. I've seen these dogs in action. They're duty dogs and if trained properly, they're on a mission 24 hours a day – to protect and serve. "I think he's scouting."

"Scouting?" she asks. "Scouting what?"

"The house," I reply. "He's checking things out before we go in to make sure it's safe."

"That's why I have an alarm," she huffs. "If anything had been broken into, the company would have been notified and called the police."

I watch as the dog returns to where we stand. As God as my witness, if dogs could puff their chests, that's what this one is doing right now as he sits in front of me and nudges my hand with his nose – giving me an 'all clear' to enter.

We move our suitcases to our respective rooms, unload our laundry into baskets and the clean clothes into the wardrobes. The boxes of things I wanted to have on hand are already in the room for me to tackle over the next couple days. The bed for the dog lies next to mine, though he hasn't tested it. I haven't unfolded his kennel yet – it took both of us to haul it inside. There's a comfortable cushion that goes inside of it. It has to be nearly six inches thick and looks like it's been handsewn and is soft. He's a little leery of what's going on but seems most comfortable by my side. If I'm uncomfortable with what's going on, I can't imagine how hard this must be for him. I'm out of my element with people I know. Poor creature is out of his element with people he's never met. I need to delve into that packet right after dinner.

Sky and I grill fish and veggies for dinner and sit outside on the patio while the dog lays at my feet. There's a large yard spread before us and this poor dog lays at my feet. He ate his food okay. He drank plenty. I offered him one of his treats, but he turned it down.

"This is crazy," I say, rising from my Adirondack chair. "He's not even fully grown yet. He needs exercise. I'm going to go see if there are any toys in his bag." As I open the patio slider, I feel the wet nose on the back of my calf. "Come on, boy. Maybe you can choose what you want to play with."

I open the duffel the lieutenant had placed in the back of my SUV. Inside is a large frisbee, a rope chew toy, two rawhide chews that look more like femur bones, and a flat black box with a ribbon tied around it. All thoughts of what I originally came in here for fly out the window as I home in on the black box and lift it out of the duffel bag. I slide the ribbon off and separate the top from the bottom of the box with shaky hands. At that moment, the dog chooses to edge closer and lay his chin on my forearm. Inside the box lies a picture of my dead husband and the dog that is currently by my side. Ben's smile is the one I lived for.

The one I'd see every time he'd come home.

Every time he'd pick me up and spin me around and hold me close.

The day we married and he said, "Now you gotta kiss me whenever I want."

Every time his eyes gleamed with the promise of a night of passion.

Every time he'd say, "I am the luckiest bastard on the face of the earth."

There's a note neatly folded in the bottom of the box under the picture.

*My darling wife,*
*Love of my life, light of my world, my sunshine. If you're reading*

*this, you know by now what it means. I didn't make it home to you this time, Sassy. What I wouldn't give to hold you right now, wipe away your tears, make love to you better than the last time, just one more time. You made loving you so easy, so amazing. You were my greatest gift, Sasha. We knew there was a chance of this happening. I know you have your friends but I wanted to leave you with a little someone to keep you company and keep you safe as you move forward. You do need to move on, Sass. Your heart is too big not to. You can never love too much. You're not leaving me behind – I'll find you someday in the afterlife. No rush, baby.*

*His name is Oscar. It means "Champion Warrior". I was going to name him Beau, but that means handsome and you already had that with me. Didn't want to give the poor guy competition before he even got started. (wink)*

*By the way, if you're wondering why he's taken to you so quickly and knew exactly who you were when Berkel dropped him off, you can either believe in fate or... tear open the handsewn cushion in his kennel or the bottom of his bed. Confession: The washing machine wasn't eating your panties, love. Nor was it eating some of your odds and ends T-shirts and tank tops. I stole them before they made it to the machine. (you suspected I was being a perv, didn't ya?) He's known your scent as much as he's known mine. He's slept with your clothing every night since he was a pup. He's heard your name every day a dozen times or more when I used it as a command. We talked about you often. He knows how I felt about you and how to honor that.*

*He's a good dog, Sass. Smart too. But like all animals, he needs guidance and discipline. I know you can do it. He will be your best friend and I can rest in peace knowing you have a loyal and protective companion. I've left all instructions, training commands, and any recommendations I could think of for you. If you have any problems, I've also left Lieutenant Berkel's contact information for you. Just watch out for him. He's a flirt and your friends are just his type. He'd never take advantage of you, though. The SEALs have a code: touching a comrade's wife is unacceptable and unforgivable.*

*If I could change anything, my darling Sasha, it would be to love you longer, love you harder, love you better. I couldn't possibly love you more. You owned my whole heart, still do, always will.*

*Don't lose your sass, baby. Tell your stories, live long and well, love hard and strong. I'll be waiting. I'm not going anywhere.*

*I loved you before I ever knew you in this life. I'll know you as soon as I see you in the next. I'll blow you kisses in the wind and toss you winks with twinkles in the stars.*
*Don't be afraid to love again, Sassy. Nobody does it better than you do.*

*All my (undying) love,*
*Ben*

My sobs are muffled by the fur I bury my face in. I want to scream and throw things. I want to hit something, but I have no idea what. We both knew the risks, the odds. But knowing and accepting are worlds apart, and my world has fallen apart.

I remove my arm from under the dog's chin and wrap it around his neck. "Oscar, huh?" I breathe through a sniffle as I pet his head with my other hand. He raises his sharp, black snout and I feel his tongue on my cheek as he licks away my fallen tears.

Sky drops to her knees beside me. "Oscar's a good name. Strong, manly." She rolls onto her butt and sits, pondering a thought as she looks to the ceiling and nods. "Rhea can only do so much damage with that." She scrunches her nose and shrugs. "At least he's not a wiener dog."

Oscar lets out a slow, soft growl. "Hey!" Sky scowls at him, cowering behind me. "It's not my fault they set you up for failure from the beginning."

"Would you not tease him?" I scold.

She double checks the laces of her tennis shoes before she rises to her feet, tugging the hem of her T-shirt, ready to bolt from the room. I see it coming. I know she's doing it for my benefit; the gloom and doom mood has been hanging in the air for days on end.

She sticks her tongue out at the dog sitting proudly next to me before she points her finger at him, sways her hips and sings – badly I might add, "Oh you wish you were an Oscar Meyer wiener," before she runs for the stairs.

Oscar takes two leaps to get to the base of the stairs and two more to make it to the top . . . where he turns and waits for Sky to join him. Good thing she has a wide staircase. First lesson for Oscar: either wait at the bottom or go first after being granted permission. Don't need any accidents.

"Ahhhh!" she shrieks, stopping on the third step from the top. "How did you get up there?"

She'll learn. These dogs are sleek, stealth, and amazingly athletic. They climb walls for Pete's sake. Oscar stands at the top of the stairs, chin tucked in challenge, strong stance on all fours as if to say, '*I dare you*'.

Sky turns to me and huffs, "A little help here?"

I shrug and grin. "Apologize."

"You're kidding! To a dog?" I arch a brow and incline my chin. "Fine!" She scowls and turns to my new bestie. "I'm sorry. No more wiener jokes."

"Oscar," I call to him. "Come." He immediately obeys and carefully makes his way around Sky and down to me where he lays down by my side.

Sky slowly walks back down the stairs and stands at the bottom. "Can I get him to do that? If we're going to be staying in the same house, he should probably get used to me too."

"Call him, see what happens."

She singsongs his name ever so gently, "Oscar, come over here." The canine looks to me as if confused. I can't order him, he has to learn on his own that Sky is in charge as well. But she also has to learn that he's not a baby. "See!" she huffs, "he won't listen to me."

"Call him sternly," I instruct her.

She scrunches her nose. "Why would I do that? His name is Oscar."

I heave a deep sigh and roll my eyes. I have *got* to find a place of my own.

# Chapter 5

## Sasha

"You've got to get out of the house," Rhea says, pouring her second cup of coffee. "You look like hell, the most sunshine you get is walking the hairball over there and throwing a ball in the backyard, and . . ." she pauses, eyeing me curiously, ". . . when is the last time you had a haircut?"

She's right. I do look like hell. My nails are chipped and scraggly. I haven't put on makeup since I can't remember when. I have more split ends than not. My leg hair is giving Sasquatch competition and Europe would be cheering for my armpits. But hey! I bathe. Well, at least every other day. I think. And with that thought, I surreptitiously lift my arm and dip my nose, sniffing the evidence. Huh, must be the day I'm due.

I've been in this house for two months now – renting with the option to buy, should I so choose. So far, it's looking less likely with each passing day. It's a nice home, comfortable, lots of yard for Oscar, but so far the only voice in it has been mine – more on that later. I managed to polish the manuscript I was working on before Ben died, but only because I had already written "The End" and only had a few edits to make. I haven't managed to write anything other than scratch out lame ideas for a couple new ones. I feel like a failure every time I open my laptop, every time I pick up my notepad and pen. My clothes are getting baggier, my skin is pale, my ambition is nonexistent, my enthusiasm null and void. I'm letting my team down. Even my dog is depressed. But he is so well behaved. I've followed all of the instructions to continue proper training. His exercise course in the backyard is topnotch and he runs it every day, three to four times . . . perfectly.

"Move it," Rhea orders, swiping my coffee cup off the counter, placing it in the dishwasher after rinsing it in the sink. "Go wash the stink off. Sky and Shae are meeting us at the spa. It's time to get your life back on track, Sasha. Ben died, you didn't. You've got one hour. I'll let Chompers out to do his duty."

"I don't want to go to the spa," I whine. "I've got too much to do and putting lipstick on a pig is not going to change anything!"

She narrows her eyes so tightly I can barely see her pupils. She takes one long deep breath and lets it out slowly. "If I ever hear you say something like that again, I will slap you so hard you'll be talking out the side of your face for a week. Go get in the shower. Do not pass go, do not stop to collect two hundred dollars, do not go to jail . . ." *All references to the monopoly game.* ". . . and get your ass back down here. You have a book signing in five days, *Sara Paine.* We're relaunching a couple as well as launching the new one."

"What?!" My shriek is enough to make Oscar jump from his position next to me. "Why didn't you say something before now?"

"I did," she enunciates sharply. "And I'm doing it again, now. It's in Charleston on Saturday."

"But…but what about Oscar? Who's going to take care of him while I'm gone?"

"Nobody," she replies. "Oscar goes where you go. He's a service dog. Those certification papers and harness apply to anywhere and everywhere, you twit."

My bottom lip trembles as the tears make their regularly scheduled appearance. "I can take him with me?"

"Don't you already?" She taps her bottom lip with her index finger. "Oh wait! You don't go anywhere!" Her face softens and she shakes her head ever so slightly. "Go get in the shower, Sash. We'll talk when you come down. Okay?" I start for the stairs when she yells out, "Oh, it's not necessarily about what they're putting on, they're taking it off too. Don't shave your legs. They need the stubble for waxing."

"Don't let Oscar out of your sight when you let him out," I shout from the top of the stairs. "He's still in training to not eat anything I don't give him!"

"I'm not still in training, and I'm not stupid!" she yells back indignantly.

An hour later we're in the car – with Oscar – on our way to meet Sky and Shae at the spa. Oscar stays with me, by my side, with every treatment, including a massage, haircut, mani and pedi, and a wax. He was made to sit at a distance for the wax, though I swear he cringed with every rip of the strips. He was a trooper. A true sailor. He stood – rather sat – the test and passed with flying colors.

We leave the spa and forgo eating at a restaurant. Instead we order takeout, go to Sky's house, and eat on the patio while Oscar relaxes at my feet. Poor guy was traumatized trying to protect me from having body hair torn from my private parts, all the while being told it was okay to watch his mistress being tortured.

"We've been talking." Sky glances at Shae and Rhea before her eyes land back on me. "We think you might benefit from seeking some help."

"Help?" I eye her warily, waiting for the suggestion of a ghostwriter. I'm a loner for my pages. I know I've been slow, but I'll get there . . . eventually.

"Maybe some therapy," Shae adds sheepishly. "Talk to somebody about everything you've been through."

"That's what you guys are for!"

"We're not trained professionals, Sash," Rhea explains. "We haven't been through what you have. You're depressed."

"Of course I am!" I yell, incensed at their lack of compassion.

"What did you expect? I lost my husband!" Oscar sits up and leans into me.

"And you've replaced him with a dog," Sky replies with a wave of her hand at Oscar. "You're using him as an excuse to hide away. He's a companion, Sasha, not a mate. He's not going to make the pain go away. You're using him as an excuse to become a recluse. You didn't go blind, you're not wheelchair bound, you don't suffer from PTSD – not in the typical way. You suffered a loss. You need to get back to functioning in the real world."

"I function just fine!" I snap harshly.

"Show me what you've done over the last three months." She arches a brow and lifts her chin in challenge. "Show me where you've put your energy. Where your thoughts are going."

I scowl and throw my napkin on the table. "Right now you don't want to know what I'm thinking."

She waves her hands toward herself. "Bring it on."

I look at the three of them one by one, their faces filled with concern and compassion. I'm bitter and broken, I know it. Oscar never tells me that, though. I never thought my friends would either. But it's not them I'm angry with.

"I want them dead," I confess with a sob, pounding the table with clenched fists. "I want them to feel what Ben did. I want them to know what it's like to burn to death at someone else's hands."

Three chairs scrape the patio concrete before I feel hands on my back. "We know, sweetie," Shae whispers.

"I don't want to feel this way." My body rocks back and forth as I wrap my arms around my stomach, staving off a round of nausea, the same way I do night after night. Oscar weaves his way under the table where he places his chin on my knee and tries to comfort me; anything to get closer short of threatening my friends with bared teeth.

"This is why we think you need somebody to help you," Sky says softly and slides a card into my hand. "Let's get the book signing out of the way and then you go see this guy. Your appointment is set up for week after next."

I look at the card she's given me. "A man?"

"He comes highly recommended," she reassures me. "He's worked with a lot of widows."

46

# Chapter 6

## Sasha

The office of Dr. Aidan Lehner is warm, inviting, private, quiet. So quiet, in fact, if the floor weren't carpeted, I believe you could hear a pin drop. The girls convinced me to leave Oscar at home; Rhea is staying with him while I'm here to have my head examined. The walls are done in a warm beige, individual chairs in the waiting room, no couches. Ah, maybe they're afraid the patients will lie down before treatment starts. The art on the walls is unalarming – a couple unknown bridges, a dark sky with twinkling stars. No Picassos. Hmm, didn't see that one coming. *Insert eye roll.* They should rethink that. Maybe hang a couple as a good reminder for a patient or two that we're not the only ones off our rockers.

The secretary, Ellen, is soft spoken, discreet, and checks me in quickly. She then walks me to a private area and has me wait to be called back.

I feel someone watching me before I hear him; a deep sotto voice from behind me. "Ms. Taylor, please come in."

I turn to see a tall, broad shouldered man with a warm smile that reaches his eyes. Eyes that only meet mine and travel no lower.

It's refreshing. I'd grown accustomed to it on the military base. Out in the general public? Not so much.

He escorts me down a short hall to his office. "Please have a seat wherever you're most comfortable." He rounds his desk where he waits to sit until I decide whether I want the chair facing him or the couch against the wall. I wore a skirt today so lying down on the sofa doesn't feel appropriate, therefore I take a seat in the chair in front of his desk and he follows onto his behind the desk.

I fold my hands in my lap and take a deep breath. "Okay, where do we start?"

He chuckles softly. I don't know why, and I can't really describe it, but it feels like a warm blanket. Soft and comforting. He feels like someone I can trust. "Why don't we get to know each other a bit before we delve into the deep stuff. Tell me a little about yourself, Ms. Taylor."

"Oh…oh," I stammer. "I don't really know how much there is to tell."

"Why don't we start at the beginning?" He smiles again – revealing slight creases at the edges of deep blue eyes that border hypnotic. Nearly black hair that is sharply groomed. Clean shaven. There's soft indecipherable music in the background that I hadn't noticed before. In fact, I swear it wasn't playing when I walked in.

"I . . . I'm from Tennessee originally," I start, incapable of peeling my eyes from his, watching him nod slowly as he prods me silently. "I . . . I'm a writer."

He places his elbows on the desk, steepling his index fingers against his lips. "What do you write?"

My cheeks flush with heat. "Fiction."

"What kind of fiction?"

My chin takes a dive as I stare at the folded hands in my lap. I've never been embarrassed about my writing . . . until now. "Romance."

"That's a fascinating career." His eyebrows rise as he tilts his head. "You must be very creative. Imaginative too."

My mouth twists, as do my fingers, and I feel the heat rise from my neck.

"Sasha," he says softly. "May I call you Sasha?" I nod. "Be proud of what you do. It's an art. Do you use a pen name?" I nod again. "May I ask?"

"Sara Paine," I whisper, immediately regretting it. Oh my God. If he reads my work he's going to see I write more than simple romance. I don't exactly write smut, but it definitely borders moan-inducing fantasies. At least that's what the reviews imply. When my readers add five hot chili peppers next to the stars, it's pretty indicative they found some thigh-squeezing scenes inside the pages.

I reach for my purse on the floor beside me and rise from my chair on unsteady legs. "I'm not sure this was a good idea."

"Sit down, Sasha." His voice is not harsh, but there's an unmistakable command behind his words. "We're not done." I turn to see his eyes fixed on me, challenging my next footstep toward the door. "Not by a long shot."

We spend the next hour in simple conversation. We don't talk about Ben, my marriage, the crash, the trauma. We don't even talk about why I'm here. Dr. Lehner explains he likes to get to know his patients first and foremost; then we'll move on to the reasons why. . . next time. He also explains we'll talk about the billing process another time, with the reassurance there will be no surprises. Having never visited a psychiatrist before, I take for granted the process differs from a regular physician. In any case, I will be seeing Dr. Aidan Lehner in three days. Since I feel better after today's appointment, I leave soberly grateful I can afford it. I also feel a bit guilty because there are so many who can't . . . and probably need it more than I do.

Three days later I enter his office again – this time in jeans and a T-shirt. He had instructed me to wear comfortable clothes for our appointments. *They have a tendency to make patients more comfortable and your comfort is my priority, Sasha.*

This time he urges me to open up about my marriage, my loss, my feelings. He hands me tissues when I cry, speaks softly and waits patiently for me to continue. He asks what I do for stress relief, what I do in my spare time. He suggests I take walks on the beach, soak up some sunshine. *He doesn't know about Oscar.*

Four days later, he asks that I lie on the couch in his office, close my eyes and take long, calming breaths before we start our session. This appointment, I talk about my best friends, how supportive they are, how close our relationships have been over the years. The fact that I'm here because of them. This appointment isn't teary like the last one. No tissues are handed out. I find myself smiling, maybe even laughing a time or two when sharing the antics of my friends. Yet, he asks that I keep confidentiality regarding our appointments until progress is significant.

And once again, as soon as I get home, everything goes back to the way it was before. I eat, shower, sleep when I'm not dreaming. I *function* . . . barely. It seems I function better while in his office than I do when I'm by myself or with my friends.

A week later, I find myself looking forward to the appointment as the elevator ascends to the sixth floor. The secretary is away from her desk and Dr. Lehner waits for me at the entrance to the hallway that leads back to the room where we meet.

"Hello, Sasha," he greets me with his usual warm smile.

"Secretary out for lunch?"

"No," he replies as he steps to the door and locks it, then waves his hand toward the hallway. "Got called out for a family emergency. Come on back."

A warning trigger niggles in the back of my brain and tells me that it should make me uncomfortable, but I ignore it and head for the hallway. He walks behind me at a respectable distance and speaks as soon as he closes the door.

"So, have you been practicing the exercises I gave you? Walks on the beach? Meditation? Sunshine therapy?"

"Some," I confess weakly, taking a seat in the chair in front of his desk.

"Ah," he drawls as he takes a seat behind his. "Some. As in not so much. Sasha, we talked about this. You need to be disciplined."

The gasp leaves my throat before I can catch it. How many times have I written that phrase in my books?

He pinches the bridge of his nose and takes a deep breath, letting it out slowly. "*Self*-disciplined, Sasha." His gaze is heated as he holds mine and that commanding voice makes an appearance. "I want you to lie on the couch. We're going to talk about Sara Paine today."

* * *

"How is therapy going?" Sky asks, lifting her foot out of the tub of solution to set it on the rest for the pedicurist to start working on her nails.

"Too soon to tell, I think." What am I supposed to say? My shrink is hot? I think he's a dom? He'd make good fodder for my next novel? I haven't gotten a bill yet?

"You've been seeing him for two months, Sash," Shae says. "You should be feeling something by now."

"Hey, at least she's showering daily and willing to leave the hairball at home by himself," Rhea scolds. "Leave her alone. We're not having to pry her out of the house with a pitchfork and threats of shaving her cootchie ourselves."

I wrinkle my nose. "My cootchie? Really?"

"Oh, I'm sorry," she replies condescendingly with a roll of her eyes. "Your sweet, pink, luscious, velvety folds of . . ."

"Shut up!"

"Just taking a line from one of my favorite author's books," she singsongs with an evil smirk.

"Speaking of favorite authors," Sky inquires. "How is the new book coming along?"

"Slowly," I answer harsher than I intend; not meeting her eyes.

"Slowly as in you've got pages to send me, or slowly as in the pages are still blank?"

"I'll let you know." I refrain from telling her the icon is still blinking at the top of the page, waiting for the first letter to be typed. Well, that's not the whole truth – I do have *Prologue* typed.

"I'll be waiting," she replies, then looks to her pedicurist.

"Changed my mind. I'll go with the red."

Rhea nudges my arm. "That's only to match the bloodshot of her eyes once she finishes her second bottle of wine tonight. Don't worry, she'll get over it. You'll write when you're ready."

I'm not sure why my writing is on hold. My mind drifts while I stare at the screen. I picture Ben, then I picture Dr. Lehner. I play Ben's voice messages over and over again. Then I cry. Then I cry some more. Then I cry myself to sleep.

# Chapter 7

## Sasha

"Sasha." Dr. Lehner says my name softly, taking my hand in his and gently circling the inside of my wrist with his thumb. "I think it's time for a change."

I'm lying on the couch while he sits in a chair next to it. I'm in tears, reticent to tell the whole truth and nothing but the truth. It's a bit more like skirting the truth and leaving out the pertinent portion – the fact that I think about him outside of our therapy sessions and wish I could call him at any given time; like at night when I'm in tears. He doesn't wear a wedding ring and I've never asked if he's married. I've caught him watching me. At first I thought his touches were simply reassuring gestures of comfort, but they seem more friendly now, even intimate at times. It should make me uncomfortable, but it doesn't.

"What?" I shoot up to a seated position on the couch, panic setting in with the fear he's seen through my façade. "A change? A change in what?"

He takes both of my hands in his – thumbs lightly brushing the tops of my fingers. "I'm going to recommend that you see a different therapist."

I stare at our joined hands, then look up into the deep blue eyes that have given me something to look forward to once a week for the last five months. I haven't admitted to anything. He doesn't know how dependent I've become on these visits – on him. The fact I've finally started writing again. How much I enjoy our time together. How the very sound of his voice lulls me into a state of tranquility when it's soft and a state of euphoria when it's low and commanding.

"Wha . . . what if I don't want to change?" I stammer. "What if I don't want to leave?"

"Listen closely, Sasha," he speaks in that deep commanding voice. "You will be fine. You'll remember your sessions here, recall my words, use the exercises I gave you. Consider a new therapist a continuation of the work we've done, not an end. You'll be surprised with the progress found. Ellen will make the arrangements for you. Do not call my office. You need to trust me. Understand?"

He doesn't give me a chance to respond and all I see is his back as he closes the door on his way out.

## Dr. Aidan Lehner

*She was a little more challenging than I had anticipated. The others have always been so easy. Sasha Taylor. Five months before I knew I had her. Her books have served as marvelous research material to dive into that mind. The southern belle determined to break free from the assumed sweet, passive, proper demeanor they're often expected to have – and become a somebody. She's in a class of her own. A body built for bending to my will. Week after week having to look at her, watch her, hear her talk about another man. Stupid husband taking chances that he knew would get him killed eventually. Leaving her behind to pine after him. What a fool. She's mine now. Two years away from my practice, two years from my last session with her. Two years and I'll be free to claim her as my own. Am I obsessed? Yes, I am. Can I wait two years? Yes, I can. I have enough women to keep my dick hard and happy until then. I'll picture her face while in the act – they don't need to know. Discretion is the secret and Sasha is my goal. Find her an incompetent female therapist, plant the subliminal electronics in her home, coincidental casual appearances in various places. Yes, Sasha Taylor, you'll be leaving my practice, but you won't be leaving my sights, nor will you be leaving my control.*

## *Fort Pierce, Florida*

"Cap," Berkel breathes heavily into the phone, "the target has eluded us again. Fuckers were already on their way out before we got there. Intel said they had choppers. Last word was they landed in Mexico."

The Captain slams his fist on the desk before swiping the top, scattering papers all across the room. "Find out where, Berkel! We're running out of time!" As he slams the phone down, Captain Graham enters the office and takes a seat in the squeaky worn chair on wheels at the other desk in the room, heaving a deep sigh.

"It's not Berkel's fault," he chides. "Give the poor kid a break. He's been working his ass off on this." He points to the scattered papers on the floor. "You're cleaning that mess up. I'm getting too old to play housemaid for you."

"I've got two months before I retire, Nash," Cap says. "I want these fuckers before I'm gone. They took six of my men!"

"In case you've forgotten, Jax, they were my men too." Nash leans forward, elbows on his desk. "If we don't get them before *our* retirement in two months, we come back as mercenaries. I'll hire you, you hire me." He shrugs and smirks. "Might be more fun. No rules to follow. No paperwork trail."

"I owe it to Arkelpaine," Cap states, throwing a pen on the half bare desktop. "Shit, I owe it to all of them."

"*We* owe them," Nash reminds him. "And it will happen. Ankle pain was one of the most patient guys we knew. He'd understand the time it's taking. So we get out, you start your business, I start mine, and wait for them to come out of hiding. They will screw up – you know that. They'll go back to Costa Rica as soon as they think it's safe. Our guys will be watching."

Cap grunts a humorless chuckle. "Ankle pain. You never could get under that guy's skin."

"That's what being happy will do for you. Too bad some of it didn't rub off on you." Nash points to the floor again. "Clean up your mess."

# Chapter 8

## Sasha

Taking to the beach with Oscar for a long run early morning today is the best idea I've had in a long time. No one is out yet, the sun is just starting to rise, and the humidity is low. I'm sleeping better, or thought I was, but Oscar is restless at night . . . a lot. I've risen multiple times to see what has him so jumpy but can't find anything – indoors or out. He's taken to hopping onto the bed with me and settling by my side every night. I've found if I move to the sofa, he sleeps on the floor next to it and calms easier, popping his head up on occasion as if listening intently.

It all started about a week after my therapy sessions with Dr. Lehner ended, and we had come back from an afternoon at Sky's where we went over my newest works. He charged past me into the house, more guarded than usual, and headed straight for my bedroom, nose to the floor, as if tracking a particular scent. That was four months ago and it hasn't seemed to relent with time.

I need to stop to dump the remnants from my shoes after I hit a soft spot in dry sand when I neglected to pay attention. Take my word for it, sand in your shoes is not the best method for a pedicure. Another quick tip: writing sex scenes in your head while running is not highly recommended. I plop my butt in the sand and untie the first of two offending foot scratchers. Oscar sits beside me, panting and waiting patiently. While I have one shoe off, tipped upside down, Oscar lunges away from me with a wicked growl, pulling on the wrist his leash is looped around.

"Oscar!" I screech, dropping my shoe and pulling back on the leash with a wrist that I now fear is sprained.

"Whoa!" I hear the deep familiar voice yell. "Down dog! Sasha, restrain him!"

I reach with my other hand and pull hard on his leash. "Oscar! Heel!" My dog stops pulling at the leash, but his growl and protective stance are as strong as ever.

"You shouldn't own a dog like that, Sasha," Dr. Lehner scolds, his tone sharp and cold. "He's a danger to people. He's also a lawsuit waiting to happen. Why would you own such an animal?"

My defenses go up immediately. I don't care who he is or how much I've missed him. This is Oscar. My gift. My Champion Warrior.

"You don't like dogs, Dr. Lehner?" I snap, rubbing the hand that throbs then reach to pat Oscar on the head and ruffle his ears. I feel the vibration as he continues to release a low growl. "It seems the two of you have something in common."

"Sasha," he breathes, calmer this time. "I'm sorry. He startled me. If you like him, I like him. He's protecting you." He lets go a megawatt smile that causes those creases at the corners of his eyes. "It's good to see you. You look lovely."

I find myself blushing at the compliment. "Thank you, Dr. Lehner."

"Please, call me Aidan. We're not in the office anymore."

He steps toward me with his hands outstretched. Oscar steps between us and bares his teeth. I'm still sitting in the sand and in a vulnerable position so I slide my shoe back on and stand to my feet, brushing the sand off my butt.

Dr. Lehner clears his throat and pockets his hands in his shorts, his brow furrowed. "Well, I guess he doesn't want me to help. I only wanted to check your wrist for injury. Are you okay?

Maybe you could leave the dog at home next time and we can walk the beach together."

"I didn't think I was supposed to talk to you anymore." He had told me not to call his office. I took for granted that probably meant I shouldn't say hello if I saw him on the street as well.

"Sasha," he says, his voice laced with disappointment. He dips his head and raises his brows. "Do you not want to talk to me? Do you not miss our sessions at all?"

"Yeah," I answer sheepishly. "I stopped seeing Dr. Kramer. We didn't have a very good rapport and I'm writing again, sleeping okay. Baby steps, you know? I've started looking for a new house. I want a fixer upper so I can do it my way. It's given me something to look forward to."

"You're moving?" He startles. "Not far, I hope."

"No. I'll be staying here. I'm looking to buy."

"I know a good realtor," he rushes to offer. "I could send her your way. Tell you what, meet me here tomorrow morning and we can talk about it. Maybe you could leave the dog at home?" He studies my face and waits for my reaction. When I hesitate, his voice deepens. "Sasha, leave the dog at home and meet me here same time tomorrow morning. We'll talk about it then."

Oscar's growl is unmistakable and I tighten the leash in my hand. I tell myself he's just being protective. Maybe he understood being left out for a walk tomorrow. He is really smart. They say dogs know people better than people know people. They also say you should trust a dog's instincts better than your own. He's never had to share me, so instead I tell myself he's jealous. We'll do the exercise course in the backyard a few times tomorrow.

"I'll see you tomorrow morning, Dr. Lehner."

"Aidan," he orders.

"Aidan," I repeat with a nod. It doesn't taste as good on my tongue as *Ben* always did. So why do I feel like I'm being told that it should? I have no desire to roll it around and savor it. It's just a name.

* * *

The next morning I meet Dr. Lehner on the beach in the same spot. He has already arrived, waiting for me, two coffees in hand. Apparently running is not what he had in mind as his clothing is casual – sandals, khaki shorts, and a polo shirt. Once again, the beach is nearly empty. Oscar had whined as I made my way out the door – familiar with my running clothes and tennis shoes – knowing he wasn't accompanying me this morning.

"Sasha," he greets me with a knowing smile and holds out a coffee for me. "Walk with me."

We spend the next hour discussing how my work is progressing, how I'm finding my inspiration. He warns that I shouldn't be looking for inspiration in men I don't know; that my inspiration should come from within, then nudges my shoulder and jokes that I can picture his face if I want. That comment triggers something in my brain I can't quite put my finger on. He hands me the realtor's card and reassures me she's top notch and can help me find exactly what I'm looking for.

"Sasha," he says as we reach my car. "No one can know that we meet for these walks. I would like to keep this between us. We can do it once a week, once a month, whatever you like. It's your call."

"Why can no one know?"

He blows a breath through pressed lips. "I could lose my license. I want to see you. I miss our talks. You were my favorite patient. I . . ." He shakes his head and chuckles softly. "I think I need this as much as you do. But it has to be two years from seeing you as a patient before we can be friends. The Medical Association has its rules. That's only 18 months away. I didn't bill your insurance for the last two months of treatment." He reaches out and brushes a piece of hair away from my face, tucking it behind my ear following the line of my jaw with a trace of his fingertip. "We can be friends, can't we?"

I'm drawn to his touch, his voice. It feels like a whisper in the dark. Yet it casts a shadow of unease as I stand here in the light of day. Still, I nod shakily. "Yeah, we can."

"Sasha." I feel a hint of warning in his tone as I climb into my car. "Leave the dog at home on the days we're going to meet."

"How will I know what days those are?"

He smiles, almost cockily. "You'll know. Trust me." My door closes by way of his hand and he walks toward his without another word.

## *Dr. Aidan Lehner*

*Bingo! It's working. I see it in her eyes, the way she melts into my touch. She's falling for me. That dead husband will be a thing of the past as if he never existed. She'll deal with my chosen realtor and I'll know the location of her new house. A fixer upper. Perfect. She won't be living in it right away. I'll have access to install my equipment and not cross paths with that damn dog. Why had she never mentioned him during our appointments? The loathsome, sneaky sonofabitch nearly took my leg off the first time I tried to get in. Never made a sound until I opened the door. I had to stalk her until I watched her leave one day with the beast. Maybe poison. I wonder . . . all in due time.*

# Chapter 9

## Sasha

***Four months later***

"I love it!" Rhea squeals as she enters the living room after touring the house. She stands in the center of the room under the raised ceiling highlighted with dark wood beams, arms spread wide, and twirls as if standing in the rain. Well, short of her tongue extended in an attempt to catch the nonexistent drops falling from the sky.

After arriving in South Carolina, I initially stayed with Sky for nearly five months. It was hard finding a place to rent that allowed dogs. I rented my last house with the option to buy. I liked it well enough – gave it a full year to grow on me – but continued to search for one that spoke to me. *Figuratively – not literally. I'm not crazy.* It didn't have the character I was looking for. Unfortunately, it was speaking to Oscar *literally*, and he didn't like what he was hearing. I don't know if it was feral cats or some other wild animals that came around during the night, but after months in that house, he was suddenly uncomfortable and I couldn't take his restlessness anymore. I seemed to sleep through any noises that may or may not have been seeping through the walls  at night because the only thing waking me up was Oscar's jumpiness.

I'm grateful my landlord gave me the extra time to find my dream home without signing a new lease. Five more months to find it, probably another two of renovations before it's ready to move into. I could move into it now – it's not unlivable – it's only been empty for six months, but it's a lot easier to work *on* it and not *in* it at the same time. Paint fumes wouldn't be good for Oscar or me.

I had my checklist:

Close to the water but elevated. Hurricanes, you know.

Three bedrooms with an office.

Three bathrooms. When my family visits, it will make things more comfortable.

A view that will knock my socks off from the ocean side. A private retreat on the back.

The master bedroom at one end of the house, the guest rooms on the other.

Persistence is key when searching for a home. Patience is the other. Let's not forget fortitude, willingness to work hard, remodel, and a damn good real estate agent. Relda Morton was patient and diligent in her search and eventually found me the perfect place.

I meet Aidan every two to three weeks on the beach in the early morning for walks and talks. He was right; I always seem to know what day he's going to be there. He says it's a pull we have to each other. He gave me a burner phone to use in case of emergency. I did show up with Oscar one day and he wasn't happy about it. Oddly, he had asked me how I had slept the night before. When I explained Oscar had a bad night and I had slept on the couch, he chastised me and told me I shouldn't let a dog dictate my life. Then he apologized profusely, kissed my forehead as Oscar growled, then bid me farewell.

He's so secretive about everything; explaining his license is at stake, but our relationship is so important to him. I've come to depend on his company, our talks, but I'm not sure how I feel about him calling what we have a relationship. He lets me chatter on about my writing, my thoughts, my work in progress. He's the only male companionship I have, unless you count my dad and my brother. And they don't live here and that's only phone conversations, so those don't really count. I don't have to explain it to the girls. When they don't rise at the ass crack of dawn – their idea of early is nine o'clock – there's no need to explain where I've been. They're still studying the insides of their eyelids while I'm walking the beach. I'm uncomfortable keeping a secret from them, but I'm afraid they're going to tell me it's too soon or I'm becoming dependent. *But we're just friends.*

"Oh Sasha," Rhea breathes, bringing her hands together and folding her fingers. "We are going to have so much fun putting this all together. I say we start with the kitchen and baths, move on to the master, then the living room. The guest bedrooms should be last."

I lean against the doorframe entrance to the living room and look to Shae and Sky. "When did she get her license in plumbing and electrical work?"

Rhea grins and waggles her brows. "I didn't. I just plan to be around to check out the vertical smiles while they work. You know, tell them where to be and where to bend. Oversee the job, so to speak." She winks. "I'll watch from behind. Maybe *crack* a few jokes with them."

"Oh my God." I roll my eyes and sigh. "You will not be allowed on the grounds while they work. You'll be a distraction and it'll be an extra six months before I'll ever get moved in."

Sky waves her hand in dismissal of my cocky marketing specialist. "You know she's an ass woman."

"And . . ." Rhea drawls, ". . . if you let them know you're watching, they flex. It's a well-known fact men work harder and faster when their ass cheeks are clenched. You need to keep them on their toes."

It's Shae's turn to roll her eyes. "That's sex, you idiot. And it's their sphincter muscles they clench while they're hammering into you."

Rhea glances around the room then to us and shrugs. "Only four holes in this room that I can detect need nailing."

"I say we leave her home while we go pick out paint." Sky narrows her eyes as she fixes them on Rhea. "Otherwise the next thing you know you'll have a red room of pain."

Rhea's eyes light up as her mouth opens to speak. "Shut it!" Shae orders with a glare, holding her hand up. "I do not want to hear it."

"I was thinking inspiration for Sasha's next books!" Rhea exclaims.

I hook the leash onto Oscar's harness. Inspiration. Hmmm . . . maybe studying the construction crew isn't such a bad idea. God knows Aidan Lehner doesn't seem to inspire any thoughts of romanticism. We're friends. That's all. And lately, I'm okay with that. I'm more than okay with that. My sofa has become quite comfortable lately and Oscar sleeps so much better on the floor next to it.

"Let's go." I head for the door, key in hand. "We'll make Rhea ride in the cart so she can't touch anything."

"Not even the stockboys?" she whines.

"I say we lock her in the car," Sky suggests with a sly grin.

"There are laws against that," I remind her.

"That's for dogs," Shae says.

"Kids too," I say and shrug. "Guess we're stuck with her."

Rhea releases an evil laugh. "I am so going to show up here every day to inspect those vertical smiles on the construction workers!" Her face lights in a wicked grin. "Ooh! Maybe we could talk them into being book cover models for the next series. You know, hardhats, chests and abs dripping with manly sweat, low slung dirty blue jeans with the T-shirt tucked into their back pocket because they had to use it to wipe the grime off their face." She waves both hands in the air like a ditzy cheerleader pumped up on Red Bull, or I don't know, maybe remnants of last night's dream of the star quarterback. "I volunteer to do the photography."

I shoot her a wry look. "Due to the fact the gentleman I spoke with sounded to be about 50, I highly doubt they're book model material."

"Age gap series?" she questions, sounding hopeful. "Viagra might be looking for someone to sponsor."

I close my eyes, silently counting to ten. "Can we just go?"

The realtor had highly recommended Callum Construction Company to do all of the work I need done inside and out. The project is huge, going to take weeks, maybe more, for the inside alone. Three bathrooms and the kitchen as well as new windows. All new lights and fixtures in the baths, all new appliances in the kitchens. The electrical in the house is in excellent condition, but I want some things added on. Dad and Trent came out a month ago to inspect things and put their stamp of approval on it themselves before I placed my final offer. They would have preferred I buy a place ready to move into, but I need a project. A mind-numbing, body-busying, emotion-capturing project that reminds me I'm only dead on the inside.

The outside is a massive undertaking that needs heavy duty thought and planning. That will be my paradise. A pool, hot tub, lounge area, shrubbery, privacy. A writer's retreat. I've worked hard for this. It will also be Oscar's paradise. An entire section cut out for his exercise yard. That comes first – before we even move in.

# Chapter 10

## Sasha

"Relda already gave me your timeline, Miss Taylor," Carl says after we've made the rounds of three bathrooms and the kitchen. "I have it fit into the schedule. She had actually taken me through the house a week ago so I could get a feel for what we were looking at. It's a big project, but nothing we can't handle. I'll take the measurements back to the office. I've got the information on all the appliances you want installed. The countertops and flooring go in first."

He's a pleasant man. My guess at his age was pretty spot on; must be about late-fifties or so. Salt and pepper hair, maybe six foot, dad bod. I bite the inside of my lip to hold back my grin at Rhea's anticipated reaction with the blow I'll be delivering. Oscar stays by my side, as always, and hasn't growled once. I like the man already.

I nod. "Okay. Do you know how long it will take?"

"Some of it will depend on availability of products, but a lot of it is what we like to call grunt work." He smiles. "My guys are good at that. As soon as we get your stamp of approval and signatures, we'll be good to go. But I'd say we're looking at six to eight weeks."

"And if all goes well on the inside," I add, "are you willing to do the outside project?"

He looks puzzled. "What are you doing on the outside?"

I blow an unintentional raspberry that sounds a bit like flatulence with my frustrated sigh over what I'm about to show him and slap my hand over my mouth. "Sorry about that."

He laughs. "Must be quite a project."

We make our way out the sliders in the dining room onto the deck and into the backyard. "Total revamp. Hot tub here, pool there, shrubbery all around," I say, pointing to the various areas of interest. "Most importantly, an exercise area for Oscar over there. I have equipment that's made for him." I wave my hand toward the west side of the yard, indicating the large grassy area to the left. "I'm much more concerned about the timeline for Oscar's area than I am any of the rest. He needs his exercise a whole lot more than I need a pool. Are you interested?"

His smile is genuine as he looks at Oscar. "I have a couple of guys who specifically do landscaping that could get right on that if you'd like." He puts his hand out slowly for Oscar to sniff.

"It's okay, Oscar," I tell him and he allows Carl to gently pat his head.

"We men need our exercise, don't we, fella?" He laughs. "He's a beautiful Belgian."

"You know the breed?"

"Best dog there is," he replies with undeniable pride. "I'll get back to you as fast as I can, Miss Taylor. I'll get a separate estimate for Oscar's yard so we can get moving on that immediately if you'd like."

"I'd appreciate that. Thank you."

"If all goes well, we should be able to get started next week. Is that good enough for you?"

"Perfect, Mr. Sanborn," I tell him, opening the slider so we can go through the house to the driveway out front.

We part ways at the driveway and I watch him leave in a white pickup truck with a logo on the door: Callum Construction.

My phone rings shortly after I step inside my front door. I smile to myself when I see Rhea's face on the screen.

"Sorry," I sing. "Wedding ring, beyond middle age, dad bod."

"What about the others?" she huffs.

I laugh. "There weren't any others."

"So not all hope is lost?"

"Oh my God," I groan. "I have to go feed my dog."

# Chapter 11

## Jaxson

"She wants what?!" I eye the estimate Carl has laid on my desk. "Why the hell didn't she go farther down the beach and build a new one? For all she's having done, she might as well. That house is nearly 50 years old."

I'm looking at plans to include refinishing of floors – for those not being replaced – rebuilding of three bathrooms and a kitchen, window replacements, and added electrical outlets.

Carl shrugs. "It's got good bones. Said the house spoke to her."

"Spoke to her? Like ghosts and demons? Is she planning on holding seances? Some old eccentric broad who has nothing better to do than spend alimony money?"

"And this is why I deal with people, and you . . ." Carl points his finger and grins smugly, ". . . don't. This isn't even half of it. She wants the entire backyard done with a pool and hot tub as well as an exercise course built for her dog."

I snort and return his smug grin. "What's she got, a poodle needing artificial turf to piss on because grass grows too tall and tickles his balls?"

He laughs cockily. "You have no idea. Attitude and latitude, Jaxson. Aim that anger where it belongs. Stay focused. You'll get them." Carl sighs deeply and shakes his head. "In the meantime, I'm going to send the figures to the lady. You want to give her a price break since she's giving us the business?"

"Aw," I drawl and smirk. "You getting sweet on her, Carl?"

He scowls. "I'm a happily married man."

"Hey, Cap," Brick greets me with his usual cheery voice as he struts in the office followed by Dusty, both of them covered in cement dust and sweat. "We got that job on Broadway just about complete. Two more days should do it. Simon's right behind us; had to hit the head on his way in."

Carl looks to me and raises his brows, a hint of warning in his narrowed eyes. "Old habits die hard, Jax."

"Shit." Brick drops his chin to his chest and grumbles low, "Sorry, boss. Eight years is a long time."

Dusty adds, "I still have a hard time with it too . . . *Jax*."

"Try harder," I remind them harshly then blow a resigned sigh. "Okay?"

"You got it," they agree in unison.

"How about I put them on the Taylor job if she accepts the bid?" Carl inquires.

"Your call." I nod. "Is she ready to get started this soon?"

"I think she would have had us out there yesterday if she could have. She wants the dog's area done first. No materials to wait for on that one. We'll start there."

"Do it," I tell him. "I'll be in Charleston for the next month working on the Kelly project. I'll check in with you. Call me if you need anything."

He gives a mock salute and leaves the office.

"Since you're the ordinary boss now," Dusty says, flashing his million dollar smile. "What do you say you buy the beers tonight?"

"Go home and shower first," I order them. "You can buy the appetizers."

I'm ex-military. I only hire ex-military. Rules: We don't

identify as such. Our mission isn't done yet. Am I obsessed? Yes. Do I persevere? Also yes. I don't have a choice. I owe it to my men. *We* owe it to those men. Six men whose remains couldn't be collected because the helicopter exploded in the air over the jungle in Costa Rica. We're mercenaries now, with one last mission. In the meantime, we stay on guard, in touch, and ready to roll at any given minute. I haven't gotten on with my life since retiring; I function until I can freely breathe again. I will breathe again, once I know the drug running assholes who killed my men aren't.

## *Dr. Aidan Lehner*

*A construction crew. Men all over the place. Couldn't keep it simple, could you, Sasha? Renovation. Damn you, Relda! I suggested you make her life simple! I suppose in the long run it might make it easier for me to get in and out. Run some wires at night without being detected. This house is secluded. I'll continue to be able to influence her thoughts while she sleeps and no one will be the wiser. Mind play. Coercion. Control. What am I going to do about that damn dog, though? Every day brings me closer to keeping my license and owning Sasha Taylor. I'm not about to let some filthy animal get in my way.*

*One day, one step at a time. I've waited this long, a little longer won't hurt. Oh Sasha, I have such plans for us. Of all the widows that have shown up at my doorstep, I knew you were the one. So beautiful, so vulnerable, so perfect. So mine.*

# Chapter 12

## Sasha

It's been seven weeks since the renovation started and the guys are putting the finishing touches on the kitchen. The bathrooms are done, the windows have been replaced, the extra electrical outlets are installed, and all flooring is finished – a combo of refinishing original oak and installing marble in the baths. The only thing left is installation of the appliances which are being delivered tomorrow.

We've alternated schedules so that the guys work during the week and we paint on the weekends. Oscar's exercise course is finished but I have yet to move any of his equipment here. It was hard enough to leave him at home while we painted, but I didn't want him exposed to the fumes.

"Holy Moses." Rhea releases a breathy whisper as we stand in the doorway. I turn to see her smiling wickedly, expecting her reaction having been to the progress made. Oh no. No, no, no. Her eyes are glued to the blue jean-clad asses in the kitchen. "The ten commandment tablets he brought down from Mount Sanai weren't that solid. Those butts are like granite. I can't decide which one I want to squeeze first."

I elbow her aimlessly, unfortunately hitting a boob in the process. "You might want to recall some of those commandments right about now."

"Ow," she grunts as she places her hand on said boob. "Stop it. If anybody's leaving marks on these babies, it's gonna be one of them." She turns to me and wiggles her eyebrows. "Or all of them." She smirks. "And number seven doesn't apply unless they're married." Being raised in the bible belt, some things were drilled into us at a young age. Nice to know she remembers which one is 'thou shalt not commit adultery'. Funny it falls right after number six: 'thou shalt not murder'. Although it makes total sense those two would be back-to-back.

"Miss Sasha," Dusty greets me with a dazzling smile from the floor where he's on his hands and knees wiping up some dust. "Come to inspect?"

Rhea murmurs beside me, "I came to inspect. And so far, God's getting an A+."

I scowl at her, then return his smile and hold up the basket in my hand. "I brought you guys some lunch." I bring lunch to the guys once a week. It gives me something to do, a nice break from my laptop, and a chance to check progress. It's never fast food, nothing greasy, and they seem to appreciate it. Today, lunch consists of chicken salad sandwiches, homemade potato salad, and a veggie tray with dip. Ah, and a slice of peaches and cream cake for each of them.

I carry it to the card table that's set up in the dining room. I brought it over weeks ago so they would have a place to sit for breaks. There is literally no other furniture in the house and it only seemed right to give them seating arrangements for eating their lunch. When I saw their size, I double checked the weight capacity on the box before bringing it over. These guys are not small. The box said each chair held up to 250 pounds, so I figured it was safe. And yes, Rhea is correct. There is not a lot of cushion on those derrieres. Not that I'm looking . . . but I'm not blind either.

"I see you brought dessert with you today," Brick says as he winks at Rhea.

Simon slaps his shoulder and scowls. "Callum's gonna have your head on a platter. You know the rules."

"What!" Brick reacts with grin and winks at Rhea once again. "I thought I saw some cream pie."

Rhea giggles. I roll my eyes. At least he's not staring at her boobs.

"Boys," Carl chastises. "I believe the proper response is thank you."

There are three men who work with Carl: Brick, Dusty and Simon.

Brick is blonde, blue-eyed, tanned, and boisterous. A bit like the boy next door, a brother's best friend, football quarterback type, aka flirt. But in an innocuous way.

Dusty is a handsome, slightly shaggy, sandy-haired, green-eyed, dimples for days smiler. The little brother of the boy next door.

Simon is quieter. Dark hair pulled back in a ponytail, chocolate eyes, deep voice. Speaks when the occasion warrants itself, but otherwise concentrated and contemplative.

"Guys, this is one of my best friends, Rhea Daniels." Before I have the opportunity to introduce them by name, they all step forward to shake her hand and introduce themselves. I watch their interaction. It's polite, gentlemanly, pleasant.

The front door opens and in walk my other two besties. Sky's eyes immediately search for my constant companion. "Where's the big O?"

I hear chuckles from the men before one of them whispers, "I'm always up for helping a woman find that."

Before I have the opportunity to find the offending mouth behind me and render a scowl, Shae whines, "I thought you were going to wait for us."

"We're right here." I laugh. "It's not like we were going anywhere."

"She wanted top choice," Rhea says with a giggle.

Brick doesn't leave Rhea's side but jokes, "I'm always top choice."

Dusty elbows him before he takes Shae's hand in his and winks. "He may be top choice, but I'm prime choice. I taste better, I'm tender, and never gristly." He kisses her knuckles. "And who might you be, love?"

"Amateurs," Simon mumbles as he moves toward Sky where he towers over her by a good six inches. "Hello," he says in a raspy voice so low it vibrates in your toes as he tips her gaping jaw closed with one fingertip. "I know exactly how to help you find the big O. Would you like to share my lunch with me?"

She glances at the table in the dining room and sees the chairs numbering only four then back to Simon. "Wh …where would I sit?" she whispers.

He leans in so close to her ear the rest of us can't hear what he whispers, but we don't miss the way her cheeks flush, nor do we miss the way her breaths stutter.

She pulls back from his mouth at her ear and stares. "H…h…how would you eat if I did that?"

His chuckle is playful and low as he kisses her forehead. "Oh, you're going to be fun."

We take a quick tour of the house and leave in a hurry while the guys take a seat at the table and start their lunch – my friends each stealing last glances before we go. The movers arrive in two days with all of my belongings.

As I'm closing the front door behind me, I hear Simon's deep laugh. "And that, gentlemen, is how it's done."

Well, that just shot the shit out of *gentlemanly*. Polite and pleasant are still up in the air – as are the hopes of my three friends.

# Chapter 13

## Jaxson

The sprawling ranch isn't quite what I expect when I pull up out front. But then, I doubt some rich broad is going to want to climb stairs every night to find her way to the bedroom. Or five times a day to find the bathroom. *"The house spoke to her"*. I guess money makes you hear all sorts of things. Can't say it looks bad though. It's got good bones. Solid structure. Carl wouldn't have bid on it if it didn't.

Dusty and Brick are loading equipment into one of the trucks as I open my door.

"Hey boss," Dusty calls out. "About time you came to check out the work of the masters. You're gonna love this one. The lady has taste."

Brick laughs and nudges him. "So do her friends."

I eye them skeptically and step toward the house. "What's that supposed to mean?"

"Nothing," Brick chimes and turns away, loading the Shop-Vac into the bed of the truck. "She brought a couple of friends today to check out the goods."

I halt my pace to the door and turn. "The goods? You guys

aren't messing around with the customers, are you?" It's not a question, they know it. Rules.

"God no, boss!" Dusty exclaims. "Miss Taylor is like a precious gem. She's special. We would never."

"Fragile old lady, is she?" I smirk.

They both burst into obnoxious laughter. "Yeah," Brick says between stuttered guffaws. "Yeah. We'll go with that."

I head for the house again. "Finish cleaning up. Sounds like you guys have a lot more to do here. Carl said you're starting outside on the back next week."

"Go check out what we've done already," Dusty yells. "It's classic!"

"Hey Cap," Brick calls out as he runs to catch up to me. Once by my side, he hesitates, rubbing the back of his neck. "Sorry," he mumbles over his repeated blunder. He can't help it. They were all active duty at the time it happened. Everybody but Carl. I was their captain. We're all waiting for the call. "Anything from intel yet?"

I look over his shoulder, out onto the water that holds no answers. "They're doing their best, Brick. It's three guys doing everything they can."

He screws his face and nods. "I know. But we're on the outside now. It's a hard place to be, Cap. I hate waiting."

Placing my hand on his shoulder, I squeeze firmly. "They're going to fuck up, Brick. And we'll be there when they do. Berkel's on top of things."

Dusty walks over and places his hand on Brick's other shoulder, squeezing. "All of us will be there. I'm putting a cap in that fucker's skull whether he's already dead or not, just for sheer pleasure. Drug runners and rapists are my favorite targets."

"Gentlemen," Simon says from behind us. "Three days, three years. Doesn't matter. We'll get 'em. There's no amount of time they could have now that will make it worth what we're going to do to them. Go check the house, boss. She's a beaut. Then we'll go get wings and beers."

"We could always ask Miss Taylor what she's fixing for dinner," Brick proffers with a grin as he rubs circles on his stomach.

"There ain't a restaurant around can outdo her cooking skills."

I pierce them all with a glare. "You've been having this woman cook for you?"

"No!" Brick denies with shocked, wide eyes. "She just does." He turns to his cohorts and grins cockily. "I think she's sweet on us."

"Let's hope her friends are too," Dusty says wistfully. "Damn, what a ride that'd be."

"Didn't think you guys were into older women. Quit yankin' my chain," I grumble as I head for the door once again. "Get your shit in the trucks. Let's move."

Crossing the threshold, I reach into the basket by the door and slip on the disposable boot covers. *Not bad, guys.* Sleek, modern, warm. I can imagine it with furniture, lamps, rugs on the floors, some nice artwork on the walls – the perfectly painted walls.

"When did painting get put in the contract?" I ask Carl as he enters the living room.

"It didn't." He chuckles. "The ladies did all the painting themselves on the weekends while we worked during the week so we weren't in each other's way.

"Ladies?" I ask, emphasizing the plural portion.

"Miss Taylor and her friends," he says. "If you'd been here earlier you'd have met them. She brought us lunch again."

"Again? So they really weren't joking." I make my way past him into the kitchen. I see the card table and four chairs in the dining room with a picnic basket on it. "Did she try and get favors out of you for it? A few extras? Upgrades on fixtures, maybe? What's her game?" I feel a hard flick to the back of my ear – like something your mother would do for punishment when you swear. I spin quickly, expecting to find one of my cocky employees. *Nothing.* "Did she ask for a discount?" Another hard flick to the other ear. I spin the other way. *Nothing.* Damnit! There must be bugs in here.

Carl pockets his hands, drops his chin and shakes his head. "You want to see the rest or shall we put out a warrant for her arrest for being sweet?"

I narrow my eyes and wait for him to look up. "Smartass."

Carl gives me a tour of each room, pointing out the projects undertaken and completed – flooring, cabinetry, shower walls and the jacuzzi in the master, fixtures, electrical. Then he takes me to the backyard to show me the exercise portion plotted out for her dogs. It's massive. The amount of land she purchased is pretty impressive, but the amount she's allowed for the dogs is even more so. She's had my guys measure spaces of turfed areas where the dogs' *exercise equipment* will go and the rest is natural grass. The area is fenced in with no access from the outside – only accessible from inside the backyard without barriers.

"What the hell does she have? It's going to take half a day every week to keep that mowed." I hold a hand up. "Wait, don't tell me. She trains show dogs. A pack of poodles, Pomeranians?" Another hard flick to the back of my ear, and this time I see my shoulder length hair move in my periphery. I turn once again. *Nothing!* "Fuck this," I growl and run my hand through my hair, rubbing my ear with the heel of my palm, and head back toward the house. If I'm going to have my ear flicked, I might as well swear and make it worth it.

I help the guys carry out any items left from the clean-up and load it into the trucks. It's my understanding the appliances are being delivered tomorrow and they're the last thing to be done . . . on the inside. Next week, they'll be back here to start on the massive project this woman has planned for the outside.

*Hope the pool boy doesn't mind wearing Speedos and being ogled by some raisin wearing a bikini while her husband bangs his secretary on his desk at the office.*

"Did you guys get bit by any bugs while you were working in there?" I ask, closing the tailgate after the last item has been loaded. I can still feel the sting on both ears, a little burn that hasn't quite dissipated.

"Bugs?" Simon's forehead creases as he studies my face.

Brick laughs loudly. "I think Dusty got bit by the lovebug this afternoon but other than that, I ain't seen any."

Dusty slaps his arm and huffs, "Simon kissed her forehead!

I only kissed her knuckles!"

I stare at Carl. "You got any idea what they're talking about?"

He nods once. "I do."

"Care to share?"

He shakes his head. "I do not."

"Do I want to know?"

He twirls his keys on a finger as he nonchalantly walks toward his truck. "See you boys in the mornin'."

Carl is a father figure to my guys. Much like one to me as well. He's their foreman – keeps them in line, gives advice when they ask for it, but never pulls the reins too tight. He's a former Marine, seen it all, closing in on sixty. Married, two daughters, hard worker. He knows what my guys have been through. He also knows what we're expecting, what we're anticipating – the call to action. He's ready for it. He won't be joining us, but he'll hold down the fort until we come home.

"You're not going to join us for wings and brews?" Dusty asks him.

He turns back and chuckles, pressing a sideways fist to his chest. "Heartburn is my enemy, boys. Talk to me when it's steak and baked potatoes. And don't forget the Tums."

## *Dr. Aidan Lehner*

*Took them long enough. I've been walking the beach for the last hour waiting for them to get the hell out of here. Tonight is my last chance. Appliances will be delivered tomorrow and the movers are coming on Saturday. Sasha has been so generous with the information, describing the layout. So excited to move into her new home. And now I'll be walking the perimeter to find my way around, without interruption or gawkers, so I'll know all access ports into her world. And her dog? Well, poor Oscar will be finding a treat or two, here and there, in his special yard.*

*Waiting for another half hour – until the sun has started to set against the ocean horizon, I pull my backpack from the trunk and make my way toward the house. It's so easy. I attract no attention from the beachcombers – all lost in their own little world of the sunset on the water, collecting token shells – or children – to take home. I make my way to the side of the house, open the privacy fence gate, and find where the master bedroom is located – the large sliding doors with a deck that leads to the patio off the back of the house. I know the doors are locked. No problem – I hadn't planned on using them. I find the high point I need for the pinpoint antenna and attach the cable under the siding corner piece, tucking it in all the way down to the bottom, and slide it underneath the last panel of siding near the foundation.*

*As I begin to stand from my squatted position, I'm suddenly catapulted forward and land face first on the deck floor with a thud, my cheek throbbing. Shit! I've been caught. I place my hands flat on the deck, capitulating, and state passively, "I'm the inspector." I wait to be given orders, be harshly pulled to my feet, handcuffed, but none of that happens. I risk a glimpse at the person above me but find no one. I'm alone. What the hell!? I must have slipped on the deck – the humidity of the day having made the wood a virtual ice skating rink. Going to have to talk to Sasha about putting some mats down. Breathing a sigh of relief, I rise to my feet, grab the backpack and head for the back door to pick the lock. Once inside, I slip my shoes off so as not to leave a trail of sand or dirt.*

*The master bedroom is perfect. Wood floors, sheer curtains that will billow softly in the breeze at night while I take my pet. I chuckle to myself as I picture furniture accommodating the positions I plan to put her in, the things I plan to do to her. All the scenes in her books I plan to reenact. Our own little love nest. You've done a good job, Sasha. Just a few more months and then you're mine.*

*I crouch down on the floor connected to the exterior wall of the house with my drill in hand – the small bit attached to the head. I angle the bit downward at the top of the floorboard and start the process. The wire is then threaded through the hole, feeding approximately forty eight inches into it so I can fish it through the wall from the outside and attach it to the cable. On the end of the wire I attach the tiny communication device and embed it into the floorboard. Virtually invisible. I repeat the process approximately five feet away from the first one; I'm not sure which side of the bed she sleeps on. Grabbing a rag from the backpack, I wipe up the dust caused by the drilling and leave the area as meticulous as when I walked in.*

*Upon exiting the bedroom, I'm shoved against the frame of the doorway from behind. I spin quickly to defend myself, but there is no one there. The room is dark, empty. I hadn't turned on any lights in order to go undetected – I worked with the small LED headlamp on my cap. After the incident on the deck, the uneasy feeling washing over me is elevating, the need to finish and get out of here intensifying. My heart pounds inside my rib cage so hard I can feel it in my head, my ears, the tips of my fingers. It's anxiety, I tell myself; the fear of being caught. It's also the rush of knowing I will still have control. Get in, get out, get the job done. Priorities, Aidan!*

*Sliding my feet back into my shoes at the backdoor, I close it behind me and return to the side of the house. Fishing the wall with the magnetic hook, I gently pull the wires down and attach them to the connectors that lead to the antenna above. I tuck all the cable and wires back up under the bottom ledge of the siding, securing them with flexible plumber's putty. I then test the connection. Perfect. I can communicate from up to two miles away. Oh my dear Sasha. You will be hearing me in your dreams. Don't let me down, love, or you will be hearing me in your nightmares as well.*

*Now, for the dog.*

*I tromp through the backyard toward the enormous open and finished area Sasha has designated for the beast she calls a pet. Pulling the container from my backpack, I prepare to toss the cyanide-laced dog biscuits from it when I'm shoved to the ground – the container and its contents spilling from my hands. I feel a strong kick to my ribs and I roll to my side, only to feel another kick to my stomach. My breath is stolen from my lungs as I try to rush to my feet, only to feel another kick to my ribs. What the fuck is happening?!? There is nobody here!*

*I gather enough traction to get to my feet and run – only*

*my backpack in my hands – leaving the container and dog biscuits behind.*

*And this is why you wear gloves.*

# Chapter 14

## Sasha

"Good morning, Carl," I answer cheerily when I see it's him calling.

"Miss Taylor," Carl says, his voice a mix of hesitation and necessity. I wait for him to tell me the appliances aren't being delivered today, that maybe they dropped one off the truck and I won't have a refrigerator for another week . . . or two.

"What is it, Carl?"

"Have you been out here on the yard with Oscar?"

"No," I say slowly. "I've been waiting until my attention is undivided before I bring him out. I wanted the exercise equipment delivered first. Why?"

"Is there a chance you could come out to the property this morning?" he asks. "We found something . . . concerning."

"Concerning?" I pause. "Is there something wrong with the house?"

"No, the house is fine," he reassures me. "We're thinking you might want to take one other safeguard. Could you come out to take a look and we'll talk about it when you get here?"

"I should be there in about an hour."

"That works."

An hour later I pull into my driveway and see Carl waiting for me.

As I climb out of the car, he wears a forced grin, more of a grimace really. "You can check the appliances first if you'd like, but what we want you to see is out back."

"Something tells me this isn't very good."

"Why don't we step out back first?" he suggests as he waves his hand toward the side of the house that leads to the backyard. "We can end the day on a good note provided you like the appliances."

We walk to the backyard where I see the three other workers at the front border of Oscar's exercise field – Brick and Simon standing with their hands on their hips, Dusty kneeling on the ground, crouching back on his heels with a container in his hands, sniffing the contents.

I hear Dusty growl as he looks to the others, "That's fucking cyanide. I can smell the almonds. Can't you guys smell it?"

"Your nose has been better than ours ever since the last . . . " Brick starts.

"Boys," Carl calls out sharply before he can finish. "Miss Taylor is here."

"Ah," Dusty says a little too quickly, too brightly as he gets to his feet. "Miss Sasha."

"What's going on?" I ask, eyeing the grounds as well as each one of them, not to mention the container Dusty tries, unsuccessfully, to stash behind him. "Whatcha got there, Dusty?"

Simon is the first to speak, and he doesn't hold anything back as he says, "Looks like somebody's trying to poison your dog."

"Dude!" Brick chides, backhanding his chest. "A little finesse. She's a lady."

"Someone's what?" I gasp. "Why would someone want to hurt Oscar? I've never even brought him here."

"You have a dog named Oscar?" Dusty asks, his face lighting with surprise. "I love that name!" My heart warms at his sentiment. I love it too.

"Boys," Carl says calmly yet firmly. "Task at hand."

"We found this," Dusty says, holding up a container half-filled large dog biscuits; some broken, the rest still whole. I reach for it, but he pulls it back. "Don't touch it!" he orders quickly. "We're going to have it tested. We think it's been poisoned. I can smell something funky in it. We've already searched the dog's," he clears his throat, "excuse me, *Oscar's* yard, and it's clear."

I point to the container in his hand. "Th . . . tho . . . those are poisoned?"

He nods. "We think so."

"Why would anyone poison Oscar?"

"You have no idea?" Simon asks.

"No! Oscar's harmless!" I cry and finish sheepishly, "Unless of course you piss him off."

Brick lifts a brow. "Piss him off?"

"W…well," I stammer. "He's protective."

"Pitbull?" Dusty questions.

"No!" I snap harshly. "He's a Belgian Malinois. It's their nature."

I swear I see Simon's hackles rise as he slowly raises his head and eyes me curiously. "You have a Belgian . . . named Oscar?"

"Yes."

He narrows his eyes. "How old is he?"

It's my turn for hackles to rise and they do, as well as my defenses. What possible difference could it make how old Oscar is? They called me out here over suspected poisoned biscuits and it has suddenly turned into an inquiry about my dog. The only people who know about this exercise field for Oscar are my friends and these guys. What do his breed and age have to do with anything? Oh my God! Tell me they don't steal dogs and sell them for fighting. Dusty said pit bull. Simon's interest grew with Belgian. They wouldn't do that, would they? Oscar is priceless!

Folding my arms over my chest, I match his narrowed eyes and raise him an arched brow, using one of my grandma's old lines. "Old enough to know better but he does it anyway."

"Boys," Carl interrupts what has turned into a stare down.

"I think we've gotten away from what we called Miss Taylor out here for. Let's get back to the reason."

I turn to Carl. "There's more? What exactly would that be?"

"Safety, Miss Taylor," he replies. "Or what we call an added layer of protection. We can install poles at the corners and in strategic points throughout and enclose the yard with a fine mesh net. You won't have to worry about wind blowing it down because it's breathable, and people won't be able to throw things over the fence and into the enclosure. We could get the poles set today and have the net up tomorrow."

I point to the container Dusty holds in his hand. "Where did you find that? And don't you think you may have wanted to leave it be until it was checked for prints?"

"Doesn't have any prints," Simon sneers.

Dusty shoots Simon a glare. "The other thing we wanted to talk to you about is a lock on your front gate. They had to have a pretty good throwing arm to get that container all the way up here from the back or . . . they brought it in from the front."

"Why on earth would anyone want to hurt Oscar?" I mutter.

"You don't have any enemies, Miss Taylor?" Simon asks cockily before he grabs his ear and rubs it as if he's been bitten.

*Good! I hope it was an extra-large mosquito.*

Up until today, he's been nothing but pleasant and kind. I'm taken aback by his attitude, not to mention his snide tone. "I'm a widow who writes books for a living, Simon." I tip my chin and flash him a snarky grin. "The only thing anyone's ever threatened me with is not reading another of my books or writing a bad review when they didn't experience the proper amount of orgasms via the pages. I think I'm pretty safe." I hadn't meant to spew my truth so freely – let's face it, I'm not everybody's cup of tea, but I make a damn good cup of coffee – and he pissed me off. I wasn't going for shock value, but due to the gaping jaw and every millimeter of irises being surrounded by the whites of his eyes, I think I attained it. I spin on my heel and look to Carl. "The netting sounds good. Please install the lock on the gate as well. Thank you. Have a good day."

As I head for my car, I hear shouts from the backyard.

"You asshole! Show some respect!"

"Dude! That was low, even for you!"

"How was I supposed to know?!"

Finally, it's Carl's voice I hear. "You got some groveling to do, son. Get your ass out there. And you'd better hope Callum doesn't find out about this."

"Miss Taylor!" Simon yells as I open the door to my car and climb in. "Please wait!"

He's barely breathing hard by the time he reaches my car, but his cheeks are flushed. *Ah, embarrassment.* He hangs his head as his arm rests on the top of my door.

"I'm sorry, Miss Taylor. I had no idea."

I slide my shades on to hide the tears that rim my eyes. I think about Ben every day, multiple times a day, every single time I look at the gift he left me in Oscar. I hurt so bad sometimes at night, I fold my body into a ball that aches from crying. I wrap myself in arms that are my own because I don't have his to hold me anymore. For the first time today, I openly admitted that I am a widow. I've never used that word before. It felt like venom on my tongue. That title belongs to little old ladies who spent a lifetime with husbands, raised children together, watched their grandchildren come into the world – maybe even a few greats. It doesn't belong to thirty-somethings who have nothing left but wishes that weren't granted, memories that had yet to be made, time saved in a bottle that will never be uncorked. Money may buy you comfortable *things*, but it will never buy you *comfort*. I would give it all up for one more day with my husband. The only words I would ever write again are *I love you, Benjamin Chase Arkelpaine*. Those vows you take? 'Til death do you part? Death didn't exactly part us – it left me behind, taking the best part of me with him. And I can't seem to find enough of what's left to make me whole again.

"And if you had known, Simon?" I stare out the windshield toward my new house in front of me, my voice breaking. "Would it make a difference?"

"Probably," he admits sheepishly. "I am sorry. I was out of

line. I love dogs, love working with them. Seeing that container and what was in it really pissed me off and I took it out on you. It'll never happen again. You deserve more respect."

"What were you doing out by the dog's area this morning?"

"Carl wanted us to give it one last inspection before we took off," he explains. "We had to water the grass and check the seams in the new sod. Guess it's a good thing he had us check, huh?"

"Guess so. But Oscar's trained to not eat off the ground." I pull my shades down to the tip of my nose and look straight into his eyes. "Simon, I don't deserve more respect than anyone else does because of my situation. And a little heads up. Should you and Sky get together at some point in any capacity, be forewarned, if you hurt her, you and Oscar will be meeting. Keep in mind, he likes her. Also keep in mind, his bite is much worse than his bark. I don't care how many dogs you've *worked* with, Oscar is special."

He scrunches his nose, which makes him look youthful and reminds me a bit of my brother Trent when he was little and in trouble. "I wouldn't think of it." He sighs deeply. "I'm sorry for your loss, Miss Taylor. It won't happen again."

*No, it can't happen again, Simon. You only lose the love of your life once, right?*

I start my car. "Alright then. See you next week."

"Can I help you move the equipment tomorrow?" He smiles apologetically. "Free of charge. It's my day off. I'll bet Dusty and Brick would help too."

Returning a smile, I tell him, "The ladies and I have done it once before. We're set. But thanks for the offer."

"The same ladies from yesterday?" His smile grows into an impish grin and his eyes light with mischief. "Now I know Dusty and Brick would be more than happy to help. Say when, and we'll be here. If you want, we can come to your old place and load it too. We all have pickup trucks."

*Of course they do. We're used to it. I think every man in Tennessee that works in construction, or doesn't work in an office, has a pickup truck. That, or a horse. And if they have a horse, they need a pickup truck to haul the trailer that holds the horse so . . .*

*oh God.*

"Miss Taylor?" Simon pulls me from my mundane – rather insane – thoughts.

My mouth engages well before my brain does. "Do you own horses too?"

His brow furrows so deeply the hair nearly meets in the middle. "Ma'am?"

My own brows nearly meet my hairline as I stare at him. Holy shit! I'm not wearing bifocals. I haven't taken to coloring my hair. My girls are perky. Cellulite has yet to become my enemy. I don't wear Spanx. I don't even own a pair of granny panties. Of all the injustices in this world . . . he has to be my age, or at the very least close to it. Sky is three months older than I am!

"Did you just call me ma'am?"

He clears his throat and nearly chokes on his own spit. "I . . . I didn't mean anything by it."

"Be here at ten o'clock in the morning, Simon." I arch a brow, then shoot him a saccharin smile. "I'm sure you wouldn't want to see me break a hip, maybe strain my back lifting something. You know how it is with us old folk."

He opens his mouth, closes it, then repeats the process once more, blushing profusely. I reach for my door, pull it closed, put the car in reverse and resist squealing out of the driveway as I take my leave. Ma'am! That title belongs to my mother, my grandmother, Mrs. Johnson across the street from my childhood home.

Ten o'clock, Simon. And bring your muscle with you. I reach up to my right shoulder and rub it with my left hand in an effort to loosen up the tightness I caused while packing.

*Power of suggestion, Sasha. That's all it is. Damn you, Simon!*

# Chapter 15

## Sasha

Walking through each room one last time, I bid adieu to the house that has been my shelter for nearly three years. The movers have the truck almost fully loaded, Oscar's equipment has been folded down and waiting to be carefully placed on the truck last — the tires wrapped in plastic so as not to stain any other items. I turn off the lights as I leave each room, Oscar at my heels with every step.

Once we reach the living room, I turn to him. "This is it. You ready to go make a house a home, buddy?" He looks up and tilts his head. The black face graced with beautiful dark eyes, the distinct shape of a brown heart on the top of his nose, a strong regal jaw and neck. The stance and carriage of a warrior. I swear he knows what I'm asking. "Now or never, Oscar. Let's go."

We arrive at the new house at nine o'clock — the movers ten minutes later. Shae, Rhea, and Sky pull up in one vehicle together and park in the street behind my SUV. Shae and Rhea exit the car with hands full of breakfast from a bakery. I know what's in them. It will consist of everything from bagels, muffins, and cinnamon rolls. The tray Shae carries will hold the fancy coffees we treat ourselves to on rare occasions.

"Is there an ounce of protein in there?" I yell, pointing to the bags that read "*Roll Over Baby*".

"You want protein? Go cook an egg. We're getting our bread on!" Rhea shouts as she holds the bags up higher, stopping to spin and swirl her hips as the stereo plays Rascal Flatts' "Life is a Highway". She swears they are not singing about cars – you know, driving and riding and all.

"She always like that?" the deep, chuckling voice behind me asks. *Brick.* They're an hour early.

"I think the exception is the dentist's chair. Then she only quivers." *I don't bother to add when she's over the trauma she does joke about being drilled.*

"What about the gynecologist?" He grins mischievously.

I smirk. "Not after they assigned her a female. When did you guys get here?"

We hear laughter coming from the direction of the moving truck and glance over, noting the men watching Rhea. "Don't you guys have a truck to unload?!" Brick shouts angrily. They immediately turn away and start the task of opening the back of the truck, preparing to unload my life from the back.

Simon and Dusty walk toward us from the side of the house as Sky shuts the car off, as well as the obnoxiously loud stereo, and Oscar whines from inside my SUV, begging to get out and join the party. "Where did you guys come from?"

"We parked down that a way." Brick dips his chin toward the end of the street and then holds up a key. "This is the key to the lock on the gate. There's a keypad lock on it as well. You can put your code in anytime you're ready. We've already been out back to check on the pooch's yard before we set it up for you."

Oscar barks impatiently and I open the door, ready to put his leash on him, but he jumps out before I can. "Oscar, stop!" For the first time since I've had him, he ignores my order and runs to Simon where he launches himself at him. I panic and shriek, "Oscar! No!"

He's not growling, nor baring his teeth. In fact, he's

wagging his tail. I think he's ready to pee he's so excited as he wiggles and dances around Simon. I look to my friends who watch in fascination and awe as my usually protective dog treats Simon like a long lost friend. Simon plops down to the ground on his knees at Oscar's level and gives him the attention he's begging for.

"Oscar, heel!" I demand, and he does. He sits by my side, though it's easy to see it's a struggle for him. He whimpers softly. Simon simply stares at him. Then all three men exchange a look I cannot discern, and one by one, they all reach for an ear, and flinch. *The mosquitoes sure seem to like them. I wonder if it's their cologne.*

"Well that was weird," Sky says, breaking the uncomfortable silence. "He never takes to anyone. He didn't even like me for the longest time and they lived with me for months."

"Lived with you?" Simon's inquisitive brows are raised and his eyes narrow as he waits for her to respond.

I flash Sky a silent plea. My name change wasn't my idea. My past and my present were never to cross. My real life and my fictitious life do not live in the same zip or area code. My publisher would have dropped me in a New York minute.

Thank God for Sky's quick thinking. We nicknamed her QT in high school. 'Quick Thinker'. Everyone else thought we were simply calling her cutie. Not that she didn't qualify – she's gorgeous – but her thought processes are faster than anyone I know. And when we needed a fast excuse, or plan, Sky was our rescue.

"Sasha's landlords never told her she couldn't have pets," she answers, feigning a scowl as if remembering something bitter. Damn, the woman is fast. "When she got that sweet little puppy, they told her it was either him or move out. He was this itty bitty bundle of fur." She holds her hands approximately twelve inches apart. Her voice is so sugary and sappy, it makes my teeth hurt. But, I must admit she is convincing. "What was she to do? I offered she stay with me until she found landlords that were dog lovers. And now, she has a home of her own that has room for Oscar and any other pet she wants."

I feel bad that she's lying for me. She was my landlord when

I was gifted with Oscar, though she didn't give me an ultimatum. He wasn't exactly a sweet little puppy – certainly wasn't itty bitty – but she did wait until I found some dog lovers to let me rent from them.

Simon doesn't look convinced, but he lets it go and looks to the moving truck. "Shall we get the equipment unloaded and set up?"

"Yeah, uh, sounds good," Dusty says, scratching the back of his head.

"Let's do that," Brick adds, eyeing Oscar a bit too long for my liking before they head for the truck.

"I only bent the truth a little bit," Sky whispers in my ear.

"Bent it? Sky, a mountain road doesn't have that many twists and turns!" I whisper back, frustrated. "What happens if he finds out?"

"Finds out what?" she quietly scolds. "They're construction workers, Sasha. I truly doubt they read romance books. What are they going to do, go tell the public they know who Sara Paine really is? You didn't tell him your pen name. Even then, it doesn't connect you to Ben. Stop being afraid of your own damn shadow!"

I pull back on her shoulder as she advances toward the house. "Did you see the way they looked at Oscar?" I scowl down at my canine hero. "And you, mister. What's with making friends with strangers?"

A sudden chill runs down my spine. *Strangers.* Oscar doesn't hate men in general – he hates Aidan Lehner.

The girls supervise the movers inside while I take Oscar with me out to the exercise yard and watch the guys as they get started setting up his equipment; the bars, the tires, the short wall for him to climb, the pilons to weave in and out of. Though, to be quite honest, they don't seem to need any guidance.

"We've got this, Miss Sasha," Dusty assures me with a smile. "If you want, you can leave Oscar with us and see that they put everything where you want it inside."

I eye him skeptically. "How do you know how to put this together?" It's a very designated and well-designed regimen for him to run. Ben sent me a recommended blueprint and I followed it down to the last hoop for him to jump through.

Brick winces and his mouth twists to the side. "Uhhh . . . Westminster dog show on TV?"

Yeah, right. I can see the three of them sitting around drinking beers and eating pizza while cheering on dogs. Toss in some hot wings and jalapeno bites and I'm thoroughly convinced. Not! Besides, that's for show dogs. Oscar and I have watched it a time or two. He actually seems to enjoy it. I think the German Shepherds are his favorite. I myself prefer the Bichons.

Simon is concentrated on his task, a scowl on his face, nary a glance in our direction as he connects the hurdle bars.

"Really?" I say cheerily, setting him up for failure. "I love that show, especially when they test the swimmers. I reserve the water night every year just so I can see which one makes it to the other side of the lake first. I was rooting for the beagle this year. Did you see how fast that little guy was?"

Brick laughs heartily. "Yeah, he was . . ."

"Brick!" Simon shouts. "Need some help over here. Now!"

I turn back to the house, Oscar still by my side, which is exactly where he is going to stay. I'm confused. They obviously mean me no harm; Oscar would sense that, wouldn't he? Even so, the winds have shifted. Something has changed. Simon apologized yesterday for his behavior and today, he can barely look at me. He's angry, dark, moody. The look on his face when Oscar ran to him; I'll never forget it. A cross between agony and delight. I felt like I was moments away from seeing a giant of a man brought to tears . . . by a dog.


## *Brick, Dusty, and Simon*


*"Not a word!" Dusty whisper shouts to both of the other men as he picks up another pole to assemble the wall climb. "We're all on edge right now. He's a Belgian. So what if he has a heart on his nose? I'm sure there are a shitload out there that have weird markings. You guys are reading too much into this. Let's just do*

*our job."*

*Simon glares at him. "You don't see this as more than a coincidence? He ran to me like a long lost friend! You ever seen a Belgian do that? They don't leave their owner's side unless there's a reason, Dusty! She's lying about something, unless Arkelpaine's wife gave him away like he meant nothing." Simon slaps at his ear. "What the fuck is with these bugs?"*

*"Hey!" Brick holds up a finger as his eyes light. "Didn't Berkel deliver Oscar to Ben's wife? He would know!"*

*"Berkel's out in the field gathering intel for us, dumbass. He's unreachable," Dusty retorts. "But then, why would I expect you to remember that?" He finishes with a smirk, "Mr. Westminster dog show. Really?"*

*"I had to think fast!"*

*"And in the process made us look like a bunch of pussies," Simon grumbles. "Sitting around watching dancing poodles."*

*"They have big dogs on that show!" Brick huffs indignantly.*

*"Alright, enough!" Dusty scolds. "We've got a job to do. Let's just do it, enjoy these ladies while we can. And for God's sake, don't mention that dog to the Cap. He's under enough pressure as it is."*

*Brick nods sharply and doesn't bother to hide the grin that forms. "Got it. Forget the dog and think pussy instead."*

*Simon's glower is enough to wipe the grin from Brick's face as he warns, "Those ladies are not barflies. They're to be wined and dined." His face splits in an impish grin. "I do plan on helping her find the big O though. It'll just be done with Merlot instead of Michelob."*

# Chapter 16

## Jaxson

Thursday evening I pull my truck into the garage and shut off the engine. I lean my head back on the seat and take a deep breath, blowing it out slowly. The Kelly project in Charleston is finally over. If Mrs. Kelly had asked for one more "fine tuning" of another item on her list, I was going to shove a hammer in her hand and tell her to help herself. That, or take a hammer to her head. I don't think I've ever been happier to be home, sleep in my own bed, in my own house. No chance of my shouts due to nightmares seeping through the hotel walls. I can find the quiet here; just haven't found the peace yet. The waiting – waiting is the hardest part. Signing on for another four years wouldn't have made a difference. My duty is to the men we lost, avenging their deaths. I've served my duty to country. It's time I served up the vengeance. I check my phone one more time on the off chance I didn't hear it while driving. I have a tendency to enjoy my music . . . loud.

*There's nothing.*

"Come on, Berkel," I mutter as I throw the door of my truck open and reach into the back to retrieve my duffel bag containing my clothes and travel items. Stopping at the laundry room on my way in, I untie my work boots and slip them off, sort through the duffel and toss my dirty clothes into the washer. I don't start it; I want all the hot water for my shower. It's them or me and quite frankly, after the week I've had, I deserve it. Besides, unless I strip where I stand, the load won't be complete.

Passing through the kitchen, I grab two beers from the fridge and head for the stairs. Why two? Because it's hotter than Hades outside, I'm thirsty, and as I stated before, I'm happy to be home.

It amazes me. I bought this house nearly two years ago. I've got a dozen and one projects I want to get started on, but I'm so damn busy fixing other people's houses, I don't have any time to put into my own. I could put one of my crews on it, order the supplies, leave it up to them. They'd do just fine, but I want to do it with my own two hands. My own sweat. I chuckle to myself as I think of my guys at the Taylor place. Kiss ups. Nobody charms the ladies like Dusty, Brick and Simon. They're good workers – my best actually. But none of my other crews have lunch being brought to them by the owner. They'd probably work shirtless to coerce her into bringing them personal choices with their next meal, but they know better. Their tattoos would give away the Navy SEAL ink they all wear. Not yet. Eventually. One more job, one last task. Then they can go shirtless all they want. And the one tattoo we haven't gotten yet is our bone frog. We're waiting. Once our duty is over, we plan to go together. Our tribute to our fallen soldiers.

My plan is to stop over tomorrow during the workday to check on progress. They've been pouring concrete for a new patio, benched seating, and flower containers, as well as installing a hot tub. *Pampered princess.* Not that I don't have my own hot tub, but damn, I work hard. My muscles pay a price. I see mine as therapy more than a luxury. The landscaping will be finished after the pool is installed, which can't be started until the permits are signed. Then we have to wait for the digging to be done, the rebar to be installed, the concrete to be poured, the electric to be installed, etc. In other words, who the hell knows? After seeing the section she had sodded for dogs, I anticipate something new this time as well.

AKA, a replica of the Kelly project I just completed in Charleston.

I remove the rubber band from the back of my head and let my dirty hair fall down around my shoulders. For twenty years I kept it cropped short without a choice; nearly shaved, but I haven't cut it since I retired from the military. What would the SEALs think of me now? I don't shave my face clean anymore either. I trim, keep it clean, but I don't think I'll ever shave my face again. It's a tedious chore that I can take or leave. At the present time, I choose to leave it.

Turning on the shower faucet to the hottest setting, I strip my T-shirt off and toss it to the side. I take a glance in the mirror over the sink. Damn. The years are really starting to show. The dark circles under my eyes, the creases in the skin on each side of them that I only wish were from laughing. Instead, they're from stress and age.

*"Hey, old man! Losin' your stamina?" I heard Ben laugh as he called out from thirty feet ahead of me as our team ran the beach. "Ain't got what it takes to keep up with the young studs?"*

*I broke into a sprint and caught him in a headlock, bent him forward and held him in place. "Excuse me, Commander? What's that you said? You're ironing my uniforms and shining my shoes for the next month? Thought so."*

I heave a sigh that carries a sad hum. I was six years his senior and that kid was fast as lightning, but I kept up. He was my incentive and he knew it. Never a bad day for him. Never a frown on his face. He was the happiest guy I knew and he gave all the credit to the woman he loved, *his Sassy.* If I had to lose any guy in my outfit, it would have been anyone but him. He wasn't cocky – he was just happy. He was what we all wanted to be.

I stare up at the ceiling and whisper, "We're trying, Ben. We'll get 'em."

Peeling off the rest of my clothes, I step under the hot water and let the pounding massage heads work on the muscle tightness, rounding my neck a few times before grabbing the shampoo and start by washing the day's grime from my hair.

Once out of the shower, I wrap a towel around my waist

and step out into the bedroom in time to hear my phone ringing on the dresser.

"What's up, Nash?"

"You back in town?"

"Just got back."

"You wash the stink off yet?" he asks cockily.

"Asshole," I grumble. "It's called sweat from manual labor."

"Wanna grab a bite and a couple beers at Tillie's?"

"Nash," I groan. "I've been eating road food for weeks. I need something that guarantees the green is not mold, the meat is not packed between two slices of bread, and the fish doesn't taste like your last girlfriend."

"You ran into Christina?" He laughs heartily.

It was a joke – one I'm currently rolling my eyes at. I have no idea who his last girlfriend was, nor what she tasted like. I'm a bit more discerning than Nash is, always have been. However, for the last couple years I haven't had to be. Burying myself in work has prevented me from burying myself in women. It's not that I'd mind it, but by the end of the day my physical and mental fatigue leaves me with no desire for anything other than a quick meal, my own bed, and a view of the inside of my eyelids. I'd love the support of a partner, a warm body to come home to, a woman to share my bed with, bury myself in on a regular basis, someone to share my life with, but I feel like that ship has sailed – pun intended. The Navy got the best of me.

Nash Graham was a captain with the SEALs as well. We served together for nearly 12 years. Best friends for just as long. We retired at the same time after twenty years of service, both moved to South Carolina – he started a security business, I started the construction business. He guards things, we build things.

"Yo, earth to Callum," Nash prompts me out of my thoughts. "How about Monte's? We'll grab a steak. Pick you up in twenty?"

Knowing he'll show up anyway, I concede, "Sure. See you then."

# MANIPULATION 101

* * *

Monte's is a bit more crowded than I expected for a Thursday night. Weekends are like a zoo here. The hostess bats her lashes, as is the usual when Nash enters a room. He flirts, flashes a megawatt smile, and barters a table in less time than it took to walk in the door. We're being seated ahead of a waiting crowd of nearly twenty people; all wearing scowls as the hostess offers us a booth that's just opened up in a quiet corner near the back. Nash turns toward the crowd, winks and whispers, "Reservations, folks."

Once in our seats, I grab the menu and hold it in front of me. "Reservations my ass. What did you promise her? A ride on the Graham rocket?"

"Actually," he drawls. "She wants you, my friend."

"What?!" I nearly growl as I glower.

He shrugs casually. "You know, if you would quit scowling so much, you'd be more approachable. Do you know how many women have been staring at you since we walked in the door? I've heard the bad boy look is in though. Is that what you're going for? Do you know how many seats will need cleaning by the time we leave? It could be your face if you'd smile."

"You done yet, asshole?"

"When's the last time you got laid, Callum?"

"When's the last time you had an STD check, Nash?"

He grins and raises his menu, poring over it from top to bottom. "So what are you in the mood for? Steak and baked potato . . ." he lowers the menu and waggles his eyebrows, ". . . or fish?"

We hear women's laughter from nearby but our view is obscured by the half wall that separates the rows of booths. Generally, normal chatter and sounds don't distract me, but there's a voice amongst the group that I'm drawn to. A soft laugh that mimics a melody yet carries an undertone of sadness. It's forced – akin to my own somedays.

"As the vicar took the lady's mouth in a heated kiss," another one speaks as if reading porn. "He pressed his throbbing, hard length against her belly and even through her thick skirts, she

107

felt his desperate need for . . .”

"Oh, shut it!” the raspy protests of the melody carrier stop her. “I don’t write Victorian romance. What on earth have you been reading?”

"Really, Rhea,” another one scolds. “She writes contemporary. Good thing Sky edits. She would know unless the *lady* is stripped down to her underwear, she couldn’t feel his *throbbing, hard length* through the equivalent of a chastity belt. Those dresses were torture. Not to mention thick as quilts.”

Nash leans forward on his elbows, his brow scrunched in mischievous curiosity. “What the fuck is that?”

"Sounds like a book club,” I mumble, though intrigued.

"Sounds like they need to get laid.” He snickers. “You want to go check them out? I’ll give you first choice.” He swats at his ear then looks around quickly. “Ouch! Damn, I think something just bit me.”

# Chapter 17

## Sasha

Leaving the restaurant, we capture the gazes, and a few scowls, from mutual patrons. *Thank you, Rhea.* Give the girl more than two drinks and the entire rodeo has heard your conversation. In our case this evening, it was half the restaurant.

"It was promo, dahling," she reassures me exaggeratedly on our way to the car. She holds up one finger, though it is the middle one. "I'm straight as an arrow."

"Why are you flipping us off?" Sky asks.

"I'm not!" Rhea yells. "I was emphasizing straight. My index finger is crooked due to jamming it into too many men's chests."

I giggle. "Due to them staring at yours?"

"You know it!" she says with a sharp nod, then brings her head back up and blinks slowly.

"Get in the car," Sky grumbles. "We're cutting you off."

Rhea giggles and puffs her chest out. "So long as you don't cut *them* off. They're my best asset. Brick loves them."

Our footsteps falter in unison and Sky grabs my elbow to steady her gait. Shae glares at Rhea. "You're having sex with

Brick? Already?"

"Not technically. It's only with my boobs!" Rhea snaps defensively.

Sky scrunches her nose. "How do you *technically* only have sex with your boobs?"

My gaze starts at the ground and my eyeballs run a full slow circle in their sockets, accompanied by probably ten blinks before they're done. They've read my books. I may write fiction, but the acts are real as rain. Boob sex is awesome, but I don't think contributing that little gem to the conversation right now is going to be very helpful.

"I don't have sex with them!" Rhea screeches. "Brick does."

I have to do something to quell the perfect storm developing in the middle of the parking lot and the catfight sure to follow. I will admit, six weeks does seem a bit fast for Rhea to jump into sex with a construction worker. We always pictured her with a college professor or a genius technology expert. She's beautiful, smart, and so sweet. Brick is a nice guy; handsome, funny. Not very quick with a thought when he needs to cover his ass, though. Westminster dog show. Oh please! On the other hand, that does mean he's not a good liar. Point to Brick.

"Guys," I plead. "We're her friends, not her parents. If Rhea wants to squeeze her boobs, let her do it."

Sky's mouth twists before enlightenment fills her eyes as she looks to Rhea. "Is that where you squeeze your boobs together and he puts his . . ."

"Yup," Rhea answers with a pop of the P and a bob of her eyebrows.

Sky looks down at her chest and studies her B cups, frowning. "Mine aren't very big."

"Doesn't take much," Rhea reassures her. "I think it's more the idea itself. You only need enough to wrap around his . . ."

"Anatomy lesson is over," I interrupt her, heading for the car. When no one follows, I glance back and see Shae studying Rhea, her eyes narrowed.

"What do you get in return?"

Rhea smiles smugly. "Check out Chapter 22 in Sasha's latest novel. Make sure you have your little buddy close." She winks. "And Dusty's phone number handy."

"So you're not having sex with him?" Shae asks her.

Rhea looks her straight in the eyes and waves a hand down her body and flips it outward in a dramatic flair as if showcasing the goods. "He doesn't get all of this art . . . until I get all of his heart."

By the time I get home, I find my fourth best friend sitting tall and proud in the middle of the living room with what looks like a ball of lint hanging from his mouth. Upon closer inspection, I find it's not lint at all. It looks to be pillow stuffing, though not from any pillows on the sofa. Those sit in their original places, fully intact, thoroughly stuffed.

"Oscar, what do you have?" I eye my canine scrupulously, bending forward and reaching for whatever foreign matter he holds in his jowls, extracting what seem to be . . . wet, slobbery feathers. The only thing stuffed with feathers is the down-filled pillows on my bed.

"Oscar!" I scold as I rush for the bedroom. He follows close on my heels, his tail wagging proudly. A tail that should be tucked between his legs. No whimper of apology, no head bowed in shame. Once in the room, I shriek in shock at the sight in front of me. My pillows are shredded, the comforter and sheets are pulled from the head of the bed and in a pile at the center. Feathers are everywhere. Oscar jumps up on the bed and starts to dig into the top of the mattress at the headboard against the wall.

"No! Get down!" I yell. "Oscar, no!" He stops his determined destruction of my bed, but only drops down on his belly with his nose poked between the mattress and headboard and growls.

"Did you lose a toy under the bed?" I ask, as if he can understand. Oh God, what if there's a snake under there? A small wild animal that got into the house?

I run to the kitchen closet and grab the broom. Wait! What am I going to do with a broom? Thwack it? Then what? I call for Oscar and wait for him to join me in the kitchen, then run to the bedroom door and close it.

"Didn't we just have dinner together?" Rhea sasses into the phone rather than greeting me with a plain old 'hello'.

"Can I get Brick's phone number?" I ask warily. I'm not sure where he lives, but my highest hopes right now are that it isn't too far. My mind went blank when searching it for someone to call. I suppose I could have called an exterminator, maybe the police. And tell them what, Sasha? Uhh… I think there's something under my bed? I can hear them now.

*"Yeah, lady, those dust bunnies are real monsters."*

"I can do you one better," she says giddily. "I can give you Brick. He's right here."

Recalling the conversation from earlier I groan, "He isn't between your boobs, is he?"

She giggles. "Not yet. Hey, you okay?"

"Not really."

"On our way," she says without hesitation and before giving me a chance to explain. Rhea is the softest of the three, the most sentimental. She would be the first to lay down and cry with me, but she would also be the first to draw blood in my defense. She's small but she's mighty. The one you want in your corner. Small wonder she has the biggest boobs. Her heart would burst out of her chest without the extra protection.

An hour later, my bedroom has been virtually torn apart – the bed, dresser, and nightstands moved, searched behind, and put back in place. Closets and master bathroom inspected. *Nothing.* Rhea helped me vacuum up the feathers and replace the bedding – I stole a couple pillows from the guest room until I buy new ones.

Brick studies Oscar for the longest time, his brow furrowed as he stands with his hands on his hips. "Something set him off," he says before he squats down and takes Oscar's face in his hands and goes nose to nose with him. A smart man would not venture such a risk. A confident man would though. "Did you chew up your mama's pillows?" Oscar's head tilts as if asking for understanding – not forgiveness. Brick leans his forehead on the bridge of Oscar's nose and whispers so softly I almost don't hear it, "You're a good boy. We'll figure it out."

"He's such a sweetheart, isn't he?" Rhea sighs as she takes in the sight.

"He was sweeter before he tore up my pillows," I grumble.

She slaps my arm and huffs, "I meant Brick."

"No," I tell Oscar as I slip into my running shoes this morning. His whimper is almost more than I can take as he dips his head and looks mournful. "You were naughty last night. You tore up my pillows. I'll do your exercise yard with you later." I think it hurts me more than him. I hate going to the beach without him – especially before the sun has risen – and he hates it when I do. Aidan will be there though. At least I think Aidan will be there. If not, I'll come back to retrieve Oscar and take him with me. I'm conflicted. Oscar is a part of me and if Aidan can't get used to that, how are we ever going to be the friends he promises?

I lock my back door to a barking Oscar and round the house to leave by way of the gate to the front. I don't need to leave it unlocked so the construction guys have access; they have the combination. As I open the gate I find Aidan standing on the other side of it waiting for me. I jump in surprise and as I shout, "Aidan!", Oscar goes ballistic inside the house and jumps up to the large bay window on the front of the house.

Aidan grasps my elbow and snaps harshly, "You have got to do something about that dog, Sasha."

"The dog is doing his job." The deep, severe, familiar voice comes from the middle of the yard as Simon makes his way toward us. There is no Callum Construction truck nearby and he's nearly an hour early this morning.

"Who are you?" Aidan sneers as he stares at him.

"Good morning, Miss Taylor," Simon greets me as he reaches us, ignoring Aidan and his question. He towers over us, his thick neck and broad shoulders intimidating at a distance, but now that he's close up, it seems Aidan is rethinking his stance and doing a double take. Simon glares down at Aidan and orders, "Take your hand off the lady." Aidan drops his grip from my elbow immediately. Simon then walks to the bay window, placing his hand on the glass and speaking to Oscar. "I've got her, boy." Oscar calms but doesn't leave his spot in the window, continuing to observe.

"What the hell is going on?" Aidan barks. "Sasha, who is this and what is he doing talking to your dog? Men that make friends with your dog are perfect candidates for rapists!"

"Aidan!" I admonish with a scowl. "Simon would never."

Simon walks back to us slowly and purposefully, a disdainful look of murder painting his eyes. "Men that lurk around a woman's house in the dark," he says, taking another step closer, "looking over their shoulder as they do," another step, "scouting the area," one more step until he's towering over Aidan, "and taking her by surprise are much more likely candidates. But then, I tend to dislike anyone the lady's dog dislikes. Seems Oscar is not a fan."

"What business is that of yours?" Aidan sneers.

Simon folds his arms over his chest, virtually making Aidan back up a step or two. "You made it my business when you insinuated I might be a rapist."

"When he what!?" Another low voice comes from the south side of the yard where Brick and Dusty round the corner. Oscar barks excitedly when he hears them and jumps up on the window; his toenails clicking loudly as he scratches at the glass.

"Aidan." I reach for his arm but stop myself. Distance feels like my friend right now. "I think I'm going to pass on the walk this morning."

His head whips toward me so fast I swear I hear the click of a vertebra in his neck. "You're choosing?" He narrows his eyes and moves close to my ear so only I can hear. "You know there are consequences for bad decisions, Sasha."

I feel the nausea rising from deep in my belly and the shiver that causes goosebumps to break out on my skin. Aidan has never threatened me but that sure felt like one. Consequences? What the hell did that mean?

"Miss Sasha," Brick says, extending his elbow for me to take. "What do you say we take Oscar out back and show him a good time? The sun's about up and he seems a little . . ." he looks to Aidan and scowls, ". . . *agitated.*"

## Dr. Aidan Lehner

*I watch as the four of them enter through the gate to the backyard – the last asshole smirking right before he closes . . . and locks it. Sons o' bitches. Where do they get off? She's mine. I spent hours last night trying to get the wires readjusted. They must have knocked things loose while working out back. Damnit! This is the second time I've had to repair the connections. That damn dog. Listening to him howl from inside while I tried to concentrate made it nearly impossible. She needs to spray for bugs! Damn things kept biting my ears so hard they're swollen and bruised this morning.*

*Funny these idiots thought they could keep me out with a combination lock on the gate. A determined man will find his way in though. Honestly, all I needed to know was her wedding anniversary. Never fails. These widows are so easy. I wasn't positive she would meet me on the beach this morning after last night's fiasco with the canine culprit, so I was prepared. My goal was to make her think the construction crew had carelessly left her gate unlocked, convince her of their incompetence. But she got the gate unlocked and open before I got to it. I saw her little blonde bimbo friend show up last night with the same muscle from this morning. I watched him carry trash to the cans.*

*And this morning I watch as he takes her by the elbow and leads her away from me. Big mistake, pal. Big mistake. There is a price for defiance.*

*Three more months and this will all be over.*

# Chapter 18

## Jaxson

The laughter is so loud and raucous from the backyard, I don't think anyone hears my truck door close. I stand by the open gate and listen for a while before I make my way toward the voices as well as the music playing.

"Miss Taylor," Simon says with a long moan, "I swear it gets better every time. You really ought to let the three of us take you sometime. We can do it together."

*Take her? The three of them? Together?*

"We could show you the best you've ever had," Brick follows. "I mean, it's nothing like you've done for us, but if you let us take you down there, you could relax while you enjoy it. No work for you while you savor the efforts of others."

*The best she's ever had? Take her down there?*

"You could relax. " Dusty laughs. "We'll do the driving."

*They'll do the driving?*

"Gotta admit, Miss Taylor," Carl says with an added warning, "But don't you ever tell Marilyn I said this, you've got some spicy tricks even she doesn't know. I'm gonna introduce you two. You'll have to teach her."

*Spicy tricks? Carl wants in on the action?*
*What. The. Fuck.*

I storm through the walkway to the backyard to find all of them sitting at a picnic bench . . . stuffing their faces. There's a table loaded with buns, meats, and all the condiments. There are a couple bowls filled with salads of some sort, chips, bottles of Gatorade and water. All the moans and compliments having been over food . . . not sex. No midday orgy taking place.

Then I see her. Apparently the infamous Miss Taylor. Fragile old lady, my ass. This woman is anything but fragile. I could talk about sex with her – anytime she wants. She is . . . breathtaking. This has to be a different Miss Taylor though – Dusty said precious gem – her daughter maybe. Blonde hair tossed up in a messy bun – yeah, I know what they are, I throw mine back in a man bun once in a while. Legs that I can only imagine because she's wearing shorts that hit mid-thigh, but her calves look pretty damn fine. She wears a T-shirt that's not too tight – though right now I'm wishing it were. You can only hide so much and what's under there looks pretty damn good. But I'd love to see the rest of that fine curvature as the soft cotton hugs . . .

"Boss!" Brick hollers, holding up a bottle of blue Gatorade. "You hungry?"

I glance at my watch, more for effect than anything – I'm well aware of the time. "Little past lunchtime, isn't it?"

Simon lifts his brows and shoots me a stern glare. "No, we take an hour on Fridays and work until four."

I slip my shades off my nose, eyeing him skeptically. "You skip your early off and work late on Fridays?"

"Yup," Dusty chimes cheerily. "If you could eat here, you would too."

*Hell yeah, I could eat here, but I'm not about to share that.*

"I'll bet there's enough for you," Brick says as he turns to the blonde. "Think we can feed the boss?"

Her mouth lights with a smile that makes me think of many things other than food. "Sure. What would you like? We have . . ."

"I'll pass," I rudely interrupt, because quite frankly, food is not what's making my mouth water right now. *Business, Jaxson, business.* "Where's your mother?"

Her eyebrows shoot skyward above the aviator shades she wears before she slowly slides them off. Puzzlement flashes across mesmerizing, gorgeous green eyes. There's a story behind them – one I can't read, though I want to.

"My mother?" Her mouth moves into the funniest little twist to the side before it twitches. "Well, if memory serves, it's Friday and that would mean she's with her bridge club." She holds up one finger then uses it to tap her chin – the chin that sits below a puckered mouth that I want to see . . . "No, wait," she holds that same finger up, "with the time difference, she's still at lunch so bridge should start in about an hour." She grins wryly. "In Tennessee. Did you want me to call her?"

The guys chuckle from their seats at the table as Carl rises from his and joins us where we stand. "Miss Taylor, this is Jaxson Callum, owner of the company. Jaxson, Miss Taylor." He directs a lifted brow at me and inclines his chin. *"Your customer."*

She extends her hand to shake mine. "Mr. Callum."

Don't ask me why, but for some reason it doesn't feel right to take it. There's a part of me that wants to pull her into a hug . . . another that feels the need to push her away. Carl clears his throat, urging me to follow protocol. Instead, I glance toward the picnic table where the guys sit with shit-eating grins plastered on their faces. *Precious gem. They'll pay for that.* I make it clear with one scowl that I won't be buying their beers tonight before turning my attention back to her.

"You make a habit of feeding strange men that work for you, Miss Taylor?" I feel that familiar harsh and painful flick to the back of my ear but I resist the urge to rub it – my determination to win the battle of our stare down stronger.

The daggers she shoots from her eyes make her a strong contender as she scowls. "I don't see you *working*, Mr. Callum. Whether or not you're *strange* is debatable. But I'll make an exception in your case. There's a sandwich at the end of the table made precisely for you." She flashes a snarky grin and holds up her thumb and finger, mere millimeters apart. "Just a pinch of arsenic and I only spit on it twice."

Howling laughter sounds from the picnic table once more, pissing me off probably more than it should, but I don't like losing. She is mouthy, challenging, and for some strange reason, too damn tempting.

"Don't you have a husband to cook for?" The moment the words leave my mouth, I feel that sting on the back of my ear again, but worse yet I see what happens.

Her smirk fades.

Her shoulders deflate.

She pales.

She trembles.

Her eyes tell the story I couldn't read but sure can now. *Loss.*

She shatters . . . on the inside. And for some reason, so do I.

"Jaxson!" Carl admonishes at the same time I hear "Damn, boss!" "Whoa!" and "Dude!" from behind me.

"Within a minute of you entering my yard, it was apparent you could be a rude, Mr. Callum," she says softly. "Within two I knew you could be a jerk when you refused to shake my hand." Tears rim her eyes as she finishes, "But now it's pretty blatant you're just downright cruel."

I hear a dog whimper then bark from inside the house she turns toward. "Please don't let him ruin your lunch, guys. I'll clean up when you're done."

"Miss Sasha!" Brick calls out as he scowls at me, then runs to catch her before she can get inside. He pulls her into a hug and pats her on the back. I turn to head for my truck to hide in shame and find a place to kick my own ass when I hear her tell Brick, "Thanks for your help with Oscar this morning."

I freeze.

It's *her* voice. The woman from the restaurant last night. I would have recognized it immediately if I hadn't pissed her off the minute I set foot in the yard. *Oscar.* This day couldn't get any worse. As if I needed another reminder of what a shit day this already was. Another failed recon mission, no leads, more waiting time. I just want it over with. Justice, vengeance, live my life in peace. No more faces that haunt my nightmares. No more guilt. I simply want to move on.

I look to Dusty and Simon, who remain at the table, glaring at me. "You clean up the mess. Don't you dare leave it for her."

"Wouldn't think of it," Simon replies cockily with a raised brow. "Sure you don't want that sandwich? I could dress it up for you before you go. You know, just in case she missed an ingredient or two."

Dusty heaves a sigh. "Give him a break. It ain't like you haven't fucked up, Simon. I remember you groveling not too long ago."

"This job is more trouble than it's worth," I mumble, sauntering to the drive where my truck awaits. Another flick to the back of my ear. This time I do rub it. "Damn bugs."

"Jaxson, wait up," Carl shouts from behind me. I stop at the side of the house, my back to him, head hung low. "News wasn't what you were expecting?"

"Is it ever?" I sigh, turning to see him, hands in his pockets, waiting patiently, rocking on his heels. "They've gone deep underground. Gonna have a helluva time finding them now."

"So you take it out on a customer?" He dips his chin and eyes me knowingly. "You owe her an apology."

"How was I supposed to know?"

He shrugs. "Doesn't make any difference. You know now. Jaxson, she's a sweet lady who reminds me of my daughters. She does what she does because she likes to be nice to people." He chuckles. "I don't think she'd know an ulterior motive if it kissed her on the cheek."

I look up at a clear blue sky that feels like it just dumped a bucket of shit on me and blow out a breath. "I'll figure out something."

He nods and laughs. "I'm sorry usually works pretty well."

My eyes shift to the left on their way back down and that's when I see it. The entire A-frame of the roofline is clean – sharp edges – but where the wall meets the roofline, a loop of copper wire peeks out from under the corner trim of the siding. I walk to the corner of the house and study the path of the connected cable that runs the length of the wall to under the siding along the foundation and ends in the middle.

I look back to Carl. "What's on the other side of this wall?"

"Master bedroom," he answers easily. "Why?"

"You been in there?"

He hesitates then squirrels his face. "Well, yeah. So have you. Showed it to you about a month ago. Refinished the oak floors and remodeled the bathroom. Why?"

My eyes follow the line of cable to the copper wire at the top of the wall and spot the tiny receiver. "You been in there since she moved in?"

"No, no reason to be." His brow furrows. "Brick was in there last night. Her dog tore up a bunch of stuff, I guess."

My blood boils and I see red. Brick would never stoop so low as to use electronics – this must be old – but the thought of him with the woman who lit my senses in the restaurant with only the sound of her voice is unsettling. A customer? He knows better – it's a company violation. This woman? It feels like a personal violation. "Brick is messing around with a customer?"

Carl gives me one of his classic *you dumbass* glares and shakes his head. "Do you have any idea what it'd do to that boy if he thought you'd lost faith in him? You're like a big brother. She needed help last night and Brick is dating one of her friends. They came over to help her. He's not in violation of company rules."

"Brick is dating one of her friends?" *Yup. This day just gets better and better.*

"You'd have to ask him about it." He smirks. "Then you can ask Simon and Dusty about dating a couple of her other friends."

I take a long deep breath and roll my neck to prevent the muscles from locking in a spasm. I don't want to ask Brick anything. I want to ask *her* everything.

"How old is she?" There, that's one question I can ask without being totally obvious.

He places a heavy hand on my shoulder and blows an exasperated breath. "Damn, son. Now I know you ain't that stupid and I know your mama taught you better. The one question you do not ask a woman is 'how old are you' and the one question you do not answer is 'does this dress make me look fat'." He laughs. "Words of wisdom if you want to make it to a ripe old age."

I glare for only a moment before I mutter, "I gotta go."

"Flowers usually earn you a brownie point or two," he says with a chuckle as I brush past him. "Don't do roses though. You'll look like every other dumbass that puts their foot in their mouth on a regular basis. Be better, Jaxson."

# Chapter 19

## Sasha

"No, Mr. Callum," I mumble to myself as I brush a tear away and close the door behind me, "I don't have a husband to cook for. Nor do I have a husband to hold me at night. Nor do I have a husband to tell me everything's going to be okay. Because it's not, Mr. Callum. Nothing is going to be okay. But thank you for reminding me of that. So much for southern hospitality and charm. Apparently you don't know what it is. Go buy your own damn sandwich. I hope the bread is hard and moldy and the meat is green. An old fashioned dose of penicillin. No, wait! I hope you choke on it. Callum Construction. What a joke. You should have named it Callous Construction. Something to match your cold and heartless disposition."

To think I actually found him attractive. Tall, broad shouldered, muscular, tatted. Sunkissed brown, shoulder length hair, well-trimmed beard, sharp facial features. Mysterious. The kind of men I put in my books. Maybe that was the pull, the attraction – the alpha connection. But then he took those sunglasses off. Icy silver blue eyes, the depth of which seemed unreachable. So much life that's already been lived. Pain. That's what it was.

Nice of you to share it, Mr. Callum. Newsflash. Kindness is free. You can throw that shit around like it's ocean water and what you get in return is worth its weight in gold. Try it sometime.

Oscar takes his usual place by my side as I walk through the house to my office; glued to my leg in a show of support. I sit down at my desk, open my laptop and stare at the screen. Do I open the file again? My futile attempt at nonfiction fiction? I stare at the two pictures on my desk – one of Ben and me, the other of Ben and Oscar. I keep them in my sanctuary, the only ones on display in my house. The others are all safely tucked away in storage with the exception of the one in my nightstand drawer. I couldn't take looking at them in every room anymore. But here, I use them as inspiration . . . incentive to keep going, to someday tell our story.

"Don't work on it when you're angry, Sasha," I mutter. "Mood is everything." Instead I open my files and click on 'The Beast and His Burden' and wait for it to pop open. Linking my fingers together, I turn my palms inside out and stretch them toward the screen, cracking a knuckle or two. "Here we go," I whisper to the manuscript in front of me. "He's a grumpy SOB. Ugly on the inside, hunky hot on the outside, and a dolphin-sized . . . " I groan when my phone rings and see it's Rhea calling. I knew that last thought was her fault. I swear the woman is telepathic. I could have gone my entire life never knowing the approximate size of a dolphin's necessary tool for reproductive purposes, not to mention knowing they're the only creature other than humans that actually enjoy the act of sex.

"Would you stay out of my head while I write?" I beg into the phone.

"Dolphin dongs?" She giggles. "You are never going to forget the nine-foot possibilities, are you?"

"Nine inches would more than suffice and my readers prefer phalluses of the human variety." I shake my head even though she can't see it. She doesn't need to know this particular beast in the book is fifteen inches and searching for a beauty that can handle his length.

"Unless," she drawls, "you want to write an aquatic animal

romance. Hmm, I wonder what sounds they would make. Skin slapping together under water doesn't make noise, scales rubbing together isn't very enticing, and glub, glub, glub doesn't sound very . . ."

"Oh my God," I groan. "Rhea, this is why I write and you market. Now, what's up?"

"You. Have you checked your rankings?"

"No, I don't do that. You know this."

"You really should. You came in at . . ."

"Rhea," I warn.

"Fine," she huffs. "You have two book signings this month. One in Charleston and one in Hilton Head. Saturday and Sunday. Same weekend. Want to stay the weekend and have some fun?"

"Hilton Head?" I ask incredulously. "Where, golf headquarters?"

She laughs. "Ever consider writing a romance series about golfers? Slow strokes, promises of lots of holes in one throughout the pages."

"And again, the reason I write and you market." I chuckle, then say, "More like *fore* strokes and a hole in one. Talk about quickies. Boring. Send me the dates. A getaway sounds like fun."

"How is your day going otherwise?" she asks, doubt creeping into her tone.

"You talked to Brick, didn't you?"

"Mm, he may have called me."

"I'm fine. His boss, on the other hand, is a jerk."

"Uh," she hesitates. "Brick said that was totally out of character for him. Said he's going through a rough time. He asked me to apologize."

"You're supposed to apologize for an arrogant ass? Pass. I'm a big girl. Don't worry about me. Now, I have to get back to work."

"You sure you're okay?"

"Never better. And Rhea?"

"Yeah?"

"Skin does make slapping noises under water. See ya later."

I disconnect before she has a chance to respond. I'm not giving her anatomy lessons, nor am I going to explain skin slapping together under water makes some delicious sounds. It's the depth that makes all the difference. You simply have to be close enough to the surface to hear it. Research is one thing – experience is everything. Besides, I'll bet dolphins make noise. Can you imagine? I wonder if I could get someone with sonar down there to check it out for me.

I manage two hours at my computer. A whopping 843 words added to my manuscript. Nothing to write home about and I'll probably edit half of them out tomorrow. My beast is still ugly on the inside, hot as sin on the outside, and still conflicted. Same shit, different day. Only, I think now he has a name. At the very least, a face, with silver blue eyes and a scruffy beard. I'll call him JC.

"You ready for dinner?" I ask Oscar, closing the lid on my laptop and tucking my chair up to the desk. We make our way to the kitchen where I prepare his dinner as well as my own; premium dog food for him, honey bourbon salmon and a salad for me.

Oscar runs to the bay window at the sound of a car door closing as I'm placing the last dish in the dishwasher. I check the peephole in the door when the bell chimes, blink twice in surprise, and check it again while Oscar stands guard at my side. *Are you kidding me?* I square my shoulders and stiffen my spine before whipping the door open to the present bane of my existence.

"Mr. Callum," I grind through a clenched jaw, then flash a snarky grin. "Change your mind about that sandwich?"

His mouth twitches before he pulls his lips between his teeth to hide it. He's still in his work clothes – worn blue jeans, tan construction boots, a green T-shirt though he's topped it with a flannel button down. His hair is pulled back in a ponytail this evening which only reveals his sharp facial features even more. He holds out a bouquet of flowers – a beautiful mix of lilies, white orchids, and a bright red bird of paradise in the center. Ahh, the florist's choice for an apology. Well, with the exception of the bird of paradise. Love and thoughtfulness. Either he got a hearts-in-her-eyes florist or he chose it himself.

*Amateur. At least he didn't bring roses.*

"Ms. Taylor," he says, remorsefully. "Can I come in?"

God, I itch to morph into my fourth grade English teacher and reply, "I don't know, *can* you?" but instead I choose, "Why?"

"Please?" he asks, his voice so low and pleading, I find it hard to say no.

I step back from the door and wave my hand, granting permission. Oscar stays planted at my side, but gives no warning growl, takes no protective stance. What the hell is wrong with my dog lately? Mr. Callum pauses once inside and stares at Oscar, scrupulously studying his features before he finally looks to me.

"You have a Belgian." His voice is filled with a mix of awe and surprise, and maybe just a tinge of suspicion. And again, my defenses go on high alert.

"How observant." I cross my arms over my chest. "What can I do for you, Mr. Callum?"

He clears his throat as if clearing his thoughts and holds the flowers out. "I felt I owed you an apology. I was out of line. I shouldn't have said what I did."

"Flowers aren't necessary."

He lifts a shoulder in a shrug and mumbles, "Brownie points."

"Excuse me?"

"Nothing," he mumbles again. "Would you take the flowers, please?"

It's all I can do not to laugh. He's uncomfortable. This is taking everything he has in him to grovel. He must be afraid of losing my business. I'm not about to fire them though. They're only weeks away from finishing my backyard and I'm thrilled with not only the progress but the quality as well. I reach for the vase, forgoing the complementary sniff I would normally give them, and set it on the end table near the sofa, my fingers brushing his as I do. I should have just told him where to set it. That touch should not have affected me. *But it did.*

"Thank you but this wasn't necessary." I avoid eye contact as I turn back, ready to open the door and release him from his misery and me from my discomfort.

"How long?" he asks.

How long? I'm not sure what he's asking. I look up into those silver blue eyes again, uncomfortable with the sincerity I see in them. "What?"

"How long has he been gone?"

Once again I look away. None of his men have asked, not even Carl. Who puts a time on loneliness? Your days and the nights run together in a blur after a while – so much so that you don't count them anymore. Old habits remain though. Wondering what they might want for dinner. Finding the banana peppers you hate and he loved in the grocery bag when you unload it; wondering how they got in there. Mindlessly set the table for two. Searching the bedroom every morning for the socks he would leave on the floor, and cry when you can't find them. Stepping over boots that aren't in the foyer simply out of habit. Picking up your phone to call him with good news then remember you can't. Rolling over in bed at night seeking calves to tuck your feet between when they get cold, then lift the blankets to search for the socks you unconsciously removed in your sleep to put them back on.

"Forever," I whisper. My mirthless snort follows. "Everybody else's calendar says a few years."

"I'm sorry for your loss." His sentiments are clearly sincere, but I've heard those words so many times, I've almost become numb to them.

"Thank you," I return, then look up at him and crinkle my nose. "Just don't send me a sympathy bouquet, alright?"

His lips tip in cautious amusement. "Deal." Even as small as that smile is, it softens every feature. It lights up those eyes that were hard as steel this afternoon. It shows a human side of him that I didn't think possible. "Am I forgiven?"

I arch an expectant brow. "You haven't asked for it."

His eyes widen in confusion. "What?"

"You said you felt the need to apologize, Mr. Callum. I haven't heard you actually apologize."

He studies my face, his gaze traveling from my eyes to my

mouth and back again. "Ms. Taylor seems so formal." He takes a step closer, stopping before we're toe-to-toe. He's a statue of a man, a head or more taller than me, causing me to look up to meet his gaze. Kinda like the Jolly Green Giant – sans the jolly and the green. "Soften it for me, give me a name."

"Sasha." It comes out a whisper, but not because he's intimidating. No, up close he's breathtaking.

"Sasha," he repeats slowly. But he doesn't say Sasha like everyone else does. No, it sounds like *Sausha*. It dips low on his tongue, deep in his throat, like a salsa dance; so deep it makes his Adam's apple bob. "I'm sorry, Sasha. I never meant to hurt you."

My nod is barely detectable as I absolve him. "I forgive you."

Oscar breaks the awkward moment with a notable bark, his head edging between us. Mr. Callum steps back and grins. Such a contrast from Aidan's scowl. He looks down at Oscar and extends a closed hand for him to sniff. "Think you can forgive me too?" Oscar nudges his hand, giving him permission. Mr. Callum reaches under his chin and rubs it. "Good boy."

"Thank you, Mr. Cal . . ."

"Jaxson," he interrupts, holding my gaze as he waits, then arches a brow expectantly. Why I indulge him, I have no clue, but I do.

"Jaxson." It sounds better than I expected it to. Feels good too. Smooth and strong, leaving me a bit breathless.

"Perfect." He turns to leave but as he reaches the door he hesitates, keeping his back to me. "Have dinner with me."

I fumble for a response before stupidly blurting, "I . . . I already ate."

He spins slowly, an impish grin painting his handsome face. "Tomorrow night."

I feel a menacing pinch in my temple but ignore it. "Y-you mean like a date?"

Step by steady step he walks back to where I stand. "Not if you don't want it to be, Sasha." *There's that damn salsa dance on his tongue again.* "Let me apologize properly. We'll call it dinner.

Okay?”

My mouth twists as a fury of thoughts race through my mind. I haven't been on a date in years. I don't know how to date, do I? Am I supposed to date? He places a finger under my chin and lifts my gaze to meet his.

“Dinner,” he says softly, as if he understands my dilemma. “Just dinner.”

“Okay,” I say as the uncomfortable pinch in my temple strikes once more, nearly causing me to flinch.

“Pick you up at seven.” He turns, heading for the door once again.

“Do you need my number in case you want to . . .”

“I have your number from the company records, but I'm not going to cancel,” he says confidently.

“Don't I need yours in case I . . .”

“You're not canceling either.” He pauses, his hand on the doorknob twisting it slowly. His shoulders rise with a deep breath and lower as he blows it out slowly. “I'll see you tomorrow night, Sasha.”

I sink to the floor against the back of the sofa once the door is closed, looking to Oscar. “What did I just agree to?” *And why is there is a voice in the back of my head telling me I should while the pinch in my temple tells me I shouldn't?*

What do I wear? He's a blue jeans kinda guy. I have plenty of jeans and ankle boots to match his construction boots. No flannel shirts, mind you, but I can finagle something. Besides, who wants to climb up into a pickup truck in a dress? It's dinner, Sasha! We'll probably go for pizza and beer. My shoulders sag and I throw my head back, looking up at the ceiling, whispering pleas for understanding, “Tell me you're alright with this.” Oscar lays his head on my lap and lets out a long and relaxing sigh. Sure glad he can find contentment. My stomach is already in roiling mode. Running my fingers through his soft fur I whisper, “Bed or sofa tonight, buddy?”

He and I have been at an impasse for sleeping accommodations. He did this at the last house too. I bought a new bed when I bought this house thinking maybe he hated the old one. It was hard replacing the bed Ben and I had slept in for four years, but it was time. His scent was long gone, my memories weren't. My dreams of Ben would always remain. But Oscar had never torn up anything until last night. I removed him from the room while we cleaned it and moved every piece of furniture to search for whatever he was digging for. We came up empty. No wild animals. No snakes. No boogeymen. No ghosts. Can't say I'm not spooked though. Maybe one more night on the sofa wouldn't hurt.

## *Dr. Aidan Lehner*

*What the hell is one of the construction workers doing here in the evening? On Friday! Alone. Carrying flowers? He probably stole them from someone's yard. Long haired hippie type – in all likelihood only bathes once a week. Probably smells like sweat and sawdust. I'll bet he drinks cheap beer and smokes pot or cigarettes, maybe both. He probably doesn't even own a suit. A black truck. I've only ever seen white ones. Callum Construction. This morning was near disaster. If only she hadn't come out of the house so early. And why did they show up an hour early? I would have been able to convince her of their incompetence, their negligence in locking her gate, leaving her vulnerable to vagrants, break-ins, possible rapists. Convince her the dog's actions last night were due to someone on the property that shouldn't have been. I could hear that mongrel trying to tear through the wall to get to me. She would have told me about it . . . eventually.*

*He's staying too long. How did he get past the dog? The damn thing lunges at me every time he gets close enough. Maybe she locked him a room. My leg bounces as I sit in my car watching the house – my patience wearing thin. What is he doing with her? Is he touching her? Is she touching him? You'd better not be, Sasha. I've told you time and again, whether you know it or not. You are mine.*

*Finally! Twenty minutes later I watch as he exits through the front door . . . alone. Ha! Trying to ply her with flowers. She's a widow, you idiot. Coercion. Manipulation. Mind play. You're in big boy territory. Go home, little boy. Leave Sasha to a real man who knows what he's doing. Because if you don't, you won't like the way this ends.*

# Chapter 20

## Jaxson

A Belgian. A Belgian named Oscar. A Belgian named Oscar with a heart on the bridge of his nose. Three strikes. My brain screams *run, Jaxson, run.* I swear to God it's an omen. A good one or bad one, I have no idea. I had only seen the dog a few times, but his marking was very distinct. It's why Ben was so damn set on keeping him, training him for his wife. I can get past this. I don't have to think of a lost SEAL every time I look at her dog. Coincidence. That's all it is. My crew has been working here for months and haven't said one word about it. If they thought for one moment the dog was stolen, they would have told me.

I was simply going to drop off flowers and apologize for being an ass this afternoon. *Simply.* Funny word that one. Sasha Taylor is anything but simple. The woman could have me on my knees in a heartbeat. The way her name dances on my tongue fascinates me. I've never met a name with a flavor. God, I want to know what she tastes like. She is fragile and delicate. But she's feisty too. And beautiful. So damn beautiful.

Dinner . . . not a date. Who am I kidding? I am such a fucking liar.

The same black Mercedes that I'd noticed when I pulled in idles at the curb about fifty yards away. It's an empty slate of land he's parked in front of, so visiting someone is questionable. If the dumbass hadn't tapped the brake pedal, I might have missed the fact the car was occupied. I hop in my truck, grab the night lens binoculars and note the number, start the engine, and back out of the drive heading in the opposite direction. Once at the end of the street, I turn right onto the only road that exits the neighborhood, make an immediate left on the next street and park at the curb, shutting off the lights. I watch in the rearview as the Mercedes passes on the main road, hit the lights, hang a quick U-turn, head back to the road I just left and follow him two cars behind. It takes seven miles and two red lights to reach his final destination. When I see the driver ring the doorbell of the house, I send the license number and address to Nash with a message:

*"ASAP. Need names of car owner and homeowner, and anything else you can get me. Thanks."*

His reply? *"She just promised me the blow job of a lifetime! Does it have to be right now?"*

Me*: "I'll tell her you're married, have five kids, and herpes. Yes, NOW!"*

Nash: *"You asshole. I'm on it."*

Me: *"Knew I could count on you."*

I'll buy his dinner and drinks next time. He'll get over it.

The guys are two pitchers, one tray of nachos, and two baskets of wings in by the time I arrive at Tillie's.

"Boss!" Dusty shouts, waving me over from the table in the back corner as if I can't see them. "Over here."

They're pretty hard to miss. They're the type women flock to; good looking, built, horny sixteen hours a day, the Navy SEAL they all want to ride. Well, in Florida they were. They'll get that status back, as soon as we finish our obligation. Here, they're construction workers – not that it makes a difference. The women still flock, they still fuck like rabbits, release their frustration in whatever way they can, and we all wait.

I pull out a chair and take a seat, reaching for the pitcher to pour my first beer. "Beers are on you, right?" Brick asks, tipping his glass up and chugging back half of it in one go.

"You blew the shit out of that this afternoon." I raise my glass to my mouth, eyeing him over the rim, take a long pull and lower the glass to the table. "What were you doing in Ms. Taylor's bedroom last night?"

His eyes and mouth pop open in unison as he stammers, "It's…it's not what you think, boss. I would never . . . she's the customer!"

"Chill out. Carl explained." I roll my eyes and shake my head, then eye the other two at the table. "Why don't you all tell me what's going on with the company you're keeping lately?"

Simon shrugs and grins cockily. "Ms. Taylor has some lovely friends."

"You're sleeping with her friends?" I question as the waitress sets another pitcher and basket of wings on the table.

She winks at Simon and leans in close, pressing her ample tits on his shoulder. "We wouldn't be sleeping if you were with me."

For the first time since I've known him, I see Simon pass on a pass. No return wink, no taking her number; his playboy smile absent.

Dusty snorts and waits for her to leave. "Hardly, Jax. We've been banished to the world of courting. They're proper southern belles."

Simon nods sharply. "They're ladies."

Brick's eye twitches and he pulls at his ear as he keeps his gaze on his glass. Aha. Two of them are courting, Brick is copulating. He must be with the easy southern belle. As long as he keeps his SEAL tattoo covered – that's all I care about.

"Tell me about the dog." I see three faces light up in unison as Brick's also relaxes with the change in subject.

"That dog is incredible," Dusty offers enthusiastically. "You ought to see him run that exercise course. Damn! He's a champ. Never leaves her side either. If he had been out this afternoon…" he shoots me a glare, ". . . when you were mean to her, he would have introduced himself . . . by way of his teeth."

Simon shakes his head and narrows his eyes, his voice filled with disdain as he adds, "Would have loved to let him out this morning just to see what he'd have done to that asshole at her gate. Rapist," he grunts. "I'd have given anything to have two minutes with him myself."

"Rapist?" I scowl. "What the hell are you talking about?"

"Some guy at her gate this morning," Brick explains. "Made it sound like he was there to go for a walk with her, but I don't know," he says, scrunching his brow and throwing a wadded up piece of napkin on the table. "I didn't like him."

"Who was he?" A churning sensation rolls through my gut. Is she seeing someone? Why hang out at the gate? Why not ring her doorbell? "And what the hell does rapist have to do with anything?"

"He told Miss Sasha that men who make friends with her dog are likely candidates to be rapists," Dusty says, pointing to Simon. "Simon explained men who lurk around in the dark are more likely to be rapists. He's lucky our boy here didn't tear him apart."

"You guys were there before dawn?" I ask them. "Why? You don't work in the dark."

Brick grimaces but stands strong on his premise. "Oscar had reason for tearing things up last night. Something set him off. I wanted to be there before daylight broke. I don't like this guy. Oscar doesn't like him either. I trust that dog's instincts more than I trust my own. If you knew him, you would too."

"What's his name?"

"Oscar," Brick replies impatiently. "I just told you."

I press a finger to my temple and squeeze my eyes closed. Brick is brilliant, he really is. But sometimes extreme intelligence can hamper thought processes, not to mention social skills. Give him a woman, he is on top of his game. Give him logistics to work with, he is tops in his field. Give him a gun, he never misses. Give him a conversation to follow – well, you see where that went.

"I heard her call him Aidan." Simon shoots a disbelieving glance at Brick followed by a quick eye roll. "And that was after I strongly suggested he remove his hand from her arm."

"He got physical with her?!" I glare at them in disbelief, tempering my anger. "And you let him go?"

"Wasn't exactly reason for justifiable homicide, boss," Dusty says. "However," he lifts a brow and smirks, "give us a green light and we can remedy that."

"Find out who he is," I tell them, reaching for the buzzing phone in my pocket where I see Nash's message.

*"Dr. Aidan Lehner. Psychiatrist. Homeowner is Greta Miller. Rich widow. Seems Dr. Lehner has a long list of patients, most of whom are widows. Been charged with unethical behavior in the past. Twice. Expunged. First case dismissed when widow committed suicide. Second dismissed when widow disappeared. Care to explain your interest?"*

*"Not tonight. Thanks."*

*"Drinks tomorrow night, seven o'clock. Don't be late."*

*"Can't. Already have obligations. Another time."*

"Sonofabitch." My phone rings with Nash's designated ringtone but I ignore it, pocketing it instead.

"You got word?" Brick's apprehensive tone and the way he grabs the table's edge and nearly bounds out of his seat reminds me how much we all want that one phone call.

"Not yet." I pat his shoulder. "Soon, Brick. I can feel it. Soon." Don't know why I say it. I have no idea when, where, how. He was best friends with two of the guys who went down on that chopper. He was good friends with Ben. The longer it takes, the antsier he gets. He needs closure. He needs *revenge*. In the meantime, I hope Sasha's friend has what he *needs* to keep his mind off things.

"How old are these ladies?" I ask out of nowhere, the conversation at a lull.

"Same age as us, give or take a few . . . months," Simon replies then winks with a cocky grin.

I eye them all skeptically. Dusty is the youngest at thirty-one. Simon tops it out at thirty-four. "Which one is it? Give or take?"

Dusty's smile spreads from ear to ear. "I like my women a little older."

"I like to teach." Simon chuckles.

"I'm a give and take kinda guy," Brick adds with a puckish grin. "I'll show her mine, she'll show me hers."

"They all went to school together. Grew up in the same town. Been friends all their lives," Simon explains.

Which leaves them anywhere from thirty-two to thirty-three. *And too fucking young for me.*

We finish the drinks and wings. I pay, as per usual. It wasn't entirely their fault this afternoon – though it was, sort of. I get it. She is special, fragile, a precious gem.

I rise from my chair and give them a warning before leaving. "Watch your step with those ladies. Don't make me look bad."

Three sets of eyebrows shoot upward as eyes narrow. Simon smirks. "Just how would we make you look bad?"

"You know what I mean," I cover quickly with a grumble. "The company. Don't make the company look bad."

Lips twitch as they exchange knowing glances.

"Pay the lady a visit, Jax. Get to the know the dog. If he likes you, she may be more forgiving than you think." Simon chuckles. "I'm sure the *company* is your only concern."

"No harm in groveling, Boss," Brick interjects.

"If you're done with the Kelly project," Dusty proffers. "You can always come join us on this one. You know, keep an eye on us." He winks and shrugs. "Or her."

*Oh, I plan on keeping an eye on her. Dinner . . . not a date.
Because she's too young.*

My phone rings for the umpteenth time on my way home.
He is relentless.

"What," I grunt as I press the button on the steering wheel.
I knew he'd call. I didn't answer his continued texts or requests
for drinks tomorrow night. Nor did I give credence to his harsh
comment that he would be at my door in an hour if I didn't pick up
my phone. That was forty five minutes ago.

"Don't *what* me, asshole," Nash snaps. "You more than
piqued my interest. This guy sounds like a psychopath. Suicide
and a disappearance and his license wasn't even suspended during
the investigation. If I hadn't put in the extra effort, I'd never have
known. To the general public, he's clean as a whistle, regular
fucking choir boy. I sent my pending blow job home in order to
further investigate. What gives?"

"I'm not sure yet," I confess. "I think he may be stalking a
customer."

His voice is light as he teases, "Taking a special interest in
our customers, are we, Jax? Since when?"

"Only this one," I mumble, asking myself the same question.

He chuckles. "She's beautiful, isn't she?"

I picture her scathing glare as she offered me an arsenic-
laced sandwich this afternoon, the tear-rimmed eyes after my cruel
blow, the mesmerizing glow when she agreed to dinner tomorrow
night. Beautiful on all three counts. "Yeah, she is."

"Be careful, Callum," Nash warns. "He sounds unstable.
Don't hesitate to call."

"Thanks, Nash."

"Uh-uh," he says. "Not how it works. You name your
firstborn after me."

"Gotta have one before that happens."

"Get crackin'," he orders with a laugh. "Just remember, if
you do want one, you don't wrap it before you tap it."

"Good night, Nash," I say before hitting the red button on

the steering wheel.

# Chapter 21

## Sasha

"You're what?!" Rhea shrieks into the phone so loud I pull it away from my ear. I believe the neighborhood could hear her if I were to step out onto my patio.

"It's just dinner," I explain defensively. "He apologized but wanted to add dinner to be thorough. It's not a big deal."

"Okay, sugar pie." She giggles, adding a bit of southern drawl. "You keep telling yourself that if it makes you feel better. So, is he hot?"

"Is he what?! I don't know," I huff in exasperation, lying through my teeth. "Look, I called to see what I should wear. If you don't want to help then I'll . . ."

"Where are you going?" she interrupts.

"I . . . I don't know."

"He didn't say?"

"I didn't ask." I'm not sure why I called her. I half expected her to talk me out of it, but so far it's turned into a game of 20 questions and she's the only one asking them. If I wanted to be interrogated I would have called my mom . . . or my dad, or Trent, or Jolie.

"Holy Moses," she lets out a breathy whisper.

"What is it with you and the bible prophet lately? The last time you spoke his name you were staring at butt cheeks, hoping for vertical cracks to make an appearance."

"I'm looking at the website of Callum Construction." I hear her fingers tapping on her laptop. "He's not in many pictures but he certainly does justice to the ones he is. Damn, Sasha. Make sure you get dessert."

"Rhea." My voice is strained as I voice out loud the same chant I've repeated over and over in my head today. "It's just dinner."

"Yeah, Sash it is," she says softly. "It's also been nearly three years. About time, don't you think? I'll be there in twenty to help you pick something out."

"Thank you."

She giggles. "Leather mini skirt and thigh-high boots okay?"

"Oh God," I groan as she disconnects.

Rhea doesn't show up to choose what I have in my closet. No, that's not Rhea's style. I should have known better. She shows up with what looks to be half of her own closet hanging from her arms – none of which I can wear. It would be like dressing an adult in Tinkerbell's clothing. More than that, not only does Rhea show up with half of her wardrobe, she shows up with the other half of our tag team – each with a bottle of wine in their hand – at eleven o'clock in the morning!

"It's five o'clock somewhere," Shae announces, holding up a bottle of red with one hand as she pets Oscar with the other. "Hey, Mutt. How's my boy?"

"On the other side of the world," I utter, glancing at the bottle then shoot her the evil eye from which she should shrivel but doesn't.

"Rhea told me this guy was a real jerk." Sky eyes me as she taps Oscar's head lightly with her fingertips in greeting.

"Oscar?" I gasp, recalling the mess in my bedroom and knowing there are no secrets between any of us. She must have told them, but I wouldn't have expected Sky to be so harsh with my canine companion. She dotes on him almost as much as I do.

"No!" She scowls and drops to her knees, pulling my dog to her in a hug. It's a good thing he tolerates her. Belgians are generally a one person dog, but he's always made an exception for Sky. I think it's because we lived with her for the first few months. "Oscar is never a jerk. A little quirky maybe, but he's my hotdog." Oscar lets out a low growl and she pulls back and ruffles his head. "Still not letting it go, are you, big guy?" She eyes me once again and smirks. "I'm talking about the two-legged beast."

"Did you come to help me pick something out or to pick him apart?"

"Do you want us to be here when he picks you up?"

"Of course she does . . . *mom*," Rhea answers for me, smirking. "She also wants you to remind him of her curfew, spew the speed course on how babies are made, and teach him how condoms are properly applied." She holds up a finger. "Oh wait! Did you guys remember to bring the banana with you?" She grins at me. "Got a big ass carrot in the fridge?"

We hear Shae from the kitchen as she pours the wine. "I'm thinkin' cucumber after studying those website pictures. Damn, how have the underwear companies not found that man to model for them?"

I roll my eyes, as well as my shoulders and heave an exasperated sigh. "Are you done yet?"

"Oh no," Shae teases. "We still have porn sites to search to see if he has a second job. We're thorough."

After running the gamut of choices and letting them believe I've agreed to the typical little black dress that every woman owns and nude heels, I bid them farewell at two o'clock in the afternoon and send them on their way. We shared a light bite for lunch, they drank the wine, and I'm on the way for a shower and a shave. The dress hangs in the closet as I've replaced it with blue jeans, a simple sweater, and ankle boots. As I mentioned before, I'm not about to try to scale a pickup truck in a dress.

*It's just dinner.*

At two minutes before seven Oscar jumps up in the bay window and studies the driveway. He wags his tail but doesn't bark. Good thing too, because the butterflies in my stomach may take flight and end up in my throat. Something tells me conversation is expected this evening.

*Husband's name was Chase – close enough, it was Ben's middle name.*

*No specific date, motor vehicle crash – helicopters are vehicles with motors, it wasn't an accident, the bastards did it on purpose.*

*Married four years, yada, yada.*

*Orr . . . I don't like to talk to about it. Yeah, I like that option a whole lot better.*

I take a deep breath when the doorbell rings, slide my palms down the front of my jeans, and open the door . . . to a well-dressed, stunning Jaxson Callum. He's in navy dress pants, a light blue dress shirt and a silver and navy tie that match his eyes. His hair is pulled back in a neat ponytail and his beard is finely trimmed. I imagine Rhea screaming, "Holy Moses!" Gotta admit, I'm kinda chanting a quick and silent, "Jesus, Mary, and Joseph" myself.

"Uh," I stammer, scrunching my nose. "Come on in."

He steps over the threshold into the living room, smiling. Oscar greets him as if they're old friends, nudging his hand. He indulges him with a pat on his head. "You look beautiful, Sasha. You ready?"

My cheeks heat in embarrassment and I hold up one finger. "Could you give me a minute? Maybe two?"

"Sure." He chuckles. "I'll let Oscar entertain me while we wait."

I set a fast pace for my bedroom as I call out, "I'll be right back."

Closing the door behind me, I throw open the closet door once in my room and pull out the little black dress and nude heels. Great! Now I have to change my bra because the peach colored one I have on is not going to work with the black dress. Oh shit! I also have to change into a thong so I don't have panty lines. I think I set a new record in changing from one outfit to another, but due to the fact I leave the original strung out across the bed and the floor, I don't think I meet Ripley's qualifications for the win. I check my hair in the bathroom mirror and do a spot check in the full length before I step out – want to make sure the hem didn't get stuck in the waistband of that damned thong. Our prom queen never did live that down before graduation. But then, she probably shouldn't have been having sex in the janitor's closet before the grand march. A bare ass in the bible belt is fodder for the masses. Her daddy was the preacher too. The last I heard, the whole family changed their last name and moved to Alabama. And here I was worried I might bring shame to mine if I wrote romance novels. Hence, the pen name. However, my family supports me wholeheartedly and my mom is my biggest fan.

I return to the living room where Jaxson sits on the sofa, a calm Oscar on the floor at his feet. He looks up as I enter and his eyes go wide as a breathy whispered, "Wow" leaves his lips.

He stands, never taking his eyes off me, and he smiles. "Sasha, you looked beautiful before. You didn't need to change."

Shrugging sheepishly I admit, "I'm guilty of assumption. I took for granted you were maybe a pizza and beer kinda guy."

He arches a brow and narrows his eyes the tiniest bit though there's a twinkle that he cannot hide in them. "I can eat pizza in nice clothes."

"Oh," I fumble, my cheeks heating in embarrassment as my mouth twists. "So we are going for pizza and beer?"

He smirks, his voice low and just a bit cocky as his eyes make a quick perusal of appreciation. "We are not going for pizza and beer. Even us construction workers know how to treat a lady to a true Italian meal . . . with wine, Sasha."

*Damn salsa tongue. He's enjoying this. A little too much.*

Not to be outdone, I cringe and add a little whimper to my voice to be convincing. "Italian? Isn't that where they put all that red sauce on a bunch of noodles?"

He stares at me, his lips parting before rolling them together between his teeth. He has the cutest eleven that furrows between his brows. "Would you rather have something else?"

I study that eleven a bit too long, entranced by the maturity and experience it must have taken to put it there, and I giggle. "Kidding. Manicotti is my favorite. You ready?"

He squares me with scolding eyes before he shakes his head. "If you behave, I'll tell them to leave the arsenic out of yours. Let's go."

I snatch my purse from the console table in the entryway, tell Oscar goodbye, lock the door behind us and nearly gasp when I see what's parked in the driveway. So much for worrying about scaling a pickup truck. He opens the passenger door and waits for me to climb into the shiny black Audi A6.

He bends down and cockily proffers before closing the door, "I can drive back home and get my pickup if you'd be more comfortable, Sasha."

"No, no," I stammer. "This is fine. I wasn't sure how I was going to get in and out of a pickup truck in this dress."

He winks. "We would have found a way."

# Chapter 22

## Jaxson

The drive to the restaurant is pleasant; conversation limited pretty much to the weather, progress on the work in her backyard, the friendly men I have working for me. I didn't ask about them dating her friends and she didn't offer up the information. The parking lot of *Crave* reveals very few open spots, but connections with the owner and an *always-open* spot in the back of the restaurant make it so (a) I have a place to park and (b) my doors won't look like someone took a hammer – or a key – to them by the time I come out. Door dings are a pain in the ass. The construction business can be quite profitable and consistent; provided you make the right connections, offer quality work, honesty, timeliness, and hire solid people. Living in hurricane country doesn't hurt either. Not that I wish for hurricanes, but the ability to turn destruction into construction and give someone their home back makes you feel pretty damn good. My business has only been up and running for two years, but we hit the ground running and started turning a fine profit at six months.

Sasha looks puzzled as I turn into one of the spaces behind the building. "You're parking in back?"

"It would seem so," I reply, shutting off the car and opening my door. "Stay put. I'll come around and get you." Our reservation is for eight o'clock, but after Sasha's *assumptions* and decision to change clothes, it only places us ten minutes ahead so sitting at the bar before being seated at our table isn't likely.

"Jaxson Callum!" Vince greets us at the front door he's just opened. "I saw you pull up out back. I thought I'd give you door service tonight as well. How are you?"

I grudgingly remove my hand from Sasha's lower back and reach out to shake his. "I'm good, Vince. You?" As soon as he's finished his typical reprimanding throat clearing and I've performed my obligatory handshake, my hand is right back where it belongs as I guide her through the doors.

"Lovely lady you're keeping company with," he says admiringly as he smiles at Sasha and dips his chin. Vince looks to his hostess and softly claps his hands twice. "Mr. Callum and his guest have arrived, Tina. Please see to it that his table is ready."

"Right away, sir," the hostess replies and darts off in the direction of apparently where we're about to be seated. I resist an eye roll. Vince loves to put on airs. If there's an audience to impress, he's there to perform. To his regular customers, he is Vincenzo. To me, as was made clear in our first meeting regarding his remodel, he's Vince, I'm Jax – not Monsieur Callum. Hence his reprimanding throat clearing. For guys like me, throat clearing is usually followed by spitting concrete or sawdust out of your mouth. Another reason I leave public relations up to my foremen. I have limited ass-kissing skills. As in . . . none. Though I could make an exception for the one below where my hand is resting at the present time. Wouldn't mind taking a little bite as long as I'm in the neighborhood either.

We hear another loud throat clearing nearby followed by, "Sasha."

She stiffens under my hand and turns in the direction of the voice where we see a dark-haired, well-dressed man with a woman hanging from his arm. "Aidan," she says, surprised. "I . . . I didn't expect to see you here."

He ignores the woman on his arm as he lifts a brow and his slow scrutinizing gaze travels from her face to her toes and back up again. "Apparently."

My hand slides from her mid back to her hip and I pull her closer to me. It's protective. So this is Aidan. *Apparently? Ballsy motherfucker.*

He extends his hand to me, eyes narrowed. "Dr. Aidan Lehner. And you are?"

*Cocky motherfucker, too.*

Glancing at his hand, not about to remove mine from her, I glower. "Sasha's dinner companion."

Sasha places her hand on my bicep, squeezing gently. "Aidan, this is Jaxson Callum. We're . . . we're just having dinner together." Her voice is shaky, lacking any and all of the confidence, as well as the spunk, I've admired.

"Callum," he says derisively. "Ah, the construction company. Did you inherit the business or are you just one of the hired help? Didn't recognize you without the blue jeans and uh . . . dirt under your nails. Are you making friends with Sasha's dog as well?"

"Aidan!" Sasha chastises though recoils as if she's made a mistake, and I hold her tighter to me. *Yeah, protective.* After the conversation with Nash, anything and everything about this guy throws a red flag and makes me see the same color.

I glare at him, the hand I don't have on Sasha's hip clenched in a fist. *Keep it together, Callum.* You don't have everything you need on him yet.

"Mr. Callum," the hostess calls from behind us. "Your table is ready."

"It's time to eat," I tell her, shooting Lehner a smirk and goad, "Maybe we'll take Oscar for a nice long walk when we're done here."

He boldly steps forward and takes her by the elbow – leaving the other woman standing behind him as if she's inconsequential. Leaning close but not so close that I can't hear, he whispers, "Three more months, Sasha."

I remove his hand from her elbow by grasping his wrist and give it a crippling squeeze at the pulse point. The only reason he doesn't drop to his knees is because I release him before he does, but he does bend a little and grimace. "Goodnight, *Doctor* Lehner."

We're seated at a table near the back where it's quiet, the voices from other tables muffled, the sounds of silverware and glasses clinking only a distraction if you allow them to be. The waiter pours our waters and Sasha lifts hers to her mouth, her hand shaking as she does. She looks like a deer in the headlights, stuck in the middle of a roundabout full of drivers confused as to which of the three lanes they're supposed to take for the next turn off. No, this one! No, over there! No, that one! I hate those fucking things. Actually, I only hate those things when they're full of said drivers who don't know how to use them. If I were the deer, I'd rest in the center circle, pop open a beer, sit back, wait for the inevitable crash, and make my escape during the traffic jam. It's what my guys and I are doing now. Waiting for the inevitable crash and burn. Then we'll make our move.

I reach for her hand and take it in mine. "You okay?"

She sits up straighter, squares her shoulders, and nods. "Yeah."

She's anything but. She's shaken, and the night is ruined. I roll his words around in my head. *Three more months.* What the hell did that mean? Determined to not let this night be wasted, I rise from my seat, keeping her hand in mine.

"Let's go."

"Wh…What?"

"I have a better idea."

She stares up at me as her lips part in a gasp. If the woman were on her feet right now, that irresistible mouth would be covered by mine. So damn kissable. "Better than manicotti?"

I pull her up from her chair so she stands in front of me, chest-to-chest, toe-to-toe. "Manicotti needs a certain mood. I don't want it spoiled. We'll save that for next time." I grin and incline my chin. "Pizza and beer sounds good right about now. Then we'll go take Oscar for a walk on the beach. What do you think?"

Her face lights in the kind of smile I want to put there often. "I think I'd like that very much."

I find Vince in his office and ask him to let us out the back door. I turn on some soft music and open the moonroof before pulling out onto Kings Highway. Sasha doesn't need an inquisition right now; she needs to sort through what happened at the restaurant. I'd rather she sit back, relax, enjoy the music and the ride; but if she sorts through it now, maybe I can have her thoughts and attention by the time we sit down to dinner. Most definitely by the time we reach the beach for a walk with the ever popular Oscar. Apparently popular with everyone but Dr. Aidan Lehner that is. Which just so happens to make him my new favorite canine.

She lays her head back on the rest and stares up at the sky, studying the stars as if looking for answers. The moonlight shines from above and casts a soft glow over her face. So damn beautiful. I remind myself again and again to watch the road; that I'll be sitting across from her with a full view minutes from now. Out of nowhere her face splits in a bright smile, her eyes close and she draws in a deep breath, letting it out slowly, and I swear I hear a soft hum as she does. She's at peace.

*Just in time for dinner.*

## *Dr. Aidan Lehner*

*How dare she! Dressed like a whore in a little black dress and high heels. Out with another man – the same one with the black pickup truck that was in her driveway last night. A construction worker! Dirty, a common laborer. Callused hands. No title, no letters behind his name, no education. What is she thinking? Why is she not hearing what I'm telling her? Why is she not following orders? She barely flinched! Did the wires get knocked loose again?*

*No other men, Sasha!*

*Greta should not have asked about her. I should never be expected to explain myself or anything I do. The nerve of that woman. To accuse me of insolence because I didn't introduce her. To expect me to put her on Sasha's level of worthiness. To lower me to the level of feigning regret, vomiting words of apology followed by adoration. If I weren't in desperate need of release, I would have walked out the door, slamming it on my way.*

*Greta Miller is a temporary fix. A rich widow who loves to lavish me with gifts and participate in the darker side of role play. It's a good thing she likes it rough because tonight I'm ready to snap. The blindfold is bigger in order to mask more of her face, the gag is tight so all I hear are whimpers.*

*I pretend it's her. I punish the woman who's not here but should be.*

*Three more months, Sasha. Three more months.*

*If Mr. Jaxson Callum needs to disappear before then – well, it wouldn't be the first time I've made someone disappear. I've done worse. I can make it happen again.*

# Chapter 23

## Sasha

I saw Ben wink at me by way of the brightest star in the sky tonight through the moonroof in Jaxson's car, just like he'd promised me in his last letter. A bright twinkle – a mini flash if you will – and then it was gone. He's done it so many times over the last couple years. They're usually followed by a gentle breeze, but since I was inside the car, I didn't get to feel it tonight. I took it as a sign that what I'm doing is okay; that dinner with Jaxson Callum is acceptable. Multiple times now when meeting Aidan for a walk in the morning, the skies have opened up in a downpour with thunder so loud I couldn't hear myself think. And rain hadn't even been forecasted those days. So strange, because by the time I reached my house, the rain had stopped and Jaxson's crew were able to work the whole day.

"He loves the beach," I say with a laugh, watching Oscar run circles around us. This is his free time; time to jump and play. He is never off guard per se, never roams more than ten feet away – he simply isn't glued to my side.

We shared pizza at an oceanside restaurant, sausage and pepperoni, and we each drank one beer. We're now on the beach in front of my house, after I changed into capris and a T-shirt and Jax slipped off his shoes and rolled up the hem of his pants. Can't say as I mind that he lost the tie, unbuttoned the collar, and rolled the sleeves to his elbows revealing delightful tats and sculpted forearms.

"Are you originally from South Carolina?" Jax asks as we walk a long stretch away from any of the lights shining off the homes, his hands in his pockets, his footsteps slow in order for me to keep a normal pace. The moon is so bright tonight, it lights our path without need of artificial supplement though we have our cell phones should the moon disappear.

"No, I'm from Tennessee." I finish with my favorite part, "Shockemall."

"Shockemall?" he repeats inquisitively.

"I took it as incentive." I nod enthusiastically. "Leave as a normal everyday person and shock 'em all with my accomplishments."

He chuckles. "And have you?"

I shrug. "For those who know what I do."

We talked about my career during dinner . . . somewhat. He didn't ask for the *fine* details and I didn't offer them up. I said fiction, felt the heat in my cheeks, and moved on quickly to say the girls and I work together. Never once have I been hesitant to talk about what I write, where to find my books, branding, etc. It's how you sell yourself. But when you're sitting across from a man you can easily picture as one of your cover models? You've heard about the proverbial cat that's got your tongue? Well, that furry little creature stole mine and left me speechless.

"What about the ones who don't?"

My nose wrinkles at the thought and I admit, "They're probably too old." I turn away and mumble, "Or would have a coronary."

Apparently I didn't mumble low enough because he laughs. "Something tells me you don't write children's books."

Good thing it's dark. My cheeks are running the gamut of all things red: cherry, crimson, maroon, skin rash. "Nope."

"Where might I find some of your work?"

"Uh," I pause. "I don't think you'd find it very helpful. I don't write about building things or blueprints or . . ."

He gently takes my elbow and turns me toward him. Oscar sits at my side, his eyes set on Jaxson. It doesn't faze him in the least; he knows Oscar is there to protect me. If his intentions were to hurt me, Oscar would have lunged by now. His grin is impish and his tone playful. "Sasha, where can I find your work?"

I roll my eyes and heave a sigh. It's only a matter of time. God knows Rhea has probably been touting it to Brick since their first date. "Sara Paine. Google me."

"Sara Paine," he says slowly as if analyzing it. He tilts his head, then shakes it. "Nah, I much prefer Sasha."

"Why do you say my name the way you do?"

He reaches out to hold back the breeze-blown hair from my face with one finger yet forgoes the typical tuck behind my ear and holds it in place while tipping my chin up with his other fingers, gently brushing my cheek with his thumb. "And how do I say your name, Sasha?"

*Salsa dance – meet goosebumps.*

"Unlike anyone else does," I whisper.

"I like the way it feels on my tongue," he says easily, as if the answer were on the tip of his and takes a step closer so that we're toe-to-toe. "I have a theory though."

"A theory?" My heart pounds hard in my chest as I stare up at him. The subject of tongues has mine nervously licking my lips.

He lowers his face so close to mine I believe we're exchanging the same air. "Usually when something feels that good on your tongue, *Sasha*, it tastes even better."

He waits, doesn't force anything, stays within a breath of kissing me, silently asking permission. I simply move forward because my vocal cords have frozen. I haven't kissed a man since Ben but I haven't wanted to . . . until. right. now.

It's almost painful it feels so good. One hand in my hair, an arm wrapped around my waist. So solid, strong, warm. His mouth on mine feels like what I've been missing for so long; filling an emptiness I've tried to ignore, breathing a life into me that I thought was long ago suffocated with the pain of loss.

He begins to release me from the kiss but I cling harder, wrapping my hands around his neck, the soft feel of his ponytail brushing my knuckles. I moan into the kiss, my eyes closed, savoring everything I fear I shouldn't. Am I kissing Jaxson Callum or am I grasping a few more moments of touch I've yearned for so long? I don't even know the man. It was dinner – not a date.

"Sasha." He breathes my name like a prayer and grips my head on each side as he leans his forehead on mine. "We should slow down."

I burst into tears without warning. "I'm sorry."

He pulls me to his chest, his fingers gently wound in my hair, his arm around my shoulder, and he holds me – simply holds me. "Don't you dare apologize."

The dampness of my tears spreads to his shirt as I cry . . . and he lets me, for however long it takes.

# Chapter 24

## Jaxson

Too fast, too soon, too much. How could I not have seen it? God, she's beautiful. Smart, spunky . . . and that mouth. She felt so good, so right. But those eyes. How could I forget the way they pierced me yesterday when I was so cruel? Way to go, Callum. You obviously just gave the woman her first kiss after being widowed. Didn't see that one coming. The least you could have done was get her to like you first. Buckle up, idiot. You've got a long road ahead of you.

By the way, *asshat*, what the hell happened to *she's too fucking young*? You know exactly what happened. Your attraction is a whole lot stronger than your willpower. Why this woman? What is it about Sasha Taylor that makes me feel like I'm breaking some sort of rule yet following an order? I can protect her, yes, but I want her too.

Loosening my hold around her as soon as she's seemed to settle, I lift her chin and offer a reassuring smile. "Better?"

She swipes at her nose with the back of her hand and nods. I swipe at her cheeks with my thumbs to brush away the remaining tears and dip my head. "What do you say we head back up to the house?"

"Yeah, it's late. You probably want to go home," she sniffles.

I wrap my arm around her shoulder, leading us back to the house, and chuckle. "Yeah, us old guys should be in bed by ten. Gotta get our solid eight hours or we need a senior nap by one in the afternoon."

She giggles and sniffles at the same time then slaps my chest. "You're not old."

I hesitate, but there is no time like the present. Might as well get it over with. Let her down easy and take my bruised and battered ego home. "How old do you think I am, Sasha?"

"I don't know. Hadn't really thought about it. You don't seem old." Her shoulders lift in a shrug under my arm. "I mean, you're not sprouting hair out of your ears."

I sigh through my nose. Is it the southern charm or was she simply born a smartass? From sniffles to sarcasm in two seconds flat. I'm not sure if I want to paddle her ass or ravage her. Scratch that – definitely ravage her – and paddle her ass . . . for totally different reasons. "I'm damn near forty, Sasha."

She halts her footsteps and stares up at me as she gasps; her eyes wide, filled with shock and awe. My heart sinks, until . . . "Forty! Oh no! We'd better call the old folks home and reserve your spot. Call the cemetery and make sure they've started digging the hole. Call the mortuary and pick out your casket, unless of course you prefer to be crema . . ." She stops suddenly and clears her throat. "Never mind. Bad joke." She wrestles out from under my arm and calls to the dog, "Come on, Oscar. Mr. Callum wants to go home." She starts off at a dead run toward the house without looking back, Oscar at her heels.

*Well, now we know. Apparently, her husband was cremated.*

"Sasha, wait!" I catch up to her in seconds; not hard to do with legs half again as long as hers, not to mention my desperation to make this right. Careful not to reach for her – Oscar and I may have hit it off, but that dog's loyalties are not to be questioned when he spins and growls at me. "Sasha, please. I never said I wanted to go home. Those were your words. I only said we should slow down."

She finally stops, breathless, hands on her knees, her back to me still. "Why?"

How do I explain? How can I make her understand? I cautiously step closer, regarding Oscar as much as he's guarding her. I put a closed hand forth for him to inspect, submitting, speaking to her as I do. "Please turn around, face me. You need to take the first steps, you know that. Oscar's going to make a meal out of me if you don't." She doesn't need to know I could handle Oscar if I needed to, not that I would want to. He's doing his job, admittedly rather well.

She stands upright and turns, taking the few steps necessary to bring us closer. I take the next few. "You want to know why, Sasha?" I tip her chin up and run my thumb across her bottom lip ever so gently. "Because when this mouth is on mine, I want it to be me you're kissing. Not a memory, not a substitute. I don't want to be a replacement; I want to be the one. Can you do that?"

Her eyes glisten in the moonlight before she glances up at the sky then back to me. "Can you give me time?"

I bring her knuckles to my mouth, kissing them softly. "I can do that."

Her mouth twitches and I see a twinkle in the eyes I'm going to see in my dreams tonight. "I'll try to be swift." She lifts a shoulder in a playful shrug. "I understand patience can be a real challenge when you get old."

I narrow my eyes before I lift her in my arms and spin her around. "Are you always a smartass?"

"Only in my downtime." She giggles and it's the sweetest sound I've heard all night long. She rests her hands on my shoulders before bringing one to my cheek, exploring my beard with her fingertips. I fight to keep my eyes open and not get lost in the sensation. "Wait! You're not going to break a hip or strain a muscle lifting me, are you?"

I hoist her up and throw her over my shoulder, and she shrieks in laughter. I look to Oscar. "Let's go, buddy. Apparently, your mom wasn't taught to respect her elders. What do you think we should do for punishment? No dessert, no bedtime stories?" I grumble quietly to myself as I carry her to the house, her warm body in my arms, that perfect peach-shaped ass that I resist biting right next to my head, "Feels like I'm the one being punished."

We spend the next two hours, side-by-side on the sofa in conversation over coffee – yeah, I won't be sleeping, I guarantee it. Movies she likes, her friends, her hometown, family. My family, my company, how it came to be, my employees, i.e. lies, lies, and more lies.

Brick "Alan" Halladay – big heart, nice guy, hard worker, speaks highly of Rhea.

Dusty "Theodore" Kemper – impish, boy scout, friendly, speaks highly of her friend Shae.

Simon Sheetz – severe, strong, loyal, speaks highly of her friend Sky.

Carl Sanborn    fatherly type to all of them. Keeps them grounded.

Nobody knows we're mercenaries waiting for word to finish one last job. No one knows they're capable of killing a man without blinking twice. Nobody knows we're former SEALs. Someday though, when the final mission is over, my guys can all claim the glory that is theirs.

I'm caught off guard and alarm bells ring in my head when Oscar drags a blanket from what I know is the master bedroom and lays it at Sasha's feet, resting his head on her lap.

"Oscar," Sasha nearly whines as she pets his head. "No, not tonight. We're sleeping in the bedroom. The sofa is not meant to be slept on."

"He sleeps on the sofa?"

"No." She releases an exasperated sigh then scowls at Oscar. "He sleeps on the floor beside me on the sofa. He's not fond of the bedroom."

Recalling the receiver attached to the cable strung from near the rooftop under the siding on the master suite side of the house, something tells me it's not the bedroom Oscar isn't fond of. Aidan Lehner's words find their way into my head once again.

*"Three more months, Sasha"*. The guys said he was on that side of her house yesterday morning. Oscar doesn't like him. They don't like him. Why the hell didn't he just ring the doorbell?

"Who is Aidan Lehner?" Knowing it's not my place, really not my business, though I plan to make it my mine, I ask. The guy was parked by her house last night, at the restaurant this evening, lurking outside her house yesterday morning. He's got predator written all over him with a side order of stalker in his off time.

Her eyes twitch as she brings fast fingers to her temple to rub it and winces. I watch as her head drops and it jerks slightly side to side. She's fighting it . . . or she's being made to. Sonofabitch. Did he hypnotize her? No. He would have been able to coerce her against Oscar. If the dog hates him, he'd want him gone. He's gotten inside her head though. Emotional and psychological manipulation with physical repercussions? I've seen it; we used to cause it. It's a psychological military tactic. But we had reasons . . . Justified reasons.

Nash's text replays in my mind. *"Psychiatrist. Works mostly with widows. One committed suicide, the other disappeared."*

Did he treat her for grief? How long did she say her husband has been gone? *Forever.* But then followed with *a few* years. *Three more months*. Is he biding his time to get past medical ethics codes? Or is he biding his time until he has her thoroughly brainwashed? Suddenly, Aidan Lehner has more than become my business. If he's done what I think he has, he's a dead man.

I do the only thing I can think of to set us back on the path we were. That, and I've been dying to do it again since we stood on the beach earlier. I take her cheeks in my palms, surreptitiously placing my index fingers to her temples – applying the perfect amount of pressure – and bring her mouth to mine. She tastes of coffee and Sasha – desire with a hint of mystery. My new favorite. She melts into my touch and the tension leaves her body. If she needs to use me for a while, I'll let her. I'll be whatever or whoever she needs me to be, so long as she finds me in the end, and as long as I can keep Aidan Lehner from finding her in the meantime.

When the kiss is over, her soft smile returns. "I was hoping you'd do that one more time tonight," she whispers.

"I was hoping you'd let me," I whisper back. I gaze into those captivating, stunning green eyes to ensure the reflection I see is my own. She searches mine as if looking for answers, sincerity maybe. If so, she'll find it. "How about you go put on pajamas, grab a pillow, and I'll stay until you fall asleep? Oscar seems pretty set on sleeping out here."

"You'd do that?" Her voice is but a shocked whisper as her eyes light up. She knows I'm not propositioning her, but rather offering comfort. It's an offer I can make while she falls asleep on the sofa, not so much one that could be made in the confines of her bedroom. And I'm a knight in need of the shiny armor with a steel-plated crotch because, well – she's beautiful, and I'm a guy. A guy who's going home – alone – to devise a plan, I remind myself. This woman will not be another one of Aidan Lehner's victims. She'll still be beautiful and I'll still be hard as a rock, after Lehner is taken care of.

I swear to God, as I sit on the sofa and wait for her, I feel a hand squeeze my shoulder. I whirl around quickly, expecting an intruder, but there's no one there.

She returns five minutes later, face void of any makeup, black tank top and short shorts; a pillow and an extra blanket in her arms. She places the pillow near my thigh, lays her head on it, and wrestles with the blanket to adjust it – unfortunately not high enough to cover the delectable crest of her breasts before she finally rolls onto her side. She releases a deep sigh as she settles in. "You don't have to stay. I've done this a hundred times. Oscar is stubborn."

I lay my arm over her shoulder and give it a light squeeze. "Good thing you have a comfy sofa. I'll be sure to lock up on my way out. Get some sleep, Sasha."

"Jaxson." She says my name so sweetly, I want to pretend I didn't hear her so she has to say it again, but I don't.

"Yeah?"

"Thank you." She rolls slightly so she can look up. "Just so you know, you're not too old for me." She adjusts herself once again on her side and snuggles in closer. "I've always been a big fan of silver foxes, and I can help you trim your ear hair when you lose your bifocals." Her giggle turns into a loud gasp with the crack of my hand on her ass. I can only take so much and her curvy ass is so close.

She pops up quickly, spinning on her knees to face me, eyes wide as she stares, speechless. I wait – it's only a matter of time. She's a writer – words are her best friend. "Did you just spank me?"

My expression remains stern, my eyebrows slightly arched, although my mouth is fighting hard to tuck that twitch away. My gaze fighting even harder to stay fixed on those gorgeous green eyes versus the pert nipples standing strong beneath the black tank top. Any closer and my resolve to not take one in my mouth will be gone.

"Fine!" she huffs, plopping back down, hoisting the pillow up onto my thigh this time as I send up a silent prayer that she doesn't get any closer to what I'm fending off. She repositions herself closer and pulls the covers up to her chin. "See if I help you trim your nose hair."

It takes her only moments . . . or so. "Jaxson," she says sheepishly.

I blow out a slow breath through my nose. "Yes, Sasha."

She draws a slow finger over the top of my thigh to my knee – *thank God she went in that direction* – her voice so damn sexy and soft. "I'll give you sponge baths after your hip replacements. And I promise not to put wheels on your walker."

In all honesty, I'm loving every minute of this despite the agony of my physical reaction. She's back to the woman I met – mouthy, confident, funny. I could do this all night. I move her hair away from her face, tuck it behind her ear, and brush my thumb over her cheek. "I'm holding you to that, Sasha. Now get some sleep."

Half an hour later, she's sound asleep, her breathing deep and even. I lift the pillow and her head off my thigh ever so gently and slide out from underneath. I steal a lingering gaze, watching her sleep. Long lashes brushing high cheekbones, soft pink lips that I can still feel against mine. So peaceful. So utterly beautiful.

Oscar pops his head up and follows me when I make my way toward the door. As I'm slipping my shoes on, I see the silk tie spread over the back of the chair and decide to leave it. Perfect excuse for a return visit whenever it suits me.

I squat down so that I'm eye to eye with the canine who watches me closely. I speak low so as not to disturb the sleeping beauty when I tell him, "You do your job well, buddy. Keep it up. I'm going to go do mine. Guard Sasha." Oscar immediately walks back to the front of the sofa, spins once, takes a position on the floor, and looks back to me as if he's done what he's supposed to do. He's a king. His ears stand straight up, eyes bright, shoulders strong and mighty. And that damn nose. The heart so prominently displayed across the bridge. I close my eyes and fight back the memory that feels like a punch in the chest every time it hits. For some odd reason, I feel he deserves a salute, so I give him one. I turn the knob quietly, flip the release on the deadbolt so it will lock when I close the door, and leave.

My senses are on full alert as I pause outside the door; the crickets chirping and the distant sounds of the ocean waves lapping at the shore not enough to offer a peaceful easy feeling. A glance to my right proves why. The black Mercedes sits on the side of the road, motor running, lights off, parked in the opposite direction it was last night. *Ballsy.* He wants a full frontal view tonight. There are no properties on the other side of the road, therefore leaving him out in the open to any witnesses that might be taking a late stroll on the beach. I make my way to my car, keeping my eye on his as I do, and slip in on the driver's side, extract my Glock from the glove compartment, start the engine, put it in reverse and back out of the drive. I see the flash of the  brake lights on the Mercedes as he puts it in gear and prepares to follow me. I indulge him – for all of three miles – before I take a fast split-second turn onto the ramp to Kings Highway and watch as he nearly loses control in his failed attempt to do the same.

"You need me already?" Nash answers with a yawn. Guess he didn't cash in a raincheck on that blow job for this evening.

"Can you put two of your guys on street duty tonight?"

I hear him groan as he sits up. "Send me the address," he says. "What are we looking for?"

"It's beachfront property. Back is fenced in but a lot of open land behind it." I take the next exit to turn around and head back to Sasha's house. I'll wait until Nash's guys get there.

"You sure two guys are going to be enough?" he asks sleepily.

"Only one way in and one way out, Nash. She's got a Belgian that's not about to let anyone close to the house. I want eyes out for the Mercedes I gave you plate numbers for last night."

"Uh . . ." he hesitates. "Did you just say she's got a Belgian?"

"How soon can you get them there?" I ignore his question, replacing it with my own. I didn't want to share that, but it is something his guys need to know. "I'm on my way back there now. I just headed the asshole off. I'll wait for your guys."

"Callum," he hesitates once again. "Just how deep are you . . ."

I sigh heavily. "Can you do it or not?"

"Text me the address. They'll be there as soon as possible."

"I'll be a hundred yards south of the house on the street waiting for them. I'm in the Audi. Thanks, Nash."

"Yeah, yeah, yeah," he mutters. "First born, Callum. First born. Nashua if it's a girl. Graham and Nashua if it's twins."

"Getting a little ahead of yourself, aren't you?"

"Knock her up, Callum. It's the only way she'll put up with your sorry ass." He laughs before he disconnects the call. I text him the address, add a *kiss my ass*, and return to Sasha's, parking the approximate length of a football field down the street, and wait until Nash's men arrive. I give explicit instructions regarding Oscar, remaining invisible unless otherwise necessary, and to call me if anything should arise.

The plan is for them to stay throughout the night, trading places with two others for the day tomorrow, then another two throughout Sunday night. Monday is a new day, my crew will be here, as will I, and by then I'll have a plan. She'll never need to know.

# Chapter 25

## Sasha

My phone chimes on the coffee table at an ungodly hour. How do I know it's ungodly? Because my eyes were not open yet, I was having the first pleasant dream I've had since I can't remember, and it's the ringtone for Rhea; Tom Petty's "Don't Do Me Like That". I'd given her a choice a long time ago. It was this or Elton John's "The Bitch is Back". She really shouldn't take offense; my sister Jolie's ringtone is a barking dog.

I hit ignore and bury my face in the pillow. She'll wait . . . or call back. It rings again . . . and again. Damnit.

"What," I whine.

"Wakey, wakey," she singsongs. "Got a body next to yours or are you all alone?"

"The only body next to mine," I groan as I open my eyes and look around, noting Oscar sitting up next to me, his breath no worse than mine I'm sure. "Is covered in fur and anxiously awaiting breakfast."

"Sooo," she drawls cheerily. "I take it he doesn't wax his back? By the way, love, a true gentleman would be cooking breakfast for you."

"It's Sunday morning," I huff. "Shouldn't you be in church confessing boob sex or something?"

"Ha! They'd lock the doors if they saw me coming. Sundays are reserved." She mimics a haughty voice as she states, "'Forgive me, Lord for snitching those four grapes in the produce aisle'. Exorcisms are only performed on Wednesdays and Fridays. Open the door, you prude. We brought carbs and coffee."

"We?" I whimper. It's too early for an inquisition – I haven't even peed yet. Come to think of it, neither has Oscar. "Hold on." I end the call and set the phone back on the coffee table. As I rise from the sofa, Oscar already sits at the door as the fast and harsh knocks start, which only causes him to bark. I'm going to murder that woman! I throw the locks on the door and open it wide, glaring at her. "You are now assigned Elton John."

"Took you long enough. I've been vying for that song for ages." Rhea reaches for my cheek, patting it gently before she pushes past me through the doorway, Shae and Sky right behind her, bags from *Roll Me Over* in their hands. They all look like they've been up for a while – showered, hair done, makeup on.

"Did you sleep out here?" Shae asks as she eyes my bedding on the sofa.

"Better question is," Rhea says with a teasing tone, holding up Jaxson's tie on one finger, "did he sleep here?"

*Shit! He must have forgotten it.*

Oscar barking at the sliding door to the backyard is my saving grace for the moment. I glance at the clock on the dining room wall on my way through. Nine o'clock. No way! I'm lucky to get past six most days. And that's only after tossing and turning. "I've got to let Oscar out," I grumble, reaching for the lock before opening the door. Oscar dashes through and runs for his usual area to relieve himself.

"We'll join you," Sky says, following right behind me. "We can eat on the patio this morning."

I look back over my shoulder. "Can I pee and brush my teeth first?"

"You're really just getting up now?" she asks, concern

furrowing her brow.

"Yeah."

"Bad night?"

A soft smile spreads across my mouth and for some reason, I don't even try to hide it. "No, not at all."

Three sets of eyebrows rise at the same time they study my face. They exchange knowing glances, slow nods, and their own soft smiles.

Rhea breaks the heaviness of the silence with a hearty laugh. "Boob sex?"

Shae and Sky groan in unison as I roll my eyes and mutter, "Somebody escort that girl to church."

"Not me!" Shae protests. "I'm not going up in a puff of smoke next to her when they throw holy water. I'll drop her off but I'm not staying."

Oscar comes back to the door before we've gotten out of it. "Can I go pee, please?" I beg impatiently, shifting from foot to foot.

"Hurry up!" Rhea shouts from behind me as I dance my way to the bathroom. "You've got some splainin' to do, Lucy. I want to check your wrists when you come out!" I hear a slapping sound before I hear her screech, "Ow! I want to make sure he didn't tie it too tight!"

Once in the bathroom, I do my business, brush my teeth, and splash some cold water on my face. Standing in front of the mirror, I take a few extra moments. Last night was more than enjoyable. There is something about Jaxson Callum, I can't put my finger on it. He knew what I needed, when I needed it. When to kiss me, when to hold me, but most of all, how to do it. Moreover, I'd let him do it again, anytime he wants.

He handled Aidan like a pro. I was so embarrassed for him. Blue jeans? Dirt under his nails? My dad is a laborer! How dare he insinuate Jaxson is beneath him due to his profession. I hate him right now. A sharp pinch in my temple shoots like a bolt of lightning through my head. Is this what a migraine feels like? I reach for the ibuprofen in my medicine chest, only to find it gone.

Where did it go? There's no Tylenol either. No aspirin.

The knock on the door is soft. "Hey," Sky says from the other side. "You okay in there?"

I open the door, still wincing from the pain in my head. "You got any ibuprofen or Tylenol?"

"I'm sure one of us does. You got a headache?"

Rubbing the back of my neck, stretching the muscles as I do. "Yeah, I probably slept wrong on the sofa."

Sky has already fed Oscar and gotten him fresh water by the time I get to the kitchen. "Let's get some caffeine and ibuprofen in you. Shae put the umbrella up but we can eat inside if it's too bright outside for you."

"No, I'll be fine." And I was. As soon as we started conversation, coffee, and carbs, the pain subsided. Until of course, Aidan Lehner happened into the conversation. My screw up.

"You ran into your old psychiatrist at a restaurant?" Sky asks. "O-kay. Shouldn't he have just said hello or nodded and maybe walked on by? How about, 'Hello Ms. Taylor, how are you?' and left?"

They all study me, suspiciously I might add, as they wait for me to explain. My avoiding their gazes and my bouncing knee under the table tells them pretty much what they're suspecting.

Sky dips her chin low before she reaches for my hand across the table, pleading for me to look at her. "Sasha, what is going on with you and your former shrink?"

"Nothing's going on!" I shriek defensively. "I only see him every few weeks on the beach for walks and we talk about things. That's all. We're friends."

"You're seeing your *former* shrink outside the office," Rhea starts with a deathly tone. "After being dismissed from his practice per his recommendation. And you don't see this as odd?"

"Why didn't you tell us about this?' Shae asks.

My eyes shift from one to the other's, speechless.

"He told you not to," Rhea speaks for me.

Sky looks to Rhea and Shae. "We alternate nights staying here until we get this figured out."

"What?!"

She squares me with a look that leaves no room for questions. "We either stay here or you come stay with me. What'll it be?"

"I – I don't need anyone staying with me," I protest. "I have Oscar."

Rhea sits back and folds her arms over her chest and smirks. "And from the sounds of it, had Oscar been *with* you outside on Friday morning, he would have made a meal out of the mysterious Aidan. We wondered how long it was going to take to get it out of you."

"What?!"

"We triple dated last night," Sky explains. "The guys told us what happened. They're worried. Needless to say, so are we. Why would you keep this from us?"

"Oh God," I groan and collapse onto the tabletop. "You told them everything, didn't you?"

"No!" Rhea jumps up and comes to my side. "We didn't tell them anything! We wouldn't do that to you! We stuck to the script."

"Sash!" Sky explains from her place at the table. "I'm the one that got you into this. It was my idea to have you seek therapy. I'm the one that let you down. I should have told the publisher to fuck off when they demanded you change your name, disconnect you from the political upheaval. Then you were sinking further and further and I didn't know what to do. I couldn't bring Ben back and couldn't fix it for you. I was trying to put a timeline on your pain. You and Ben were so different though. I should have just let you ride through your grief."

"We were all guilty of it," Shae adds.

Tears pour from a place they hadn't before. You suffer many cracks in your heart with loss. Pain, anger, devastation, denial, loneliness, emptiness. Each one has its place, each one needs its own healing, each crack gets filled in different ways. The one crack I had discounted was understanding. I prayed my friends would never feel what I felt. That's what it would take to understand. But today, I feel a little more understood, for the first time.

"So they don't know anything?"

All three shake their heads in unison as Rhea says, "No more than they did Friday morning. I think they were simply concerned and let us know what happened. It took us more than a New York minute to figure out who he was. It's been what, two years since you'd seen the guy?"

Twenty one months, but I don't bother to state it out loud. I know exactly how long it's been – he reminds me constantly. And hearing him say *three more months* last night was disturbing. Is it Jaxson? I wince as the pain in my temple returns.

Sky reaches for her purse and obtains a bottle of ibuprofen. Popping the top, she asks, "How many?"

"Better go with three," I reply and hold out my hand.

"How long have you been having headaches?"

"Just the last two days." I take the pills and toss them back with a shot of the coffee, burning my tongue in the process, unaware they had reheated them in the microwave while I was in the bathroom. "Damnit!"

Shae gets up and hurries for the kitchen. "You really should have done that with water. I'll get it. I'm booking you an eye appointment for this week."

Once settled with an ice water temperature-tongue which has somehow made me forget all about the headache, Rhea redirects the morning's mood. "Speaking of hot things." She holds up a chocolate croissant and grins. "Eat and tell us all about the sexy and mighty Jaxson Callum."

I snatch a bite before I take it from her fingers and she jumps. Crumbs fall into my lap and gather at the corners of my mouth. Huh, guess I am hungry. I shrug casually. "He's nice."

Rhea snort-laughs. "Elaborate. The man left his tie on the back of your chair."

"And he left his shoes by the front door." I roll my eyes with a huff. "And he rolled up his pantlegs and shirt sleeves. What's your point?"

Shae scrunches her nose. "Did he at least take his socks off?"

Rhea shudders. "Oh! I hate it when they leave their socks on."

I ponder for a moment before saying, "I don't think he wore socks. I know we were both barefoot when we . . ."

Sky gasps. "You did the deed? On the first night?!"

"The deed!?" I screech. "We walked the beach, you moron!"

"Oh, thank God!" Rhea breathes in exaggerated relief, placing both hands over her heart. When she finds us all staring at her, she lifts her hands in defense. "What!? After her dry spell, if they had done more I'd expect her to be limping and using a donut pillow." She narrows her eyes and tips her chin indignantly. "Otherwise, those website pics are photoshopped."

Sky drops her head in her hands in exasperation. "I give up. Sasha, just tell us how the date went last night."

"It wasn't a date," I reply, though my voice is wistful as I think back to the kiss on the beach followed by the one on the sofa. I lift one shoulder in a shrug. "It was an apology dinner." Yes, he kissed me. Let's not forget the smack on the ass either. And he stayed with me until I fell asleep on the sofa. He locked up before he left, made me feel safe. I'd have had to be stupid, not to mention blind, to miss what I'd done to him. And no, I don't think those pics are photoshopped. But he also emphasized he was too old for me. Talk about tossing a wet blanket on a flame. You are hardly too old for me, Jaxson Callum. I haven't felt so right in someone's arms since . . .

Sky snaps of her fingers in front of my face. "Earth to Sasha."

"He thinks he's too old for me," I say softly, picking at the last of my croissant. It was delicious, but my appetite has escaped as the thoughts have moved in.

"How old is he?" Shae inquires.

I roll my eyes and use air quotes, "Damn near forty."

They all laugh in unison but Rhea blows a lengthy raspberry as I swipe the resultant crumbs off my tank top and glare. "Come on," she says, laughing so hard I fear she may choke. "That's another twenty five years of good dick. Has he not heard of Viagra?"

# ANNIE MICK

# Chapter 26

## Jaxson

"Brick!" I call out as soon as he pulls up to the house on Monday morning. The three guys usually ride together in one company truck to the worksites after arriving for work in the morning, unless one of them has an appointment during the day. Carl drives his own company truck to and from work, taking it home at night – a perk that goes with being a foreman. It's my first day on the Taylor job. You can bet it won't be the last. Oscar jumps up in the bay window and barks as a woman exits through the front door.

Brick's face lights up like a damn Christmas tree and he holds up a hand as he runs toward the woman. "Be right there, boss." He picks the woman up and spins her around. "Mornin' beautiful," he greets her before planting a big sloppy on her mouth. "Thanks for waiting for me. I gotta go, but I'll call you tonight."

She giggles. "Can't wait, big guy."

A grinning and apparently pussy-whipped Brick runs back to where we wait, but only after turning one last time and blowing her a kiss. He points his thumb back toward the woman who's climbing into her car. "That's my Rhea."

I consider retrieving the air compressor from the rear of the truck to help him reinflate his balls but settle instead on a wry look and a sarcastic, "You don't say."

He laughs. "What's up, boss? Decided to join us after all?"

"Open the gate and give me the combination," I tell him as we make our way toward the backyard.

Simon is right behind us, his voice low and grave. "1-1-8-1-6. It's her wedding anniversary. Your turn. You want to tell me why you have two of Graham's men stationed close by?"

I flash him a side-eye and inquire, "Is that a January or November anniversary?"

He smirks. "Your curiosity is intriguing. Answer for answer, boss. You first."

"Excuse me, Sheetz?" I snap, keeping my voice low. "That sounds a bit like defiance."

He snickers sarcastically. "Drop the rank, *Cap*. Out here we work as equals. In case you forgot, I've got a woman who visits here regularly. If something's going on, I'd like to know. Come to think of it, I'd bet Brick and Dusty would be interested as well."

I scrub my hand down my face and over my beard before raking it up and through my hair, grabbing the band from my wrist and wrapping it in a ponytail. He's right, and I'm tired. I may have managed four hours sleep all told between Saturday and Sunday night. All three men stand before me, arms folded over their chests, waiting expectantly.

"I think she's being stalked." I rub the back of my neck. "The guy from Friday, his name is Aidan Lehner. He's a psychiatrist." I watch as their interest increases with the information. "Brick, I believe your instincts were right. There's something off about him. Let me in the yard, I want to show you something. Close the gate behind you."

"Keep an eye out." I nod to Dusty. "I don't need her coming out here right now." I point to the mostly hidden cable on the side of the house. This side of the house is solid, no windows, so we're hidden. Brick and Simon study the path from the rooftop to the ground for a moment before Brick drops to his knees and crawls along the foundation and peels the cable away from under the siding until he comes to the end where it enters the house.

He stands to his feet, takes a few steps back, gauging the length of the wall before whispering, "Motherfucker." He brushes the concrete dust off his hands and swipes the back of one across his mouth. "He put it through the wall at the head of her bed. I knew Oscar had a reason for tearing up that room. I missed it." He looks to me; his teeth bared. "Can I rip it out?"

I hold up a finger. "Hang on." Then I look to my communications expert. "Can you reroute it? And," I add, "make it look like nothing's been touched? I want him to continue using it, make him think it's still working."

Simon sucks in a breath between his teeth, hands on his hips. "I can trace and copy, listen in, but if I disconnect those wires, I may not be able to get the communication back. It depends on the detection system he has. You think he's doing a little mind play and need proof?"

I nod. "Yeah, I do."

"I don't need any more proof," Dusty sneers from where he watches for Sasha. The fire in his eyes is unmistakable. "Say the word, boss. Wouldn't be the first time."

Looking to Brick, I ask, "What wall is the head of her bed against?"

He nods toward the side of the house we're concentrated on. "This one."

The wheel on the gate lock starts to buzz and turn after Carl has entered the combination. He flips the second latch and opens it. "Mornin' boys," he greets us, then takes in the cable lying on the ground. He looks from it to us, then specifically to me, arching a brow, "I take it that wasn't the cable TV hookup after all."

"Nope," I tell him. I'm not sure how involved I want Carl in this. It's not about trust. I've no doubts about that. It's about accountability. The less he knows, the safer he is. He's not young and he has a family. Oblivion is a good place to be sometimes.

"Hmmm," he hums knowingly, nodding slowly then lifts his brows at me. "Did the roses work?"

"I didn't take roses," I huff. "You said not to."

"So, what did you take?"

"How the hell should I know?" I shoot him a look of disbelief. Flowers are flowers, aren't they? Unless they're roses, apparently. "They were white. A couple different kinds. The florist threw a red one in the middle for good measure. Looked like that origami shit. What difference does it make?"

Four sets of eyes stare at me in shock. In those eyes is written *you are such a dumbass.*

"How are you going to know what to give her every year on your anniversary?" Brick asks, his face folded into fifty shades of confusion.

"Anniversary of what?"

He gasps – his eyes big as saucers, his mouth a gaping hole – and slaps his cheeks, dragging his hands downward until his fingertips fall off his chin as he stares at his cohorts. "What do you think, boys? Is he salvageable?"

I clip the back of his head with my palm as they all laugh before I head for the backyard. "Simon, do your thing. Brick, tuck the cable back where it belongs when he's done. Dusty, we let him live for another day. You'll be the first to know if I need help."

Dusty lost his little sister to suicide from a drug overdose a few years ago. At least that's what the paperwork read. Her friends told Dusty a different story after the funeral. She had a boyfriend who stalked her, bullied her, gaslighted her – until she ended up dead in an alley one night. Dusty had no idea what was happening until it was too late. She hid it from him. He was on base, signed in for active duty, tucked safely into his quarters the night the boyfriend succumbed to a brutal death. The records proved he was in his quarters. Yup, that's exactly where he was. He and Brick and Simon all were. At least that's what the paperwork read. I saw to it myself.

"Hey boss?" Brick shouts after me. When I look back over my shoulder, I see him grinning. "How was the date?"

I see his face fall when I answer, "It was dinner, not a date." Though when I turn back around I can't help but grin to myself, because that was the best non-date dinner I've ever had.

Dusty walks beside me as Simon and Brick work on the cables at the side of the house. "You're not too old for her, Jax."

My thoughts from Saturday night return with a vengeance. If it occurred to these guys, even if only for a fleeting moment, the fact remains. Or did they sit and weigh the pros and cons?

"Yeah, I am," I concede with a grumble, hastening my steps to uncover the equipment in the backyard.

"Why would you think that?" he asks, pacing to keep up with me. "You can still run sprints around the rest of us most days. You show up at the bar and the women want to know if you're interested before caring if we are. What's the problem?"

"What the hell are you talking about?" Reaching for the plastic tarp on the treated lumber, I throw it off and begin to fold it.

"You hurt her feelings . . . again!" he accuses. "For such a smart guy, you can be such a dumbass." I glare. He shrugs. "What can I say? The women talk."

"The women talk," I mimic sarcastically.

"They care about her, Jax," he says quietly and carefully as he looks around so as not to be overheard. "Shae said you're the first guy she's gone out with since she lost her husband. She also said she was pretty disappointed when you told her you were too old for her." He grins wryly and shakes his head. "God knows why, but the lady likes you. Why ask her out if you think that? Why lead her on? If you screw things up for me I'm going to be pretty pissed. I like my southern belle. She's got class. That's hard to find. I ain't getting any younger." He smirks. "And if I ain't getting younger, you're about to roll over the proverbial hill, old man. We won't be putting candles on your cake anymore for fear of burning the house down."

"What about when we get called away, Dusty? The one last mission we've all committed to?" I'm not testing his loyalty, I know it's there. I'm simply tossing out food for thought. "I don't want you to have to lie to your women."

"Emergency call for work," he replies with a shrug, and without hesitation. "Storms happen all the time all over the world.

We're in construction. We can call it cleanup duty. You know . . ." he follows with an evil smile, his fists clenching and unclenching. "Ridding the world of one stormy scumbag at a time."

The sliding doors open and out runs the ever popular Oscar followed by his even more popular owner. She's fresh faced, hair up in another messy bun, T-shirt, mid-thigh length shorts, and tennis shoes. Modest, but undeniably beautiful. A welcome reprieve from the Kelly home where the typical daily attire consisted of see-thru tank tops, barely there shorts covering only half her ass cheeks, and the occasional *whoops* trip through the house in only a bra and panties. Did I mention the customer was *Mrs.* Kelly?

"Oscar!" Dusty greets him cheerily, petting him under the chin as he reaches us before he smiles brightly and waves. "Mornin', Miss Sasha."

"Good morning, Dusty." She chuckles, then looks at me. Her eyes flash with surprise as her lips part, her tongue making a quick appearance to wet them before it disappears, and I'm suddenly tasting her again. "Ja . . . uh, Mr. Callum. I wasn't aware you'd be visiting this morning." Her mouth tips in a teasing grin. "I'm sorry, I didn't fix sandwiches today."

Dusty snort-laughs then feigns a throat clearing cough and mutters, "Viagra," right before he howls, "Ow!" and reaches for his ear and rubs it. He turns a glare on me, but quickly realizes I'm too far away to be the guilty party. Welcome to the world of bugs, Dusty. You had that coming. If I could find the mosquito and thank him, I would. Damn good timing. He then turns his full attention back to Oscar.

"Good morning, *Ms. Taylor*," I return, lifting one brow, emphasizing the formality with a hint of cockiness.

"Mornin' Ms. Taylor," Carl greets her, tipping the bill of his cap as he passes and grabs Dusty's arm. "I think the boys need help unloading some equipment from the trucks."

"But aren't they . . ."

"Boy, I could not pay you to be this stupid," Carl mutters, pulling him along by his shirt sleeve as they walk away. As they get around the corner of the house I hear Carl announce, "Anybody walks in that backyard until the all clear and I will dock every one of you a day's pay."

# Chapter 27

## Sasha

I bid farewell to my first appointed watchdog as soon as the work crew shows up in the morning. Rhea had promised Brick last night that she would wait until he arrived, using the excuse of working on a campaign for staying the night with me. Technically, it wasn't a lie. Assuring reservations were sealed for next weekend, to include accommodations for Oscar and that the books for signing had arrived at the stores, is work.

When I step out the back door I'm greeted with a sight I most definitely didn't expect on a Monday morning. Admittedly, Jaxson Callum in dress clothes is quite handsome, but Jaxson Callum in faded jeans, T-shirt, and work boots? Well, let's just say the hamster wheel in my brain is circling through every description I've used in my books to paint the perfect male physique, and creating a few new ones at the present time as well. He is definitely inspiration. I was too mad at him last Friday to take real notice, but today is a new day. I've kissed that mouth. I've felt those arms hold me while I cried, while I laughed, when I needed a distraction.

He walks slowly as he makes his way to where I stand – so tall he blocks the sun from my eyes once he reaches his destination.

"Mr. Callum, huh?" he says playfully, tipping my chin up. "What happened to Jaxson? And you should know by now, I'm a pizza and beer kinda guy."

"I wasn't sure you wanted your crew to know."

His thumb caresses my jaw ever so gently as his fingertips steady my chin. "What is it my crew shouldn't know?"

"You left your tie here," I say weakly, his touch distracting me from any semblance of reason, or conversational skills.

"I know," he whispers, leaning in and brushing his nose against the side of mine. "I needed an excuse to come back . . . after hours." His mouth feels just as good if not better than before. One hand on my hip, his fingers at the base of my neck. He doesn't tear my messy bun from its confines – though I wish he would. The kiss isn't overbearing. It's . . . just enough.

He draws back from the kiss and leans his forehead on mine. "Let's try this again, shall we? Good morning, *Sasha*."

*Salsa tongue, meet squeezing thighs.*

My chuckle is light as I respond, "Good morning, *Jaxson*."

He kisses my forehead. "Much better." He studies my face for a moment before he asks, "Where did you sleep last night?"

Odd question, but after Saturday night, it doesn't seem too unreasonable. My shoulders deflate, shooting a scolding glare at my ever faithful canine who sits at my feet. "On the sofa . . . again."

"Have you thought about rearranging the bedroom?" he asks. "It might be the placement he doesn't like. I don't know where the furniture sits, but it's worth a try. The guys and I can help you right now if you'd like." He shrugs as if it's no bother. "It'd probably takes us a matter of minutes."

I ponder his offer. The arrangement I have is a perfect fit, but if changing it gets me back in my own bed, compromise is worth it. Oh shoot! Unless of course I want to watch TV from the foot of the bed or settle on sound without the picture.

I heave a sigh. "I have a wall-mounted TV on the other side of the room from the bed. That's not going to work."

"Is it wireless hookup?"

"Yeah," I say. "But the mount would have to be redone and

then I'm left with all the holes to patch and . . ."

"You got the paint?"

"Yeah."

He wraps his arm over my shoulder, leading me toward the sliding door. "Go get your naughty things put away. We'll get the supplies ready."

I giggle. "What kind of naughty things do you think I have?"

He takes my cheeks in his palms, studying my face before he lands a kiss that takes my breath away. The heat in his eyes is undeniable, his voice so low it rumbles. "I'm giving you time. Don't make me want you more than I already do."

He walks away, leaving me to stare at a custom built backside that I can't tear my eyes away from, short of a quick glance up to the sky to whisper, "Good job."

"Anytime you're done there, Sasha," he warns playfully. "We do have our regular work to do." He rounds the corner of the house and I hear him begin to give instructions for the new project.

ANNIE MICK

# Chapter 28

## Jaxson

This is perfect. We'll rearrange the furniture, get a look at the communicators the asshole wired into the bedroom, and see if inside access helps Simon in the process.

"Little side trip on work today," I tell them in passing, waving my hand toward the path to the front of the house, leaving Carl to putter in the backyard. The farther we are away from Sasha, the better.

"Are we going somewhere?" Brick asks as he follows me to the gate.

"No." I look to Simon. "You've got an in. We're rearranging the bedroom furniture for her. Oscar refuses to sleep in there so she's been sleeping on the sofa. She needs a wall-mounted TV moved to the wall her bed is currently up against." I tip my chin. "You're up. Take your time and check the floorboards to see what you're working with."

"On it," he says, reaching into the back of the truck, extracting the power tools he'll need for the transfer of the wall mount while Brick grabs the painting supplies, then lifts an eyebrow and smirks. "Just one question."

His tone as well as his smirk tells me I should probably forego entertaining him, but I bite. "What?"

"How do you know where she's been sleeping?"

I narrow my eyes in warning. "Simon, do you know how often HR haphazardly loses direct deposit information?"

He snickers. "I'm good with cash until they get it straightened out." He rolls his eyes. "For God's sake, Callum, will you just admit you're into the woman? You spent half of Saturday night with her. We're not asking if you got laid. Although if you want to share those details . . ." He swipes a hand at his ear and yells, "Ouch! Damnit! That last rain must have cropped up a new batch of mosquitos."

Dusty stares before asking, "Did you just get bit? On the ear?"

"Yeah," Simon grumbles, rubbing his ear once more.

"I just got bit in the backyard!" Dusty exclaims.

"Is that code for on the ass, Dusty?" Brick teases.

"Kiss my ass, Halladay," Dusty grumbles.

"Mark a spot, buddy. You're all ass." Brick retorts.

Dusty throws a roll of masking tape at him and storms toward the backyard, Brick on his heels, pleading, "Come on, Dust, I was only kidding."

"Those two having problems?" I ask Simon, watching Dusty stomp away as if the last piece of candy was snatched out from under him.

"Nah," Simon replies with a chuckle. "He's jealous Brick got a morning kiss and he didn't."

"Hey Dusty!" I yell before he turns the corner to round the back of the house. "I can see if Oscar has a little extra tongue to give today." His only response is flipping me the bird before he turns the corner. Simon laughs behind me and I join him as I shake my head. "You guys are so fucking whipped."

"It's not a bad thing to be, boss. Dusty's just having a little problem with the art of patience." He grins. "And chafing."

# Chapter 29

## Sasha

I make a mad dash into the house to gather any items from the tops of the dresser and nightstands so they can rearrange the furniture. Reaching for the picture of Ben that I set out on the nightstand once again after Brick helped me look for the nonexistent monster that Oscar had been seeking last week, I study his face once more, tears rimming my eyes as I look at the love of my life. The playful smile, the twinkling green eyes, the dimples I used to tease him about. *Used to*, Sasha. Bringing my fingers to my mouth, I kiss the tips and transfer it to the glass, feeling a pang of guilt for kissing a man in the backyard just minutes ago. "Gotta tuck you away for a while again, but only from my sight, never from my thoughts. I miss you." I slip it into the drawer and turn as four bodies appear in the doorway.

"Are you going to supervise?" Dusty asks with his usual boyish grin.

"I think we can handle this without an extra body in the room," Simon grouses and pushes past him. "Come to think of it though, she probably is stronger than you. What do you think, Miss

Sasha?"

I surreptitiously wipe a stray tear from my cheek and sniffle. "I think I might have missed a feather from the other night. Excuse me, I believe I'm about to sneeze. I trust you to figure out a good placement." I hurriedly slip under someone's propped arm against the doorframe and rush past them. Not sure whose arm it is – my only concern is concealing my feelings regarding the kisses I miss and the one I just shared on my patio.

"Sasha." I hear the concern in his voice as he calls softly from behind me. As I reach the door to my office, I close it before he can see inside. I don't need him seeing Ben's pictures in here either – the two of us, the other with Oscar. I'm not ready to share that part of my life. It's mine and mine alone. I'm Sasha Taylor – not Arkelpaine. Ben isn't Ben – he's Chase. Oscar wasn't a puppy when I got him. My husband trained him for me.

"You okay?" Jaxson asks, taking my shoulders in his hands. "You don't have to do this. I thought it might be worth a try to get you back into your own bed."

His concern is overwhelming. The way he cares, the way he wants to help but won't push if he thinks it's too much. Yet he pulled back when he knew it was too much on Saturday night. He seems to know what works, what's best, even when I don't.

"Moving the furniture is something I should have thought of. It's probably some animal that creeps into the yard at night that has him upset." I place my hand on his cheek and brush my fingers lightly over his short beard. It feels good, a little like a teddy bear. Not that my teddy bears ever gave me tingles. "Do it. I'll be in my office. Just knock if you need anything."

"It won't take too long. If this doesn't work, we can switch it back," he promises with a light caress of my shoulders, then turns back down the hall.

See? No kisses. No dramatic displays of affection. Simply reassurance. It's like he knew now wasn't the time.

As soon as he's down the hallway, I open the door to my office and slip inside, closing the door behind me. I pick up the pictures from my desk and stash them in the drawer. I did tell him if he needed anything to come and find me. Oscar and I can hide in here, out of the way, far from the chaos, or so I thought . . . until the burner phone in my desk drawer rings an hour later.

I pull the drawer open and stare at the phone. I don't want to answer it. But as soon as that thought enters my mind, I feel that newly familiar searing pinch in my temples. My hand moves of its own volition, reaching for the phone and touching the green button.

"Hello?" I answer, though I know exactly who is on the other end.

"Where were you this morning, Sasha?" His voice is harsh and demanding with his inquiry. "I waited on the beach for an hour. Where were you?"

"I – I didn't know I was supposed to be there," I stammer. "I didn't know you would be there."

"How could you not know I would be there, Sasha?" It doesn't sound like a question, it sounds more like an accusation. "I thought we had a *connection*."

He says connection like it's some kind of code word and I blink with the pain it causes in my temples.

"Where are you sleeping, Sasha?" he snaps. "Are you letting that dog dictate where you lay your head at night again?"

"No – no," I answer, but don't give him any details. "I'll be back in my bedroom tonight."

"Meet me on the beach at six o'clock tomorrow morning," he orders.

"I – I can't. I have company staying the night, Aidan."

"Who?!" he yells into the phone so loudly I have to pull it away from my ear.

"The girls are staying with me," I answer sheepishly, struggling to withhold the truth. I can't tell him they know about him.

"Why are they staying with you?" he demands. "Are you sure it's not the man you were out to dinner with, Sasha? That grubby construction worker?"

I fight through the pain in my temples with help of the anger I feel all the way to my bones. "How dare you judge a man by what he does for a living! You don't know him. My own father did the same thing. I need to go."

"Sasha wait!" he pleads, then sighs heavily and his voice softens. It's like a Dr. Jekyll and Mr. Hyde moment. "I'm sorry. I didn't mean it that way. You deserve the finest of things. I worry about you being taken care of by the right man. I don't want to see you taken advantage of."

"And just who is the right man, Aidan?"

"We both know the answer to that." He surprises me with his next words, his voice low and velvety smooth. "See me this weekend. I'll take you to dinner. We'll go dancing. Let me show you off."

My head spins with thoughts that range from shock to discomfort. "I can't. I have a book signing. It's out of town and I'll be gone for two days. We're friends, Aidan. You have nothing to show off."

"The weekend after this one, then. You let him show you off."

"No," I protest. "We're not like that. I need to go."

His tone is reminiscent of one I've heard him use before but can't pinpoint an exact time of when it was as he says, "Don't defy me, Sasha."

I end the call with shaky hands, dropping the phone back into the drawer. I stare at it as if it's just bitten me. Show me off? Dinner and dancing? For the last twenty one months, we were not supposed to be seen in public because I was a former patient. He caught me at my worst and took full advantage. I've done research on this for my books. Capture your victim in the midst of their grief, take full advantage of their weakness, prime them for dependence. Stay just far enough out of reach to make them need you. He's been grooming me! How could I have missed it? I am such a fool. Two years to avoid medical ethics code violations. Aidan Lehner is a walking talking ethics code violation! And now, he's jealous. This is what the girls suspected without voicing it out loud.

My head pounds so hard it feels like it's going to explode. Pressing my fingers to my temples is a futile attempt at pressure relief.

My breaths are coming fast and hard. I know I'm hyperventilating but try as I may, I can't stop it. My vision sparks with bright lights and I hear Oscar's spastic barking before my world goes black.

# Chapter 30

## Jaxson

We enter the house one-by-one, equipment in our hands, ready to move furniture and transfer the TV to the opposite wall. I arrive just in time to see her place the picture in the nightstand drawer. It'd be so tempting to take a peek, see who my competition is – *was*. I won't do it though. That would be a betrayal of epic proportions. With my luck he was her age; business type – maybe even a professor. She's a writer. I could see her with a book smart, clean cut, suit-wearing kind of guy. But I'd rather see her with me. That kiss the other night was mind blowing. It's all I've thought about since. Yet, it didn't feel like it was all for me. She'd been missing that human touch and I was the mouth and hands to help her find it. I can't imagine her with that fucking psychiatrist, Aidan Lehner. What has he done to her? What is he doing to her?

I see the wetness on her cheeks as she turns, the tear she swipes with the back of her hand as she rushes from the room; Oscar at her heels as always. This is why she needs slow, why she needs my patience. I shouldn't have kissed her this morning, teased her the way I did. If twenty years in the service didn't teach me patience, the last few certainly have. If I can wait for vengeance on my men's behalf, I can certainly wait for Sasha Taylor.

"She okay?" Simon's voice but an uttered whisper as he eyes the doorway she's just slipped through.

"Don't start yet." I pinch the bridge of my nose, releasing a sigh. "Let me go check on her first. She may have changed her mind." I know she hasn't changed her mind. This has nothing to do with the furniture. It has everything to do with the man she lost and the picture she has just hidden in the nightstand drawer.

Following the general direction she and Oscar went, I find her in the hallway at the other end of the house containing five doors, one of which she is about to enter.

"Sasha," I say softly, not wanting to startle her.

She pulls the door closed before I can chance a glance at what's inside. It's not a secret; simply a part of her world she's not ready to share. . .yet. As she turns and I get closer, I see it. The sadness, the hesitancy, the guilt. I should not have kissed her – not this morning anyway. But not touching her isn't so easy, so I settle for a reassuring touch because I promised her I could wait. And my crew and I have got to get to the baseboards in that bedroom.

I return to the master bedroom minutes later and instruct the men to get started. "We're good to go." I point in the general direction of where the furniture is to be moved, but my main objective is to get Simon where he needs to be – down on the floor to see where that sonofabitch placed the communicators.

An hour later, the TV has been remounted on the opposite wall, the bed has been moved, the dresser and nightstands have been placed, the rugs have been moved accordingly, the wall has been patched and painted, and the painting that was originally above the bed will be above the bed again after the paint has dried. Not once did I try nor consider opening that nightstand drawer–it was twice. But I didn't.

Best part? Simon found the tiny, nearly undetectable speakers attached to the baseboards and covered them with caulk. Now, they really are undetectable. They're also dysfunctional, inside the bedroom. He'll crack into the receiver and trace the communications once they start again. It's going to be a long couple of nights.

The muffled, panicked barking coming from the opposite end of the house pulls all of us away from packing up the supplies in the master bedroom and running toward the sound of Oscar.

"Sasha!" I yell on my way down the hall. Without waiting for an answer, I open the door. Oscar runs back to where she's slumped over her desk, her coffee cup tipped, the contents spilled over the top and onto the floor.

Her skin is flushed but not overly warm, pulse is rapid but steady, breathing is even and clear. Oscar jumps up on the arm of her chair on the other side from where I stand, whimpering as he nudges her shoulder with his nose.

"She'll be okay, boy," I whisper. "Simon, lift her chin." As he does, I slide my arm under her shoulders and the other under her legs, lifting her out of the chair and cradle her in my arms as we move out to the living room to the sofa. She murmurs softly against my shoulder on the way, slowly regaining consciousness. I would much rather prefer to hold her on my lap but concede and lay her down flat on her back on the cushions. There's a small goose egg forming on her forehead, soon to be a bruise, and I flinch. It'd be innocuous for one of us, but her? Not cool. This beautiful face should be adorned only with kisses and caresses.

Simon hands me a throw pillow for her head while Brick slides her shoes off her feet and tucks a pillow under them. Dusty arrives from the kitchen with a glass of water and a wet cloth wrapped around a sandwich bag filled with ice for her forehead. Carl comes up behind me and holds out the tiny bottle of smelling salts while Oscar struggles between letting me take the lead and biting my balls off to get me out of his way.

*Yeah, we're a team.*

Her eyelids flutter open and closed multiple times before she tries to sit up. "Whoa there, Spitfire." I hold her down gently and chuckle. "Let's take this one step at a time."

Her eyes flit from man to man and her breaths become stuttered as her eyes water. I hear Carl behind me. "I do believe Jax has this under control, boys. Let's head outside and get to work, shall we? Feel better, Miss Taylor."

Simon gently squeezes her shoulder, Brick taps her foot lightly with his fingers, and Dusty smiles, adding, "Lunch is our treat today, Miss Sasha. We'll get takeout. Let us know when you're hungry."

*It's not quite nine o'clock, but it's all Dusty had.*

"What happened?" she whispers once they're gone. Oscar lays his head on her thigh – lucky dog – and whimpers. She reaches for the top of his head and smooths his fur back and I watch as he calms with her touch. Yeah, I can see how that works.

"I think you passed out." I lift the icepack from her forehead and inspect the goose egg which has increased in size slightly. I lean in and drop a soft kiss on it before replacing the icepack. "Did you bump your head before or did that happen after?"

"My head?" she asks, reaching for the pack. She scrunches her brow and winces with the pain the movement causes. "No, I don't remember bumping it."

"Wanna tell me what happened?" I'm not going to tell her I saw the open drawer with the burner phone in it. I know Simon saw it too. I also know Aidan Lehner hasn't had access to her since at least Friday night if she slept on the sofa again last night, the girlfriends were here yesterday, and Rhea stayed overnight last night. Is the burner phone his access to her otherwise? My own phone buzzes in my pocket and as much as I want to ignore it, I can't. There are too many things at stake right now to let it go. I hold a finger up and grudgingly look at the screen and see Nash's text.

*"Heads up. Mercedes boy was on her beach this morning."*

I tap a quick *thumbs up* emoji button in response and pocket my phone.

"Something important?" she asks.

"Just another job. Letting me know the guys showed up on time. Now, where were we?"

She slowly starts to rise and I help her until she's seated

comfortably. I take a seat next to her – close enough for her to lean on me should she need to – and place the icepack back on her forehead. "You need to keep this on for a while."

"How bad is it?" She raises her hand and tries to remove the icepack to feel the bump underneath.

I lower her hand gently and hold it in mine. "Uh-uh," I tease. "The ink might not be dry yet. Dusty worked hard on that third eye. Blending the greens to match your others was pretty hard."

Sheer mortification, as well as fresh tears, fills the eyes that have visited my dreams and my thoughts since I first saw them.

"Hey," I whisper, moving the icebag away for a moment. "I was kidding. There is not a bruise in the world that could taint your beauty."

She buries her face against the side of my chest, grasping my T-shirt in her hands, and sobs. "I've been so stupid, Jaxson. I don't know how I didn't see it."

"Talk to me, Sasha." I wrap one arm over her shoulder and hold her head to my chest with the other hand. "Tell me what Aidan Lehner did."

She stiffens in my arms at the mention of his name – a repeat reaction of Saturday night. Without hesitation, I pull her onto my lap until she straddles me. I need her in the proper position for this for it to work. She buries her forehead against my chest and reaches for her temples, but I draw her head away from my chest, discreetly sliding my thumbs under her fingers, applying pressure to both of her temples, moving them in slow synchronous circular motions. My fingertips move to the back of her scalp, seeking the pressure points I need to make her melt into my touch, and she does. Her hands fall gently onto my forearms, relaxing with my touch.

*Use me, Sasha.*

When I hear her deep intake of breath, hear the light hum and relaxed sigh that follows, I press my mouth to hers, delivering a kiss that not only gives her the comfort she needs, but drains the pain she's been trained to feel. Her hands move to the back of my neck as she straddles my lap, pulling me tighter to her; as if to draw more comfort, more pleasure, more amnesia, and less pain.

*Use me, Sasha. Just find me at the end.*

When the kiss is over, she leans her forehead against mine, tilting it slightly to avoid the swollen, sore spot. "You do that so well."

"Only for you, Sasha." I place a light kiss on her mouth. "You ready to talk?"

Oblivious to the sudden reversal of symptoms, she proceeds to explain how she ended up in Aidan Lehner's care – therapy after the death of her husband. He treated her for months, transferring her care to another doctor after ensuring he knew her deepest secrets, held her utmost confidence, locked her into a state of emotional transference and dependence. Then played with her insecurities and met with her for the last twenty-some months outside of a medical setting and made it personal. Early mornings where no one would see them, hear them, know them; under the supposed guise of friends – my deduction; not hers  Then, she explains this morning's phone call.

Narcissistic sonofabitch. *Don't defy him?* He hasn't been playing with her. No, this asshole is in it for full control.

"He's been using me," she says, as if she's just figured it out.

*Oh, sweetheart, he's been doing a lot more than that. But I keep that thought to myself for now. I need to know how much long term damage he's done. Admittedly, she's brilliant if he's had this much time to manipulate her and she's figured out what she has. Oscar deserves a gold medal for keeping her out of her bed. First chance I get, I'm fixing that dog a T-bone.*

"He's been manipulating you, Sasha."

"Now that I think about it, it might have been him who tried to poison Oscar." She winces. "Oscar hates him."

"Someone tried to poison Oscar?"

"Before we moved in, after his exercise yard was finished, the guys found a container of poisoned biscuits next to it." She shrugs. "We thought it might have come from out back but that's why they put up the mesh covering on his yard and installed the heavy duty lock on the gate. So no one could throw anything in from the back or have access by way of the front."

This is the first I've heard of it. Can't say I'm not pissed either. Admittedly, I'd been in Charlotte for the last couple months, but something like that is nothing to take lightly. It happened on one of our worksites. They should have informed me, or possibly even reported it to the authorities.

"I won't let anything happen to you," I promise her as I nod at the canine at the edge of the sofa eyeing us intently. "Or Oscar." I lift her off my lap and set her on the cushion next to me. "Would you let me have the burner phone from your office?"

Her eyes widen in near panic. "How do you know about that?"

I realize my mistake as soon as I hear the tremor in her voice. *Another Aidan Lehner manipulation.* Sometimes a lie is all you have to protect someone, and I don't think Oscar is going to hold it against me. "You left the drawer open. Oscar tried to bring it to our attention, but we were a little distracted at the time." I shrug. "You know, unconscious lady and all. He's the one who called us to begin with."

Her eyes fill with tears as she reaches out to the faithful canine who looks at her as if she's the eighth wonder of the world. She brushes her fingers over the heart on the bridge of his nose. "He is pretty special."

A familiar pang hits me in my chest as I think *there's another one out there just like him.* I only hope he's loved as much as her Oscar is.

"You can have the phone, Jaxson."

I rise from the sofa to go back to her office to retrieve the phone. I collect it from the open drawer and pocket it – tempted to look around the room while I'm here – gather a little more insight into her world. But I respect her space instead and leave the room as I found it other than grabbing her own cell from the desktop. I stop in the living room before heading back outside and hand her the other cell phone that was left behind.

"Open it so I can put my number in." She does as I ask and I add my number to her contacts and send myself a text. "Is there a code to get into the burner phone?"

"No," she replies with a shake of her head. "It's never left my office."

"Put the icepack back on your forehead for a little while longer." I lean in and kiss her once more because – well, I can't help myself. "Can I get you anything before I head outside? Something to drink?"

"No, I'm good. I have a water right here."

"I'm leaving the glass slider open so I can hear you. Call if you need anything. Don't get up and start running sprints, okay?"

She laughs. "I promise."

I wink. "Good girl."

A tiny shudder envelops her body – in a good way – before I turn to leave followed by a soft whimper once I reach the kitchen. I shake the thought of her under me while I repeat those words in her ear.

*Time, asshat! You promised her time.*

# Chapter 31

## Jaxson

Stepping outside onto the patio, I see four concerned faces as they look up from the lumber they're measuring, cutting, and hammering. "She'll be okay." Keeping my voice low, I then concentrate on three of those faces and scowl. "We, however, need to have a little chat." I tilt my head toward the side of the house. "Over there."

Carl gives me a mock salute, dismissing us. "You're not off the hook, old man," I tell him. "Details to come."

He smirks. "Can't wait."

The other four of us walk to the side of the house. "Is there a reason you neglected to tell me about poisoned dog biscuits?"

They exchange very wary, uncomfortable glances as their feet shift from side to side. Brick's eye twitches and he pulls at his earlobe. Dusty sniffs. Simon thumbs his nose. Yup, all tells. They're nervous. Damnit! They've been away from their stations too long. *Stoicism is the rule.* Time for some retraining.

"Well?" I ask impatiently, my arms folded across my chest.

"We were gonna," Brick answers sheepishly, toeing the ground with his boot.

Dusty pockets his hands and blows a breath, avoiding eye contact.

Simon furrows his brow. "I pissed her off that day. She told us she had a Belgian named Oscar. It seemed strange, ya know? Caught me off guard. I was mean to her, said things I shouldn't have. She put me in my place real fast though; made me feel like a jackass. I don't think I've ever groveled like that in my life. I begged to let us help her move the next day. Then she shows up with a dog that looks just like . . ." His eyes mist over with the memory and I can't help but feel his pain. I felt the same way when I saw the dog. "We felt it best if we didn't say anything at all. We took all precautionary measures and made sure he was safe."

We all stand in silence for a few moments, probably in honor of a man we all lost. The memory of circumstances which still gut us, the vengeance yet to be served. The wishes for a call we all wait for.

"Alright," I say. "I get it."

"Was there something else?" Dusty inquires.

"Your instincts were right. Aidan Lehner is a problem. It seems he's left two dead women in his path and I'll be damned if Sasha is going to be number three."

"What!?" Brick shouts before I shoot a glare in his direction. "Sorry," he mutters, then whispers, "Lehner's a killer?"

Simon's scowl is murderous as he clenches his fists. "I should have snapped that fucker's neck when I had the chance. You knew about this?"

"No," I answer. "I had no idea what his role in Sasha's life was until ten minutes ago. I only had a partial on him up until now."

"What partial did you have?" Simon asks accusingly. "You knew our women are here on a regular basis. Did it not occur to you they could be in danger as well? We could have taken care of this asshole last week!"

"Hold it," Dusty says, holding his hands up. "Let's get the whole story first. Arguing isn't going to solve anything. Just shut up and let him explain." He flashes angry eyes at me. "Make it fast, Jax."

"He was Sasha's psychiatrist after her husband died." I run my hands through my hair, fisting them in frustration. "I have no idea how much damage he's done. He's not after your women, he's after her. You know about the lines wired into the house already. He's been stalking her as well. It's why I have Graham's men watching the property. He was on the beach this morning." I yank the burner phone from my pocket. "I have to see if he's left any voicemails. Simon, you have to monitor the feed that was going into the bedroom. See what he's been saying."

"Why are we bothering?" he snaps through gritted teeth. "You just said he's killed two women. What the fuck, Callum!"

The scruff on my face is going to be sparse with the way I'm scrubbing it. "They couldn't pin anything on him. One committed suicide." I grimace at my words and glance at Dusty, seeing the instant mix of fury and pain in his eyes. "The other disappeared. They haven't found her."

"What the fuck are we waiting for?" Dusty growls. I should have realized these particular circumstances might affect him harder than the others. It hits too close to home.

"We need proof," I warn them. "Have him arrested and brought up on charges. We can't just kill him."

Dusty takes a step toward me, his hands clenched so tight his knuckles are white, the fire in his eyes undeniable. "I can."

"Wait a minute," Brick says as if a thought has just occurred to him. "We asked the women about him on Saturday. They would have known if Miss Sasha was seeing a psychiatrist." His angry eyes flit from Dusty to Simon. "How many guys do you know named Aidan? They told us they had no idea who he was. They lied."

"They were probably covering for her," I say in their defense, then arch a brow. "Would any of you be so quick to share about one of your buddies being treated for PTSD?"

"None of their therapists are psychos!" Dusty whisper-shouts.

"Look," I say calmly in an effort to mollify them. "We'll get this handled."

"My *hands* around his throat sound good," Simon grunts.

"And when it's over, my *hand* across Rhea's ass for lying to me is in order. Damnit, that woman never takes anything seriously. We're dealing with a killer and she made a joke about Miss Sasha finally gettin' some."

"I doubt they have any idea what's really going on." I dip my chin in warning. "And it's best it stays that way."

"No way," Dusty snarls. "Until that sonofabitch is six feet under or I've fed him to the sharks myself, my girl gets Graham's protection too."

"Same for ours," Simon demands.

"We can do that." I pull my phone out of my pocket and open up the contacts list. They've got reason to be worried. Once Lehner realizes he doesn't have access to Sasha, there's no telling what he's going to do. I hadn't bothered to voice I have no intention of letting Lehner go free – if he's gotten off twice, he's found a way around the system. He's slick. A suspended license or revocation of it is only going to make him a looser cannon than he already is. No, the only way guys like Lehner go away is if they disappear, permanently. But I'm not about to let my guys take the fall for a problem I consider to be mine.

Graham bypasses a hello when he answers, "Don't tell me the beach boy made it past my men."

"Nope," I tell him. "We're good. I need a few more though. I'm on my way, we'll talk about it then."

"A few more?" He laughs. "Why don't you just call in the National Guard, Callum?"

"Long story. I'll see you in about an hour." I pocket my phone and nod to the guys. "Text me their addresses."

"What about next weekend?!" Dusty demands.

"Graham's guys work weekends. What's the problem?"

"Are they going to travel?" he huffs. "Go wherever they go?"

"Are they planning a trip?"

"All next weekend!" he exclaims. "Book signings for Miss Sasha. They'll be out in the wide open in Charleston and Hilton

Head. Who knows what that nut case will do?"

This is news to me. Not that Sasha had reason to tell me, but it would have been nice to know. The big question is whether or not Lehner knows. "I'll talk to Graham and let him know about it. In the meantime, I'm going to check on Sasha."

"Hey boss?" Brick calls after me once I've stepped away. The hint of taunting in his voice and the fact he's waited until I'm far enough away for him to dodge a punch gives me pause.

"What?"

"Why do you say her name the way you do?"

I feel the smile tip my lips, but I keep my back to him, hiding it. It does feel good on my tongue, tastes even better. My theory was spot on. Definitely a flavor I could savor every day.

"Get back to work," I order them as I slide the screen door open. "I'll be back later. Keep an ear out for . . ." I turn one last time, emphasizing her name for them, her flavor for myself ". . . *Sasha*." I hear their chuckles as I close the screen behind me, leaving the glass door open.

She's still on the sofa, calves tucked to her side, icepack off. Oscar is stretched out beside her, though his head pops up in full guard mode when I walk in. Her forehead looks good; less swollen, a slight purple discoloration about the size of a quarter. I hate that she got hurt; that anything other than a soft caress or kiss would touch that beautiful face.

"How are you feeling?"

She flashes an impish grin. "I was a good girl. No sprints."

Dropping to my knees in front of her, I take her cheeks in my palms. "I'll be sure to put a gold star on your chart."

She giggles. "How many do I need to get a reward?"

My mind races as I consider all the possibilities for a reward I'd love to gift her with. Good thing I'm on my knees. Adjusting Jax jr. without being obvious right now would be quite the feat. Shifting without resultant zipper burn? Impossible.

"Ten," I reply with restraint I want to pat myself on the back for. "You only have five. Behave yourself, Sasha."

She reaches for my beard and gently runs her fingertips

through it. Relishing the feel of her touch, I close my eyes, taking a slow, deep breath through my nose, and let her treat it like her playground. She seems fascinated by it. One would think she's never had facial hair to play with. Unfortunately, the current climate is not helping Jax jr.'s current disposition.

"I need to run some errands." I reach for her hand and drop a kiss on her palm. "I'll be back later this afternoon."

"Okay." Her voice is but a faint whisper and her smile is so soft it's nearly undetectable, but her eyes hold everything. Every secret, every emotion, every unspoken thought.

I whisper a kiss across her lips. "I'll see you later."

"I'll be here." Her soft smile grows into a full spread heart stopping face filled with mischief. "I promise I'll be good."

Placing another kiss on the tip of her nose, I smirk. "I'll place another gold star on your chart."

She rolls her lips between her teeth as she tries to hide the teasing grin that longs to peek out. "How many did you say I need?"

Reminding myself the main goal at the present time is safety over satisfaction, I narrow my eyes. "Twenty."

She gasps, adding a scowl, and huffs, "You said ten!"

Brushing a knuckle over her cheek, I gaze into eyes that hold a story I want to hear, a story I want to know page by page. "And you said time, Sasha. It's not a race. I'll be here." I plant a kiss on her forehead and rise from the floor. "I'll be back this afternoon."

Her lips twist and her shoulders deflate slightly. "I'll still be good."

I smile and wink. "I know you will."

# Chapter 32

## Jaxson

"Alright, let's hear it," Nash says, leaning back in his chair, hands folded over his stomach as he eyes me curiously. "Then you can buy me lunch."

"I need more of your guys." I take a seat in a chair in front of his desk. "I bought your lunch last time, and dinner at Monte's if I remember correctly." I narrow my eyes and smirk. "Filet mignon because fish was still tainting your taste buds."

He laughs then throws a pen at me. "You never did go check out the book club on the other side of the wall. Never know, Jax," he bobs his eyebrows. "A writer could teach you a few tricks. Well-read and well-written. Hmmm," he hums and wiggles his fingers. "Ever wonder if they do hands-on research?"

Nash did go check them out, initially peeking over the partition for a looksee, then making a special trip around the wall and past their table . . . slowly. As none of them leapt out of the booth and grabbed his dick, not to mention the fact he was my ride, he simply enjoyed the view for a moment or two and probably went home to whack one off. I didn't ask, nor did I care.

I shoot him an icy glare. "You done yet, asshole?"

"Not really." He grins slyly yet eyes me curiously. "Apparently, neither are you. Tell me, Callum, how is the little bookworm?"

"You did a background check? On my client?" I don't know if I'm more pissed that he took liberties or that I can't see this as him simply performing a favor for a friend. I knew Sasha was the same woman from the restaurant. I didn't ask for a background check on her. I got to know about her Saturday night, on my own. I also don't need Graham babysitting me. Granted, above and beyond is in his nature, but I'm not the one who needs protection.

"You didn't?" he says casually. "That's not like you, Callum."

"She's a customer," I offer somewhat defensively. "I saw some things at the house that caught my attention which have led to conclusive evidence she's being stalked, groomed, and manipulated by her former psychiatrist." I scowl and add, "Aidan Lehner."

His eyebrows nearly reach his hairline as he soaks in this information before they furrow deeply. "Ah, Mercedes man." He tips his chin and inquires, "How did you get in so deep?"

I scrub my hands over my face for the hundredth time today before running them through my hair. "I don't know. There's something about her that draws me in. I felt it the first time I saw her. She's so damn different, Nash. It's almost like I know her from somewhere." I lift my eyes to see him observing me.

"Drawn to her, huh?" He narrows his eyes. "You're never drawn to anything."

I nod slowly. "I know. Feels good though. What did you find on her?"

He studies me with one eye half closed – his tell for deep thought – then lifts one shoulder and shakes his head. "Not much. Tennessee born and raised, family's still there, successful writer, got a string of bestsellers, widow."

"How did her husband die?"

He shifts in his chair uncomfortably before he looks out the window. "Tragically," he utters. "*Chase Taylor* was murdered." He flinches and reaches for his ear, rubbing it harshly. "Damnit," he swears. "The mosquitos are bad this year."

My lungs squeeze tight in my chest and my stomach roils. Murdered?

"How?"

He keeps his gaze on the window but I see him wince slightly. "He was shot."

"Let me see the report," I demand.

He fidgets for a moment and then opens and closes a few drawers of his desk. "Oh shit, I must have left it at home. I can get it to you later. In the meantime," he says, his voice changing a pitch. "Tell me about these extra guys you need."

I shake off the uneasy feeling caused by suspicion. Nash doesn't leave things at home – not without reason. "She's got three friends who happen to be dating my crew that's working on her house. They need protection too. All four will be traveling this weekend for book signings that Sasha has in Charleston and Hilton Head."

"Whoa, whoa, wait a minute. Which crew is dating her friends? Let me venture a guess. Alvin, Simon, Theodore? The chipmunks?" He belly laughs so loud it rings throughout the office and probably into the hallways. His reference to the old cartoon is rather comical. It doesn't go over as well with the guys, but it has always made for some good razzing amongst the men. "Damn," he breathes on a heavy sigh. "I knew I should have introduced myself when I went past their table."

"You done?"

"Who's dating the one with the . . ." he holds his hands in front of his chest mimicking large breasts ". . . bazoombas."

I pinch the bridge of my nose. I haven't met the other two, but I'm assuming it's Rhea. Not that I was looking this morning, but let's just say the woman's endowments enter the room a full two seconds before she does.

"That would be Brick."

"Lucky sonofabitch," Nash mutters.

"Nash," I groan. "Can we get back to the subject at hand?"

He singsongs in a cocky voice as he uses his hands like a

balancing scale, "Subject *at* hand, subject *in* hand. Pretty much the same."

"Graham," I snap.

"You got 'em," he replies. "Tell me where and when."

I slide my phone out of my pocket and write down the addresses the guys have sent. "I need a guy posted with each of these women 24/7. I have no idea what this psycho is capable of. My impression is he only wants Sasha, but we both know what loose cannons can do if they feel like they're losing their grip." I pocket my phone and square him a look of sheer determination. "He's going down, Nash. And I'm taking him down myself."

He narrows his eyes as he lifts one brow. "You want him down or do you want him out? High tide comes in handy. This guy is dangerous, Callum. We'd be doing the female population a huge favor."

"I'll take him down," I proffer. "You can take him out."

"Hmmm," he hums and bends his ear forward. "I do believe I hear the sharks sharpening their teeth right now."

Pulling the burner phone from my pocket, I open the voice mail messages, hit the speaker button, and set it on the desk.

The recording starts with "You have nine new messages."

His voice is nauseating as it waxes and wanes from sappily sweet to anger to scolding to intense fury from one message to the next, not necessarily in that order.

*"Sasha, you must not be close to the phone. I know the light blinks to indicate messages so I'm sure you'll call me back as soon as you get this."*

*"Sasha, why weren't you on the beach this morning? I waited for over an hour. You know I'm a busy man. I'm an important man. People depend on me to help them through tragedies. Just like I did for you. I set aside special time for you. I wouldn't do that for just anyone. You know how important our walks are. I certainly hope this doesn't happen again."*

*"Sasha, I'm losing patience. How do you not know when to meet me? You've always known. Is that dog interfering with your sleep again?"*

*"Sasha, this morning's incident at your gate was inexcusable. I refuse to deal with those filthy construction workers! I told you there are consequences for bad decisions. Do not defy me, Sasha."*

*"Do you have any idea what it did to me to see you with another man tonight, Sasha? A grubby construction worker of all things? Imagining his dirty hands all over you? I might have to find another woman to take my frustrations out on. I didn't mean that, Sasha. No one could replace you. Please don't let him influence you in any way. Call me, please."*

*"Sasha! Pick up the damn phone!"*

*"I saw you on the beach tonight, Sasha. I saw you kiss him. I saw his hands all over you! Did you let him fuck you? Did he take you hard, Sasha? Did he make you scream? What would your dead husband think?"*

*"I'm sorry, Sasha. I'm so sorry for my behavior. Please forgive me, darling. You deserve the best of everything and I only want to ensure that you have that. I promised you friendship. I want to promise you the world. I'll even make friends with Oscar."*

*"Sasha, I'm on the beach waiting for you. Where are you? The sun is about to rise! I have patients to see this morning. I told you to be here. If it weren't for those damn construction workers, I would be at your house right now! You'd better not be with him again. Get rid of him, Sasha. Damnit! Do not defy me!"*

The phone beeps and we hear, "End of messages."

Nash chapels his index fingers to his mouth and his eyes narrow. "Well," he says slowly. "I don't think his mental health is in question. Do you?" He leans back in his chair and waves his hand at the phone. "This fucker's crazy."

My knuckles are white from clenching my fists and my teeth feel the pressure from the tightness in my jaw. Every time I heard him say her name, I wanted to throw the phone across the room.

"I'm glad I confiscated the phone before she heard the messages," I tell him. "He's in her head too deep as it is."

He pierces me with a glare. "In case you missed it, his

problem is with you as much as it is her. Watch your back, Callum."

We finish the details of the security for Sasha's friends, but when I stand to leave Nash scowls. "You owe me lunch, asshole."

"I bought you dinner at Monte's."

"That was last week," he complains. "New day, new food. Besides, I'm not picky. You know me, I'll eat anything."

"Well aware, Nash. I just can't remember the last one's name."

"It was . . ."

"Don't care." I hold up a hand to stop him. "I was going back to Sasha's to have lunch with the guys."

"And the problem would be?" He grins. "I'm mobile. Haven't seen the chipmunks in a while. This could be fun."

Yanking my phone out again, I text Dusty.

*"You order lunch yet?"*

*"Nope. About to. Miss Sasha wants lobster rolls from the Crab Shack. You in?"*

*"Order an extra five of them. Add fries. On my way."*

*"Five???"*

*"Good job, Dusty. I now know you can read."*

*"Who's buying?"*

*"See you soon."*

*"WHO'S BUYING???????"*

I slide my phone back in my pocket once again and look to Nash. "Let's go. You can follow me. Hope you've kept your palate clean since Monte's. We're eating fish."

# Chapter 33

## Sasha

"Nope, sit down," Brick says, gently taking my shoulders and leading me to the picnic table. "We're serving you today. Lunch is on us."

He'd come into the house ten minutes ago to gather the plates and silverware for lunch – after washing his hands, of course. Dusty and Simon made the trip to the Crab Shack for the lobster rolls I'd requested and are minutes from arriving with the food.

I hadn't run sprints to the bathroom, but I had managed to get there and apply a spot of foundation to the bruise on my forehead to hide the purple mark that sits dead center from temple to temple and hairline to the bridge of my nose. I should still qualify for good girl status. Oh, that man's voice. I wonder if he would do an audiobook for me. Hmmm, I could fall asleep to that every night. Maybe just the sex scenes. No! Wait! Countless other women would be doing the same. I'll tuck that little tidbit away for myself. Maybe have him record it and never publish it?

As thoughts of depriving the female population of Jaxson Callum's deep baritone vocal cords dance through my petty, selfish brain, the sound of four car doors closing out front capture our attention.

"The boys must be back," Carl says, taking a seat opposite me at the table.

"Long time no see, Nash," I hear Simon say.

"How's the lead chipmunk, Simon?" an unfamiliar voice returns.

"Who's got my fifty bucks for the extra rolls and fries?" Dusty asks impatiently. "I'm a dating man now. My money goes for my woman."

"You having to pay for it these days, Dusty?" the unfamiliar voice asks with a laugh. "Losing your touch with the ladies?"

"Nope," I hear Jaxson answer for him with a chuckle. "Poor guy's living up to his name. Dusty's in a bit of a dry spell. He's dating a proper southern belle."

"Asshole!" Dusty hollers as they round the corner to the patio, his hands loaded down with bags from the Crab Shack

"Gentlemen," Carl says dryly as he spots them all with a stern glare.

My back is to them, but I hear their boots scuff on the concrete as their footsteps falter and Jaxson mutters, "Oh shit."

Oscar is chomping at the bit to greet them all and wiggles next to me. "Stay," I order him firmly. "They were naughty. They don't deserve the honor of your welcome." Keeping my back to them, I proffer, "Don't have any shit, Mr. Callum, but I'm pretty sure I can find that arsenic. Care for a little sprinkle on yours?"

Brick cackles while Carl smiles. Loud unfamiliar laughter rings from behind me, ending in a quick *"oomph"*. I soon feel warm callused hands lightly squeeze my shoulders before his mouth drops a light kiss on my neck and a whisper reaches my ear, "It was a joke, Sasha."

I turn my head slowly and drop my shades to the tip of my nose. "My offer wasn't. We proper southern belles value our virtue."

He nuzzles a little closer and whispers, "I value your virtue too, as well as everything else about you." He extends his hand for me to take. "Come here, I want you to meet somebody."

I stand and turn to see a strikingly handsome man. Strong jaw surrounded by well-trimmed facial hair, broad shoulders, tall, well built. He's standing with his hands in his pockets, shades on his face, but it's apparent he's staring at Oscar. His lips are parted, his thick arched brows prominent above the rim of his shades as he takes in my four-legged companion.

"Nash," Jaxson says curtly, drawing his friend's attention away from Oscar.

"Hmm? Oh, sorry," he says, slightly distracted. "That's a beautiful dog you've got." He extends his hand. "Nash Graham. You must be the lovely Sasha Taylor. Jax speaks highly of you." He takes my hand in his before he lifts it to his mouth and kisses my knuckles.

I smile brightly then smirk at Jaxson. "I'm sure he did. I'm one quarter of the proper southern belles Mr. Callum spoke of."

Jaxson scowls at Nash and reaches for my hand, gently pulling it away while shoving his shoulder. "Knock it off, Romeo. Lunch is ready. Let's eat."

"So how do you two know each other?" I ask once we're seated and halfway through lunch. Jaxson sits next to me while Nash sits across from the two of us.

"Scouts," Nash answers quickly, eyeing Jaxson. "Earned all our badges together, wore the same geeky uniforms, camped out, peed in the woods. I don't think we ever brought out the tape measure though, did we?" He smirks at Jaxson, then winks at me. "Jax was shy. He knew I'd win anyway."

I scrunch my nose and feign puzzlement. "Measuring who could pee the farthest?"

"Uh," Nash clears his throat and scratches his head. "Yeah, sure."

"Oh," I say as if enlightened, and nod. You know, *southern belle and all.* I look to Jaxson. "What size shoe do you wear?"

His forehead creases in confusion but he still answers, "Thirteen."

Looking to Nash I ask the same, "And you?"

"Uh, twelve."

"Huh." I shrug. "Well, that answers that. No tape measure needed."

Jaxson snort laughs as Nash gawks at me, stunned.

In my periphery I see Simon's head drop to his chest and hear his drawn out murmured, "Burn."

A voice calls out from the gate at the side of the house and I hear my best friend call out, "Hey! Let me in. I didn't bring my key. Are you keeping those vertical smiles to yourself?"

Brick nearly trips over himself rising from his seat, his face lit with a smile a mile wide as he runs for the gate. "That's my Rhea."

Nash wears a puckish grin and waggles his brows as he looks to Jax and inquires, "Brick's? So I get to meet the girls?"

"No," I answer on his behalf. "It's only one of them."

Nash smirks. "Not from what I remember."

Jaxson scowls and Nash suddenly jumps and yelps, "Damn." He scowls back at Jaxson. "Can't blame a man for appreciating." He snickers. "I'm sure Brick and Rhea make a nice *pair*."

Grateful for the interruption of my confusion, Brick and Rhea enter the yard – his arm around her shoulder, her thumb in the loop of his jeans. It's the best they can muster as the top of her head lands just above his armpit – but she swears he always smells good.

"What happened to your forehead?" Rhea rushes to my side, swipes her thumb on her tongue, then spit washes the makeup off of my bruise – like your mother would do before a mad dash into church on Sunday when she eyes that wayward drip of syrup on your chin after pancakes for breakfast.

"Yuck!" I double swipe her spit off my forehead with the heel of my palm, then reach for my napkin and dab it again. "What are you doing here?"

"I brought the usual books over for you to pre-sign so you don't have to do it Friday night in the hotel." She shrugs. "This way we can eat, drink and be merry while we binge watch porn instead."

Mine is not the only jaw at the table that drops, but my eyes are the only ones that glare. The others are filled with amusement.

*We have never binge watched porn! Well, not since college, and my excuse then was for research. Theirs was for . . . support, on my behalf. And if you believe that, I've got real estate in the middle of the Indian Ocean I think you might be interested in.*

She glances around the table. "Which one of you klutzes hit her with a two by four?" She points a finger at Oscar and frowns. "And why aren't you protecting her?" She looks to Jaxson and narrows her eyes. "You must be the infamous Jaxson Callum. I found your tie on Sunday morning. Nice taste in clothes. Not one mark on her wrists either. Kudos to you." She then turns her head slowly and shoots a seething glare at Nash – who happens to be looking exactly where he shouldn't – and directs her index and middle fingers toward her eyes. "My eyes are up here, dickhead. Look at my boobs again and I will slap you silly."

*Yes, folks. This is my bestie.*

Brick places his hands on her shoulders and says proudly, "For those of you who haven't met her, this is my Rhea." He nuzzles into her neck and in pure Brick fashion, offers a simple lunch in a sensuous way, "You want my lobster roll, baby?"

She giggles. "Do I have to swallow?"

"Oh God," I groan and lower my head in embarrassment. I know they're joking; Brick doesn't get her art until she has his heart. "Go eat and then I'll sign."

Her face turns serious and the crease between her eyebrows deepens. "You sure you're not going to see triple? Want to tell me what happened?"

"Later," I answer with a nod.

As she and Brick find their way to the end of the table, Nash shakes his head and eyes Jaxson. "There is not a pair worth the ball bustin' that would bring." He laughs heartedly. "Give Brick my regards."

* * *

Lunch is over, the wrappers are gathered and disposed of, and Nash is about to leave. His draw to Oscar is not alarming per se but does seem a bit unusual. He explained it as a love for dogs, having had them for years, but asking to take him out to the exercise yard to see how he performs in it? Yeah, unusual. It only lasted for fifteen minutes, but he seemed to know exactly what to do with him. And Oscar? He loved it. Me? Not so much.

As Oscar pants by my side after a good workout in his yard, Nash pulls his phone from his pocket when it buzzes. His brow furrows as he reads a message, then he looks to Jaxson.

"Think I'd best be going. Miss Taylor, it was good to meet you. Hope to see you again soon." He reaches for my hand once more and this time only gives it a gentle shake. "Jax, can I see you out front for a bit?"

# Chapter 34

## Jaxson

"He's on the beach as we speak," Nash informs me once we reach his truck. "My guy said he's scouting the house with a pair of binoculars. Care to go give the peeping psycho a visit?"

"You think it's wise to rile him up?"

His shoulders lift and drop. "Wouldn't hurt to know exactly what he can see from where he stands. If he sees us coming and runs, we'll know how familiar he is with the comings and goings. He may have been doing this for weeks now."

"And if he doesn't run?"

He arches a brow. "Then we know what we're working with. He's either obsessed with her or he's obsessed with winning. We know how this works, Jax. He's put in his time. He's not about to accept losing. If we push him to make a move, we'll be a step ahead of him. We'll be better aware of how this particular one operates."

"Let's do it." I turn in the direction of the beach, knowing my boots are going to be filled with sand by the end of this journey. Won't be the first time; truly doubt if it will be the last. I used to live for getting sand in my boots. Sometimes thought I'd die doing it. One more mission . . . after this one.

"I know what you're thinking, Nash," I say on the way through the sand. "I saw the way you looked at the dog."

"Not gonna lie, Callum," he admits. "That just about knocked me on my ass. I'd have loved to have been around when you and the chipmunks saw him."

"He's older than Ben's dog would be," I explain. "Simon said his girlfriend told him Sasha's had him since he was just a puppy. Gotta be more than one of them with similar markings."

"Why the setup for the training yard?" he asks. "He's damn good, by the way. You'd think he was militarily trained." He rubs at his ear with his index finger and thumb and yells, "Damn these bugs!"

"Researched it, I guess. Gotta admit, she does a good job with him. That dog would kill for her."

He places a hand on my shoulder as we approach a scowling Aidan Lehner. "Let's make sure he doesn't have to, shall we? I wouldn't want to deprive you of the pleasure."

Lehner's in a dress shirt and tie, rolled cuffs on his pants, barefoot. Compact expensive binoculars hang from a lanyard around his neck which he doesn't go out of his way to hide. Attire that screams, *"lunchbreak stalker"*.

"Aidan Lehner," I address him with the same amount of disdain he held for me in the restaurant Saturday night, and eye his binoculars. "What brings you to the beach midday? No patients to treat?"

He pockets his hands and looks around casually, ensuring he has witnesses. "Ah, the construction worker." He shoots me a snarky grin. "Did you decide to come down to the water for a bath?"

Nash doesn't flinch. His arms are folded over his chest, shades over his eyes, feet planted firmly in the sand. He could do this for hours on end. He could also snap Lehner's neck in a heartbeat. Either one of us could – but we'll save that for later.

"You always visit the beach with binoculars?"

He looks down at his chest and tugs at the lanyard. "Oh

these?" he says casually. "I'm birdwatching. It's one of my favorite pastimes."

"What are some of your other favorite pastimes, Dr. Lehner?" I take a step toward him. "Stalking former patients?" I see his quick intake of breath and watch his fists clench. Giving him the impression I'm now only aware of her being a former patient – after all, I am just a dirty, uneducated construction worker – I ask, "What did you mean when you said, 'three more months' to Sasha?"

"That's none of your business!" he snaps.

"I'm dating her, Lehner," I say with a low growl. "Everything is my business. She's mine now." *Just enough to set him off. Perfect.*

He takes one step forward, hands fisted and chest puffed, but thinks twice about it with the faltered second step when he realizes I have a good three inches and probably thirty pounds on him. Not to mention, mine is muscle. "You need to stay away from Sasha."

"Too late," I tell him. "You know how it is when you find the right one, doc. You'd do anything for them. Find another spot on the beach to . . ." I flick the lanyard around his neck, ". . . *birdwatch.*"

I turn first while Nash watches my back for a quick minute, ensuring the dumbass doesn't pull a weapon. I don't think he's that stupid. Crazy? Maybe. Stupid? Nah, this sonofabitch is crafty. He schemes. Let the game begin, Lehner. Two women are dead – I know the missing one is never coming back. Maybe I can squeeze out the location of her body while I squeeze the life out of you.

Halfway back to the house Nash says, "I do believe you've set the wheels in motion. Nothing like pissing off a psycho and taking away his favorite treat. Did I hear they're going away for the weekend?"

"Yeah." My shoulders tighten with the thought. "Sasha has book signings to do in Charleston and Hilton Head." I shoot him a side eye. "Your guys will be on this, won't they?"

"Of course," he reassures me. "You know, it's been a long

time since the chipmunks and us have taken a bike ride. What do you say we make a weekend out of it?"

*Ah, the Harleys. Damn! A bike ride through the mountains sounds like a vacation right now. Open road, rumble under my ass, freedom.*

"I'd rather be close and on-call if something happens with that asshole, Nash. No telling what he's capable of."

He nudges my arm. "You'd be a whole lot closer and *on-call* if we were in the same towns they are. Might not be a mountain ride, but a ride is a ride."

"I was going to ask her if she wanted me to take Oscar for her so she doesn't have to kennel him."

Nash laughs loudly. "Something tells me where she goes, Oscar goes. My bet is that dog has never seen the inside of a kennel. Besides, if that asshole shows up, he's going to be a lot easier to tail with a bike than a vehicle."

"What if Berkel calls?"

He sighs heavily. "Jax, it's a half day prep minimum just to get on the damn chopper. We'll be good, I swear."

"Do you know where they're staying?"

He tosses me a sly grin. "I will as soon as I'm at my computer."

"Think we can get rooms in the same hotel? It's tourist season. What if they're fully booked already?"

He looks to the sky and feigns a sad hum, smiling cockily. "Oh ye of little faith." He slaps my shoulder. "You in?"

Blowing a deep breath, commonly known as a sigh of relief, I nod. "I'm in."        I stop before we reach the house. "Nash. Sasha and I, we're not, we . . ."

He snickers. "Yet."

"We're not like the chipmunks and their . . ." My voices trails as I shake my head.

He laughs. "I thought I was the only one who called them that." He eyes me with severity doused with a touch of confusion. "So, this is all about protecting her? Because I gotta tell you, Jax, from what I saw, there's a whole lot more than protection going on between you two. I've never seen you look at a woman like that."

*Yeah, Nash. Tell me something I don't know.*

"I'm too old for her," I mumble.

His eyebrows nearly reach his hairline. "Did she tell you that?"

"No," I admit with a shrug. "She doesn't seem to have a problem with age."

"Does your dick still work?" He laughs as he backslaps my arm before he reaches for his ear once again. "Ouch! Sonofabitch!"

"You get bit again?"

"Apparently." He scowls, rubbing the back of his ear. "I gotta get out of here before I get eaten alive." We walk the last hundred feet or so to get to his truck when he turns and blows a deep breath. "Jax, you know age is mind over matter. If she doesn't mind, it doesn't matter. Why should you? Go with your gut. We've lived by the rules all our lives. 'Yes, sir. No, sir. Whatever you say, sir.' We gave them twenty fucking years, Jax. We're never going to get that back. How many more do we have? We've seen it disappear in a heartbeat. You want to tell yourself this is all about protecting her? You do that. I'll be back to put my foot up your ass when you screw it up. Stop beating yourself up for what wasn't your fault and enjoy the chance you've been given. I've never seen you smile like you did in that backyard. It looks good on you. Don't be an idiot. You're worried about age? Check out Botox. Oh!" He snaps his fingers and his eyes light up, "They have this stuff called ky-a-liss, too. I hear that shit is a miracle drug."

Rolling my eyes, I correct his pronunciation, "It's called Cialis, dumbass."

He roars with laughter and points a finger. "You have been doing your research."

Why I hadn't seen that coming, I'll never know. I hardly need any enhancement drugs. I narrow my eyes and scowl. "Fuck you, Graham."

He grins as he opens the door to his truck. "Save it for her, buddy. At your age, you never know when you might run out of steam." He climbs in and starts the engine, revving it a few times.

"Hear that?" He smirks as he rubs his hand over the dashboard. "Purrs like a pussy. Just gotta know how to pet 'em."

"Goodbye, Graham."

"Hey!" he calls out once I've turned my back. "What kind of books does she write?"

"Fiction," I answer gruffly. No way am I going to tell him what she writes, nor what her pen name is. I've spent the last two nights up late reading Sasha's books. Fiction, my ass. That's fantasy . . . waiting to become reality. Screw Cialis or Viagra. Open a page or two of Sara Paine's world. Trust me, it works.

"Tell the chipmunks to get the bikes ready," he says. "We're going for a ride. Yeehaw!"

## Dr. Aidan Lehner

*Who the hell does he think he is? She's his now? She's mine, Callum! She has always been mine! Damn you, Relda! Another woman who can't follow orders. You couldn't just find her a house to move into, could you? A fixer-upper? A total renovation is more like it. This is your fault. Construction workers in and out day after day. They've probably broken more than they've fixed just to have reason to be around her. Look what you've done. I slept with you! I suffered your irritating laugh, your howls of ecstasy while I pretended you were her, shutting down my brain and letting my animal instincts take over, perform without conscience.*

*And how did you pay me back?*

*You placed my little lamb in the hands of wolves.*

*Insubordination has its price, Relda – time for you to pay.*

# Chapter 35

## Nash Graham

As his best friend, I should. I really should.

Also, as his best friend, I can't. I simply can't.

I've never seen Jax so happy. There's a shine in his eyes that I've never seen before. Jax and I have had our share of women over the years. We've had fun – the lust and leave type – but never have I seen him treat a woman with such gentility as he did today. The way his hands found their way to her in one way or another; be it her back, her shoulders, the nape of her neck, her hand in his. The most spectacular change though? His smile. Jax never smiles. He smirks. He also never laughs – not outright anyway. But he did today.

He should have known the moment he saw that dog, though. But he looked past it, over it, around it, through it. I don't know, maybe he was too enamored with Sasha Taylor to even consider the possibilities. And what's with the chipmunks? How did they miss it? What. the. fuck! They're special ops, for God's sake. Navy SEALs – not that they look the part. Which may explain why she hasn't put two and two together. If Ben wasn't a *bring your work home with you* kind of guy, their names and faces are all new to her.

They're all single. Their downtime wouldn't have been spent with married couples. I know mine sure wasn't. And Jax? Socializing has never been in his stratosphere. His idea of being sociable was buying her dinner, a couple drinks, getting her off a few times, himself at least once, and going home after. Not sure he's ever spent the whole night with a woman. I'm pleading the Fifth for myself. His men were his top priority – their private lives were their own.

I know who Sasha Taylor is . . . or was. *Sassy Arkelpaine.* But why the name change? Why take back her surname? The one thing my investigation did not uncover. Ben never referred to her as anything but Sassy. He also never disclosed the fact she was a writer. Dipshit! If he had, we might not be where we are: his former captain falling for his widow, and me anticipating the loss of my balls – if not my life – when Jax finds out I knew.

*"Code of Ethics" You do not touch another officer's wife.*

But does it apply to a *dead* officer's wife? Does it apply when you're no longer active military? Shit! I never had reason to study it closely; I made damn sure my dick was dipping into the off-base, single, female population. I know the officers' wives also have their own code of ethics. Don't ask me what it is, but I'm pretty damn sure it runs neck and neck with the men's.

How in the hell did we end up in South Carolina? Our original plan was to start our businesses in Key West, Florida. We can channel out as far as we want in either of our businesses, but to make the home port for both of them in South Carolina?

My eyes lift skyward on the way back to the office as I speak out loud to the one guy I miss a helluva lot. "You couldn't just call her Sasha, could ya? Did you never tell her your senior officer was Captain *Callum*? It's no wonder I called you ankle pain. Should have just called you pain in the ass." I reach for my ear as a familiar sting strikes once again. "Damn bugs!" I look up once more and scowl. "You probably sent those too, didn't you?"

# Chapter 36

## Sasha

"Oh my God!" I gasp and try not to choke on my dinner as Sky and I watch the news Thursday evening. It's her turn to stay with me tonight, not relenting from the mutual decision they cast on Sunday to alternate spending nights with me.

I eye the screen closely, observing the flashing lights on the dual screen in the background, while the desk reporter shares the name of the woman found washed up on the beach early this morning.

"What?" Sky turns her head from the TV to me. "Did you know her?"

"She was my realtor." My eyes are fixed on the screen, soaking up any more information I can glean, but the report ends. No conclusive cause of death yet; just a name, a body, on the beach, this morning. They didn't say she drowned. Wait a minute! Relda said she hated the water – wouldn't even go out on tour boats. She would take the long way around rather than drive the coastal highway. She lived five miles inland. "She hated the water," I mutter.

"You look like you're gonna be sick." Sky rises from her

seat and heads for me. "You need help to the bathroom?"

I swallow hard and feel the bile rise in my throat. Sliding the TV tray away from me, I rush to my feet, run toward bathroom and barely make it over the bowl to empty the contents of my stomach. She was so young, close to my age. Why was she in the ocean? How did she get so close to the water when she hated it? Was she driving the coastal highway? They didn't mention a car. Why am I so upset by this?

Once she feels it's safe to let go of my hair, Sky runs a washcloth under water at the sink, wrings it out and hands it to me. "Did you two become friends?"

"No," I say, swiping the washcloth over my face, breathing through my mouth so as not to set off my tastebuds and cause another round of regurgitation. I step to the sink, grab a cup to fill it and rinse my mouth before slathering toothpaste on the bristles of the brush. "We hardly knew each other but for the house. She was really nice. She's the one who recommended Callum construction. Aidan recommen . . ." My words get caught in my throat and I shove my toothbrush in my mouth as a quick cover for being speechless. *Aidan.*

Sky folds her arms across her chest, brows pinched. "Aidan recommended her."

I nod carefully around the toothbrush moving inside my mouth and wince. There's no reason to think there's a connection, is there?

"And she's the one who recommended Jaxson's company?"

I nod around the toothbrush once more.

"Rinse and spit," she orders coldly. "Rhea told me what happened today. I think we need to call Jax. Actually, you call Jax. I'll call Simon."

On my last swish and rinse, before I can wipe my mouth with the towel, I try to ask but it comes out more spittle. "Why would we call them?"

She gives me a cold, hard stare. "I think this guy may be dangerous, Sasha. Maybe even more than Oscar can handle. Do you want to take that chance?"

"No," I whisper, guilt washing over me that I would give a second thought to risk over safety for my friend. But Jax and Simon are construction workers. We should call the police. Then again, what would tell them? It's conjecture, suspicion. Pretty farfetched at that. "Let's call them."

Sky puts her call on speaker phone. "Hey, sweet cheeks," Simon answers with a flirty tone so apparent in his voice I can almost picture the smile on his face.

"Um," she stutters nervously. "I'm at Sasha's. I think we may have a problem."

We hear a car door slam as Simon tells her, "Open the door, Sky."

"What?" she asks moments before pounding on the door starts and Oscar goes crazy.

"Open up, Sky," Simon bellows through the door and the phone simultaneously.

Sky throws the latch on the deadbolt and the knob lock, turning the doorknob to an anxious looking Simon. He moves her aside, opens the door to make his way in, closes it with his foot, and slides his hand under the back of his shirt while he scopes the room over her head.

"What's going on?" he asks, not once looking at either one of us.

"Uh," she stammers, eyeing me sheepishly. "We saw the news tonight."

He removes his hand from behind his back and releases what appears to be a relieved breath. For those of us paying close attention – meaning me – it also looks like he took his hand off a gun he has tucked back there. Holy shit! He dips his head and lifts her chin to face him. His dark full brows furrow together. "You saw the news tonight?" His face softens and he shifts his hands to her shoulders. His voice is sweet and gentle as he uses her nickname – well, the one other than *sweet cheeks*, "Blue, was there something on the news you want to tell me about?"

She nods slowly, so smitten by the man in front of her. "Sasha's realtor died."

"O…kay," he says slowly, his eyes flashing to mine. "I'm sorry to hear that."

"Oh," she adds quickly, grasping his sleeve and pulling him toward the sofa. "But there's more. They found her body on the beach this morning."

"She drowned?" he asks, taking a seat next to her.

"They don't know yet," she explains . . . sort of. Her mouth twists when she looks at me and she heaves a sigh. "Would you take over?"

"Simon," I start hesitantly. "Relda Morton was recommended to me by Aidan Lehner. She hated the water. She wouldn't even drive the coastal highway."

He stands quickly and pulls his phone from his pocket, ensuring his shirt tail is tugged down in the back. *Yup, he's hiding something.* "Have you called Jax?"

"Not yet." I shake my head. "You were here before Sky barely said hello. Speaking of which . . ."

"I got it," he interrupts and steps toward the kitchen, his fingers making fast work on the keypad. "Yeah, think we may have a problem. I'm at Ms. Taylor's." His voice becomes muttered as he steps deeper into the kitchen, and I can no longer hear him clearly while he apparently gives more details to Jaxson. He ends the call with, "See you soon." He lingers in the kitchen for a few minutes before he returns to where we are.

"Dusty and Brick are with Rhea and Shae," he informs us.

"What do they have to do with this?" I nearly shriek, then point to his midsection. "And why are you carrying a gun, Simon?"

Sky gasps and stares at him. "You have a gun?"

He places his hands on his hips and looks down, blowing an exasperated sigh. "I know how to use it."

"So do we, Simon," I retort with a touch of snark. "Do you really think our daddies would turn us loose this far from home defenseless?" *I don't bother to add my husband reinforced my skills exponentially.* "You still haven't answered my question."

"I'll let Jax explain," he grumbles as he looks at his watch. "He should be here soon." He lifts his eyes to Sky. "You know how to shoot?"

Sky crinkles her nose and her eyes travel the ceiling above her. You know the look – the little girl who gets caught with her hand in the cookie jar but if she looks cute enough, daddy will give her one anyway.

"Oh for God's sake!" I scold her and answer Simon simultaneously. "She's a crack shot. Two-time Tennessee state champion in the clay pigeon competition. She cleared the shooting gallery of all the men every Saturday morning when we went for practice."

I've never seen a man glow the way Simon does as he crosses the room, yanks her up from the sofa, and places his hands on her hips. His voice is so low it's nearly a growl and I swear I see her toes curl. "Damn, baby, I don't think I've ever been this turned on."

Shooting him a wry grin, I snort. "Yeah, well, turn it off while I'm sitting here. Now answer my question. Why are you carrying a gun?"

# Chapter 37

## Jaxson

"Callum," Nash answers cheerily. "We didn't talk this much when our desks were in the same room. Miss me?"

"Relda Morton," I start, bypassing a greeting or entertainment of lack of the same. "Washed up on the beach this morning. Can you get me a cause of death?"

"You don't think she drowned?"

"She was Sasha's realtor." I sigh heavily and finish, "Recommended by Lehner."

"Kind of a stretch, don't ya think? Could be simple coincidence."

"According to Simon, and I'll get the rest of the story in a while," I explain. "She also recommended us for the reno."

"Ahh," he drawls. "You think Lehner went off the deep end." He chuckles. "Okay, bad choice of words."

"I'm feeling guilty as shit that I pushed him too far on Monday and may have gotten a woman killed for it!" I snap. "Damnit, Nash. If this is my fault . . ."

"Breathe, Jax," he commands in an all too familiar tone. "You don't know that. Not sure they'll have any info yet. It's a little soon for results if she washed up this morning, but I'll call Thompson and see what he's willing to divulge."

Chad Thompson is the state medical examiner. He's also Nash's inside contact for all things dead people. If there's a reason Nash needs to know, he's usually amenable to releasing the information to him as soon – sometimes sooner – as he is to law enforcement. Nobody needs to know and it's not like dead people talk, so in the end, no harm - no foul.

"Thank you. Get back to me as soon as you can." I end the call and grip the wheel tighter as I enter the ramp onto Kings Highway. Simon had tapped into the late night whispered voice being fed through the now muted lines into Sasha's bedroom over the past few nights. The ones she no longer hears. I hadn't shared the details with Nash yet.

Sick sonofabitch.

*"Aidan Lehner holds the key to your happiness, Sasha. He knows all your secrets. He'll keep you safe. That's why your husband sent you to him."*

*"Meet Aidan on the beach in the morning, Sasha."*

*"Aidan Lehner is your only chance at a happy life."*

*"No other man can make you as happy as Aidan Lehner can."*

*"Meet Aidan in the morning on the beach."*

*"Leave Jaxson Callum, Sasha. He'll only hurt you. He's dirty. He's using you for your money. Aidan Lehner knows what you need."*

Every word is spoken in the third person as if the orders come from on high. As if a wiser entity is advising her and guiding her future. Now I know why Oscar tore up her bedroom; why he made it virtually impossible to sleep in her own bed.

*Good boy, Oscar. T-bone, I promise. As soon as I can fire up the grill.*

Only now does his panicked and angry voice mail message left on the burner phone this evening make perfect sense.

*"Sasha, you need to call me! I need to see you! You're making me do things I shouldn't have to do!"* His voice went from

anger to pleading in seconds flat. *"Sasha, baby, please. I need . . . I need you now more than ever."* Then back to anger. *"You know there are consequences, Sasha. Do not defy me."*

I had been staked out in front of his high rise awaiting his arrival when I got the call from Simon, which in turn explains his immediate response to his girlfriend's call as well as Brick and Dusty's not so coincidental watchful eyes on their women at the present time. We were all watching.

I stop to speak with Nash's man out front who informs me there are now two out back keeping guard due to the vast open area and lack of lighting. I should be surprised, but I'm not. This is Nash. If something is important to me, he makes it important to him. He employs approximately fifty, all vetted thoroughly, and just like me, only hires veterans. The ones who don't get around as well, i.e. disabled, work for us in other capacities, be it office work, IT systems aka hackers, drivers, etc.

I ring the bell and turn the knob in unison and Oscar is there to greet me long before I have the opportunity to step in. I use the term *greet* loosely. Oscar is at the door to inspect; on guard, ready to shred any intruders.

"Good boy," I whisper, extending my downturned, closed hand for his inspection. Three sets of eyes find mine, but there's only one I'm seeking. "Talk to me."

The story Sasha shares doesn't take but a few short minutes. Her realtor, nice lady, searched high and low to find her the right place, recommended by Aidan Lehner. Those connections alone make me suspicious, but the fact Relda Morton hated the water and recommended Callum Construction is far too coincidental.

*Did I just get a woman murdered? Was the price of keeping one safe the cost of another?*

The whisper in my ear should be audible to everyone in the room, but no one – other than Oscar – seems distracted from their exchange. "He would have done it anyway. He's a psycho. Focus. Your job is Sasha."

My head whirls to the left, anticipating Simon – maybe even Nash – to be sitting next to me. *Nobody.* I note Oscar's eyes fixed on me as if to say, *"You heard it too?"* He whimpers softly and lays his head at my feet. I reach down and pet him on the head and note the goosebumps on my arm. My eyes follow the line of what is visible of the floorboards, searching for tiny speakers embedded in the wood. *Nothing.*

"You okay?" Sasha's soft touch as she puts her hand on my forearm and the sound of her voice brings me back to the here and now, the air filling my lungs again as I breathe deeply and release it slowly.

*You are not crazy, Jax.*

My best effort is put into offering her a reassuring smile and a nod, though it's a struggle. He's been in her head for how long now? Months? I've had her on one date, kissed her a few times – not that I don't crave a thousand more – and now I'm hearing voices? I'm pulled from my thoughts by the phone ringing in my pocket.

"Yeah," I answer, unsure I want to know what he has to say.

"You alone?"

"No."

"Might wanna be," he warns. "Step outside."

Rising from the sofa, I nod to the others and make my way to the front door. "I'll be right back." As soon as the door closes behind me, I glance up and down the street, noting Nash's man where I left him minutes ago. No Mercedes, no signs of unwanted company. "Let's hear it."

"Thompson's still in the preliminaries. No toxicology report yet but he did share the fact she had major bruising around her neck. Two massive crossover bruises either side of the larynx. Said they look to be about the size of thumbs. No water in her lungs."

"Sonofabitch," I utter, running my free hand through my hair and yanking at the roots. "She was strangled."

"That would seem to be the case," he states flatly. "They found a rope tied to her ankle. Seems our doctor friend planned on keeping her at the bottom . . . or feeding the fish. Pretty apparent the stupid fuck didn't know how to tie a knot. Think it's time we showed him how it's done?"

When the metallic taste floods my mouth I realize how hard I've bitten the inside of my cheek. "He's mine," I growl low and slowly.

"Wouldn't have it any other way," Nash agrees lightly, then ends with a chuckle, "You dirty, grungy construction worker."

There are times I miss the desk phone, even the old style flip phones. A desk phone you could slam into the cradle. A flip phone you could slap shut. The most I can do now is hit the red button to end the call. I suppose I could slam it onto the concrete, but the feeling of satisfaction would last all of a nanosecond until I realized I no longer had a form of communication. Good God, I miss the old days sometimes.

Stepping back inside, I'm met with three expectant gazes – *in all honesty, I think Oscar already knows.* "Sorry about that," I say, taking a seat next to Sasha once again and add, "Business." If Oscar had lips I'm pretty sure he'd be frowning in disappointment right about now as he eyes me skeptically. I swear to God, he just rolled his eyes.

"Do you carry a gun, too?" Sasha's gives me a once-over from head to toe as if searching for the weapon in question.

I glance at Simon and I see him cringe. *Good going, sailor. Apparently discretion wasn't high on your list of priorities this evening.*

"It's open carry here, Sasha. We're all licensed and well trained. We work in some questionable areas sometimes." I shrug as if it's nothing unusual. "Better safe than sorry. We haul some pretty expensive equipment. It's simply a safeguard."

Sky chimes in with a laugh. "Come on, Sasha! You ratted me out. Are you going to tell him or should I?"

Sasha clears her throat and sits up straighter, her cheeks a pretty flushed pink. "I think we should get back to the matter at hand, don't you?"

"Oh no you don't," Sky says with a waggle of her finger, then looks to me. "She can shoot the fly off a horse's butt at fifty paces without singeing the hair on its coat. And Sasha's hus . . ."

"Sky!" Sasha screams, her eyes big as saucers and filled

with horror.

Sky does a one-eighty as her cockiness dives with a throat clearing cough. "Sasha's *hustled* half of Tennessee's male population on skeet shoots. Usually came home with an extra five hundred bucks in her pocket and sent them home with a good dish of humble pie." She tips an indecipherable look at Sasha as well as her chin. "Came in handy for college funds."

Sasha scowls. "You're such a cutie." It's definitely not a compliment, but her shoulders relax. She turns in her seat, her face now filled with worry and what appears to be . . . remorse. "Do you think Aidan killed her?"

*Oh yes, I'm sure of it. Am I about to tell her that? No. Her expression says it all. She will carry the weight of Relda Morton's death on her own shoulders forever. She will piece it together. Aidan recommended the realtor, the realtor recommended us. In the process, we found each other. Was Relda Morton a component? Maybe. I would have sent her a thank you card for it. Was she at fault? Hell no! Aidan Lehner is an asshole; never stood a chance.*

*A **narcissist** needs someone to blame though. I thought he would blame me – even anticipated being his target. I wasn't aware there was another woman in this particular drama he created. Relda Morton was collateral damage.*

*A **psychopath** will leave a trail of destruction to feed their illness. I hadn't planned on giving him that opportunity.*

*A **pussy** goes after women; they don't have the balls to go up against men.*

*And now that we are where we are, Aidan Lehner will find himself at the bottom of the ocean – well, until the sharks find him. We do know how to tie those knots; it's one of the first things we were taught in the Navy.*

Taking her hand in mine, I lie, "I don't know."

"What do you suspect?"

Shaking my head because I'm finding it really hard to look her in the eye, "It's too early to tell. The autopsy results aren't back yet."

She's on her knees on the sofa cushion next to me in one

swift movement – giving her the height advantage of approximately three inches – grasping my chin as she crinkles her brow. "That isn't what I asked. Do you think Aidan killed her?"

It's been six days . . . six freaking days and those eyes melt me. They've pierced me with a glare so hard I physically felt it. I've seen her smile, watched her cry, heard her laugh, giggle, and sob. I've held her in my arms and nothing has ever felt so damn good. I've kissed that mouth and deemed it my favorite flavor the moment my lips touched hers. Her name feels like a dance on my tongue. I've smacked that peach shaped ass and shown more restraint than a fucking choir boy. And now, as I study the hypnotic green graced with tiny flecks of gold, all I see is a plea for truth.

Blowing a deep sigh, I nod slowly. "Yeah, I do."

The change I see in her expression is a new emotion I don't ever want to see again . . . fear. "Is he going to kill me next?"

I pull her to me so fast and so hard she has to straddle my lap, and I hold her so tight she can't possibly not believe me. "Over my dead body, and I don't plan on dying anytime soon, Sasha." I draw back from my hold on her so I can see those eyes, possess her gaze, and guarantee her reassurance. "I will not let anything happen to you."

"Promise?" she whispers, her eyes glassy with tears.

"I promise." I kiss the first tear that falls from her eye, then the next before my mouth finds hers. I know there are two other people in the room – three if you count Oscar – but our bubble is our own. She sniffs in the middle of the kiss, followed by what seems to be a stifled snort, and I feel her shoulders shake. I break the kiss and give her a puzzled look.

She shoots me a forced impish grin, running her fingers gently through my beard. "Be really careful, okay? You are damn near forty."

*Sniffles to sarcasm in two seconds flat. One more page in the book of knowledge on Sasha. This is how she handles stress. I almost wish she wouldn't though. It's avoidance – her way of shelving pain, fear, and loss to be dealt with later. Maybe that's why it's taken so long for her to move on. But this is my Sasha.*

My eyes narrow and I take a deep breath through my nose while my hand resists smacking that pretty little ass of hers. I slide my hand around the nape of her neck and pull her close, whispering in her ear, "Do you remember what happened the last time you made fun of my advanced age, Sasha?" I feel her thighs stiffen on top of my own. *Oh yeah, she remembers.*

"Mmhmm," she hums, her lips tucked between her teeth, her eyes big as saucers.

I smile cockily and wink. "Be a good girl."

She swallows hard. "How many stars do I have now?"

"You just lost five," I say, reluctantly lifting her off my lap as she huffs in protest, placing her back on the cushion beside me. I really don't need an audience, nor do I want to spend another evening with balls as blue as sapphires. My phone vibrates once more and I look to see another message from Nash. I stand so as not to share what might be on the screen.

*"Beach. One mile south of the bookworm's house. Bring your chipmunk. Stay low. My men will stay there."*

My thumbs tap out a quick, *"On our way."*

I pocket my phone and see my *chipmunk* raise his brows in question. "Simon, let's go."

"You're leaving?" A panicked Sasha stands and rushes to my side, gripping my sleeve. "You said you wouldn't let anything happen to me."

I take her cheeks in my palms. "No," I murmur as I kiss her forehead. "I promised you. And now, I'm going to go make good on that promise. Stay here," I order harshly then look at Sky. "Neither one of you leave the house." Without giving it a second thought, I give another order to her faithful canine, "Oscar, guard Sasha." He immediately takes his place by an ashen Sasha who suddenly looks like she's going to pass out as she stares at me. She breathes hard as Sky reaches under her arm, shouldering her weight. I move back to her, scooping her up in my arms and delivering her to the sofa where I lay her on her back, Oscar planting himself at her feet on the end cushion.

"She'll be okay, Jax," Sky reassures me. "It's not what you

think. I've got her."

"You're sure?"

"I'm positive." She narrows her eyes at me and her mouth twists before she shakes her head. "Coincidence," she mutters low.

"What?" I ask.

"Nothing," she grumbles, returning to Sasha's side. "Just go! And be careful." She turns one last time. "Simon?"

His face lights in a grin and he winks. "We're good, Blue. I'll always come back to you."

ANNIE MICK

# Chapter 38

## Sasha

"Breathe, damnit!" Sky scolds me, flipping the cold washcloth on my forehead. Jaxson and Simon left just minutes ago together – one truck, tires squealing. "It didn't mean anything. A lot of people tell their dogs to guard the house, guard the liquor, guard the kids. Hell, maybe guard the liquor *from* the kids. You have got to get over the triggers, Sash. It was such a simple thing."

I scowl at her. "The last *simple* thing from my husband."

She rolls her eyes. "As if Jax would know that. It's not like he called you Sassy and it's not Jax's fault Ben taught Oscar what *guard* meant."

Throwing the washcloth off my face, I sit up and glare. "And you, Miss Cutie. What were you thinking, flapping your jaws about my husband?" I hold my thumb and forefinger a centimeter apart. "You were this close to telling them Ben trained me to sharp shoot. What the hell, Sky? Do you spill our secrets to Simon when you're cuddled up in the dark?"

"No! I don't tell Simon anything!" she shrieks in defense.

Rolling my eyes, I grouse, "So much for southern belle charm."

Her expression falls into one of concern and worry once again. "How long do you think they'll be gone?"

"I don't know," I whisper, reaching for the top of Oscar's head, running my fingers through his fur. "I'm not even sure what they're doing, Sky." I rise from the sofa to head for the bedroom. "I think it might be a good idea to have the gun handy while we wait though."

Pounding on the front door brings us a breath of relief and Sky shoots out of her seat, rushing to open it. Oscar jumps up from his place, but Sky unlocks the door before I can stop her.

"Sky, don't!" I shriek as I rush behind her. But I'm too late. She didn't even check the peephole. She didn't verify it was safe before turning the lock. She didn't ask who it was . . .

The door is shoved open and Sky is knocked backward onto the floor, taking Oscar with her before he can maneuver around her. He anticipated Oscar, though. He was ready. And as Oscar quickly regains his footing and lunges for the intruder, the gun shot pierces through the air quietly – the silencer he uses muffling the noise. Oscar's whimper and the sound of his body falling to the floor is deafening though.

"Oscar!!" I scream as I fall to the floor at my best friend's side. The blood is rushing profusely onto the floor from a wound just behind his shoulder. I apply firm pressure with my hand and watch as Oscar looks at me, his breathing rapid, his gaze growing weak, his whimper softening. I look up at Aidan who glares at me. "You bastard!"

He holds the gun on a stunned Sky – who's sitting up now staring at me – and reaches for my arm, yanking me up to my feet. I shake my head at Sky and mouth "don't". He doesn't want her. The last thing I need is her dying because of me.

His voice is cold and harsh as he orders, "Let's go, Sasha." I struggle, but his hold on my arm is brutal, his fingers digging so tightly it feels like the blood supply is being restricted. I don't dare kick and aim for his crotch, his shin, his nose, his chin; everywhere I was ever taught to aim. His gun is aimed at Sky. If it goes off due to my struggling, it's my fault . . . by default. He suddenly wraps his arm around my neck and drags me backwards against his body. Oscar lifts his head and whines, struggling to rise but he's too weak.

"Your little boy toy is down on the beach, Sasha," he growls in my ear. "He won't be coming to your rescue. So stupid."

Aidan suddenly screams as if something is hurting him. He bends in pain, taking me with him, but only tightens his grip on me. His head rears back, but my body stretches with him as his stronghold doesn't lessen, and he moves me . . . out the door.

"Sky!" I shriek a begging plea, tears spilling as I stare at my last living reminder of Ben on the floor. "Take care of Oscar! Please!"

# Chapter 39

## Jaxson

"Over there." Simon points to the group of men gathered in a circle near the water. I slam the gearshift into park and we exit together.

Nash rushes up to meet us. "Think we may have a problem."

"What!?" I hasten my footsteps toward the soon-to-be-dead murderer on the beach when Nash grabs my arm.

"Callum," he says with caution as he's left with only my shirt sleeve to cling to. "It's not him. Looks like he may have sent a decoy. This guy is drunk as a skunk, ready to piss his pants, and can only tell us some guy paid him a thousand bucks to wait on the beach. I just got here myself. I was about to message you."

Simon and I exchange a quick *holy fuck* glance and run back to the truck.

"Sonofabitch!" I yell on my way. "He's at Sasha's."

"My men are there!" he calls after us.

"Damnit!" I white-knuckle the steering wheel with one hand and put my truck in gear, screeching out of the lot. "Did you see Graham's men when we left?"

"Massey was out front," Simon reassures me. "I didn't

check the back. They were there before I went in earlier though."

"Let's hope to hell they're still there." I push the gas pedal to the floor, wishing my truck would move as fast as the adrenaline flowing through my veins.

What greets us when we arrive couldn't get much worse. I shut off the lights before I turn the corner and stop the truck in the street. If I spook him, there's no telling what he'll do. Massey is lying on the ground up ahead. Lehner is backing out the front door dragging Sasha with him while pointing the gun at someone inside the house with his free hand. No sign of Oscar, no sign of Sky.

Simon growls as he grabs the door handle. "Motherfucker. I'm going to kill him."

"Hang on." I grab his arm and pull hard. "Slow and steady. Don't startle him. He's gotta be holding that gun on Sky. Oscar wouldn't be standing down. Keep your emotions out of it, Simon. Let him get out of the house and away from her."

He glares and yanks his arm away then throws the door open and slinks down to the ground on his hands and knees, and I join him. On our hands and knees we make our way closer and closer to the crazed lunatic; guns drawn, ready to spill blood.

Since I don't hear her faithful canine, my only guess is Lehner's already done irreparable damage. Oscar would tear through walls for Sasha. I watch as Lehner's head rears back and he howls in pain, but the sonofabitch is relentless in his pursuit to get Sasha out of the house.

"Aidan, let me go!" Sasha sobs, struggling to get out of his hold. "I have to help Oscar!"

"You won't be needing that damn dog, Sasha," he sneers, pulling her out the door and into the yard. Once out of the house, he quickly turns the gun on her. "I told you to get rid of him a long time ago. I hate that mongrel! I had everything planned. You couldn't wait three more months? You whore yourself out to that filthy construction worker?"

He uses her body as a shield as they move toward the street, jerking her back and forth, his arm wrapped around her neck, all the while holding the gun to her temple. His eyes dart from side to side, watching and waiting for someone to show up. I can't take a shot at this distance, not with Sasha in the middle and not with his finger on the trigger.

"Hold still and turn around, you sonofabitch," I whisper to myself as I move in closer. He's a half head taller than she is – one to the forehead and he'll be down. I only need one shot.

I note low movement in the tall, sandy grass across the street. I know it's Graham's men, but by God, they'd better not get in the way. Massey hasn't moved and the best I can hope is he's not dead.

"He's all I have left, Aidan," she begs. "You can take me but let me help Oscar."

"Dogs don't live that long anyway, Sasha," the cruel bastard says with a wicked laugh. "They're a little like husbands. You would have been crying over him sooner or later. May as well get it over with."

His emotional cruelty is unrivaled. The poor woman seemed to find solace in a dog after her husband died and this asshole is mocking her. It almost makes me wonder if he didn't have something to do with her husband's death. Nash said he was murdered. I stand to my feet once I've reached the edge of the yard; my gun cocked and aimed directly at my target with minute wiggle room.

"Let her go, Lehner."

My appearance takes him by surprise, but he only clings tighter to her and ducks his head down. He is predictable though. He stops his trek toward the street; merely twisting back and forth using Sasha as a shield.

*See? Pussy.*

"Did you know Sasha is a championship skeet shooter, Lehner?" I creep forward at a snail's pace, my eyes fixed on his so as to keep his attention off my movements. "Tell him, Sasha. Tell him how you shoot those clay pigeons right out of the sky. What do they do when they get hit?"

"Shut up, Callum!" Lehner screams. "You don't get to talk to her!" He's crazed, his eyes glassy and void of all emotion. But his paranoia has surfaced.

"Th – they shatter," Sasha stammers softly.

Ignoring his demand, my eyes zoning in on what feels like the most important shot of my life; my words meant only for her. "They do. After they shatter, what happens?"

*Take my cue, Sweetheart. They fall to the ground.*

Her body suddenly goes limp, taking Lehner by surprise, and he can't bear her weight in the one arm holding her up. *Good girl, Sasha.* It's just enough to give me what I need and the bullet that leaves the barrel of my gun sails through the center of Aidan Lehner's forehead.

Sasha doesn't falter as her knees hit the ground. She bounces to her feet like a rubber ball – bare feet no less. She doesn't bother herself with a glance back at the body lying on the ground, nor does she scream and run to me to gather her in my arms. No, she runs for the front door of her house, screaming for Oscar.

The men move in from several directions, a couple checking Massey where he lies near the street, others rushing around the fence line toward the back, Simon running for the front door.

A grim Nash reaches for my shoulder as I flip the safety on my gun and tuck it into the back of my jeans. "Callum."

My glare should be enough – his guys fucked up big time – but I tack on a fast, "Not now, Graham," and run for the front door.

Inside I find Simon with his hand pressed hard over a bloody cloth on a rapidly breathing, nearly unconscious Oscar. Sasha is on the phone in a panic trying to reach the vet clinic. A bloodied Sky rushes from down the hall with fresh cloths to press to the wound.

I yell out the door to Graham, "Get my truck up here!"

Reaching under Oscar as gently as I can, I lift him into my arms. He raises his gaze to me, weak as it is, his eyes half shut, and a small yelp escapes his throat. "Don't you dare die," I whisper as I carry him out to my truck which is now on its way. "Sasha needs you." He wriggles in my arms but I have a good hold on him and Simon continues to press on the wound with the cloth in his hand.

"Come on, Oscar," Simon's voice is low beside us, keeping an even pace and steady pressure on the wound. "You're tough, buddy. Be a good warrior."

Sasha and Sky follow us out as Sasha directs us as to where we're going. Lehner's body isn't in the front yard anymore. Don't know where they took him – don't much care. An ambulance turns the corner at the end of the street and drives past us to the far edge of the yard – apparently arriving for Massey.

Nash opens the back door for a sobbing Sasha and me. Oscar stays on my lap, Sasha holds his head in hers, gently circling the heart on his nose with her fingertips and whispering, "Stay with me, Oscar, you're all I have left." Sky sits up front with Simon as he squeals out of the driveway and heads for the vet hospital. The ride is otherwise tense and deafeningly silent . . . and far too long.

As soon as we pull into the lot of the vet hospital there are two assistants rushing to the truck to help with the wounded patient. Simon throws my door open and I climb down out of the truck, turning away from the assistants with Oscar in my arms. "I got him." The less he gets shuffled around, the better.

They run ahead to hold the doors open, and we're met by the vet who stands at the entrance of the hallway leading to the exam rooms. He allows me to gently place a weak and limp Oscar on the exam table, but after that the rest of us virtually become invisible as they get to work on the patient. Or so I thought. We're not invisible at all.

"Please wait in the waiting room," the assistant says as he opens and closes cupboards, removing supplies and setting them on a cart.

The vet looks up from where he's examining Oscar's shoulder and offers a quick, forced, sympathetic smile to the woman I'm trying to hold up. "Sasha, let us do our thing. I'll be out to see you as soon as I know what we're dealing with. Okay?"

*No promises. No false hopes.*

She's resistant to leave, but reluctantly concedes and lets me lead her out into the hallway where Simon and Sky wait just outside the exam room, and we walk to the waiting room together. There are individual chairs, a few benches along the wall, and a couple double vinyl seats. I lead Sasha to a double chair and take a seat next to her. She doesn't need to sit alone, and when she crashes after the adrenaline rush from this night from hell, she's going to need a place to land. That place will be me. I reach inside my pocket to pull out my phone and start tapping on the keypad. There are a shitload of texts I should answer, but I'm on a quest.

Over six hundred reviews, a five star rating, and Dr. Lancaster is the preferred veterinarian at the clinic. One breath to release . . . sort of.

"What did they say?" Sky asks.

Sasha simply shakes her head then drops it in her hands, sobbing. I pull her onto my lap – a secret hope this chair doesn't collapse beneath our weight – and lean her head on my shoulder. I can't promise her Oscar will be okay. I won't shush her sobs or muffle her cries. I'll wipe her tears, try to ease her pain, but I know I can't take it away – I simply eliminated one of the causes tonight. If I only knew how to eliminate the others. The only widows I've ever dealt with were the wives of dead sailors, and that was by way of quick condolences at a funeral and recognition of their husbands' service. Once again the familiar pang in my chest strikes – knowing I never made it back in time to express my condolences to Ben's wife. I've yet to even honor the man himself by avenging his death. I suck at emotions, tenderness, and personal relationships. But for some reason, Sasha Taylor makes me want to be a better man. Be those things I've never been, have all the things I never knew I wanted.

Simon's questioning gaze catches my attention as he rests his chin on the top of Sky's head and holds her close. I simply squeeze my eyes closed. I have no answers.

"Hey, Blue," he whispers, reaching for her blood crusted hands with his own. "Let's go get your hands washed, shall we?"

They're no more than turned around when the doors to the clinic blow open and four people rush inside.

"What the hell happened?" a panicked Rhea shouts as she takes in the scene before her. Her eyes land on Sky's blood-covered hands, then Simon's.

Before she can inquire any further, Simon shakes his head

and continues to walk Sky toward the bathroom and simply says, "It's not hers." As Rhea takes a step toward them, he shakes his head vehemently before he opens the door and narrows his eyes. "I've got her."

She turns her attention to us; her steps slow and cautious as she moves forward. "Sash?" Sasha lifts her head to acknowledge her friend and bursts into tears once again. Rhea rushes in for a hug and pulls her off my lap, soon joined by the other one who came with her. I haven't met her yet, so this must be Shae – Dusty's girl. They run their hands through her hair, swipe the tears off her cheeks, whisper encouraging words, exchange hugs. They pull disposable wipes out of their purses to clean her hands off. Something tells me I'm not getting her back anytime soon.

*And the dire reality of this situation is squeezing the air out of my lungs. My name in the news. Construction worker shoots psychiatrist. Low profile, my ass.*

Dusty and Brick both stand with hopeful inquisitive expressions aimed at me. I scrub my hands over my face and blow a resigned breath, shaking my head. "Waiting for the doc to come out."

They plop down in the chairs on either side of the double I'm sitting in. "What the hell are you guys doing here?"

Brick leans forward, elbows on his knees. "We took the ladies out for dinner tonight. They said Sky was staying the night with Sasha but Rhea suddenly got this feeling something wasn't right." He scrunches his nose. "I swear those women are psychic. When we got there, the ambulances were being loaded up. Nash caught us before we could get out and told us to come here. Nothing more."

Dusty rolls his neck a few times as if to work out the kinks. His whisper is angry but controlled for the sake of the women. "Who the fuck shoots a dog?" He looks up at the ceiling and blows a sigh through pressed lips and puffed cheeks, his eyes misty with unshed emotions for a dog he's become attached to. "I wish I'd been there. I could have helped." Our medic. Heart as cushy as a marshmallow and balls made of steel.

"How do you know Oscar got shot if Nash didn't tell you anything?"

He waves his hand around the room. "Since we were sent to a vet clinic and you guys are all standing and or sitting . . ." He grimaces. "Not to mention covered in blood. Deduction brings us to the conclusion it had to be Oscar. Am I wrong?"

"What the hell happened?" Brick huffs. "I've never seen Nash so pissed."

"Did he say anything else in front of your girlfriends?" I eye them both. "How much did they see? You two didn't slip up, did you?"

They glance at each other and I see dawning bloom on both of their faces. Dusty shakes his head, takes a quick look over his shoulder at the women still gathered in a circle, then back to me and scowls. "We're not stupid, Jax. We're still simple everyday construction workers. Nash only said to talk to you. They were loading up ambulances when we got there. We were a little busy trying to keep the ladies in the car without having to tie them down." He shoots a glare at Brick. "You have to remember, Rhea was in there."

"Hey!" Brick snarls. "She was worried."

"Knock it off." I reprimand both of them with a low growl. "More than one ambulance?" There is no way Lehner lived through that.

"They were loading up three guys total," Brick says. "Two were being brought up from behind Sasha's house. I think they were all Graham's men. Nobody was covered up head-to-toe though so they were all alive. What the hell happened, Jax?"

My voice is low and my jaw clenched so tight I swear I hear a tooth crack as I grind out, "Lehner happened." I nod toward the women standing together. "Go tear those three apart and reroute that conversation any way you can. We've got damage control to tend to."

Dusty huffs, "How the hell are we supposed to . . ."

"Figure it out," I order brusquely and take my phone out of my pocket, stepping to the other side of the room. There's more than one victim and I've neglected to check on the others. Apparently, Lehner did a lot of damage tonight.

"How's Oscar?" Nash answers after the second ring. I hear the sound of elevator dings and a page for a doctor in the background.

"In surgery, I'm sure. Doc hasn't come out yet. How's Massey?" I return, then sigh. "Sorry, Nash. The adrenaline was pumping."

"That'll happen when you put a bullet in somebody's forehead," he says with a chuckle. "Nice shot, by the way. Dead center."

"What did you do with his body?"

"What body?" he asks cockily. "Only thing collected tonight were three men involved in a random shooting by a house on Seaview Circle. They're going to make it. It's my understanding it was dark and nobody saw a thing. Odd though, witnesses only heard one shot."

"Shit," I utter, knowing it was my gun shot they heard. "Are your guys okay?"

"They will be. Told you that fucker was crazy."

"Speaking of which . . ."

"Shark food," he interrupts to save me from asking. "I understand they were extremely hungry tonight."

"What about the yard?"

"Good thing it's rock," he informs me. "Bleach. Lots and lots of bleach. My guys hosed the ground before the officials showed up. They'll get the bleach down as soon as they leave. Make sure Oscar stays off of it for a while. Should be good to go with a few days of rinsing."

"Thank you."

"Callum," he says, the warning in his tone loud and clear. "The two women involved need to understand that tonight didn't happen the way they saw it. Oscar got caught up in the middle of a nasty drive-by. Our culprit is gone. A news story about a heroic rescue would not be in our best interests right now."

"How the hell am I going to do that?" I ask myself as much

as I do him.

"She might surprise you. Make it happen, Callum. Just don't blow our cover. Ten to one says the bookworm probably doesn't want her name in the news either. Low profile would probably suit you both." His voice is cryptic as he finishes. "We've got a lot riding on this. Your name in the news might bring out a lot of fifteen minutes of fame seekers who want to sing your praises and scream. . ." his voice rises an octave as he singsongs, 'I knew him when he was . . .''

"Sasha?" I hear the doctor call for her behind me.

"I gotta go, Nash. The doc just came out."

"Let me know how Oscar's doing," he says. "He's been trained by the bes. . ." He grunts and yells, "Ouch!"

"What is it?"

"Damn mosquitos," he complains. "They even got 'em here in the hospital."

# Chapter 40

## Sasha

"Sasha?" Dr. Lancaster walks toward us in the waiting room. His next words will either shatter my world or give me hope, and I feel the breath catch in my lungs while I wait to see which it will be. He waves his hand at a set of chairs. "Let's sit, shall we?"

I swear Jaxson pushes my friends out of the way to get to me and leads me to the closest chair, taking the one next to it. Dr. Lancaster pulls one up to sit in front of me, elbows on his knees, and leans in close, taking my hands in his.

"The bullet lodged in his lung on the left. That's why there was so much bleeding. He has a couple broken ribs, but no other organ damage. We've stopped the bleeding, removed the bullet and sutured him up. Things look good as far as I can tell. We're going to need to keep him for a few days."

"Can I – can I see him?" I stammer through fresh tears.

He grimaces and shakes his head. "We have him heavily sedated, but if he hears you or is aware at all that you're close, it's going to cause him stress. Seeing him in this state will probably cause you a lot of stress as well, Sasha. I don't want to put you through that. It's probably not a good idea."

"You don't think he's stressed not knowing where I am?" I protest. "He's going to think I abandoned him!"

He squeezes my hands a little tighter. "Sasha, Oscar is post-op, heavily drugged. He's probably not going to remember most of this. At least I hope not." He lets out a sad yet understanding chuckle and winks. "He may not ever want to come see me again. Whatever would I do without my favorite canine and his mistress?"

Jaxson clears his throat and eyes our connected hands. "How long do you think you'll be keeping him?"

Dr. Lancaster releases my hands. "At least three days."

"Three days!" I panic at the mere thought. "Who's going to stay with him? He's used to being with me all the time. How will you know if he . . .? I'll stay with him. I'll pay extra for someone to stay . . ."

"Sasha," Dr. Lancaster speaks with ease. "He'll be watched closely. I have a fulltime weekend staff for emergency cases. Oscar won't be here alone. I promise."

"Can I just stay with him?" I plead pathetically.

He takes my hands in his again. "Sweetheart, he'll be okay. I've been taking care of Oscar since . . ."

"Since he was a pup," Rhea interrupts before he can finish. "They're the best of friends. You can trust him." She shoots him arched brows and narrowed eyes simultaneously. "Right, doc?"

He nods and smiles. "Yes."

"Can I just take a peek at him?"

"She's not going to rest until she sees him." Jaxson's low, stern voice resonates next to me as he reaches for my hand, removing it from Dr. Lancaster's, and holds it in his. "Let her look through the window on the door. You can do that, can't you?"

He barely hides a smirk but falls short of an eye roll as he looks at my hand that Jaxson now holds in his. "I can do that. I'll take her back."

"Thanks for the offer," Jaxson says with a touch of snark. "But I'd kinda like to see my buddy too. Besides, Sasha might need someone to hold her hand." He kisses my temple and whispers in my ear, "I'm that guy, right?"

A couple of short snorts followed by immediate silence when Jaxson rears his head toward his crew makes my friends giggle.

I look at the man next to me and think of what he'd done for me this evening. He saved me from a crazed lunatic. He stood in the line of fire, ready to take that bullet, and had enough faith in me to follow an order without giving it directly. He carried my dog like a baby, held me while I cried on his shoulder. For the first time all night I finally find a smile, small as it may be. "Yeah, you're that guy."

Holding the same hand he hasn't let go of since he confiscated it from Dr. Lancaster, he helps me from my seat. "Let's go check on Oscar."

Oscar looks to be more dead than he does sleeping peacefully. He has a tube down his throat, a drainage tube in the side of his chest, and an IV drip. I want to run to his side and hold him, cuddle him, reassure him that things will be okay. Bury my face in that fur coat like I did the first day we met; feel like a part of Ben is still with me. Staring through the window, watching his chest move up and down in a slow steady rhythm, I see his left ear slowly moved from its natural pointy position, like I do when I pet him. Then it happens again, and again. My heart literally bursts in my chest. *He's not alone.* I fold my hands together and hold them in front of my mouth so as to stifle my sob. His ear is pinched softly and wiggled back and forth to wave at me – as if to reassure me and indicate it's okay to go. I press my fingers to my lips, blow a soft kiss, and exit the room. No one needs to know what I saw. They'd probably think I'm crazy anyway. Was it Ben? I'd like to think so.

Oscar is not alone. That's all that matters.

On our way back out to the waiting room, Jaxson wraps his arm around my shoulder and pulls me to him. "He looked pretty good. Feel a little better?"

"Yeah." I nod against his chest as I fall into his touch. I have no idea how Jaxson Callum has become such a fixture in my life so quickly. My attraction to him was instantaneous; despite his offensive behavior and all. And he did return to apologize that same day – with flowers! My attraction *is* to him. That first night on the beach was all him. His voice, his arms, his mouth, his kiss. He's so severe, so rugged, rough around the edges yet so gentle and caring. He held that gun tonight with precision, like he'd done it a thousand times. He's tactical. He's . . . *oh shit!*

"What did you do before you worked in construction?"

His answer is fast as he chuckles. "You mean besides school? Always been into navigating my way around puzzles and construction of some sort, Sasha."

"Where did you go to . . ."

"How's he doing?" Brick asks as soon as we reach the edge of the waiting room, thereby interrupting my inquisition. *Fine, I'll ask him another time.*

"He looks good," Jaxson offers before I can, not that I fully agree with him.

Brick heaves an audible sigh of relief as does everyone else in the room.

"Where's Sky?" I ask one and all.

"She's still in the bathroom with Simon," Shae replies. "Are you going to tell us what happened?"

"Still in the bathroom?" My eyes drift toward the bathroom door. They've been in there an awfully long time. They wouldn't be . . . No.

Jaxson takes my elbow and leads the way. "Let's go."

"Wait!" I pull my elbow back from his hold. "What if they're . . ."

He arches his brows and dips his chin. "What if they're what?"

I wave my hand toward the bathroom door and crinkle my nose. "Well, you know."

His shakes his head and eyes me curiously. "Can't say as I do, Sasha. How about you spell it out for me."

I stand on my tiptoes and whisper in his ear, "S-E-X." Don't judge! He did ask me to spell it out for him. It certainly is how I used to spell relief. Since I've been in a drought for nearly three years, I've had to use sarcasm or dry humor – there is a difference, but you do what you gotta do.

He rolls his eyes, takes my elbow again and grumbles, "Even Simon has a moral compass." He frowns and shakes his head. "Most days."

Jaxson knocks twice and speaks softly. "Simon, open up. It's me."

"A little busy in here, Jax," he answers brusquely, though not breathlessly, so I don't think they're doing the deed. "Not a good time."

*Then again . . .*

"Open the fucking door, Simon, and let us in." Jaxson's tone is no longer soft nor is it friendly. "Damage control."

The lock turns and the door opens only a few inches. Simon's face comes into view and he eyes Jaxson curiously.

"Vital," Jaxson mutters and the door opens enough to allow the two of us to walk in, but Simon closes it immediately behind us and locks it once again.

The bathroom isn't large and barely provides shoulder room for the four of us. One toilet, a single vanity with a sink, and an air dryer next to a dispenser for pull-down hand-drying sheets on the wall. A tall contortionist could probably flush with their foot and wash their hands at the same time. Two people in here would be crowded. The four of us is a claustrophobic's nightmare. Sky leans against the vanity; her eyes red and swollen from crying, her shirt wet and still blood soaked from Oscar. It's now I realize I haven't thoroughly washed my own hands and Jaxson and Simon still wear the blood of my dog on theirs.

"Sky." I push past Jaxson to take her in my arms and hug her tighter than I ever have. She kept Oscar alive while I was dragged out into my front yard by a madman. Her trauma was as prolific as mine. Aidan held a gun on her while dragging me out the front door. "God, I'm so sorry," I cry against her shoulder.

"I killed Oscar," she whimpers against me.

"What? No!" I draw back from my hug, moving her hair away from her face. "He's out of surgery. Dr. Lancaster said he'll be okay."

"I- I opened the door, Sasha. If-if I hadn't opened the door, h-he wouldn't have gotten in and this n-never would have ha-happened," she stammers through a fresh wash of tears. "I-I thought it was Simon and Jax coming back."

"Blue," Simons whispers as he sidesteps me and takes her in his arms. "He would have found another way in. He would have shot the lock off, he would have come in through the back, he could have . . ." His breath stutters as he buries his face in her hair. "You could all be dead. My God, baby, breathe."

His words shatter like thin glass in my heart, the splinters burying themselves in all four corners where they will fester for the rest of my days. We could all be dead. Oscar was his first target in order to get me out of the house. Sky could have been collateral damage. I would never be able to forgive myself.

Simon raises his head from where he has it buried in her hair. "I'm taking Sky home with me."

"Understood," Jaxson tells him. "We need an agreement first."

"What?!" Simon growls as if his patience is ready to snap.

"Tonight never happened," Jaxson replies, his eyes set on Simon with a hard gaze. "At least not the way we know it did. It was a drive-by shooting that Oscar got caught up in."

Simon's cold, hard stare is matched by the others Jaxson is getting from Sky and me in the tiny room we stand in. Jaxson's eyes don't leave Simon's and I see the slightest movement in his brows as he arches one. It's a silent message; apparently one that Simon receives because his nearly nonexistent nod is mixed with a slow blink.

Jaxson bows his head, hands on his hips as he explains. "Lehner had already killed two women and gotten away with it. After tonight there is no doubt Relda Morton was his third victim." His eyes flit from Sky to me. "You two could have easily become the fourth and fifth victims. There may even be more. We don't know." He concentrates his gaze on me. "With your career, coupled with what happened tonight and the publicity it will bring, it might be in your best interests to let this go. Lehner has been dealt with.

He shot three other people tonight, too. They're in the hospital as we speak. They'll make it."

My jaw hangs agape as I stare at him. "H-how do you know all this?"

He avoids my eyes as he answers, "There were men out looking for Lehner."

"W-why?" I ask, my questioning gaze darting from his to Simon's. The longer we stand here, the more apparent it becomes they're both privy to this information.

His frustrated sigh precedes the explanation he reluctantly offers. "Nash runs a security agency. It's a long story. We were just looking out for you, Sasha."

Sky and I exchange looks of '*let's hope looking out for me and not into me is all they did*' and nod in agreement. "Okay," she says for the both of us. "Drive-by shooting that Oscar got caught up in." She shoots me a look of caution as her business persona makes an appearance. "Sasha and I know nothing. Didn't see a thing." Her face crumples and her tears make a reappearance. She swipes her cheeks and sniffles. "My big O really is going to be okay?"

"You saved him, Sky." I collect my friend in my arms and deliver a hug that leaves no room for doubt. She sobs in my arms, but this time sounds of relief are mixed with the sadness.

"I'll buy him hotdogs," she promises.

"All beef from the butcher shop," I tell her, matching her attempt to find light in the dark places. "No tubes of mystery meat. Okay?"

She giggles softly and sniffles again as she wipes at her tears. "Deal."

# Chapter 41

## Jaxson

After scrubbing up as best we could in the tiny bathroom, we make our way out into the waiting room where – well, everyone's waiting. Hence the name. We're exhausted, emotionally spent, and both Sasha and Sky have experienced a nightmare from hell.

I tilt my head in the direction of the exit. "Let's get out of here."

"Sasha." The vet stops us before we can get out the door. "May I see you for a moment?"

*Gee, doc, not sweetheart? You plan on holding her hand again? So, Oscar's your favorite patient, huh? I'll bet Oscar's mistress is your favorite eye candy too. Good God, what's wrong with me? The guy just saved Oscar's life! Let go of her hand, Callum. She's a big girl. And for the first time in my life, I have to admit to myself I'm jealous. New feeling, odd sensation. Can't say as I like it, can't say as I hate it. It's simply . . . foreign to me.*

Reluctantly, I release her hand and watch her walk toward the hero in white. I feel Simon's firm grip on my shoulder before he mutters in my ear, "You can either walk over there and claim what's yours or you can stand here and murder him with your glare.

Your call, Cap." My feet move before giving myself a chance to back out, and Simon's soft chuckle is left in the dust behind me.

"We're obligated to report gunshot wounds, Sasha. Just like we would with people," the vet explains as I approach.

"Drive-by shooting," I offer before Sasha has the chance. "The police report should be in by now." I lift a brow in challenge. "It's not like we had time to stick around and talk to them. There were other people on the scene to take care of it for us."

"Okay," he replies slowly and aims his gaze at Sasha. "And this took place on your property?"

She's a pro. I couldn't be prouder of her than I am right now as I watch her answer with a nod, "Yeah, Oscar was in the wrong place at the wrong time."

"Not in your home though, right?" he asks with wide eyes as though aghast at the thought. "You're not in danger, are you?"

"It was a drive-by, doc," I emphasize with a scowl. "The bullets didn't come through the windows. There were three people shot tonight, outside. Oscar was trying to be a hero. I think we've covered everything." Might not have been the whole story, nor the whole truth, but it was close enough. I gently place my arm over Sasha's shoulder and turn her toward the door, looking back over my shoulder. "Thank you for everything you did for Oscar. It's been a long night. I need to get her home."

He simply nods, seemingly disappointed that her care is in my hands. "You're welcome." I gotta give the guy credit for persistence as he calls out one last time, a sad glimmer of hope in his voice. "Sasha, I'll be in the clinic tomorrow if you want to call me. You know, to check on Oscar."

It takes everything in me to not roll my eyes. I also resist a smirk. However, when Sasha turns her head and forces a smile, that voice I want for me and only me, and tells him, "I will, Todd. Count on it," I lose the ability to avoid sinking my teeth into the inside of my cheek.

*Todd? Really? What happened to Dr. Lancaster?*

My hand drops from her waist to her hip as I lead her away – feeling the soft curve under my palm – the temptation to squeeze overwhelming. But I don't, because now is not the time and here is not the place. I know he's watching though. I've laid claim – he knows it, I know it. It's enough . . . for now.

"Book signings are postponed." Shae holds up her cell phone before dropping it into her purse. "Explained you had a family emergency." She shrugs with a tilt of her head and a teasing grin. "Told them your big O had fallen ill."

Sasha's jaw gapes and she huffs, "You what!?"

"Would you rather I had told them your dog got shot?"

"No," she concedes with a sigh.

"Which is why I do public relations and you write," Shae says. "We'll deal with the fallout later. When your readers find out you put your puppy first, they'll understand. We all love our fur babies. A lot of readers prefer them over children. No interruptions between the pages. They never leave the toilet seat up, no diapers to change, no clothes to buy, and no expensive boarding schools to pay for." She snaps her fingers. "Oh! And they don't destroy your body by birthing them."

Sasha presses her fingers to her forehead. "Can we go now?"

The four women wrap arms around each other and walk ahead of us through the parking lot. I watch as Rhea directs them in a clumsy side-to-side skip and a couple of them start singing a song about a wizard.

"What the hell are they doing?"

Brick stares at me, wide-eyed. "You've never seen The Wizard of Oz?"

"The what?"

He gasps and looks at the other two grinning morons walking with us, then back at me and throws his hands in the air. "Where did you grow up? He's the guy behind the magic curtain that grants wishes. He got Dorothy back home to Kansas. He gave the tin man a heart, the lion courage, and the scarecrow a brain!"

I side-eye him as we continue our trek toward the vehicles. "Scarecrow get the last one before you got there, did he?"

Brick squirrels his face as the other two break into laughter.

Suddenly reminded why I'm grateful it wasn't Brick and Rhea in the bathroom tonight – it probably would have been S-E-X – his face splits in a grin as he grabs his crotch. "Nope, I got the balls."

The ladies stop at my truck, their process of saying goodnight something I guess I'm going to have to get used to. It's like their trips to the bathroom in a public place: never go alone and take long enough to leave your date wondering if you fell in. When guys say goodbye, it's a speedy process. A quick 'see ya' or a wave, hop in your truck, take off, done. When we need to take a leak, we walk in, whip it out, and go. Some are even known to wash their hands. However, ten minutes later we're still standing here with our hands in our pockets waiting . . . patiently.

Not being one for chitchat, I take a gander at our surroundings then to my cohorts and quietly ask, "How much longer do you think this is going to take?"

"Gee, boss," Brick says condescendingly. "If I only had a brain." Dusty and Simon chuckle as we watch Brick saunter toward the women. He nuzzles into Rhea's neck and wraps his arms around her waist from behind, whispering in her ear.

She nods and says, "That's a brilliant idea." She pulls Sky in for a hug. "Simon said you're staying with him so Shae and I will stay with Sasha tonight. We don't want her to be alone."

*Brilliant, my ass. What the hell did he just do? I didn't plan on her being alone!*

Brick tosses back a quick look as he makes his way toward us and Dusty's truck. "You ladies call if you need anything. Miss Sasha, we'll be over to professionally clean the floor first thing in the morning. You fix the coffee and we'll bring breakfast." He smirks when he reaches my side. "Top that, boss."

"You asshole!" Dusty whisper-growls. "You just cost me my night with Shae."

"Oh please." Brick rolls his eyes. "Stress sex is not the way to win a woman's heart, Dust. You'd regret that forever. Never take a vulnerable woman. You send them bubble bath, chocolate, flowers."

"Riii-ght," Dusty drawls. "Like you haven't been banging

Rhea."

"Hey!" Brick scowls and jabs his finger. "Show some respect. And FYI, no I haven't."

Dusty snorts loudly. "The guy that offers his lobster roll and she asks if she has to swallow? Yeah, I'll believe that . . ." he glowers as his nostrils flare, ". . . when hell freezes over."

Brick shrugs. "Believe what you want, Dusty. We may play, fool around, but I won't be *in* her until I *win* her. Call me a sap, but I came from a broken home. I sure as hell won't be the cause of one. She's not a one-nighter; she's a whole-lifer. I knew it the minute I saw her. I ain't gonna fuck it up."

His words hit hard. Brick has always been one of our biggest players. He's never had to try. For the first time in his life, he's willing to put in the effort.

Dusty gives a sharp nod, humbled. "Sorry. You're right. I'm gonna go tell Shae goodnight."

*When the hell did my guys grow up?*

The ride to Sasha's is quiet – three ladies in the backseat, Simon and Sky up front with me. BAPUTs (big-ass pickup trucks) come in real handy at times. Keeping a couple blankets for emergencies in the carryall in the bed come in handy as well. The backseat had a few smears of Oscar's blood on it, but the blankets covered it. Why in hell it hadn't occurred to me to have Rhea and Shae ride with Brick and Dusty is beyond me, but hindsight will forever be 20/20 and as useful as tits on a boar. Not to mention the fact a second goodbye for them would simply add more time to a night that needs to end.

Sasha sits in the middle so I aim my rearview mirror at an angle that allows me to catch a glimpse of her reflection every so often. She leans her head back, staring up at the sky through the moonroof as if stargazing – the same way she did the night of our *dinner – not a date.* As if she's found what she's looking for, a sad smile lights her face and she blows the softest relieved sigh I've ever heard. When she props her head back up, a lone tear falls down her cheek, only detectable by the way she swipes her cheek and the sniffle that follows.

Yeah, my girl is tired. She needs a shower, her bed, and a pillow to lay her head on. A healthy Oscar wouldn't hurt either, but I'll be here until he comes home.

When we turn the corner onto Sasha's street, the flashing lights of two police cars sitting at the edge of the property serve as immediate reminders the night is not over yet. Nash's truck sits in the driveway and his door opens as soon as we pull up next to it. He pulls my door open and tosses a couple T-shirts at me.

"Whoever has blood on your clothes, swap out or cover up. Now," he orders. "Get the women in the house as fast as you can. Heads down, not a word." He slams the door shut and walks away quickly to distract the officer making his way toward us from across the yard.

Simon snatches a shirt out of my hands and slips it over Sky's head in one fell swoop as if it's second nature. I toss the other in the backseat. "Help Sasha put this on." Simon and I both yank off the ones we're wearing and tuck them under the front seat, hoping like hell our jeans aren't covered in blood. I glance toward the back. "All done?"

"Yup," Rhea answers for all of them.

I pull open the handle on the door. "Let's go. You heard the man. Inside. No chitchat."

"Excuse me, folks," the officer calls out as soon as we exit the truck.

"Follow my lead, ladies," Rhea whispers, then giggles and sways as she pulls on Sasha's arm. Shae joins her in the act of total rebellion, grasping Sky's hand. *This right here is why we train sailors to follow orders! I killed a man tonight and her antics are going to blow an entire operation!* She's loud as she drags them toward the side gate as if she hasn't heard him. "Hot tubby time! Oohh, those drinks were strong." The quiet whirr of the lock opening is fast and the gate slams shut moments later. The laughter and obnoxiously loud fake giggles continue as they make their way into the backyard.

"I wanted to talk to them," the cop nearly whines. He's short, thinning hairline, bit of a belly. I'll bet he wanted to talk to them . . . for a long time.

Nash scratches his forehead with a backwards thumb and chuckles. "Doesn't sound like they'd be of much help." He glances at Simon and me. "Have you guys been home at all tonight?" Honest question to which we can give an honest answer.

"Nope." Simon glances down at his bare torso then looks up and grins. "We've been, uh, busy with the ladies."

"No," I reply, shaking my head. "Why?" I've got to play straight man. The cop watched me get out on the driver's side.

"There was a shooting," the cop grumbles. "We wanted to know if you saw anything."

"Day-um," Simon drawls, as if shocked and awed. "Anybody hurt?"

The cop gives him a once over followed by what can only be described as an *are you for real* look. "It was a shooting. What do you think?"

Simon's eyes go wide as he plays dumb and dumber in one scene. Put a blonde wig on him and I'd call him Brick. "Is he dead?" Good job, Simon. We know there were three.

The cop's brow furrows before he narrows his eyes. "What makes you think it was a he?"

Simon looks dumbstruck. "Who would shoot a woman? They're made to . . ." he moves his hands in an hourglass shape, ". . . caress." He nudges my arm and bobs his eyebrows. "Am I right?"

The cop points his thumb down the street at the silver truck parked on the opposite side. *Simon's truck.* "Any idea who that might belong to?"

Simon smiles proudly. "That's my baby. I parked her down there so I could surprise my girlfriend this afternoon. Been there all day." He gasps and his eyes go wide before he whines openly, "Ah man, they didn't shoot my truck, did they?"

Water splashing and giggles interrupt our conversation as well as our thoughts as it rings out from the backyard. "We're done here," little cop sneers before he turns and heads back down to his car.

Nash waits until he's down at the street before he turns his eyes on Simon. "We are never playing poker again. That was just downright scary. Simon Sheetz turned surfer dude. Get outta here. I need to talk to Jax."

Simon runs for the backyard with a hoot and a holler, all for the benefit of the officer who continues to watch us from his spot at the end of the yard. "Get your panties off, ladies! I'm coming in!"

Nash stares as he watches our normally severe and contemplative special ops mercenary run to the gate. "It's been a helluva night, Nash. Watching that crazy sonofabitch hold a gun on his woman just about did him in. Not being able to take the shot, the feeling of helplessness. It made him human. I don't think he knows what to do with it yet."

"What about you?" he asks, sounding more concerned than curious.

"I knew exactly what to do with it," I sneer. "He's dead."

"Not what I meant and you know it."

"Are you asking if it's taken my eye off the goal?"

"Maybe."

"Not a chance." The internal rage and need for revenge resurfaces as if it all happened yesterday. "I will not sleep peacefully until those fuckers are dead. Nothing has changed. As soon as the call comes, I'm ready to roll. Ben's death is meaningless if we don't take them down. We're all waiting to put those bone frogs on our skin."

"Speaking of which," he says, eyeing my bicep which has always held my treasured mark, now covered with a dark shark. "What happened to your SEAL tat?"

"Still there. We all have them covered with hennas every two weeks. Until this is over, no association with the service. Why? Aren't you covering yours?"

He laughs. "I just do my women in the dark or wear T-shirts."

I roll my eyes. "More than I needed to know, Nash."

His voice drops an octave as I learn why he sent Simon away. "I heard from Berkel."

"Why didn't I get a call?" I snap harshly. Berkel has two

points of contact: Nash and me. It pisses me off he didn't use both.

"I told him not to. Things are getting heated. The less airwave communication, the better. One point of contact from here on out. They're on the move again, Jax," he informs me. "They're headed back to Rica. They've got about half of their men moved and almost ready to start up operations. It's only a matter of time now. Shouldn't be too long." He quirks a brow. "You think the chipmunks are still in?"

"I have no doubts."

"I hope you're right." He slaps my shoulder. "They're the best we got. Come on over to the truck, I brought you some clothes."

"Clothes?"

"You're staying here, aren't you?"

"I thought I probably should."

"Yeah, thought so. I brought you some clothes as well as some sweats to, uh, *sleep* in," he emphasizes, then grins mischievously. "Wouldn't want you to end up naked with the lovely bookworm." He reaches for his ear and slaps it as if he's been bitten. "What is with the damn bugs around here?"

*Good question.*

"Nash," I groan. "I'm not sleeping with her."

His wicked laugh is one I've heard a thousand times as he opens the door to his truck and throws a duffel bag my way. "Yet." His smile drops and that air of concern returns. "Which tells me you're hesitant. Figure out why, Callum."

"What the hell is that supposed to mean?"

"You're falling for her. But ask yourself this," he starts. "Is she everything you want or does she remind you of something someone already . . . whoa!" he shrieks as his truck starts to roll backwards down the driveway. "Holy shit!" he yells, jumping into the driver's seat and slamming on the brakes. "It slipped out of gear!"

"You good?" I stare at a frustrated, pale, rapidly breathing Nash. It's an automatic. It didn't slip out of gear – it slipped into neutral.

"How in the hell did that happen?" He stares at the dashboard then looks at the gear shift. "I always put it in park and set the brake."

"It's been a long night for everybody, you included." I nod toward the backyard. "You want to come in for a drink before you go?"

He ponders for a few moments and rubs his scruff before his face splits in an impish grin. "There were four of them and only two of you, right?"

"Nash," I warn with a low growl. "They're Brick and Dusty's girlfriends."

He shrugs casually. "I could take two for the team." He lifts a finger and laughs. "Oh wait! If it's Brick's girl, she alone could give me two, couldn't she?"

I roll my neck – the instant muscle spasm this guy manages to give me setting in once again. "Go home, Nash."

"Are they in the hot tub?"

"I have no idea."

He double checks the shifter and resets the parking brake. "No time like the present to find out." He hops out of the truck, hits the lock, and slaps me on the shoulder. "I hate wearing trunks in a hot tub. I wonder if the bookworm would mind if I . . . damnit!" He rubs his ear again. "She really needs to spray for bugs."

When we enter the backyard, we find Rhea and Shae at the edge of the hot tub splashing water with their hands and laughing as loudly as they can. The other three sit at the patio table, Simon with his arm around Sky as if he's afraid to let her go, Sasha leaning back in her chair. There's an open bottle of wine and filled glasses in front of them which look to be untouched.

Rhea looks over her shoulder at me. "Is he gone?"

On instinct I scowl, but then temper my anger. "Yes. Why didn't you just do what you were told to do and go inside?"

She shakes the water off her hands over the hot tub, walks to where we stand, places her hands on her hips and tips her chin up. If she were any shorter, she'd have to stand on a chair to make eye contact. "I may look like a stunted Barbie doll, but I'll have you know I graduated with a 4.3 GPA, was on the dean's list every semester throughout college, and have an IQ of 163. Had we walked inside as you ordered, that officer would have found his way in and seen Oscar's blood on the floor. Tell me, gentlemen, who's the genius tonight?" She waves a hand up and down at me. "Put a shirt on, Jax, it's hard to be mad at you when you look like that." She spins on her heel and walks toward the table but stops halfway there and turns back. "You can thank me and apologize simultaneously whenever you're ready, although I hear you kinda suck at apologies so flowers will be acceptable. I like roses. Yellow are my favorite."

Sasha's jaw hangs agape as she glowers at her friend. Apparently there are no secrets amongst this group. I turn to see a stunned Nash. He crinkles his brow and whispers an astonished, "163? Do those come in double D?"

"I hope her liquor cabinet is full," I grumble as I make my way slowly to the table which now reveals an empty glass in front of Sasha. "Rhea's staying the night. I'm going to need something a whole lot stronger than wine."

# ANNIE MICK

# Chapter 42

## Sasha

Jaxson Callum in a T-shirt is something to behold, but Jaxson Callum shirtless? Oh my! Oh my, my. The perfect amount of hair on his chest, tapering on its path downwards. And dummy me closes my eyes for two seconds to stash this picture in my memory bank – definite book cover material – before my short-stack friend steps between me and the real thing. I really wish she would get out of the way, or shrink even more, maybe stand in front of Nash while she reads them the riot act. Come on, Rhea! Lean to the left or lean to the right – just get the hell out of my way!

I reach for the glass of wine in front of me to take a sip. Huh, guess I was thirstier than I realized. Down and gone in one gulp. As if that weren't bad enough –  sucks at apologies? Yellow roses? That does it. Rhea will be woken with a cold glass of water in her face come morning. Who needs alarms when you have a vengeful bestie you've pissed off the night before? It might be meaner than an airhorn, but it's a whole lot nicer than your hand dipped in warm water. I'm not a monster.

"How are you doing?" Jaxson's soothing voice is the calm I need as he bends and drops a kiss to my forehead then takes the chair next to mine, setting a duffel bag on the ground next to him.

"Okay." I eye his chest and fight the whimper that longs to break free, reaching for the hem of the T-shirt he threw into the backseat. "Do you want this shirt back?"

His mouth twitches. "Do I need it back, Sasha?"

"Wine or beer, you guys?" Simon says a little too loudly from across the table as he rises from his seat and reaches for Sky's hand to follow him.

"I'll take a beer, poker face," Nash replies with a laugh.

"Coming right up," he tells him. "Sky is going to get a shower."

I whip the T-shirt off over my head and hand it to Jaxson. "I think Rhea would rather be mad at you."

"And you?" He grins impishly.

Taking advantage of one last fast perusal, I close my eyes. "Put the T-shirt on, Jaxson."

Simon returns with two beers moments later and sets them on the table in front of Jaxson and Nash. "Sasha, you got a minute?" he asks. I follow him to the sliding doors and we step inside. Once over the threshold, he stops and takes a deep breath, letting it out slowly. "Sky has decided to stay here tonight, but I'd like to stay with her. You okay with that?"

"Sure," I reply without hesitation.

"I can sleep on the floor next to her bed," he offers sheepishly and I watch as a boyish flush overtakes the cheeks of this mountain of a man. "She's had a helluva trauma. I want to be here if she wakes up with nightmares."

"Of course." I chuckle. "You don't have to sleep on the floor, Simon. It's a queen size bed. No sense washing two sets of sheets."

He rubs the back of his neck and stammers, "Oh, I didn't mean, I wouldn't disrespect . . ."

I hold my hand up to stop him. "Not my business. Besides, it might be a source of comfort to all of us to know there's a man in the house tonight." I point a firm finger at him. "Not that we can't handle ourselves, but we are one Oscar short."

He grins and lifts his brows. "*A* man in the house?"

"Well, yeah, unless you carry extras in your pockets."

He laughs heartily as he turns my shoulders toward the table outside. "Let me know your master plan to get that one to go home. Wild horses couldn't drag him away. You've had a helluva trauma tonight, too. You're stuck with us, Sasha. Don't make the poor guy sleep in his truck."

*I do have a pull-out sofa with a memory foam mattress. I hope Rhea and Shae don't mind sleeping in one bed together because I certainly don't plan on Jaxson sleeping in his truck, and I'm certainly not ready for a bed partner.*

After Sky is finished with her shower, it's my turn. I try not to take too long, but the water feels so good, the massage heads doing their job; relaxing muscles I hadn't realized were so tight — the deep breaths I can finally take. Once the steam is built up in the bathroom, a faint yet overwhelming scent of Aidan permeates the air. He's here! I can smell his cologne. He's not dead! He's . . . not . . . dead!


"Sasha." Jaxson's voice is a soft whisper next to me, soothing, coaxing me out of slumber. "Baby, wake up." His hand caresses my cheek, his thumb brushing lightly over my forehead.

Voices in the background are muffled but I hear Rhea clear as day. "My God, I'm glad you caught her before she fell. One head knock this week was enough."

Another voice announces, "Spinner's on his way up from the beach. Should be here in five."

"Who's Spinner?" Rhea asks the voice.

"He's our best med . . . uh, best medical doctor on call," the voice answers.

"I'm calling an ambulance!" Rhea yells. "She's been out for over five minutes! That's too long."

"It's syncope," the voice says. "After the shock of today, it's not uncommon."

"What shock?" Rhea demands. "What the hell happened today? Nobody's told us anything and you'd better start talking, mister!"

*"Wake up, Sassy," Ben whispers softly inside my head. "You're okay."*

I fight to open my eyes and feel them roll inside the sockets.

"She's coming around," Jaxson announces, then soothingly speaks to me as brushes his fingers over my cheek, "That's my girl."

His face is the first thing I see when I open my eyes. Those silver blue eyes surrounded by the creases of experience, now joined with the furrow of worry – that eleven between the brows that I long to smooth away.

"What happened?" I breathe weakly.

"You fainted." He smooths his thumb over my forehead and grimaces. "Again."

Disturbance in the doorway attracts attention as a man enters the room. "Got here as soon as I could. Clear the room and show me the patient."

"I'm not going anywhere!" Rhea yells and grabs hold of the footboard, holding steadfast and strong.

"Yes, you are," Simon growls, lifting her off her feet and removing her from the room in the midst of being kicked and scratched. "Let the doctor check her. Kick me again, Einstein Barbie, and you will be his next patient."

# Chapter 43

## Jaxson

"Where are my clothes?!" Sasha screeches, gripping the throw we put over her tighter in her fists, and pulls it higher as she sits up on the bed, realizing she nearly flashed the doctor as well as me when she shoots up quickly. Thank you, baby, but I've already been flashed and it was a sight I will live and die with – happily now that I know you're okay. "I'm nekked!"

Hearing the panic in her voice and seeing the mortification in her eyes, not to mention the drop-dead sexy southern twang I've never heard before, I do believe now would not be the proper time to inform her I carried that *nekked* body to the bed. We all heard her scream and came running. I, however, barreled over and through Rhea into the bathroom. It could have been a spider, could have been a snake. Whatever it was, she was terrified. I caught her before she fell in the shower. I may have even had a boob in my hand. Who the hell knows? It wasn't exactly top priority at the time. You reach for the nearest body part and hold them up.

"Nekked?" My voice is light as I arch a brow. I feel the twinkle in my eyes, though I can't see it as there isn't a mirror in sight.

She narrows hers and scowls. "I don't have any clothes on, Jaxson. Naked," she draws out slowly. "As in nude."

"You fainted in the shower, Sasha. Most people take those in the *nude*."

A loud throat clearing captures our attention and I turn to see the doctor with his back to us, his eyes aimed at the ceiling. The *doctor* is actually Brent Parker aka "Spinner" – one of Nash's team – and a damn good medic. He was part of the team involved with, shall we say, dissecting the problem from earlier tonight.

"Mind if I examine the patient, Jax?" an entertained Spinner asks. "I'll let you two iron out the verbiage details on your own time."

He proceeds to introduce himself as Dr. Spinner, as ordered by Nash, and performs a conscientious general exam i.e. BP, pulse, lungs, cognition, etc. He explains that he is aware of the evening's circumstances and listens attentively as she explains what happened in the bathroom to set off a panic attack. He expounds on the effects of trauma and reassures her it won't last. He leaves her with a card for a therapist and politely asks to use her bathroom.

Once done, he steps back into the bedroom. "Do you want your friends to come back in and help you get dressed?"

She only nods.

What the hell? I could have helped her get dressed. Not that I should, but I could.

He opens the bedroom door and calls for the rambunctious runt to come back in. He looks at me and surreptitiously tilts his head toward the living room for me to exit. Aha. He wants me out, but for reasons of his own.

"His scent is on the clothes in the bathroom," he says quietly once we're in the living room. "I recognized it from the ones we took off of him. The asshole must have bathed in his cologne. Probably transferred onto hers when he had hold of her. It's most likely what she smelled once the steam rose. Remove them as fast as you can, burn them if you have to. Just get them out of there."

"Will do," I tell him. "I'm up for the next shower. I thought it was odd you asked to use the can."

He shrugs. "Something triggered her. Had to figure out what it was."

"Why did you give her a referral for therapy? That's what got her into this to begin with. That asshole was a psychiatrist."

Nash steps up and places a hand on my shoulder. "No, he wasn't." He shakes his head and dips his chin. "He was a cold blooded psychopath with a degree and lots of fancy letters behind his name. He killed women who got in his way." He narrows his eyes and lifts his brows in harmony. "You might be a Band-Aid, Jax, but we both know wounds can fester. Let the lady get help."

Rhea and Shae exit the bedroom behind us. Rhea wears a smug grin as she yanks on my arm to pull me down so she can whisper in my ear. "She won't come out until she sees yours."

I nearly suffer whiplash between turning my head sideways and downwards at the same time. Damn, she's short. "Sees my what?"

She waves a hand up and down from my head to my toes and huffs as if I should know. "Your nekkedness."

Spinner nearly chokes on his own spit as he snorts and mutters to Nash, "I could handle buck nekked with that one."

Nash pinches the bridge of his nose and winces. "Uh, Spinner, that's Brick's girl."

Spinner pales, stunned. "Brick's? As in Halladay?"

"Uh huh," Nash replies, nodding slowly.

"Oh . . . oh," Spinner sputters as he extends his hand to Rhea. "Uh, nice to meet you, ma'am. I think I'd better be on my way." He tips his chin at me. "Things look good here. Let me know if you need anything else. 'Night guys."

And he's gone. As in ass on fire, seeking water to extinguish it, gone. Officer to officer, SEAL to SEAL, you do not, under any circumstances, approach a comrade's wife or girlfriend. **Code of ethics.** With Nash, it's a joke. Any offhanded comments or sexual innuendos he's ever made have been in jest and in private – to me and me alone. He appreciates the female form. Nash also sometimes admires statuesque mannequins so . . .

I tap on the bedroom door and wait for her to respond before

I open it. No, I don't plan on stripping down to *nekkedness*. But I think I have figured out why I feel the need for a drink when Rhea is around. Her humor is as dry as the Sahara desert and having something in my hands prevents me from strangling her. 163. I think I need proof. She's smart; I don't doubt that. But I think sixty of those points should be accredited to smart . . . ass. A little like Brick. A genius in his profession – a "Forrest Gump" in social skills. It's no wonder they complement each other.

Sasha sits on the edge of the bed in virtual pajamas – simple lounge pants and a tank top. She's exhausted. Her hair is still wet, dark circles under red rimmed eyes. I knew this would all catch up with her. She shouldn't have been left alone for a minute. Trauma like this evening doesn't leave you unscathed and has a tendency to rear its ugly head when least expected. Sky had her share, but Sasha had the gun to her temple, was dragged out of the house into the yard. Lehner was shot while he still had hold of her. Oscar is at the vet hospital. Her beloved companion almost died tonight – we still don't know the final outcome. It's one o'clock in the morning. The adrenaline is gone and we're all running on fumes.

I take a seat next to her, wrap her in my arms, and kiss her temple. "How are you doing?"

"Did you see me naked?"

Whoa! Not at all what I expected. How do I answer this? Yeah, baby, I sure did? Spank bank material for the next decade? Burned into my retinae? You've got a body I want to explore for the rest of my life? I could spend ten minutes on your tits alone? Nope, probably not a good segue.

"I saw *you*, Sasha," I whisper as I hold her tighter to my side. "I saw you were in need, struggling, about to fall. I saw the panic in your eyes before they closed. I felt the bend in your knees as they folded on my forearms. I felt your head against my chest instead of hearing it hit the shower floor. I cannot describe the rush of relief that gave me."

She lifts her gaze, those green eyes I see every night in my dreams searching mine, that perfect cupid's bow moved to the side as her mouth twists. "So you didn't see me naked?"

"You're not going to let this go, are you?"

She picks at the hem of her tank top and shrugs sheepishly. "Well, it wouldn't hurt a woman's confidence to know what you thought."

*Segue, Callum, I think to myself. Segue!*

Lifting her chin with two fingers, I release a half groan. "You need to come with warning labels."

Her nose scrunches. "What would they say?"

Remembering where we are and her state of vulnerability, I kiss her forehead and whisper, "The first one would read 'Fragile, handle with care'."

"And the others?"

"You only get one at a time."

"Did I earn any stars?"

Arching a brow and dipping my chin, I warn her, "Be a good girl, Sasha."

I see her shoulders sag slightly but I rise in spite of it and reach for her hand, pulling her to her feet. Once at the door, I pause before turning the knob and take her cheeks in my palms.

Why she needs approval, I have no idea. Particularly my approval. This woman could have prospects anywhere from the grocery store to Paris. She's gorgeous, smart, funny, and kind. She's so fucking real it's unreal – if that makes any sense. As far as she knows, I'm a construction worker. A simple, dirt-under-my-nails, blue jeans wearing, beer drinking, pizza eating, damn near forty construction worker. And yet, what I think means something to her.

It's not just her body I'm thinking about – though it does deserve kudos – when I tell her, "A hundred, Sasha. A hundred stars. I'm pretty crazy about you."

"You make me pretty crazy, too." Her smile alone is worth a thousand stars, but the giggle that follows is music. Pictures may paint a thousand words, but Sasha's eyes tell whole stories. You simply have to know how to read and interpret. I'll tell her every day how beautiful she is, how strong and resilient she's proven to be, how the world – my world – is so much better with her in it if it makes her smile like this. The way her name dances on my tongue, has its own flavor, its own area and zip codes that no one else will ever occupy. How, in such a short time, she has managed to own me.

The kiss isn't as long as I'd like, but it is enough . . . for now. "You're beautiful, with and without your clothes. Now let's go get these guys tucked into bed. It's been a long day."

Days, I think to myself as we leave the bedroom. Brick said he knew the moment he saw Rhea – *my sympathies, Halladay* – but I am starting to understand.

A quick pleasant memory flashes through my mind. I'd only heard such conviction once before: Ben.

*"I knew Sassy was my one and only the minute I saw her," he'd told us. "Found her in the kissing booth when my cousin dragged me out to a fair after a family reunion. She was doing some college fundraiser for literacy for kids. I asked her how much they needed to raise. She told me what their goal was. I sent my cousin back home to get five hundred from my dad and grab another five hundred from my duffel bag. Paid a dollar for every kiss until he got back, handed her the thousand dollars, and waited for her to turn it in. I picked her up out of that booth and threw her over my shoulder. Took her for a funnel cake, asked her for a date, and the rest was history."*

*"Why didn't you just go get it?" Simon asked him. "Why send your cousin?"*

*"I wasn't letting another man touch those lips!" Ben told him. "Soft, fine, and all mine after the first one. You find a woman with a flavor," he pointed a hard finger at Simon, "then you'll know you've found your soulmate."*

*Simon laughed, hard. "I know how women taste, Arkelpaine. You've had one, you've had them all. Pussy is pussy."*

*Ben picked up a roll from his tray and threw it at him. "Her mouth, asshat! Try kissing them first, Sheetz. My Sassy didn't give it up for months. I could kiss my wife for hours on end and still not get enough."*

*I laughed. They were young. Women had flavor, no denying*

*it. But in a kiss? On the mouth? Simon had a point. You didn't get to the good part until you went down on them. The fastest way there was via ripping of clothes, a nip here and there, dirty talk. Intimacy had eluded me all my life. I never was a kisser.*

Until now. There was truth in Ben's words – apparently knowledge as well. Sasha most definitely has a flavor. In her name, in her mouth with every kiss, on her skin. Hell, there's even flavor in my thoughts about her.

"You okay?" Her voice is soft, her touch electrifying yet calming at the same time.

"Yeah." My answer is swift as I smile and glance around the room and find Simon, freshly showered and sitting next to Sky. His arm around her shoulder, tucking her close into his side. Has he found his flavor?

Nash sits next to Simon. Rhea and Shae sit on the sofa tapping away on their cell phones. The remnants of Oscar's blood is still visible by the front door. The rug has been tossed outside. Rhea looks up from her phone. "Brick and Dusty will be here first thing in the morning with breakfast and the machine to clean up."

"Tell him anything before nine will land him in the unemployment line," I fire back, reaching for the duffel bag next to the sofa. "I'm going to get a shower. Nash, hang on before you leave. I'll be out shortly."

He laughs. "No rush. I've got nowhere else to go."

I cut him a wry look. "Yeah you do. We've run out of places to sleep. Unless you want the patio."

He lifts both arms in the air, palms up, and grins. "I'm easy."

Simon and I both shoot him a glare and in unison respond, "We know."

"Jax," Nash calls out, "I packed a plastic bag in there for your dirty clothes." He smirks. "Wouldn't want you getting the clean ones all . . . *stinky*." For the others in the room, it's supposed to be humorous. For me, it's a reminder to get Sasha's clothes out of the bathroom.

Unfortunately, when I enter the bathroom, it's void of any clothing she would have left behind. And now we have double the dilemma. If they're tossed in a hamper with any others, she's not only lost more wardrobe, but a hamper as well.

I poke my head back out of the bedroom door. "Nash, you got a minute?"

"Need help scrubbing your back, Jax?" the pint-sized motor mouth asks with a giggle. "You do realize Sasha's not running a bath house here."

I take a long deep breath and let it out slowly. Four seconds in, five seconds out. Nope, not working. The day has been long, the stress high, the results excruciating. She doesn't get it, but there is a time and a place and now and here are not it. I slowly turn to face her, replacing my seething glare with a smug grin. "I would have asked you, Rhea, but being so vertically challenged I figured you'd have trouble just reaching my ass."

Huh. Might not have gotten her to shut her mouth – her jaw is gaping wide open – but her vocal cords have frozen temporarily. Good enough for me.

"Her clothes are gone," I tell Nash once in the bathroom. "They probably tossed them in a hamper somewhere. I need you to search while I grab a shower."

He rolls his eyes. "Lovely. They probably stunk up the whole thing. Any idea where she keeps it?"

It's my turn to roll mine. "Yeah, Nash, I take inventory and make note of everything other than her when in Sasha's bedroom." I wave my hand toward the door. "Get your ass out there and find it. Take it out the sliding door and stash it in your truck. You can take it with you when you leave. I'll explain it to her later."

He snickers. "You want me to take your girlfriend's pretty little underthings home with . . . damnit!" He slaps at his ear once again and scowls as he looks around the room. "Where is that damn bug?! I'm gonna squash that little fucker! I swear to God he's following me around."

*Gotta admit, it is a little on the spooky side. Maybe it's his cologne.*

By the time I finish my shower and dress in the sweats Nash brought me, he's found the hamper, taken it out to his truck, and made it back in through the sliding doors without notice. Knowing Nash, he's regaling Rhea with a story of cute little dimples on my ass cheeks that required extra attention. *Asshole.* Before I leave the room to join the others, the overwhelming niggle to open that nightstand drawer strikes again. I know the picture is in there. Just one tiny peek at the man who came before me. A little insight into the shoes I'm looking to fill. The ghost I sometimes feel I'm trying to chase. A professor? An artist? A businessman? Clean cut? Is that why she likes my scruff...because it's a change? Or does she miss his? I hear their voices as they converse and laugh together in the room next to the one I'm in. They'll never know. They're distracted.

The lamp on the nightstand is on, the light a soft glow casting just enough illumination that I'll be able to see. My fingers itch and tingle as I reach for the handle on the front of the drawer and gently tug. I'm met with a strong resistance at an opening of approximately two inches as well as a whisper in my ear. "Don't do it." I swear on my life, it's not a voice in my head; not my conscience. It's a warning. I whirl quickly in the direction the sound came from but there's no one there. Maybe it was my conscience after all. Whatever it was, I close the drawer, pick up my duffel, and walk away. She'll tell me about him . . . someday.

# Chapter 44

## Sasha

"Goodnight, everybody." I watch as they file down the hallway one by one. It's three o'clock in the morning. Nash has left, the sofa bed has been pulled out and fresh linens have been placed. There are two pillows in case Jaxson wants extra head support. Rhea and Shae are sharing a bedroom as well as a bed, Simon and Sky are sharing the other spare bedroom. The police are long gone from the street out front. I've double and triple checked the locks on the doors and windows. I don't know why – he's gone. *He's dead.*

"You going to be okay?" Jaxson asks as he ducks his face down to meet my gaze. It's tender, really. He conforms to me instead of bending my head back to look up at him. As if he's afraid I might break. *Fragile – handle with care.* It wasn't like this with our first kiss – that was all heat and desire – but he knows what I need right now. Only one other man has ever . . . Stop it, Sasha! Don't go there. It's not a competition. He deserves better.

I nod slowly. "I'll be okay."

"Call me if you need anything," he says before he kisses my forehead. "I'll be right out here."

"I'll know where to find you." I laugh lightly before I turn to head for my bedroom. "Jaxson." I stop at the door. "Thank you, for everything."

He dips his chin. "Goodnight, Sasha."

Slipping out of the lounge pants I wore in front of company and releasing the girls from the confines of the bra I strapped them into under the tank top, I settle into bed in the boy shorts and tank I usually wear. Long pants and wrestling with sheets is not a sport I'm fond of. I pull up the vet clinic number before I lay my head on the pillow and call. I'll never sleep until I know.

*"Lancaster Vet Hospital."*

*"Hi, uh, this is Sasha Taylor. I was calling to check on Oscar."*

*"Oh, Sasha!" the cheery voice replies. "This is Clint. I was here when you brought Oscar in. He's sleeping soundly. We're keeping him sedated, but he looks good. Dr. Lancaster should be able to take the breathing tube out tomorrow."*

I don't think I've ever cried so many good tears in my life. I want to hop in the car and drive there right now, give my dog a big hug. I've heard people say, "Dogs are people too". It's true, you know. They're like children to some. They give the elderly a purpose when the kids are grown and gone, the lonely a companion, children somebody to whisper all their secrets to, and a widow an extension of her soulmate. I should know, I'm one of them.

*"Sasha, you there?" Clint asks, a hint of worry in his tone.*

*"I'm here." I wipe the tears from my cheeks and sniffle. "I just needed to check on him before I went to sleep."*

*He chuckles softly. "You can call anytime but sleep is a treasured commodity. Put your head down and get some rest. We'll worry about Oscar. Dr. Lancaster just left about an hour ago but should be back in about nine o'clock."*

*"Okay." I sniffle once more. "Thanks, Clint."*

I end the call and finally lay my head on the pillow and sob. There's a soft tap on my door before it opens slowly and closes behind him. He walks to the bed and drops to his knees beside it. "I heard you crying."

"I called the vet clinic."

He gathers me in his arms and holds me tight as I wrap my arms around his neck. I feel his heart pound against his chest. "Oh, Sasha. I'm so sorry."

"Wh – what?" I pull back and look into his eyes, startled. "No! He's okay. Oscar's okay."

He places a hand on my cheek, that eleven between his brows making an appearance. "Then why are you crying?"

"I'm happy," I blubber before burying my face against his shoulder.

He wraps his hand in my hair and pulls me closer with his other around my back. "Ah. Any chance you could teach me to distinguish between the two?"

"Would you stay?" I whisper against his neck, breathing in the masculine scent of his soap. His soft beard against my neck and shoulders is foreign to me, but so damn delectable. "Just hold me."

He stands as I lift the blankets and invite him in. His eyes follow a path leading from my bare legs to my toes. "Where did your pants go?"

"I don't sleep in them," I explain. "They get all tangled up in the sheets and the bed looks like a war zone in the morning."

He looks as if he's fighting an internal battle as he studies me, the raging war within – the devil on one shoulder, the angel on the other, each one eyeing the trident in the middle to use as a weapon. His voice is strained as he concedes, "Scoot over."

Once he's settled beside me; my head on his chest while he lies flat on his back. "Did you lock the door?"

"There is no reason to lock the door, Sasha. Every guestroom in your house is full."

"Exactly," I huff. "What about privacy?"

"For sleeping?" He lifts my chin with two fingers and narrows his eyes. "Which is exactly what we'll be doing. Roll over and go to sleep."

My index and middle fingers dance up his chest playfully. "Are you going to kiss me goodnight?"

His eyes close and he lets out a slow exhale through his

nose. "One, short, sweet and simple kiss. Got it?"

"I suppose," I teasingly mumble and shrug one shoulder. "I forgot, it is far past your bedtime. You'll probably need two naps tomorrow to make up for lost sleep."

His entire body stiffens next to me and his harsh exhale mixed with a low growl indicates I probably did poke the bear, because the next thing I feel is the blanket being stripped off and a hard hand landing on my ass before Jaxson rolls me over, pulls the blanket back up, and tucks himself behind me. He places one bent arm under my pillow and his other around my stomach. "Be a good girl, Sasha. Goodnight."

Well! If that was supposed to be calming, somebody needs to deliver the message to my brain – and a couple of body parts – because it didn't work. I'm tempted to run into the bathroom to see if there's a handprint on my butt. Instead, I concentrate on settling in and getting comfortable; the pillow wedged between my shoulder and head – after I've punched it a time or two, a little wiggle to situate my back against his chest, and . . . hello! Seems I'm not the only one struggling.

I can literally feel his clenched jaw as he growls in my ear, "If you don't lay still, I'm going to put a pillow between us."

"I'll bet I could still feel it," I grumble.

"Sasha." His whisper sounds agonized, but that damn salsa tongue is making my lady parts sing. "Not tonight."

Doesn't he get it? If not tonight, when? I'm alive tonight. Sky didn't die. Oscar made it. Who knows how many tomorrows we have?

I reach for his arm around my waist and slowly guide his hand upwards toward my breast. "Touch me, Jaxson. Please," I whisper, a plea so desperate it would put a starving beggar to shame. "I need to know I'm still alive."

# Chapter 45

## Jaxson

*"Touch me, Jaxson. I need to know I'm still alive."*

I assumed she was teasing with her sarcastic comments when I crawled into bed with her. But that's Sasha – it's how she handles stress. So much to learn about her. My conscience is screaming "no" as she guides my hand past her ribcage and arches into my touch; the weight of her firm breast filling my palm like it was made for it. The stiff nipple an invitation for my mouth.

She wanted time. It's not selfish to give and not receive, is it? This is for her; she needs release. I scoot away just enough to roll her onto her back, sliding my hand under the hem of her tank top. She sits up quickly, yanking it off over her head and throwing it to the foot of the bed. She lies back, reaching for the waistband of her shorts to slide them off.

"No." I grasp her hand firmly in mine. The moonlight shining through the window casts a glow on her face, reflecting the disappointment in her eyes. "I won't let you regret this in the morning," I say softly, placing a hand on her cheek and tipping her chin up. "Baby steps. I'll let you moan tonight," I wink, "but screaming my name will have to wait until the house is empty."

I would love to have my mouth on every inch of this woman. But if she were stripped naked in this bed right now, my sweats would be peeled off in seconds and I would sink so deep and so hard into her, I wouldn't come up for air for days. Her parted lips are an invitation for mine so I start there. My mouth travels to her jaw, to her neck and finally to a pert nipple that begs for attention. My fingertips slowly edge their way across the soft, creamy skin of her ribs, down the curve and dip of her belly, and into the waistline of her shorts. Her hips buck in an effort to expedite my journey, but I've always found the trip to be half the pleasure. The tease, the buildup, and lest we forget. . . the end result. When she lets out a pleasured moan, I clamp my mouth over hers in a hard kiss – we don't need an audience. Somewhere deep down inside, I had a feeling Sasha was a moaner. And now, not only do I have a favorite flavor but I have a new favorite sound. I'll bet we'd make damn good harmony together.

The tent in my sweatpants is nearly unbearable, but as she moves in rhythm against my hand, I'm okay with it. This is for her. I feel her grasp the front of my T-shirt, seeking something – anything – to hang onto, or so I thought. She was seeking alright – a definite goal – inside my sweatpants. And her firm grip on my dick has me close to exploding.

"Sasha," I scold a deep and low warning, though my hips are moving with her rather seemingly skilled technique. When her thumb rubs over the tip I nearly scream with ecstasy.

"Sh-shut up, Jaxson," she stammers through broken heavy breaths. "I-I'm a mul-multi…tas…tasker." She breathes hard as she pumps her hips and her hand in sync, and I find myself easily keeping rhythm with her movements. She clenches hard around my fingers at the same time I explode against her hand. She buries her head against my shoulder to muffle her moans and I bury my face in the crook of her neck to do the same.

And now I know. We sound fucking delightful in harmony.

"Well," she says breathlessly. "I know what your warning label should be."

"Oh yeah?"

She giggles softly as she squeezes my now sensitive yet still hard and, unfortunately, willing dick. "Contents under pressure. May explode on contact."

Resisting the urge to smack that peach shaped ass once more, I laugh. "That mouth. Wait here." I climb out of bed and head for the bathroom. Opening the cabinet I collect a washcloth and run it under warm water. Glancing in the mirror above the sink I mumble to myself, "Asshat."

Returning to the bedroom, I find a half asleep Sasha turned back on her side away from me. Taking her hand in mine, I gently wash it off as well as her fingers, one by one, and tuck it under the covers. "Get some sleep."

"The hamper's in the closet," she offers quietly. *No, it's not.* But I don't bother to tell her that.

"I need to grab some fresh sweats," I tell her instead.

She rolls over to face me, her brows pinched and that kissable mouth twisted. "Are you still going to stay with me?"

"Of course I will."

Her face softens instantly and a shy smile appears. "Okay."

I exit the bedroom and find the duffel exactly where I left it. I need to change my pants and T-shirt, clean up the mess from a hand job I'll never forget, and try and get some sleep. I'll tuck that washcloth inside the duffel once I'm done with it and explain why her hamper is gone, later. Tomorrow. There's always tomorrow. Right now, I need to get back to Sasha, hold her for the rest of the night.

Climbing back under the covers as gently as possible, I take a position next to the blonde beauty and settle in comfortably. She's put her tank top back on, *damn shame,* and curls into me like a second skin. She fits. She simply fits . . . perfectly.

"Jaxson?" she whispers so softly I almost miss it. I want her to say it again. The last time she said it, it was preceded by "shut up" but then again, she was in the middle of administering a hand job and on her way to orgasm, so I really shouldn't complain.

"Yeah?"

"Are you still crazy about me?"

Lowering my mouth to her shoulder, I drop a gentle kiss. "Still crazy, Sasha."

She sniffles. "You still make me crazy, too."

Tucking her into me closer, I chuckle. "Go to sleep."

Six o'clock is my usual time to wake, no matter when I fall asleep the night before. It's been an internal alarm for years – one I can't shake. She's still in my arms. Her body curled into mine, one leg tucked in between my calves, her arm resting softly over the one I have wrapped around her waist. Is this cuddling? Why have I never had the desire to do it before now? I gingerly back my hips away first – morning wood has a mind of its own – and remove my arm from under the pillow her head is lying on. Lifting one leg, I gently slide hers forward and off the other underneath it. I'd like to think my body is free from hers, but it's not. It's bereft. It's lacking. It suddenly feels like it's missing something.

Stealthily sliding out from under the blankets, I take one glance back at the soundly sleeping enigma in the bed. I'll figure you out someday, Sasha. How you've managed to wrap this coldhearted bastard around your fingers with a flavor, your eyes, your tears, your voice.

Closing the door gently behind me, I pass through the short hall to get to the dining room and see Simon already in the kitchen and smell the welcome coffee as it permeates the air.

He eyes the hallway from which I've arrived then back to me, the eyebrows meeting his hairline and dipped chin silently questioning.

I ignore it. "How do you know where to find the shit to make coffee?"

He waves a hand around the kitchen. "It ain't that hard, boss. She's pretty organized. Coffeemaker there." He points to the machine. "Tray underneath with all the supplies." He grins like an idiot and points to the sink. "Oh, and the universal tap that delivers water every time."

I flip him off and grumble, "Smartass."

"Did you call Carl last night?" he asks. "He's going to be

here in less than an hour, business as usual, if you didn't let him know."

Rubbing a hand through my scruff, then up to my hair as I brush it away from my face. "Shit, I forgot. Wasn't exactly first thing on my mind."

"Yeah." He snorts sarcastically. "Killing a man isn't exactly a regular day at the office . . ." He narrows his eyes and deadpans, "Lately. Nice shot, by the way."

I yawn and stretch, keeping my voice low. "He was practice, Simon. One more job, then on to civilian life. Can't come soon enough."

He scans me head to toe . . . twice, then arches a brow.

"What?" I grouse.

"Forgive me if I'm wrong," he says with a smirk. "But if I'm not mistaken you went to bed in navy sweats."

I square him with my decades old Captain's gaze, well aware my gray sweats are not the ones I went to bed in. However, seems I'm not the only one who's had a change in attire. Folding my arms over my chest, I eye his bottom half, the vision of gray as he sat on the sofa with Sky last night returning; now navy as he stands before me. "And I believe yours were gray, Simon."

He holds up a cup. "Coffee, boss?"

"Sounds good."

"Comin' right up."

*Subject closed. It's how we roll.*

I fold up the sofa bed in a tidy hurry, placing the cushions in proper order with throw pillows lined in the corners while Simon pours my coffee. Who the hell have we become? Three years ago we would have already been out for a five mile run, showered, fully dressed, and ready to start our day. Or, we would have been in the field, on a mission, un-showered for days, killing without conscience, and serving the way we were trained. Granted, last night we did kill a man, saved a dog, and catered to women who suffered at the hands of a crazed lunatic. Three years ago? Killing was all in a day's work, child's play. Lately? Itching to do it again . . . one last time.

Simon and I decide to sit on the patio with our coffee so as not to wake the others and to discuss what comes next.

I glance over toward the walkway leading to the front. "The wires on the side of the house need to come down today. Tear them out, make it look like they never existed."

"You ever going to tell her?"

Eyeing him over the rim of my coffee cup, I take another sip. "Think I should?"

He tilts his head slightly, his forehead creasing. "Yeah, I do. Before I take the wires down. You know how this shit works, Jax. Show it to her, let her know what that asshole did. Might help her get past it. It'll also let her know why Oscar tore up the bedroom. He was trying to protect her."

"You're pretty attached to that dog, aren't you?"

A sad smile is partnered with glassy eyes as he shakes his head. "Watching that dog damn near die last night brought it all back. Made me wonder where the real one is; if he's as faithful to Ben's wife as this one is to Sasha."

"Belgian's are a pretty unbeatable breed, Simon."

"They are," he agrees. "But Ben's dog was special. The way he trained him. The genius he put behind it. It's almost like he knew he wasn't gonna make it."

*See what I mean? Itching to do it again.*

The whirring of the lock on the gate stirs us from our conversation and Carl makes his way into the yard. *Damnit! I forgot to call him.*

"Mornin'." He tips the bill of his hat and greets us in his usual neutral but friendly fashion. He pauses as he does a double take and nods. "I take it you boys had a slumber party last night. Hope you didn't wear yourselves out too much to work." He continues toward the workbench to set his lunchbox down.

Simon doesn't hesitate to share at least a portion of last night's events. "Oscar got shot last night."

Carl freezes in his tracks and turns back to Simon. "Is he okay?"

"He will be," I answer for him.

His face is stern and two shades redder than ten seconds ago. "Did you catch the shooter?"

"Yup."

"Is he six feet under?" he sneers.

Hiding the grin that longs to peek out in admiration of the animal lover in front of us, I tell him, "Deeper than that, Carl."

"Good," he grunts. "World ain't got no place for somebody who'd shoot an animal like that. Tell Miss Taylor I'll buy him a steak when he's ready to eat it."

We both laugh. "Hey Carl, Brick and Dusty are bringing breakfast but they won't be here until nine. They have a little cleanup to do inside first before we start work too. Come and have coffee. May as well take a load off. It's going to be a while."

"What are they cleaning up inside?"

Looking back over my shoulder, I grin wryly. "It's a long story."

He shrugs. "What the heck, I'm salaried. I got time. Go pour me a cup, Simon." He holds up a hand. "Oh, call them boys and tell 'em I want biscuits and gravy with extra sausage. And for God's sake, don't tell Marilyn. That woman made me eat oatmeal this morning. Wouldn't even put syrup on that shit. Peaches! Who in the hell eats peaches on oatmeal!?"

306

# Chapter 46

## Sasha

Rolling over onto my back I can feel the benefits of the stretch from my fingertips all the way to the tips of my toes. My spine feels longer, my muscles feel looser, my mind less foggy, my . . . oh shit! I'm on the wrong side of the bed, and the other side is cold. Jaxson! What was I thinking? I shoot off the mattress so fast my feet get tangled in the blankets and I nearly faceplant. My phone! Where is my phone? I need to check on Oscar. Grabbing it off of the nightstand, I see it's only eight o'clock. Clint said Dr. Lancaster would be in at nine this morning.

Okay, Sasha, pee first. You can't dance and concentrate at the same time.

Brush your teeth. Your tongue is sticking to the roof of your mouth.

Brush your hair. The birds could probably make a nest in there.

Clear the cobwebs out of your brain. Good luck with that, dipshit. You had hand sex with Jaxson Callum last night!

Voices ring out from the kitchen. I'd like to be able to say they're all friendly, but . . .

*"Overgrown tree trunks!"*

*"Midget with attitude."*

*"You coffee hogs! You didn't even make a fresh pot!"*

*"It's brewing now. Don't you know coffee stunts your growth?"*

*"I think her mother must have bottle-fed it to her."*

Oh God, I'd better get out there. Rhea can shoot the gnat off a skeeter's ass. She knows where I keep my guns and she is not a morning person. I find my lounge pants, lose the boy shorts, and pull them on. Opening my bedroom door, I find Shae at the dining room table with her head in her hands and Sky seated next to her observing the two barefoot, sweatpants wearing giants with the little sprout in the kitchen in a standoff. Carl sits at the end fighting a grin behind the rim of his cup as he watches them.

"Good morning, all," I say cheerily from the short hallway's entrance I stand in.

Rhea glares and waves her hand at Jaxson and Simon as the coffeemaker makes its telltale gurgling noise and the final drips fall into the pot. "You want to rein in these baboons? They drank all the coffee!"

Simon pours a cup and holds it in front of her. "Here. Something to keep that mouth busy. It's hot. Be sure to drink it fast." He looks up and sweeps his gaze from one face to another and smiles slyly. "Anybody know if a burnt tongue works like a gag?"

He proceeds to pour two more as Rhea growls, "You're an ass!"

He glances at her as he heads toward the table. "And you're a pain in it." He sets both cups on the table; one in front of Shae and one in front of Sky as he drops a kiss on her head. "Be careful, Blue, it's hot. If you burn your tongue, let me know and I'll cool it off with mine." She smiles so sweetly at him it makes my heart melt. He adores her. The two of them will make the most beautiful four foot tall two-year-olds I've ever seen.

Jaxson stares at me. Well, sort of. His gaze takes intermittent trips from my eyes to my chest as his brows rise. The longer he stares, the harder my nipples get. It's a tease, isn't it? He's reminding me how much he enjoyed . . . until his brows furrow. Simon has his back to me as he sips his coffee at the counter. Carl sits sideways in his chair and stares out the sliding door. Rhea's smile shines like a beacon as she holds her hands up to her boobs, finger-guns me and says, "Bang, bang." I whirl around quickly and hightail it back to my bedroom to put on a bra.

Living with only Oscar has made me careless, not to mention a little carefree. He's never complained about my scanty jammies, whether or not I wear a bra. Oscar doesn't even care if I shave my legs or not. I think it took me two months to put a razor to my legs after Ben died. It just didn't matter. Other than when my dad and Trent visited to approve my purchase of the house, I haven't had men in my home before I was up and dressed for the day since my husband. Lesson learned.

I reenter the kitchen, this time with the proper two layers covering still taut nipples but hidden much better. I'm greeted with a cup of coffee being offered by a hand that I recognize probably more than I should.

"Thank you." I take my first sip and moan lightly, the hot liquid coating my throat in the most delectable way. It's fixed perfectly with a slight touch of cream. "How did you . . ."

"Last week." He winks. That's right. We had coffee after the night at the beach. He remembers how I take my coffee. Gold star for you, Mr. Callum.

"I need to call Dr. Lancaster to check on Oscar," I inform him.

He arches a brow as he emphasizes, "*Doctor* Lancaster? Not *Todd*?"

I feel all eyes in the room watching our exchange with slight amusement. My grin is playful as I match his arched brow. "You're not jealous, are you, Jaxson?"

His voice is low and his gaze is heated as he states, "I may be feeling a little territorial."

"Territorial?" I scrunch my nose. "You're not going to pee

on me, are you?"

The room bursts into laughter. He shakes his head slowly and his lips twitch  before he takes a step closer and brushes his knuckles over my cheek and his thumb over my bottom lip. "That mouth."

"We're southern belles, Jax," Rhea chirps. "We're not as discerning about what comes out of our mouths as we are what the male species begs to put in them."

"Rhea!" I gasp and glare at her as do my other two besties.

Jaxson simply closes his eyes and breathes a sigh. "Does she ever shut up?"

"When she's asleep," Shae offers. "Unless snoring counts."

"I'll bet Brick put gags on her," Simon grumbles as he walks to the front door to answer the chime that alerts us to Dusty and Brick's arrival. The two men enter the kitchen carrying three bags from *Roll Me Over* filled with carb lovers' dreams, and a Styrofoam tray for Carl with a special order of biscuits and gravy.

Dusty greets Shae with a warm hug and a loving kiss. Brick picks Rhea up off her feet and she wraps her legs around his middle. It's sweet, enchanting, heartwarming. Every one of my friends are in love. I've been where they are. Maybe someday I'll be there again.

Rhea pouts as she tells Brick, "Simon thinks you put gags on me."

Brick laughs loudly. "Aw, baby. Have you been telling people about our kinks again?" He holds his face back from hers, winks and smiles that boyish smile that wins her over every time, waits for her to giggle, then kisses her hard. He squeezes her tightly to him once again and shoots Simon and scathing glare over her shoulder mouthing, *"knock it off".*  Simon only chuckles and proceeds to dig into the bags of baked goodness.

Slipping back to the bedroom, I make the call.

*"Lancaster Vet Clinic."*

*"Hi, it's Sasha Taylor. I called to check on Oscar."*

*"Ah, Sasha. Dr. Lancaster wanted to speak with you. Hang on."*

*"Sasha,"* Dr. Lancaster greets me in a way that immediately puts me at ease. *"Oscar looks really good this morning. I removed his breathing tube and I'm going to lower his dosage of sedatives. He should be more alert soon. Should have him up and walking within the next couple hours."*

The tears find their way to my cheeks once more. I feel myself rocking back and forth as I look up. "Thank you," I mouth to the ceiling. Ben. He smoothed that ear back, he wiggled it to wave at me. He was there last night, I know it.

*"Thank you, Dr. Lancaster. When can I pick him up?"*

He sighs. *"Todd. And Sasha, let's not rush anything. As much as I would love to see you, it would not be good for Oscar. I need to keep him confined and calm. Let's plan on Monday afternoon. He should be good to go by then. If anything changes, I'll be sure to let you know."*

*"But somebody is always with him?"*

*"Somebody is always with him,"* he reassures me. *"Staff in the building for emergency cases, even throughout the weekend. I'll stop in and check on him myself. Promise."*

*"Thank you, Todd."*

*"It's what I'm here for . . . Sasha. I look forward to seeing you Monday."*

The bathroom mirror stares back at me. *"Fairest of them all,"* I mumble to myself. I'm a mess. My eyes are swollen and red rimmed. My cheeks are puffy. Good thing my hair and scrunchies are friends because they're spending the day together. I put on real clothes, my full intention of tossing the dirties into the laundry hamper only to find it gone. Who in the hell would want my hamper? The only other person in here was . . . wait! The girls were in here to help me get dressed after that doctor left.

"Rhea!" I call out to my bestie.

She's at the door and in my room in no time. "What's up?"

"Where's my hamper?"

"In your closet." She steps forward and looks at the same spot my eyes are fixed, noting the empty space. "Well, it was last night. I'm the one who put your clothes in it after the shower incident. Did you move it to the laundry room?"

"No. If I had, I wouldn't be asking you where it is."

"By the way," she singsongs, "where did Jaxson sleep?"

My cheeks flush to a heated crimson. "I prepared the sofa bed for him. You were there."

"Uh huh," she drawls ever so slowly. "Not what I asked. But tell me, is that where he changed from the navy to the gray sweats, too? Maybe he didn't pack extra undies and borrowed some from you." She runs to the doorway and hollers out into the kitchen, "Guys! We got ourselves a laundry thief. Who stole Sasha's panties?"

*If Brick doesn't gag her, I'm going to. That's only if I don't murder her first.*

"Rhea, I'd like to talk to Sasha." A fully dressed Jaxson stands in the doorway, hands in his pockets as he waits for her to leave. It's not a request, she knows it.

Rhea glances at Jaxson then back to me and smirks. "I think we've found our bandit." Her head is tilted back as far as humanly possible as she glares at him on her way out. "I hope that thong is giving you a wedgie."

Jaxson closes and locks the door behind her, showing the restraint of a saint not hitting her in the butt with it. He hasn't gained her trust yet. I know Rhea. She's pushing him, she's testing his limits. She adored Ben. Pretty sure she feels it her duty to inspect every pair of feet that might want to fill his shoes.

Jaxson takes my hand in his. "Come and sit for a minute. We need to talk." We take a seat on the edge of the bed. "Spinner thinks the trigger for your spell last night was Lehner's scent on your clothes. He thinks it got stronger with the steam from the shower. By the time I went in to get my mine, your clothes had already been collected and were in the hamper. I had Nash take the whole thing with him in his truck because the other clothes in it would have smelled the same. It was safer to just remove the whole thing. I'll buy you a new one. I was going to tell you this morning."

"Oh." I suppose it makes sense. I did think he was in the bathroom with me – just no idea why or how.

"There's more," he says softly, but it somehow sounds like a gentle warning.

"More?"

"Sasha," he hesitates. "I need to show you something. Then maybe you'll understand the headaches, Oscar's behavior, sleeping on the sofa . . ."

My fingers fly to my temples as the searing pain strikes again. "Let me," he soothingly orders, removing my fingers and replacing them with his thumbs, massaging my temples. His fingers find their way into my hair, pressing firmly as each digit caresses circular motions in areas that relax and soothe me. He tilts my head back and brushes his nose against the side of mine. "He's gone, Sasha," he murmurs against my mouth. "Find me."

"Don't let go," I hear myself whisper.

"Never," he breathes, taking my mouth in a kiss full of promises; granting wishes I've yet to make, suffusing the hole in my heart with color versus the darkness that had taken up residency three years ago.

# Chapter 47

## Jaxson

"You've done this for me before." She stares at me in wonderment as she breathes deeply. "On the sofa. How did you know what I needed?"

*At least she remembers.*

How in the hell do I tell her? It's acupressure treatment to combat psychological abuse? There are eight points on the skull . . . ten if you count the temples? I know because I've inflicted the abuse . . . but mine was justified? I can help you with the physical pain, but I'm not sure how much psychological damage he caused?

It's not a painful flick to my ear this time. No, it's a pinch. A rather uncomfortable pinch, then a tug. What the hell?

"I've been reading, trying to find the best treatments." *Yeah, I'm going to hell for sure.* "I think you've been suffering migraines." *The deepest, darkest depths of hell.* I take her hand and pull her to her feet. "We need to take a walk outside."

* * *

"Why didn't you just tell me about it when you found it?"

she asks incredulously. I've explained what we found, the steps we took to disconnect it, the reason Oscar didn't want her sleeping in the bedroom. I've explained why we rearranged her bedroom furniture that day. I did not elucidate the communications Lehner attempted after Simon rerouted the wiring – the things he'd said, the instructions, the threats. Some things just don't need to be disclosed.

What I hadn't anticipated was the inquisition mixed with a shit ton of skepticism as she eyes us one by one. "How do you guys know about stuff like this? Bugging someone's house and receivers and wiring?"

Remember when I said Brick is a genius at his job, but often a little late to the party when it comes to social skills . . . or something like that? I take it all back.

"Simon and I used to work at an electronics store before Jax hired us to work for him," he tells her. It's not a total lie; it just wasn't in a store, it was on a ship. And now I'll rescind my statement of taking it all back. Brick has an off switch, we just haven't found it yet. "We were getting a little flabby around the middle and figured manual labor might be better than standing at a counter all day."

Rhea beams with pride, wrapping her arms around Brick's waist. Simon fights wrapping his hands around Brick's neck and instead clamps one on the back of it and leads him away from us. "Better grab that *manual labor* equipment to tear this shit out of here."

Sasha doesn't seem thoroughly convinced, her eyes searching mine as if I might be harboring a secret. *I am, sweetheart, but it has nothing to do with you.* Maybe someday – soon I hope – my life can be an open book. I'd love to have you read it.

Simon and Brick remove the wiring from the outside of the house while Dusty and I spend the next hour inside cleaning Oscar's blood off the oak flooring in Sasha's living room. We cleaned the rug in the driveway – it had already been set outside last night. The floor had been wiped up last night and it was simply a matter of a professional treatment this morning.

After that, it's business as usual in the backyard. The permits have been signed for the pool to be finished. The plumbing will be done next week. Electrical installed after that. Concrete will be poured as soon as they finish. The tile will be set and sealed. If all goes according to plan, in one month Sasha will have her pool installed and Callum Construction will no longer be needed. The bigger question though . . . will Jaxson Callum be needed?

The ladies are spending the weekend together as was originally planned, minus the book signing. "Who needs a hot tub in a hotel when there's a perfectly good one in Sasha's backyard?" *The midget's words, not mine.* We men spend Saturday on motorcycles. Can't say I don't enjoy it. Can't say the idea of a sidecar with a Belgian in it and a blonde on the seat behind me doesn't enter my mind. *Who the hell am I?*

Monday afternoon arrives, after a long and somewhat lonely weekend. We enter the vet clinic together, Sasha nearly running for the desk once we're in the door. Dr. *"Todd"* Lancaster is already at the desk and flashes his pearly whites as soon as he sees her. However, that smile fades when he notes me behind her.

I grin. "Afternoon, doc. How's our boy?" Gotta give the guy credit. His jaw doesn't clench but honest to God, the hair on his neck rises. Must be a characteristic he's picked up from being around animals.

"Sasha's boy is doing fine," he grinds out. Nope, must have missed it – he is definitely clenching that jaw. Bet the sphincter muscles are pretty tight too.

Sasha is so excited she is oblivious to our exchange, bouncing on her heels as she virtually pleads, "Can I take him home now?"

The doc's animosity toward me is quickly forgotten when he looks at her and beams. "Come on back, Sasha."

My feet don't move as she starts for the door leading to her canine companion. I'm just along for the ride, right? I didn't want her distracted on the ride home, able to give Oscar her undivided as much as she deemed necessary. The doc holds the door open for her and she crosses the threshold, but she turns back and stretches her hand out to me. "Aren't you coming with me? He's going to want to see you, too."

Swear to God, I have facial muscles I've never used before this woman came into my life. I didn't have a reason to. But I sure do now. Yeah, I want to see Oscar, but I want to see her happiness a whole lot more. The moment she sees he's okay, the happy tears I foresee her shedding. You know, the ones I need to learn to decipher from the sad ones. Sasha Taylor. My enigma. The puzzle I want to take apart one piece at a time, replacing each one before I go on to the next; exploring, experimenting, savoring every moment along the way.

Taking her hand in mine, we walk down the hallway together. "Let's go take our boy home, shall we?"

We get back to the house – after a five thousand dollar vet bill – at three o'clock in the afternoon. Sasha didn't even blink twice. You can bet your ass I did, give or take a hundred more. Oscar is worth every penny, but five thousand dollars?!

The guys are still working – their day almost at an end. They're gentle and slow in their approach to the truck, not wanting to rile a healing Oscar.

Simon is the first to reach the truck and waits for me to open the door. "Does he need to be lifted down?" he asks Sasha. She nods. He reaches for him and has him halfway into his arms before asking, "Can I do it?"

She chuckles softly as she looks at me. I simply smile and shake my head, amused with the gentility shown by a guy I know to be capable of many things, though nurturing would not be on the top of that list.

"He can walk just fine, Simon," Sasha tells him as he continues toward the house, Oscar held tight to his chest. "He's not supposed to jump for a while but he's good to walk. You can set him down."

"That's alright," he says with a laugh as Oscar licks his face. "I don't mind.

I pull my phone from my pocket as I watch the three of them enter the house.

*Me: Get into that asshole's accounts. Extract five grand. Get it to me in cash. Vet bill. He owes her!*

*Nash: Holy shit! You sure you don't want twenty to cover emotional distress? A court would find in her favor.*

That's Nash. On-call humor 24/7, calm and cool on the outside, friend to anyone in need; compassionate, a ladies man, but don't ever piss him off. He was feeding the sharks Thursday night. It's why he brought me fresh clothes; he'd already showered and changed his own – after burning the others. He knows where to bury bodies or, in this case, dispose of it properly.

*Me: Can you do it?*

*Nash: You know I can. I'm on it.*

*Me: Thank you.*

*Nash: How is our four-legged friend?*

*Me: Doing great.*

*Nash: He'd make a damn good SEAL.*

*Me: Already has a job as a civilian, Nash.*

Two weeks have gone by. My guys have put the fine polish on all the projects outside of finishing the tiling on the pool. Still waiting for the concrete to be poured. It never fails. When you count on the weather to dictate your schedule, you may as well dress for success with Speedos for underwear. Don't forget the scuba gear while you're at it. It has rained for seven days straight. We're not talking sprinkles here and there. No, we're talking seven more days of this shit and somebody better call Noah. We've been called out to brace up retaining walls before they collapse, cover roofs before the interiors of homes are destroyed, move dirt and rock for sink holes to be filled because the state can't keep up. The storm is a gift that keeps on giving. My people are working 12-hour days and we've been on for ten days straight. It's not a hurricane, not even major thunderstorms – just massive relentless downpours and destruction. On day eight the sun finally decided to make an appearance, but the damage is extensive and we continue, even if it's temporary fixes until the ground is stable enough to replace those retaining walls.

In those ten days I've managed to talk to Sasha seven times – late at night, my head on a pillow, the demon known as exhaustion fighting to take me before I've heard her voice.

"How's Oscar?" I've asked for an update every time we talk. I miss him. I miss her. God, I miss her. My arms have never felt so damned empty. I woke up with her in my arms once . . . and it's all I've wanted to do since. I want to wake to that scent of coconut and spicy vanilla filling my senses. I want to feel her feet between my calves, the way her body snugs so tightly against mine. I want to sleep the way I did the night she was next to me; so damn peacefully. I don't want to toss and turn. I want Sasha Taylor. For the first time in my life, I don't want to sleep alone.

"Even better than the last time you asked," she says, chuckling. "I think he misses you though. Would you let me fix you dinner tomorrow night?"

"God, that sounds good," I groan. "We're all taking the weekend off."

She laughs. "I know. Rhea already called me. She had threatened to turn you into the Labor abuse department last week."

"Is there such a place?"

"I don't think so," she says with a giggle. "But you know Rhea."

I refrain from saying I wish I didn't. Rhea's not all bad, she's just a pain in my ass. Sasha loves her so I guess I can *tolerate* her?

"I'll see you tomorrow night," I say instead. "Seven okay?"

"Sounds good."

"Sasha," I whisper, my body begging for sweet relief. I'd take breakfast, lunch and dinner but right now I need sleep and I've got a shit ton of paperwork to fight through tomorrow.

"Yeah?"

"Make it five. I've missed you."

ANNIE MICK

# Chapter 48

## Sasha

Sitting on my patio, Oscar at my feet, I recall the conversation. "Make it five, I've missed you." I've missed him too. We spent two evenings together before the rain hit. Lots of conversation, a couple walks on the beach. Then the state was inundated with storms, causing disaster up and down the coast. Jaxson and his crews have been working diligently for the past ten days without a break, other than to collapse at night in shared motel rooms, only to start again the next morning. It has, however, given me plenty of time to write and contemplate those conversations. One on the beach in particular:

*"No, I've never been married. I've always been too dedicated to my work."*

*"Have you been with a lot of women?"*

*"Define a lot."*

I shrugged a limp shoulder, letting it fall aimlessly. *"I don't know, hundreds?"*

Tongue in cheek, he sighed. *"No Sasha, not hundreds."*

*"How many?"*

*"I didn't keep track."*

*"Any steady relationships?"*

*"No."*

*"Why not?"*

*"Never found the right woman."*

*"When was your last?"*

*"She was this mouthy little thing. Hands of a magician. Now that one…"* He waggled his finger and winked. *"That one was unforgettable."* He stopped walking, tipping my chin with two fingers, his eyes cast with undiscernible emotion. *"Before her, it had been nearly three years."*

*"Why?"*

*"Maybe someday we'll talk about it."*

*"Was it because of a woman?"*

*"No, Sasha, just circumstances. Tell me, were you happy in your marriage?"*

*"I was,"* I answered without hesitation. *"I got lucky."*

He gently placed his arm around my shoulder and kissed my temple. *"I'd say he was the lucky one."*

The moon is full, the sky lit with a blanket of stars. The perfect night to detect a twinkle – see if I can get some answers. I speak to him as if he can hear me.

"I really like him, Ben. It's odd, I know. He's so unlike you. You were always clean shaven, your military haircut, a smile cemented on your mouth, never short on conversation. Jaxson is broody, doesn't talk much, scruffy, long hair, so severe. Maybe that's what it is. I don't want somebody like you. I can't even compare the two of you, other than kindness. He's considerate and gentle, just like you. But other than that, you're polar opposites. He saved my life, you know.

"I'm lonely, Ben. We were supposed to grow old together, have babies. I knew the risks but I never wanted to believe that fate would be that cruel. I'd give anything to have you back. For months I wanted to lay down and die, and you knew I would. That's why you sent Oscar." I reach down and brush back the ears of my canine companion. "It worked. He's a good boy. Jaxson saved him too. I would never leave you behind. I will never not miss you, but I want to move on. I need to move on. I don't want to be alone anymore." I swipe at the cascade of tears as they fall but it's fruitless. The more I swipe, the more they fall. "You will always be my first love. My first real *in love*. But I need that human touch. Please tell me you're okay with this."

Leaning back in my chair, I study the sky and wait. *Nothing.* Five more minutes pass before I narrow my eyes in frustration and huff, "So damn stubborn." As the words leave my mouth there's a sudden whoosh of wind in the trees that startles me and I look up once more. How the man does it, I'll never know but a formation of stars glows brighter than all the others against the backdrop of the black sky, in the shape of a perfect smile. Maybe it's a smirk.

My giggle and cry mix together as I stare at it. "You did that on purpose, didn't you?" One star – the one I usually seek – blinks quickly. *His wink.*

Rising from my chair, I blow a kiss to the sky. "I love you, Benjamin Chase Arkelpaine. You'd better be there waiting for me, just like you promised."

* * *

They say the way to a man's heart is through his stomach, and I am a pretty good cook – especially barbecue. But Jaxson Callum is eyeing me with a hunger far beyond what he had for that New York strip he ate, and he nearly licked that plate clean. Admittedly, the short denim cutoffs and thin strapped, braless camisole tank I'm wearing might be playing a role, but it's hot. Fine, it's hot outside and we're inside, but still . . . Even Jaxson wore cargo shorts and a button down this evening. See? Hot.

"You wore this on purpose, didn't you?" Jaxson nuzzles my neck from behind and squeezes my hips as I rinse the last dish at the sink to be deposited in the dishwasher. Dinner is over and he refused to sit and relax while I cleaned up, assisting me with every last task until it was completed.

My head tilts of its own volition, giving him access to that sweet spot that drives me crazy. "It's what I didn't wear that was intentional, Jaxson." I shut off the water, leaving the long forgotten dish in the sink, and spin in his arms. "Are you going to make me go change," I say sweetly. "Or are you going to help me take it off?"

He studies my face for signs of unsurety, hesitancy, maybe conflict. But he's not going to find any. I'm ready for this. "Off sounds good to me," he says, reaching under my butt cheeks and hoisting me up so I'll wrap my legs around his waist. He glances behind him once inside my bedroom before he closes the door with his foot. "Sorry, Oscar. You take care of the house, I'll take care of Sasha."

I giggle as he walks me farther into the room, gently setting me on my feet. His mouth is on mine before I can take another breath, as if giving me air and taking his own at the same time. He wraps his hand in my hair and bends my head slightly to maneuver the perfect angle. I melt into his touch and moan against the kiss.

"Another label, Sasha," he mutters against my mouth. "Flavor is addictive." He holds my head firmly in his grasp. "You're sure about this? There's no going back." I nod against his grasp. He shakes his head and whispers, "Words, Sasha."

"I don't want to go back."

He leans his forehead on mine and breathes deeply. "I'll try to be gentle."

"You must have missed my label that says unbreakable, Jaxson." I clasp the front of his shirt in my fists and challenge him. "Show me what you've got."

He smirks before he takes the spaghetti straps on my top and twists them around his two index fingers and strips them off my shoulders, down my arms, and pulls the bodice to my waist, leaving my breasts bare. "Game on."

"I'm half nekked!" I shriek, eyebrows meeting my hairline, my damnable southern drawl rearing its ugly head.

He slips a finger into the top of my waistband, popping the button, his voice a deep growl that makes him sound wickedly sexy. "And only half as *nekked* as you're about to be."

"When do you get naked?" I huff, though without resistance

against his smooth handling of my attire.

His hands continue to free me of my wardrobe as easily as if he were pouring me coffee. "As soon as you undress me, Sasha."

*Salsa tongue – meet nether regions.*

"It's not a race, you know," I grumble as I reach for his shirt button.

"Good thing." He laughs playfully, then picks me up and out of my cut-offs that have fallen to the floor and tosses my thong-covered – rather uncovered – ass on the bed. "You would have lost."

He pulls the back of his half unbuttoned shirt up and off over his head. *Oh God – just like in my books.* He takes the infamous condoms out of his wallet and tosses them on the nightstand. Apparently he's feeling lucky; there's more than one. He unbuckles his belt and lets his shorts fall to the floor before he lands on the mattress on his knees.

"Uh-uh, big guy," I warn, wagging a pointed finger. "Lose the skivvies."

He stares as his eyebrows rise. "And yours?"

I lift one shoulder in a shrug. "I wasn't the one undressing me."

He smirks and without further ado he stands again and drops his jerseys. *Impressive . . . heavy. . . hard . . . and proud.*

"Good thing it wasn't a race." I wink and smile as I snap the strap on the side of my thong. "I guess I would have won."

He pounces before I see him coming, flips me quickly and lands one hand on my right ass cheek. "Be a good girl, Sasha."

He flips me back over as I giggle. "Will I get more stars if I am?"

"How about I make you see some first?"

His mouth starts a slow path from my lips to my jaw, my neck to my collarbone, on to my breasts where he nips and tugs gently on my nipples. My back arches with every slight sting and pull, and low groans leave my throat as heat and desire build. He is painstakingly slow as he makes his way to his target, whispering words of adoration, anticipation; describing what I do to him with every kiss and touch of his tongue – how he's waited for me. He slides my thong off ever so slowly, kissing the inside of each ankle before laying it back down. His kisses and tongue take turns as he works his way back up my legs.

*"So fucking perfect."*

The man has had me on edge since he had my nipples in his mouth. Between his tongue, his dirty talk, the way he curls his fingers and finds that sweet spot, it doesn't take long for the orgasm to hit.

*"Jaxson . . . I - I'm going to . . ."*

*"Mmhmm."* His low growly hum against my throbbing bundle of nerves sends a vibration throughout my entire body and I explode. But he doesn't change pace, nor does he stop or loosen the grip his mouth has on my . . .

*"Jaxson! I'm doing it again!"*

He's relentless as he continues until my legs have loosened their grip on his head and I'm a whimpering mess. But then he does this little twisty scissory thing with his fingers and hits a spot I didn't even know I had that sets off a whole new round of *Holy Moses.*

I fist his hair in my hands and tug hard. Problem is, I don't know if I'm tugging him to me or away from me. I'm so sensitive I'm not sure if I want more or can't take anymore, but due to the fact my heels are digging into his back in an effort to gain lift, I'd bet it's more.

*"Jaxson, plea- ea- ease."*

*"You don't have to beg, Sasha. Just let go."*

And I do. I. just. let. go.

He's slow to return, savoring every inch on his way. My skin is sensitive with every touch, every kiss, every brush of his scruff that causes a fresh tingle as he works his way up my body. He rises to his knees to reach for a condom on the nightstand. I'm so tired of latex – just ask my little buddy in the drawer. I haven't been skin to skin for so long. Do I dare?

I grasp his forearm before he can open the foil package. "You said a long time, right? You haven't been with anyone?"

His forehead creases as he hesitates. I see the reservation and concern in those silver-blue eyes, but there's curiosity too. "No I haven't."

"So you're clean?"

He nods slowly, that eleven between his brows dominant as ever. "Of course I am. I've never not been clean. I wouldn't risk that with you."

"I'm on the shot," I tell him. "It's generally used for birth control but I use it for regularity because I've had adverse reactions to the pill."

"You want me to go without a condom?" His tone isn't one of suspicion and his eyes are filled with wonderment.

I shrug sheepishly. "It's your choice. I simply wanted to . . ."

"To feel what's real," he interrupts.

"Only if it's the same for you." I nod and swipe at a pathetic tear that has found its way to my cheek. "Tell me we're not just playing here."

He cradles my face in his hand, his eyes burning with emotion. "I'm not playing, Sasha. It's very real. You are everything I never knew I wanted."

He tosses the condom back on the nightstand. "First time for everything," he mutters, then looks to me with raised brows and blows out a breath. "If I don't make it last long the first time, I'll make it up to you the second time. I've never done this without one."

"I can be forgiving," I whisper against his mouth as I take him in my hand and squeeze as he positions himself on top of me. "I'm generous that way."

"Don't be too generous," he warns as he moves my hand away and his hips move closer to his target zone. "Another label, Sasha," he moans as he slowly slides in an inch at a time. "Enter" . . . *a little more* . . . "at your own" . . . *more* . . . "fuuucckk" . . . *and he thrusts* . . . "risk."

"Jaxson!"

# Chapter 49

## Jaxson

She's curled into me – a perfect fit. Her back to my front. Naked. Or is that *nekked*? After what we did, I'm going to go with the naughtier of the two. Oscar is on the floor at the side of the bed. He didn't even scowl at me once we opened the door. Good boy. I don't imagine being left outside the bedroom for three hours is something he's used to.

"Ask me to stay," I whisper in her ear from behind.

"I took it for granted you were going to," she replies softly.

"I will never take you for granted, Sasha." I pull her closer to me and slide my hand against hers, locking our fingers together. "Ask me to stay."

Her voice is light with a hint of playfulness as she puts her own spin on the answer to my question. "How do you take your coffee, Jaxson?"

That's an invitation if I've ever heard one, so I go with the flow. "In a mug right next to yours."

"See you in the morning," she singsongs.

Kissing her shoulder lightly, I whisper, "Goodnight, Sasha."

The melodic sound of her voice rings out before I drift off

into sweet slumber. "Jaxson?" I know what's coming. I would love to make her say it again, but I won't. It was my name she screamed in the throes of passion, my name when she pleaded for more.

So instead, I breathe her in deeper, hold her closer, and relish the feel of this beautiful enigma in my arms. "Still crazy about you, Sasha."

She takes a deep breath and hums softly as she lets it out slowly. "You still make me crazy too."

An hour later her breathing is deep and even as she lies in my arms. God, she feels good here, folded into me. I don't want to sleep. I want every minute I can get with her. Sex used to wear me out, knock me into a deadass sleep for at least a couple hours. With Sasha, it's euphoria. That's not to say I'm not relaxed; I'm relaxed alright. But I could do it again, and again.

*"Chase's been. . ."* Her whimper sounds pained as she moves restlessly in my arms. *"Don't leave. I love you. Chase's been . . ."* Her words are slurred but the meaning isn't hard to decipher. Chase has been? Been what, murdered? Isn't that what Nash said? *"Find me. Find me. Don't let go."* Then she softly breathes a relieved, *"Thank you."*

My stomach roils. I told her I wouldn't be a replacement. She wasn't ready for this. Is she feeling guilty? It's been years! How long does it take to get over a dead husband?

Slowly removing myself from under the blankets, away from her, I roll out on the other side of the bed. Yeah, I remember doing this a time or two . . . or twenty – sneaking out before the sun rose. But I never felt guilty about it. Those were one-night stands, shore leaves, women I knew I would never see again. Women I didn't want to ever see again. Meaningless hookups.

Karma has finally bitten me on the ass. And she is, without a doubt, a true bitch.

Oscar raises his head and watches me as I collect my things. I forgo collecting the condoms on the nightstand; don't foresee the need for those anytime soon. They'll be expired, I'm sure, before my dick shows any interest again. Hell, my dick will probably expire before they do.

I leave the room, closing the door softly behind me, and get dressed in the living room. Finding a pad and pen, I leave a note on the kitchen counter. It's the least I can do. I'm not that big of an ass. Years ago, yes. Today, I'm a changed man, but only because of her.

*My dearest Sasha,*

*I told you I'd wait. Apparently I didn't wait long enough. It wasn't an hour after I'd been inside you and you were calling out his name in your sleep. Last night shouldn't have happened, at least not yet. I wish I could have been the one, but from my perspective, he already was. I've never understood true love, only heard about it once. I always wished I could be that guy. Maybe someday, but you're not ready. I told you before, I can't be a replacement. I'll be waiting. When you're truly ready to let go of him, I'll be here to catch you.*

*Still crazy about you,*

*Jax*

Making sure the deadbolt is set to lock as I close the door, I take one last look around the room. Never have I wanted to stay in one spot more than I do right now. The sting to my ear is harsher than any I've felt before and literally makes me cringe. Even the mosquitoes are on her side. I close the door in a hurry before I wake her with the grunt of pain I feel the urge to release as another bug bites my ear.

The drive home must have been done on autopilot because by the time I arrive, I don't remember a bit of it. I collapse on the bed in a heap of remorse, shut my eyes, and don't wake until morning.

Whoever deemed Sunday a day of rest hasn't been to my house. Restless? Maybe. Paperwork, laundry, site organization for my employees for the next week, and food. Yeah, let's not forget a couple hours in the hot tub and the bottle of Jack next to it. Anything to help me forget, soothe the pain, ease the guilt.

* * *

Tuesday afternoon while on the job site, Brick's phone rings during lunchtime. He grins as he pulls it from his pocket and answers, "Hey, baby. Miss me?" His grin vanishes as high-pitched screeching from the other end comes through loud and clear for anyone around him to hear. It's not intelligible – just ear piercing. He quickly jumps off the tailgate of the pickup, his lunch forgotten, and walks even faster away from the rest of us. "Whoa, Rhee, slow down. Baby, take a breath. I can't understand you when you're all worked up. Start over." His back is to us as he listens intently then slowly turns and sets his gaze on me. He scratches the back of his head with one hand and holds the phone with the other. "Uh huh," he replies as he drops his chin, then looks back up at me, scrunching his face. "Uh huh. Okay, okay. Um, can we talk about it when I get off tonight?"

I start packing my unfinished lunch. There's no question as to what, rather who, they're talking about. But my personal life is not open for discussion; here or anywhere else. I might not be their captain anymore, but I am still their boss. "Five minutes," I order the gawking Simon and Dusty whose phones pinged in unison approximately two minutes ago. "Then back to work." Not a word is spoken about whatever text messages Simon and Dusty received, nor is anything said about the phone conversation between Brick and the screaming midget. We do our jobs, go home at seven, and will start all over again tomorrow.

Wednesday morning isn't quite so calm, or quiet. The howling midget visits the office before I get the opportunity to leave for the job site. She virtually tackles my assistant on her venture into my office without checking in first. Keep in mind, my assistant is male, stands six foot-two, a former marine, and beefier than a grass fed buffalo. The only gratification I get is when she struggles and kicks against his hold as he picks her up from behind and suffers more damage than he does. Joke's on you, Rhea; he wears prosthetics. Titanium doesn't feel very good on sandaled feet, does it?

"Put her down, Tim, she's harmless." He smirks as he sets her on her feet and closes the door behind him. I stand from my chair, turning my back to her, and open the file cabinet drawer. "Don't have time for you today, Rhea. I've got work to do."

Letting her in was my first mistake. Turning my back? A dangerous one. The stapler flies past my head by only millimeters, leaving a nice sized dent in the wall.

"You egotistical, pompous, self-centered asshole!" she shrieks. "What's the matter, Jax, she didn't compliment your fucking skills? Didn't worship your dick enough?"

Keeping my back to her – hell, I have enough trouble looking at myself in the mirror – I grind out slowly, "You have no idea what you're talking about."

"No idea what I'm talking about?" she yells, indignant. "Do you have any idea what she's been through? Any idea what she's lost? And you? You have the audacity to get a little butt hurt because she calls out her husband's name in a dream?" She literally growls in frustration before continuing. "A husband she never got to bury because there wasn't anything left of him? A husband who worshipped the ground she walked on simply because he loved her that much and she the same for him?"

"Enough, Rhea." I don't know if it's a plea or an order, it comes out so weak. I don't need to be reminded I'm competing with a ghost. But it doesn't stop her.

"A husband whose name she had to forfeit because her publisher didn't want connections with the political fallout that might damage their reputation and her career?!"

My ears perk at that piece of info. Political fallout? It sounds too close to home.

"She was broken. It took us months just to get her to leave the house. It took forever to help her pick up the pieces." Her voice breaks as she unknowingly shatters my world. "The day Ben died in that helicopter crash, a big part of Sasha died with him."

Every part of my body freezes with the exception of my stomach, which is ready to heave the breakfast I ate. I turn slowly, the file in my hand dropping to the floor, papers flying everywhere. "I thought her husband's name was Chase."

Rhea's mouth twists as she blinks fast, her eyes searching for anything to fixate on . . . but me. "That was his middle name."

A flashback of initials written inside the rim of a Navy cap runs through my mind. *BCA.*

I step toward the door and stand in front of it, blocking her access. She's in flight mode, and I'll let her fly . . . as soon as I get the answer I already know but need confirmed. "What name did she forfeit?"

"Th-that's not im-important," she stammers.

"What name did she forfeit?" I ask again slowly. My stance as well as my arms folded over my chest and steely glare must not be as convincing as it always was with newbies, because she tips her chin and matches my glare with one of her own.

"Name!" I demand loud enough to rattle the walls, and I watch as she shrivels. In the service we did not discriminate. Male or female, we were equals. Short or tall, a command was a command.

She jumps at my outburst but stands her ground; shaky as it may be. "I've said too much."

My voice is but a low growl as I make it clear she is not going anywhere until I decide how much is too much . . . or just enough. "Answer my question."

"P-promise y-you won't say I-I told you?" she asks weakly, tears rimming her eyes. For a short stack with balls, she certainly doesn't look so mighty right now. I only nod. "Arkelpaine," she whispers.

My knees nearly buckle and my head swims, but before I let her see my weakness I grip the doorhandle behind me, using it for stability, and yank the door open. "Get out."

"Please don't say I told you," she begs. "Don't tell anybody."

Taking a deep breath as I rest my shoulder against the door, gripping the knob tighter, I swallow hard. "You have my word." Every ounce of restraint I have goes into not shutting the door before assuring she's through it, but as soon as she is, the walls shake as the thunderous sound of wood splintering resonates throughout the office as I slam the only divider available between us closed.

Who would I tell, Rhea? I've hated myself for my men dying. I've hated myself in particular for Ben dying. I never knew I could hate myself for loving . . . but I can, because I do. Sasha

Taylor. Sasha Arkelpaine. Ben's Sassy. An officer's wife. The ultimate ethics code violation among men of honor. And I just shot it all to hell.

*What the fuck have I done?*

I told her I'd be waiting, but I won't. I told her I'd be here to catch her, but I can't. No matter how many times I roll her name around on my tongue, I can't make it taste bitter. The longer I go without tasting her, the hungrier I get. The more time that passes without holding her, the emptier I feel.

*She's not yours to have, Callum.*

The leaded glass paperweight from my desk is fisted in my hand so tightly my knuckles are white. I throw it at the wall, hitting the exact spot my stapler landed when Rhea threw it. It doesn't leave a dent though. No, there is now a gaping hole approximately six inches in diameter. My eyes drift to the ceiling. "I swear to God, Ben, I had no idea."

The knock on the door interrupts my thoughts and my voice is harsh as I call out, "What!"

The chipmunks enter single file, eyes downcast, looking more as if they're waiting for punishment than instructions. That is until they note the scattered papers on the floor from the dropped file as well as the hole in the wall, then exchange wary glances. The mood around here has been like walking on pins and needles since Tuesday but they haven't asked. It's a good thing they don't this morning either because I'm literally pulling out of my reserves to keep my shit together right now.

"We're ready to go." Simon eyes the wall then looks to me as he flips his thumb toward the parking lot. "You going to ride with us or take your own?"

What would they think if they knew? How would they feel about their former captain fucking their fellow SEAL's wife? Scratch that . . . their dead fellow SEAL's wife.

"I won't be out in the field today." I tip my chin toward the door. "I want you off the site at four. Be back here to park the truck by four thirty." I'm met with three sets of surprised eyes. "Brick, hang on for a minute. I want to talk to you before you leave." He glances at the other two and shrugs. "Go on," I nod to Simon and Dusty, "he'll be right out."

"Did I do something wrong?" Brick asks as soon as the door closes.

"No," I answer sharply then sigh. "I need you with Rhea tonight. Keep her away from Sasha's until I call you." I glance at my watch – a futile attempt of estimating how long it takes to tear a woman's world apart. "Figure about six o'clock. I'll send a text to give you a heads up, but you're going to have to be on standby and close. She's going to need her but I need a little time with her first." I give him a hard stare and finish, "Alone."

He grimaces and rubs the back of his neck. "What if I can't get Rhea to leave?"

My eyes are cold – a look he's familiar with. I don't blink and neither does he. It's not a power struggle. He knows I need him, he doesn't need to know why. As a little incentive just in case she's difficult. "Remind her that I gave her my word."

He looks thoughtful and a bit confused before he nods. "I'll make it happen." He moves toward the door, stopping before turning the knob. "I sure wish I knew what was going on."

"No talk of this while you're out there today, Brick."

He forces a halfwit grin in an effort to lighten the extremely somber mood. "So I can tell them you gave me a big ass raise?"

"Get to work, Halladay."

He shrugs. "It was worth a try. See you tonight, boss."

Four hours later I walk into Nash Graham's office where I find him on the phone. I'd gone home to use the punching bag in my personal gym. It was that or use his face. Twenty years in the military will teach you self-control, means to control your temper, but I've never been so close to losing mine. He waves a hand for me to take a seat then holds up one finger indicating he's about finished. I close the door behind me and choose to skip the chair, standing instead.

"Jaxson Callum," he says cheerily after ending his call. "A little early for booze, but you can buy me lunch if you want."

"Buy your own lunch," I deadpan. "What I want is the file."

He looks uneasy as he shifts in his chair. "The file?"

"You know the one, Nash." I narrow my eyes. "The file on *Chase Taylor*. If you left it at home again, you can give me your keys and I'll pop on over and pick it up myself." We hold a solid stare for a good half minute or more – neither of us blinking – before he flexes his jaw a few times, blows a deep breath, and breaks it.

"There is no file," he grumbles.

"Because there is no Chase Taylor." I rake my hands through my hair and yank at the roots. "What the fuck, Graham? How could you not tell me?"

"You didn't ask me to do the investigation, Jax." He shrugs casually. "I was under no obligation to report my findings. I hinted a couple of times."

The temptation to leap over his desk and put him in a chokehold is suddenly overwhelming. "You sonofabitch! She was Ben's wife!"

He dips his chin and lifts his brows in challenge. "Say it again, Callum." He waves his hand in a circular motion. "Well, skip the sonofabitch part, don't insult my mother. Key word, *was*."

I sink into one of the chairs across from his desk and drop my head into my hands. "I slept with her, Nash. I slept with Ben's wife."

"Ben's dead, Jax."

I raise my head and pierce him with a glare, my jaw set so tight I feel the burn in my ears. "You think I don't know that? It's the weight of the fucking world on my shoulders until we finish what we need to do."

He tilts his head. "What's after that, Callum? What then?"

I stand and walk to the door, pausing before I open it, my back to him. "Then I'll be able to breathe. Maybe even sleep at night."

"Breathing and sleeping are necessary evils for staying alive. They don't have a damn thing to do with living."

Shaking my head as I heave a pathetic sigh. "Let me guess.

Samuel Clemens? Winston Churchill?"

"Nope." He chuckles. "Straight from the mouth of Nash Graham."

I roll my eyes. "Could have gone the rest of my life without those words of wisdom."

"She made you happy."

"She sure as hell did," I mumble as I reach for the doorknob.

"Jax," he says cautiously, "We good?"

"Still got your six, Nash," I reassure him as I turn the knob and open the door. "Even if I do hate you a little."

"Might want to recheck those codes of ethics," he calls out after me, his voice echoing in the hallway as my footsteps carry me away. "Everything has terms and conditions, even time limits."

"Wouldn't make a difference," I murmur to myself. "She's going to hate me in a few hours anyway."

*I never met her, I wasn't at her husband's memorial, I didn't reach out after Ben's death. I never sent personal condolences, never sent flowers. I never even sent a fucking sympathy card!*

*I was trying to catch his killers!*

*Hell, I still am.*

# Chapter 50

## Sasha

Four days since he left me with a note telling me I needed to move on – to let him know when I did. Four days since telling me he'd wait, that he'd be there to catch me when I fell. Too late, Jaxson, I've already fallen. Good going, Sasha, you hit the ground running. Unfortunately, you landed flat on your face. And here you sit; bruised, battered, and broken.

Sunday was spent wallowing in self-pity, Oscar by my side. I swear he has eyebrows. They lift when he's listening intently, furrow when the subject turns sour. I pretty much spent Monday doing the same thing; no desire to open my laptop, no desire to cook or clean. I couldn't recall any dreams. Probably confused the hell out of him wondering who *Ben* is. Or have I conditioned myself so well that I called for Chase? My mom called me Monday afternoon just to chat. I didn't share the deep dark secrets of the weekend, but the next thing I knew, Rhea was at my door with Ben and Jerry's – three pints no less – and four lobster rolls with fries from the Crab Shack. *Moms always know.* No Shae, no Sky – until Tuesday. Rhea stayed until this morning; give or take a couple errands to run, and now I'm by myself again. By Wednesday evening, I've surrendered to the blinking icon on my laptop and shut it down when my doorbell chimes.

I didn't think my world could implode any more than it already had. How much more can someone take from you when you don't have any more to give? How can you look forward to a tomorrow when your yesterdays hold you in their grasp? How can you start over when your past keeps pulling you back? How do you let go when there's nothing to land on?

"Can we talk?" His voice is so soft and pleading, the fleeting thought of turning him away I had moments ago dissipates and I open the door fully to let him in. He studies Oscar for a moment, then brushes the tips of his fingers over his head and lightly trails his thumb over the heart on the bridge of his nose. I wait for the usual 'good boy', but it doesn't come. His lips roll between his teeth in a flat line as that famous Callum eleven forms between his brows.

"I think we'd better sit down, Sasha." Oh God. No more salsa dance on his tongue. He says my name like everyone does.

"What do you want, *Jax*?" I emphasize using only half of his – the way everyone else does. If I can suffer, so can he. Apparently it works because he squeezes his eyes closed for a moment before he gently takes my elbow and leads me to the sofa. He doesn't sit beside me though – he kneels in front of me.

"I have never seen a man's face light up the way his did when he talked about you," he starts, taking my hands in his, studying them instead of making eye contact. "You were his favorite subject. He never told us what you did, never told us your real name. He never called you Sasha. You were only ever his Sassy. I swear to God, I didn't know."

He leans his forehead into my hands that he holds as I try to catch my breath. "I swear to you, Sasha, I had no idea. I would have never approached you if I had."

"Wha – what ?" I yank my hands from his grip and try to scoot farther away, but there's nowhere to go. He places his hands on my knees as if to hold me in place.

He looks up at me from his knelt position. I swear I see his eyes rim with tears and hear his voice break as he whispers, "I was Ben's captain."

"No," I gasp in denial as I stare at the man in front of me. I had never met him before that day on my patio. My brain scatters to recall Ben ever saying Captain Jax or Captain Callum over the four years we were together. He only ever referred to his commanding officer as "Cap". And I've gone and fallen in love with the man. I slept with him; the repercussions of which . . .

"Sasha, we didn't know."

I lift my eyes to meet his, my heart not prepared for the blow that I know is coming. "And now that we do?"

He props up high on his knees, wrapping my hair in his hands, pulling me to him, and captures my mouth in a searing kiss as if he can't help himself. It's one I'll never forget, because that's what it feels it's meant to be. Not to be forgotten . . . because it's the very last one.

The kiss over, he releases a deep sigh and leans his forehead on mine. "Ben and I were two men given the privilege of loving you, but only one of us ever had the right to. I'll miss you, Sasha Taylor," he whispers; *the salsa dance with my name returning*. He kisses my forehead, holding his lips there as he breathes deeply then murmurs, "It's been an honor, Sasha Arkelpaine." *The salsa dance gone.*

He rises to his feet, takes one last lingering gaze into my eyes then turns his back to me, making his way to the door. Oscar follows and he bends to pat him on the head. "Guard Sassy." I'm suddenly taken back to the parking lot at the hotel in Florida. If only I knew then what I know now:

*Jaxson Callum knew the best part of my life without ever knowing me.*

The door closes behind him and so does my heart.

I curl into myself on the sofa, racked with sobs – memories of a life that once was, a new one I thought held promise, and the reality that is mine. I have no landing place.

*Oh God, Ben. I'm so sorry. I had no idea.*

Shouting from outside comes from a familiar voice before

the front door flies open and moments later Rhea rushes in. "Sash?" she says tentatively as she makes her way to my side. The door opens and closes again. Not sure who it is but I'm pretty sure who it isn't.

Rhea engulfs me in her arms. No idea how she does it, as little as she is, but she's mastered the art. "What did he do?"

"Jaxson was Ben's captain," I sob into the knees I have folded against my chest.

"What?!" Rhea wheezes.

"*Holy shit.*" I raise my head from my knees as Rhea whirls hers toward the gasp. "You're Ben's Sassy?" Brick stares wide-eyed with his jaw agape, then turns to my four-legged friend. "That really is Oscar? I'll be damned, Simon was right."

Rhea and I stare – her through flared angry eyes; me through blurry, bloodshot ones. "Oh no," Brick breathes worriedly as his eyebrows furrow. "I gotta find Cap."

"Excuse me?" Rhea snaps.

"Rhea, baby listen." Brick holds his hands up defensively as an alarm rings in his pocket and his eyes nearly bug out of his head. It sounds like . . . a siren. *Oh God, I've heard that ringtone before.* He pulls the phone from his pocket and stares at the screen. His breaths quicken as his shoulders rise and fall and a look of sheer determination paints his face. He nearly growls before pocketing his phone, "Showtime."

"Rhea." Brick's plea is desperate as he holds out his arms to the woman he loves. "Come kiss me goodbye, baby." He winces. "Please."

She only scowls before I grab her arm. "Go kiss the man and make it good enough to last for a while." She stares at me, her eyes filled with unsurety and distress. I tilt my head sharply in Brick's direction. "Do it, now."

He meets her halfway and picks her up off her feet. I don't observe the rest; it's not my place. When it's over and they're both on their feet, I see tears rim their eyes as they both say, 'I love you'.

"Brick!" I call out before he gets the door closed. "That wasn't goodbye. You'd better come home." He nods only once –

the boyish grin replaced with a hard set jaw and steely cold eyes – and closes the door.

That siren ringtone was a call to action. Who the hell have I had in my house for the last five months? *"That really is Oscar? Simon was right? I gotta find Cap?"* Construction workers, my ass.

Rhea and I sit in stunned silence for the longest time – could be minutes, could be hours – before she turns to me. "What the hell just happened?" Her phone rings before I get the opportunity to respond – not that I would have. That ringtone has haunted me for years. Never did I think I'd hear it again. It preceded Ben's last kiss. I just pray it wasn't Brick's for Rhea.

Rhea puts the phone on speaker, her voice nearly cracking as she answers with a with a feigned cheery, "What's up?"

"Dusty texted to cancel our date and now his phone is going straight to voicemail," a sniffling Shae tells her. "I swear his message sounded like he was breaking up with me. He begged forgiveness and said he would someday hopefully explain. What the hell, Rhea? Is he married and didn't tell me?"

"Yes," Rhea replies bluntly as she rolls watery eyes at me. "He also has fifty children. One in every state of the union. Are you done being a dumbass?"

The call waiting alert sounds and Sky's pic fills the screen. Rhea blows a silent breath. "Here we go again." Before pressing the button to answer, she interrupts an upset Shae, "Get your ass over to Sasha's. We'll figure it out. See you soon." She answers the incoming call without ceremony. "Just come to Sasha's. We'll figure it out together. And don't forget the wine."

# Chapter 51

## Jaxson

"They're at Fort Pierce waiting for us," Nash informs me of the remaining SEALs set to join us on this trip when we hop out of my truck after parking it inside the hangar next to his. The chopper waits on the pad outside of Charleston, fully loaded with the gear that's been stored in his warehouse. Simon, Brick and Dusty grab the backpacks from the rear of the truck and we set a fast pace for the bird that's about to drop our asses on old stomping ground we haven't been on for a long time.

I stop them at the hangar door before we head for the chopper to board and turn to face them. "One last chance. A hundred percent head in the game or you can turn around now. No judgment."

Simon steps so close we're all but toe to toe as he arches a brow. His eyes are nearly black as he stares into mine. "I don't play games and that is the last time you get a freebie for a stupid remark, *Jax*. Now, let's roll, *Cap*."

"Yeah," Brick grunts behind him then tips his chin. "What he said."

Dusty narrows his eyes. "Don't forget, dead or not, I get to cap that fucker's skull. Been waitin' a long time." He hoists his bag onto his shoulder and heads out.

Nash shoots me an impish grin. "I ain't worried about 'em. You?"

"Not anymore." I take my first step out onto the tarmac, smelling the adrenaline pumping through their veins as I walk behind them. There's no anxiety here. This is blood curdling, bone crushing anger. Good. It matches mine. More so now than ever.

## *Costa Rica*

"Five houses on the compound," Brick says, pointing to the blueprints laid out in front of us. "Every one of them built out of stone. All of them surrounded by the water with one bridge in and out. However, this entire inlet here is loaded with small boats. Five tunnels leading from one house to another all throughout the compound. Main house has its own helipad on the roof." He looks up and spots us with a wry grin. "Looks like the boss wants a quick way out if he needs it."

Nash and I study the layout together before he takes a deep breath and nods slowly. "Take out the chopper first?"

"After we rig those boats and spread and tie off the wire nets in the water if any don't blow. Not one of these fuckers gets out this time." I turn to our lead intel man since this circus started. "Berkel, any women in there?"

"Haven't seen any, Cap." He grimaces and adds, "They've all moved in after dark though. I can't guarantee it."

"Callum," Nash warns as he eyes me knowingly. "Years in the making here. This isn't a rescue mission. They're not sex traffickers, they're drug runners. Ten to one says they're not comfortable enough to move their women in yet. It's why we've moved so fast."

Knowing he's right, I turn to Berkel once more. "What's the count?"

"Eighteen have slowly moved in over the last two weeks, but Chavez didn't arrive until last night and he had twelve more with him.”

“That’s thirty-one to our ten,” Dusty voices without waver and nods confidently.  “We can do this with our hands tied behind our backs. We got this, no problem.”

I side-eye my co-captain. “Did you hear that, Nash? Not only can our boy read, but he can count, too. You lost the bet; you’re buying his lobster rolls next time.”

Nash chuckles as Dusty glares. “You still owe me five bucks from last time!”

Nash reaches around Dusty’s shoulder before he pulls him into a headlock and ruffles his hair. “Name your firstborn after me and I’ll buy you the whole Crab Shack, Dust. Tell me the southern belle finally turned a hose on your dry spell.”

Berkel snorts. “Dusty with kids? Has our man found a woman who will tolerate him? Whoa, I have got to meet her.”

“You’ve already met her, Berkel,” Brick mutters to himself, studying the blueprints in front of him as if no one can hear. The two in the room that shouldn’t have heard him though, do, and as their eyes meet, a thousand silent *what the fucks?* are exchanged. However, as enlightenment fills their eyes, they show the wisdom of a thousand scholars and remain silent. Brick looks up to see them staring at him and narrows his eyes. “Guess Westminster dog show guy didn’t have such a dumb idea after all, huh?”

What the hell that was supposed to mean, I have no idea, but I’d put a hundred bucks on the table it has something to do with Oscar. I should have seen it. I think I did see it; I chose to ignore it. I chose to ignore a lot of things. I only saw her. Why didn’t I open that damn nightstand drawer? She wasn’t saying ‘Chase *has* been’ in her dream. She was saying ‘Chase *is* Ben’. ‘Find me’. Those were the words I spoke to her. ‘Thank you’. That was for *me*.

*She’s not yours to have, Callum.*

“Round up the scuba gear and the nets. We go in after sundown.” I look to my co-captain, ignoring the questioning gazes from Dusty and Simon. We’re not here to discuss Ben’s *wife*; we’re here to avenge Ben’s death. “Nash, I’ll let you determine the best divers for the job. Simon and Dusty, take out the rotors on that chopper." I lean over the table and study the prints, then point. "Best vantage point is from here. Wait for them to come running to the rooftop and open fire. We'll be on the ground so I don't care who you hit, just hit 'em hard and make it count."

Simon steels me with a firm glare before his eyebrows pinch together.

"What?"

"Any chance we got a ground rocket laying around?" He arches a brow. "Let 'em take off. I promise you, I won't miss."

He wants an eye for an eye. I get it. "Simon, I gotta know that we get him. I can't risk it. He could put anybody on that chopper and take another route out."

He nods once in agreement before Dusty slaps his shoulder. "Come on, buddy. We got thirty-one scumbags to take out. Then Nash owes me a restaurant." He turns to Graham, scowling. "And five more bucks."

"Guys," I call them all in before we head to our designated posts. "We all come back in one piece, come hell or high water. Got it?"

* * *

It is a bloodbath – for them, not us. The body count is only twenty eight, so we're missing three, including Chavez. The perimeter is clear, we've found the tunnels – a total of five – and four have been cleared. Therefore, I wait in the last one. Brick is twenty feet away, Simon and Dusty scour the grounds near the exit. The sound of heavy rushed footsteps draw closer, two men, neither of whom are Chavez but they go down easy. That leaves us one more; the one I want most.

"That's all of 'em," I tell Brick loudly as I put a finger to my mouth, indicating we are not done. "Let's get out of here." We wait and wait. There is no other way out. They know it, we know it. They just don't know we know it. A portion of the stone wall begins to move slowly. I'll be damned; a panic room. Best start to panic, Chavez. You have no cameras, your communications were cut off hours ago. Brick and I move away from the door and out of sight – well, out of his sight. Only one man leaves the room. Chavez. He left the others to fend for themselves.

As he rushes toward us in the tunnel, I step out in front of him; my gun aimed dead center, middle of his forehead, while his is pointed upward due to being surprised and – well, stupid. He may not have shot the ground rocket off, but he ordered it. It was his men who killed Ben and the five others on board that helicopter. "Go for it, I dare you."

The second his arm twitches, I fire my gun; the bullet making a clean entrance; the exit wound leaving a bloody mess of brain matter on the wall behind him. I stare at the body on the ground and mutter, "For Sasha." The sudden juxtaposition hits hard. Since the day Ben died, this had been all about justice for him. Since the day I learned the truth, it somehow became all about her.

"We did it, Cap." Brick places his hand on my shoulder before he spits on the body before us. "Ben can finally rest in peace. Let's get outta here." He turns before I do and steps toward the exit where Simon and Dusty wait, and I follow.

There's a quiet scuffing sound behind me but before they can fire . . .

"Brick!" I launch myself over him to take him down and shield his body from the bullets. Chavez was supposed to be the last man standing. He was number thirty one. I let my guard down. Bullets ricochet off the walls – too many to count – but it's the ones I feel pierce my body that burn. I feel the painful jolt as Brick shoves me off of him and hear more gunfire as well as angry shouting from familiar voices before blackness starts to take me under.

There's a whisper in my ear; a voice I haven't heard in years, *"Sorry, Cap. I had a choice between your ass and your brain. I can only stop so many bullets at a time. Don't you dare fucking die. I am not playing poker with you while I wait for her."*

"Move it, move it, move it!" Simon's deep timbred shout is unmistakable as is his concern.

"I got this end! Let's go!" Dusty's holler is just as loud.

"Med evac's waiting," Graham yells. "Berkel, you got

Halladay?"

"Got him!"

I struggle against the darkness as every sharp jolt fires through my body, but finally succumb to it when I have no fight left.

This must be my punishment . . . for falling in love with another man's wife. With an officer's wife.

For breaking the **Code of Ethics.**

# Chapter 52

## Jaxson

The machines beeping in the background offer no solace nor reassurance as I wait for an answer. We must have a man down. How bad are his injuries? I can't see who it is. I only feel his pain. Everything is so foggy . . . everything but my thoughts of her. I murmur her name and it dances on my tongue, my favorite flavor. *Find me, Sasha. Please, find me.* I slip back into deep slumber, but this time she has my hand in hers as we walk the beach.

"About time you woke up, princess," Nash says as he stands over me. "I was about to go eat fish and breathe on you. Remind you of the good ol' days."

"I ain't taking your leftovers, asshole. Where's Brick?" I groan then cough, reaching for the pain in my side as scenes of the tunnel return. My mouth is so dry my tongue sticks to the roof of it. There's a stabbing pain in my ass as I try to adjust myself.

"Brick's fine," Nash reassures me, holding a glass with a straw in it to my mouth. "Took one to the shoulder. We got 'em, Callum. We didn't lose any men."

"Where are they?" My voice is barely a whisper, my body feeling every ache and burn, but as clarity returns, all I want is to know my men are alive. I reach for the blankets covering my body. "Let me up."

"Whoa, whoa, whoa." Nash pins my shoulders down. "Hang on there, Superman. You took four bullets. Your men are all waiting outside. They've been bunked out here for three days waiting for you to wake up."

"Three days?" I rub my eyes with the heels of my palms, in the process pulling at the IV stuck in the top of my hand and knocking the oxygen tube out of my nose. "Where the hell are we?"

"Fort Pierce," he replies, then smirks. "Your ass ain't perfect anymore but the nurses have had a lot of fun dressing that wound. I've caught a few of them patting it gently and telling you what a good boy you are."

The hair on the back of my neck rises and a shiver runs up my spine. *"Sorry, Cap. I had a choice between your ass and your brain. I can only stop so many bullets at a time. Don't you dare fucking die. I am not playing poker with you while I wait for her."*

"Oh, come on," he scolds. "Your ass will heal just fine. If you'd seen the number of spent bullets lying around, you'd be pretty damn grateful it was your ass, leg, and shoulders that took the brunt of it. A bit of rehab and time and you'll be good as new." His eyes glint with mischief. "Well, that and a war wound that gives you the perfect opportunity to drop your pants to show it off."

I lift a weak hand just high enough to flip him the bird. "Where's Berkel?"

He winces. "He's been checking in quite often. I think he's struggling."

I knew he would be. The count was wrong. Who knows how it happened? They could have come in by way of the water, under the bridge, a passageway they were unaware of. "Tell him I want to see him."

"Will do," he reassures me. "In the meantime, got a few others itching to make sure you're still alive."

They file in one by one – Simon, Brick, and Dusty. *The Chipmunks.*

Brick grins impishly as relief washes over his face. "Do we

get raises now?"

Simon slaps his arm. "Nothing like hitting a man when he's down."

"What?!" Bricks drawls in protests. "I want to buy her a ring."

I drop my head back on the pillow and pretend to snore.

"Good ploy, boss but we know you're awake," Dusty says cockily. I peek one eye open. "I don't need a raise, Nash is buying me a restaurant." He holds his hand out to Nash. "Now give me my five bucks. I saw a Milky Way in the vending machine that's calling my name."

"Have you guys called your ladies yet?" My question is met with furrowed brows after they all exchange wary glances. "What?"

Brick rubs the back of his neck nervously. "Yeah, we called them."

"Why aren't you back home?"

Brick shrugs the shoulder that's not in a sling. "We were waiting for you, Cap."

Simon chuckles. "More like waiting for you to pull your head out of your ass. You need to talk to her."

"Simon," Nash chimes in. "He's got one more surgery to go before he's discharged. They haven't finished with his ass yet." He side-eyes me with a wry look. "We can recommend a cavity search while they're in the area."

I lay my head back on the pillow and close my eyes. "Go home to your women. Carl will have plenty for you to do. I'll get there when I get there." I glance at Nash. "Call the nurse. Tell her I need some painkillers."

Who knows? Maybe if I sleep, I can forget. If nothing else, I can pretend.


I'm awakened by a wet nose and a whimper in my ear. Can't say I'm happy about it. I was so close; my dream taking me to the best place I'd ever been – about to enter…at…my…own…risk.

My eyes fly open at the intrusion and Oscar releases a nice

helping of dog breath in my face. Nothing has smelled so good in days – damn I've missed that dog. But what stands right beside him takes my breath away.

*Sasha. No! She's Ben's wife. She's not yours to have, Callum.*

Her eyes flit from my face to the painful tent under the sheets caused by that damn dream. If she's trying to hide a grin, she's failing miserably as she pins me with a knowing look. "Miss me?"

My eyes squeeze closed and I grimace with the pain as I try to adjust myself.

"You look like hell," she says with a touch of humor mixed with concern.

"Sasha." Her name feels like a prayer, but reality snaps me back to what we cannot be. "Why are you here?"

"Uh-uh-uh," she responds lightly. "You're supposed to say, 'you should see the other guy'."

Oscar jumps up on the mattress with his front paws again and nudges my hand with his nose. Automatic reflex has my fingers lightly brushing the bridge of his nose. I don't have to wonder how she got him in here. I'd bet my left nut he's registered, chipped, allowed on the base before most humans. Once a SEAL, always a SEAL.

"Go home," I plead with the most conviction I can manage with a body full of drugs and pain. "You shouldn't be here."

"Do you not want me here, Jaxson?" She reaches for my hand and I swear her touch alone provides more healing than any surgery these doctors could perform, but I pull away quickly, cringing with how she flinches at my rejection. She soothes my pain and all I do is cause her more.

I clench my fist and turn my head away. "It doesn't matter what *I want*. It's wrong. Go home, Sasha. You were Ben's wife."

"Ah, code of ethics." She chuckles sarcastically. "Honor. I guess we didn't matter enough for you to read the fine print. So that's it, huh?"

"Yes it is," I snap harsher than I want to – it's more for me than for her. "Don't make it any harder than it has to be."

"If I walk out that door, I'm not coming back," she says softly. "One trip was hard enough for me."

"It was one trip too many." I chance one last look into the eyes I will see in my dreams until the day I die. "Go home, Sasha."

Tears rim her eyes as she nods slowly. "Then I guess I'll just say thank you for what you did for Ben and leave it at that. Take care of yourself, Jaxson." The jingle of Oscar's collar as he moves toward the door with his mistress is as loud as combat boots tromping on concrete, but I feel it in my heart. The door swings open and I feel like my one chance at happiness is being ripped from my world.

"Sasha," I call out to her before she can leave. She stops, her back to me. "I need you to understand I don't regret a moment of us, but only because we didn't know. I am sorry for any pain I caused you."

She turns slowly, studying my face for the longest time. "I didn't regret any of it either, until now, because you make me want to forget it ever happened. At least I checked the rules. We wives had a code too. I would never dishonor that by showing up here, nor would I ever dishonor my husband. Goodbye, *Captain* Callum."

358

# Chapter 53

## Sasha

*Two days ago*

It's been five days since they've been gone. The girls are beside themselves with worry. They finally stopped asking questions when they saw the stress it was causing me. I lived this way for four years. I grew used to it, sort of. Reliving it is something I never foresaw. The difference? Jaxson tore my world apart before he left. Brick kissed Rhea like she held the lifeline he would tether to until he returned. Simon and Dusty sent texts that promised they would be back. Jaxson kissed me *goodbye* with no intent to ever see me again.

Navy SEALs. They'd have to be, wouldn't they? How did I miss it? There's a demeanor, a confidence, respect, a camaraderie you won't find anywhere else. Never mind the scruff and long hair. Jaxson isn't just their boss – he's their leader.

I open the door to a sullen looking Nash Graham, then see Simon beside him. My hand flies to my mouth as the air leaves my lungs. I've seen these looks before. They've come to tell me Jaxson is gone. I've been here, done this. They just aren't in uniform and didn't bring a chaplain.

"No," I whimper as my knees go weak, and before I fall Simon catches me in sturdy arms.

"He's okay, Sasha," he reassures me. "A little beat up, but he's okay."

"Damn, Sasha," Nash utters. "I'm sorry. That should have been the first thing out of my mouth. I wasn't thinking. Can we come in?"

We take a seat in the living room, me on the sofa, them in the two chairs across from me, and they explain what's happened. Everything they've done was for Ben. Years in the making; tracking, intel, waiting, and finally, revenge. And now Jaxson is in the hospital post-surgery, still unconscious.

"Jax has been fixated on this since the day Ben died." Nash heaves a sigh. "It's why we weren't at his service. We were in the field trying to catch them before they went into hiding. We were supposed to be back two days earlier but didn't make it. Jax and the rest of us have never forgiven ourselves for that."

My eyes flit from one to the other. "Did you know who I was?"

Simon scowls as he glances at Nash then back to me and softens. "I didn't."

Nash pinches the bridge of his nose before he looks back up at me. "I've known for a while." He scrubs his face in frustration. "Sasha, Jax is a grumpy bastard. You made him happy. I weighed the pros and cons of telling him so damn many times and the cons won every time. You gave him something he'd never had. I couldn't take it away."

"What was that?"

"Something to look forward to, a real smile." He shrugs sheepishly. "Then I looked further into the code of ethics. You're not off limits. Ben has passed. Those same rules don't apply. You're welcome to check them yourself."

"Did you tell him that?"

He shakes his head. "The timing wasn't right. When we're

on a mission, it's tunnel vision. Maybe I should have, I don't know." He dips his chin and lifts a brow. "I will tell you this though, Jax was calling your name before he went under. He needs you, whether he knows it or not. Will you come back with us?"

"Where?"

"He's in Fort Pierce."

My throat tightens so fast, I'm afraid if I try to swallow I'll choke. Fort Pierce. The one place I swore off years ago. The land of misery and memories. Oscar leaves the attention he's getting from Simon and is by my side in no time.

Nash must notice my discomfort because he drops to his knees in front of me and takes my hands in his. "We'll fly in by helicopter, take Oscar with us, and go directly to the hospital. I know this can't be easy for you, but I'm asking you to help me save my friend. Talk to him, hold his hand. We can't get him to wake up."

"How soon do we need to leave?"

"As soon as you can pack a bag," Nash says. "The helicopter's waiting."

"I'll take Oscar out for you," Simon offers. "Have him do his duty and then we can take off."

"Hel-helicopter! I don't know how he'll do on a helicopter, Simon."

He laughs and ruffles Oscar's fur as they head for the sliding doors. "He'll do just fine, Sasha. It won't be his first time." He looks down at Oscar with the brightest, biggest smile I've ever seen him wear. "You ready to fly again, buddy?"

*Oh my heart.*


I've sat by his bedside for the entire first day, held his hand, talked to him about walks on the beach, kissed his forehead. I spent the first night in the room with him. Talk about a battle with the staff regarding privileges. If it weren't for Nash, they would have booted me out of here and off the base entirely – dognapping Oscar at the first opportunity. Something must have worked because after one chat with a couple doctors on staff, I've been treated like near royalty since, with the exception of a few nurses that really seemed to enjoy dressing Jaxson's wounds.

Nash took me to quarters where I could shower and brought me a meal. Simon took care of Oscar for me. Former lieutenant – now Commander – Berkel was delighted to see Oscar again.

And then my day of reckoning arrived. *"Goodbye, Captain Callum."* There is no more Jaxson, no more salsa dance on his tongue. He doesn't want me. I will always be his mistake – another officer's wife.

As I'm exiting the hospital – Oscar's leash in one hand, my bag in the other – Nash is walking in. "Sasha, where are you headed?"

By sheer determination and soul crushing anger, as well as an agreement with myself that I will no longer cry, I simply answer, "Home. You can either have arrangements made in the next half hour or I will rent a car. You brought me here, Nash, the least you can do is get me back."

He clasps firm hands on my shoulders. "Sasha, wait." Big mistake, Nash. Given my emotional state and his fast moves, Oscar once again proves I am his priority. His teeth are bared, the warning bark is given but Nash doesn't pay heed fast enough. Oscar is between us and has Nash flat on the ground in seconds, standing on his chest. It's a good thing I've a hold of his leash. I yell his command and he retreats, leaving a breathless Nash on the ground with his hand over his chest.

"Holy shit," he breathes hard, relieved.

"So, Nash." I loosen my hold on Oscar's leash and remind him of his vulnerable position as I narrow my eyes. "A fast flight or do you call for a rental car?"

"I'll get you a chopper. The chipmunks can head back with you." He rises to his feet, keeping a wary eye on my guardian. He shakes his head and rolls his eyes. "What did that dumbass do?"

# Chapter 54

## Jaxson

Sasha left, taking my heart, my future, and every hope of happiness with her. *No, she didn't leave, asshat – you sent her away.* She wasn't unbreakable after all. I saw it in her eyes. I broke her. God, I wanted her to kiss me, even if for one last time.

*"I had more faith in you than that, Cap."*

That same voice; the one from the tunnel. I must be dreaming. I hear the machines beeping, I feel the pain pump button in my hand. I push it once, twice, three times. I can't get too many drugs out of it – it's controlled – so I must not have enough.

*"Don't bother," the voice says. "I ain't letting you out of this."*

Reaching for the call button, I press it hard over and over. Maybe the pump is broken or I administered too much. Whatever the case may be, I need the nurse to fix it.

*"Don't bother with that either," it taunts. "I disabled it. You know, for a guy I held in such high regard and thought was so smart, you sure are a dumbass."*

"Ben?" I look up at the ceiling, searching for the voice I'm sure is in my head. Maybe it isn't the drugs – maybe I have died.

*"On your left, ol' man."*

I slowly turn my head in the direction he's ordered and nearly shit my pants. Ben Arkelpaine, as I live and breathe, is sitting in the chair against the wall. I blink fast and do a double take. "Ben? Is that really you?"

*"I'd love to say in the flesh," he says as he holds his hands out and laughs. "But ethereal is the best I can do these days."*

"I'm sorry, Ben," I whisper. "So damn sorry you died."

*"Oh quit." He waves a hand in the air. "Shit happens. It wasn't your fault." He tips his chin toward the door. "She's really something, isn't she?"*

Looking away in shame, I whisper, "I didn't know she was your wife."

*He chuckles. "That was the plan. If you had, you wouldn't have fallen in love with her. As it was, you sure were taking your sweet time with that job up in Charleston. I was starting to think you were enjoying that hag shaking her goods in front of you. I'd considered setting Sassy up with Nash, but that guy's got a thing for fish that I never did figure out. He's a good guy, but I'm afraid his dick is going to shrivel up by the time he's fifty from overuse. Yours is still working, isn't it?"*

"My dick works just fine." I shoot him a death glare until it dawns on me it's fruitless; he's already dead. It then dawns on me, I'm talking to a dead man. And he's talking to me! It's the drugs; has to be.

*"Oh! Before I forget, good on you! Two dead center forehead shots." He gives me a thumbs-up. "Guess the old man's still got aim even if he doesn't have game. You saved my Sassy. Kinda wish you'd gotten there before that asshole shot Oscar, but you saved him nonetheless so no hard feelings. And you got Chavez."*

"You saved my ass in Costa Rica," I breathe, recalling the voice in my ear.

*"Eh." He tilts his hand back and forth. "Technically, I saved your life in Costa Rica. Your ass has a hole in it." He smiles cockily and holds up a finger. "Good thing they patched the correct one. You were already anal retentive as it was. You'll heal though.*

*Now, you can concentrate on what matters most."*

"Meaning?"

*"Sassy," he says as if I should know.*

The air leaves my lungs in one huge sigh and I cough once again. "She's your wife," I grind out for the hundredth time since I found out. "You know the code."

*"She was my wife in the flesh and blood life," he corrects me. "She's not technically my wife anymore, Cap. The rules don't apply once I'm dead. You're the first man she's been with since I died, you know. That says a lot about you."*

"Wait . . . wait a minute." I hold up a hand while my stomach roils. "You weren't there when we . . ."

*"God no!" he exclaims on a shudder. "I'm not a masochist. Dying once was enough for me. Seeing Sassy happy is one thing. Seeing Sassy in the throes of . . ." He shudders again. "I'm not a pervert, Cap. Just a man who wants to see her happy again. I left her behind to pick up the pieces on her own. Not intentionally, mind you." His voice is wistful as he sighs. "She's got so much love to give and she's been so miserable. She's suffered more than anybody."*

"Did it hurt?" I study his face for hidden truths. "The explosion?"

*"Nah," he says, sounding as if he's reassuring me. "One minute I was flying, the next I was floating. Have been ever since. But the thing is, Cap, I don't want to float anymore. I'm tired. I want to rest in peace. I don't think I can do that until I know Sassy is taken care of. I worked hard to get you to South Carolina." He shakes his head and chuckles. "What in the hell were you thinking wanting to set up shop in the Keys? Those blue hairs would have been dropping right and left from palpitations. Probably fakin' chest pains just to get you to pump their titties and give 'em mouth-to-mouth."*

I roll my eyes. "What do you mean to get me to South Carolina?"

*"You and Nash both," he says. "Well, and the chipmunks. They all needed to start tuckin' 'em in anyway. I knew Sassy's*

*friends would be good for them. Nothin' like a Southern belle to bring a man to his knees."* He pauses and grins. *"Or his senses."*

"Ben," I whisper, my voice low and apologetic.

*"Hey! It's my turn. I don't have many left,"* he confesses. *"I'm tired of shifting trucks outta park into neutral, catching bullets, flickin' you guys' ears."* He rolls his eyes and groans, *"Mosquitoes, oh please."*

I stare at him in amazement. "That was you all along?"

*He smiles mischievously. "Somebody had to make you mind your manners. I knew my Sassy would be good for you. Moreover, I knew you'd be good for her. I wouldn't trust just anybody, Cap. I saw the way you looked at her the first time you laid eyes on her. Then you made an ass outta yourself, but you were back the same day to apologize. Captain Callum took flowers to a woman. Will wonders never cease?" He laughs. "I knew she had you right then and there. She's like that, you know? One day you think you've got it all. Then you meet Sassy, and you realize you're only half the man you could be because she would make you whole. Am I right?"*

A slow nod joins the pitiful huff I release. "Yeah, you're right."

*"She loves you, Jax. I know Sassy. She used to look at me that way."* He waves a hand in the air in what I determine as defeat but I'm quickly corrected when he says, *"I don't mind. It makes me happy. I want the best for her. That's you. I'll give you one week in this bed to heal. Pull your head outta your ass and go after the best thing that's ever happened to you. I loved you both. Now, go love each other."*

"You don't think I'm too old for her? You're okay with this?" I strain to sit up a little straighter and he stands from his chair to walk to the side of my bed, leaning over me.

*"I'm more than okay with this, Cap. She'll keep you on your toes."* He eyes me with the impish grin that was always associated with Ben Arkelpaine then points his finger hard. *"But be assured, she is only on loan to you in this life, because I promised her the afterlife. And you can bet your ass I will be waiting for her. Got it?"*

"I'll do my best, Ben. I promise."

*"It was always enough for your men," he says. "Just love her, Jax. It's so easy to do. Make her happy. It's all I ask."*

"Am I going to see you again?"

*"No." He shakes his head and smiles. "And as far as anyone else knows, you never did. It's time for me to go home and wait. I think I'll rest for a while. A nap sounds pretty good right now. Take care of yourself, Cap."*

I hold out my hand to shake his and while I feel the slightest tingle in my skin as we make contact, there is no actual grip. He walks toward the door and vanishes through it. I'm left breathless, dizzy, shocked, and awed. I was just given a gift I hadn't realized I needed – a chance to apologize to Ben.

I need one more. Sasha. No: *Sausha.*

ANNIE MICK

# Chapter 55

## Sasha

Not one chapter or page, or even a line. Can't say I've even opened the laptop in weeks. No drive, no desire. I've got a story in my head – a story in my heart as well, but I feel broken. My head is so full of thoughts, I can't separate one from the other and my heart is so shattered, I'll never be able to piece it back together. I had always held out hope that maybe someday I could fall in love again. Now? I want to sink under the covers and hide. Maybe build a blanket tent like we used to do as kids at grandma's house. The problem is, grandma isn't here to bring me cookies and milk.

Oscar and I sit on the patio under a blanket of sky tonight. It's warm. I can hear the ocean waves if I listen closely on nights like this. Maybe I'll find some solace with a light breeze and a wink from the twinkling stars above. Everyone's left – their need to try and feed me, soothe my tired and aching heart via barbecue and friendship fulfilled. I hear the car doors close and engines start out front as they head for home. My three best friends and the loves they've found. I'm happy for them, I really am. It's a bit uncomfortable on nights like these. The ladies stay crowded around me while the guys look like sad, forlorn puppy dogs waiting to take a bite of their favorite treat, but don't dare for fear Sasha may feel left out.

Oscar rises from his place beside me and walks toward the side of the house where everyone had gone to exit through the gate; probably doing a security check of the yard as is his usual. I hear the quiet jingle of his collar when he makes his way back to me.

"I have only been terrified two times in my life." *Jaxson.* He must have come in the gate as the others were leaving. "The night in your front yard when he held that gun to your head was one of them. Knowing all it would take was one wrong move and I could lose you forever. That was the night I realized I was in love with you." His voice cracks as he continues. "I had been on so damn many missions, but suddenly that became the most important one in my life."

"What was the other?" I keep my back to him – glued to my chair for fear my legs won't hold me up – and wait for him to tell me it was the journey he just made to avenge Ben's death, maybe a military coup involving heavy artillery fire.

"Right now," he answers instead. "Terrified you won't give me another chance. Afraid you won't be able to forgive me for hurting you. Scared to death I will never find a way to fill his shoes."

On my feet without hesitation, I find that strength I need and round the table to make my way toward him. He's trimmed his facial hair, his hair is tied back into a neat ponytail. He wears his usual blue jeans with an untucked button down rolled at the sleeves. He's using a cane for stability.

"I don't want you to fill his shoes, Jaxson," I gently scold, "I want you to walk in your own." I reach for his beard, incapable of resisting, and run my fingers through it, holding back the tears that rim my eyes. "Ben was my first love, I want you to be my last."

He gazes into my eyes, his pleading forgiveness. "I'm sorry, Sasha. I never meant to hurt you. Exploring any options never occurred to me. The pain and shock from both directions was just too much. I felt like I'd let you both down."

"I know," I whisper, having felt exactly the same things he

had. But since then I've reread Ben's letter multiple times. He told me to move on, to not be afraid to love again. I also checked the code of ethics. We did nothing wrong.

"I'm new at this, Sasha," he confesses. "I'll do better. I'm a grumpy old asshole."

"You're not an asshole," I protest, then sniffle.

He palms my cheek with his free hand, that eleven of wisdom and experience creasing his brow. "But I am grumpy and old, huh?"

Dipping my chin to better hide the grin I can no longer suppress, I tease, "You are walking with a cane."

"It's temporary," he grumbles.

"Okay." I tilt my head to the side and straighten the collar of his shirt. "What would it take to resolve the grumpy?"

"You," he whispers. "I know it's fast, but I swear I will put you first, be your last, make every day your best, and be there to wipe away the sad and the happy tears. Marry me?"

Happy tears appear from a place I'd forgotten existed. It is fast, but for some reason, I have not one doubt. "Yeah, I'll marry you."

He swipes at my cheek with his thumb ever so gently. "These are the happy ones, right?" I giggle without measure and nod. He smiles. "See? I'm a fast learner."

Running my hand through his beard, I snicker. "I'm so proud of you. I hear kids can help with the grumpies. They help keep you young, too."

His face softens with a smile like I've never seen him wear and his brows lift in surprise. "You'd want kids with me?"

"I could do a couple."

"Yeah?"

"Yeah." I nod and shrug casually. "Probably don't want to wait too long, though. Wouldn't want you watching their high school graduations on a big screen TV in the nursing home."

His jaw drops as he stares at me for only a moment before he grips the back of my neck and turns my face up. "That mouth."

"Is begging for a kiss."

"I love you, Sasha." *And the salsa dance is back.*

"I love you too, Jaxson."

The cane falls to the ground as his fingers twist in my hair and his arm wraps around my waist, pulling me forward. It's okay – I'll hold him up if needed. He buries his face in my neck after the kiss and holds me – simply holds me.

I open my eyes for a moment to look up and offer a silent 'thank you'. A soft breeze sweeps through the air and I watch as a bright light appears in the sky, blinking once, then shoots straight toward heaven . . . as if to say a final *'goodbye'* – maybe an *'I'll be waiting'*.

* * *

"How bad is the pain?" I ask as I  slowly strip the shirt from his shoulders after he's lifted mine and thrown it across the room. He stands with his legs against the mattress for balance and stability – cane be damned. He took one bullet to his butt, another to his thigh, one to each shoulder ten days ago. Thank God for body armor.

"Not even thinking about it, Sasha." He reaches for the hooks on the back of my bra and in one quick flick, it falls forward and he slides the straps down my arms and palms my breasts. "Beautiful," he whispers.

"So," I say, reaching for his belt buckle, masterfully conquering it as well as the button and zipper in less than ten seconds, "do you want top or bottom?" I slide my fingers under the waist of his jeans and jerseys, and slowly lower them over the bandage still sealed to his left cheek with one hand, while paying special attention to the firm salute I'm receiving from the front.

He hisses as his head tips back. "Why do you ask?"

"Because I want you feeling more pleasure than pain." I lean my forehead on his chest where I drop a kiss. "I want it good for you."

He lifts my chin with two fingers. "You are nothing less than perfect." He lifts his feet out of his jeans one at a time while using my shoulders for balance, and slowly lowers himself onto the edge of the bed. I pop the button on my shorts and let them drop to the floor. He leans his head on my belly, his hands on my hips. "God, I missed you."

I slowly remove the band from his ponytail, watching the hair fall loosely around his shoulders – the long hair one less reminder of what he used to be. Tonight he needs to be a man without memories, without regrets, without agony.

He slides up onto the bed gingerly, adjusting himself so his head is on the pillow. He smiles, running his tongue along his bottom lip, and bobs his eyebrows. "Guess I'm on the bottom. You've got two seats to choose from."

Narrowing my eyes, I take a deep breath and let it out slowly. *So tempting.* "You're still maimed."

His bottom lip puffs in a pout. "Raincheck?" He sees the worry in my eyes, the hesitancy to attempt sex with his battered body. His shoulders can't hold his upper body weight for any significant amount of time, so it only makes sense for me to take the top. He reaches out and whispers, "Come here."

Acrobatics have never been my thing, though I'm not a bad contortionist, so I put my best foot forward – literally – and ease one leg over until I'm on my knees above him, hesitant to drop any weight for fear of causing him pain. His shoulders and chest are in the stages of healing bruises – a mix of purple and green – clear tape over the sutures from surgery.

"How about if I just . . ." I frown and try to lower myself between his legs.

He grasps my biceps and pulls me down on top of him. "Don't even think it." His voice is gruff and demanding as he warns, "I am fine and if you truly need convincing, I will flip you over and take you six ways to Sunday." He slides his fingers into my hair and pulls me down for a kiss that truly is convincing. If he's feeling any pain, it certainly isn't affecting his performance.

I break the kiss and look him straight in the eye. "So, you're willing to enter at your own risk?"

His face lights with every glimmer of hope and love I could

ever want to see in his eyes. "The only risks worth taking are the ones with the highest payoffs. I got you, didn't I?" He guides my hips as he slides in slowly, setting a pace that matches the beat of my heart.

*Yeah, Jaxson, you got me.*

Two hours, two orgasms, a shower, and one settled in Oscar, we lie in bed; my head on his chest because he can only lie on his back or belly – he says he's not a stomach sleeper.

"I'm not going to make you ask me to stay, Sasha. I know how you take your coffee. There will be two mugs side by side in the morning, I promise." He kisses the top of my head and settles in easily. "Goodnight."

I wait in comfortable silence, his soft breath in my hair. "Jaxson?"

He doesn't miss a beat. "Still crazy about you, Sasha."

"You still make me crazy, too."

He hums softly. "Sounds like a match made in heaven."

# Epilogue

## Jaxson

I really did want to treat her to two mugs side-by-side this morning though something tells me the ass crack of dawn at six a.m. is not what she may have had in mind. We were awake until two. Oscar pokes his head up at the edge of the mattress as if to say, *"You coming? I gotta pee."*

I gingerly and very slowly – for her sake and my own – climb out of bed and snatch my jerseys off the floor with the tip of my cane, and edge my way to the door, Oscar following close behind. I slide my jerseys on once outside at the patio table – don't judge! – I'm not limber at the present time. I wait for Oscar to relieve himself, tempted to join him in order to simplify things, but I'll wait until I'm back inside.

Finding his food and the universal faucet that dispenses water – thank you, smartass Simon – I set him up for his morning rations and make my way back to the bedroom, closing the door softly behind me.

*So much better than coffee.*

Sasha may not be a fan of six a.m. but she apparently doesn't mind six thirty. . . at all. Turns out not only is she a moaner, she's a morner as well. Perfect harmony.

Finishing our second cup of coffee on the patio, she sets her cup down and rises from her chair. "I'm going to take Oscar out in his yard. We won't be long." She drops a kiss on my mouth before heading for his exercise course, leaving me to watch.

The doorbell chimes a few minutes later and I grab my cane next to me. There's no point in calling her away from what she's doing – it's probably the midget with full intentions of pushing my buttons this morning. I did slip my jeans on, but I remain shirtless. It's the equivalent of a half muzzle, so she should be somewhat tolerable.

Upon checking the peephole, I roll my eyes to what have to be early morning bible thumpers standing outside. A couple in their sixties with fixed smiles on their faces ready to spread the good word. Must be illiterate as well because the sign is unmistakable.

Yanking the door open I shoot them a harsh glare. "In case you missed it, the no solicitors sign applies to everyone. Pretty sure the owner already knows Jesus, she's not interested in a new roof, and the only things she likes is cookies and chocolate. Since you don't look like Girls Scouts, my bet is she's not buying whatever you're selling."

The man tucks his hands in his pockets; a hard, unbreakable, stone-cold stare as he takes a slow deep breath through flared nostrils while the woman snort-laughs behind him; her eyes making a slow perusal of my bare chest.

"Then it's a good thing I'm not selling anything." His heavy southern accent slips through a clenched jaw as his eyes narrow. "Now tell me, son, where is my daughter?"

*I've read about balls shriveling inside a man's taint. I've heard stories of assholes puckering out of sheer fear and mortification. Mine must be doing something because the gunshot wound in my left ass cheek is throbbing at the moment. Ah, the wrath of fathers. It's what legends are made of.*

The jingle of Oscar's collar sounds like a respite until the man in front of me bends down and greets him. "Oscar! How's my boy?" The tail thumping against my leg as the man pats him on the head is a strong indicator Oscar is happy to see him as well.

"Daddy!" Sasha's delighted shriek behind me as she rushes to the door is one more indicator I've just put myself on a shitlist I may never be able to get off of. Sasha is still in a tank top and short shorts, aka pajamas, because it was just the two of us.

"Hello, sweet pea," her dad greets her with a hug – after virtually pushing me out of his way in the door.

"Mama!" Sasha nearly cries, wrapping her arms tightly around the woman that follows.

"Hello, sweetheart," her mom returns, squeezing her eyes closed as she relishes the hug and returns one just as tight.

"I – uh," I stammer, "I'm going to go put a shirt on."

"Oh, you don't have to on my account," her mother nearly sings.

"Mama!" Sasha teasingly scolds at the same time her father snaps, "Libby!" And of course, mom giggles.

"Daddy, mama," Sasha starts. "This is Jaxson Callum. Jaxson, my mom and dad, Tom and Libby Taylor."

I dip my chin in a humiliated greeting and extend my hand to shake her father's.

"I think he thought we were Jehovah's witnesses," her father says with a laugh as he looks at his daughter, then glares at me. "If he had suspected Girl Scouts, the least the man could do is put a damn shirt on!"

I heave a deep sigh and tell her, "I'll be back in a minute."

"Do you want some help?" Sasha asks so sweetly I can't just walk away. I asked the woman to marry me last night, and she said yes.

Placing a soft kiss on her temple, I whisper, "I've got it." Leaning closer to her ear and mutter, "This has Rhea written all over it."

As I reach the entry to the short hallway to the bedroom I hear her father's harsh yet concerned inquiry. "Sasha Rae, what kind of company are you keeping? Was that man in a knife fight?"

*Yes, Mr. Taylor, I was. Those surgeons' scalpels are a real bitch.*

Two hours, a southern breakfast, a shitload of coffee, and a lengthy explanation later, Mr. Taylor and I sit at the patio table while Sasha and Mrs. Taylor clean up in the kitchen.

"I was very fond of my son-in-law," Mr. Taylor says wistfully.

"So was I, Mr. Taylor." I look him straight in the eyes. "He was a good man. I lost a brother when we lost Ben."

"You gonna love her as good as he did?"

How do you answer a question like that? Going to do it better? Until the day I die, just like he did? I only get her in this life so I'm going to give it my all? I'd like to think so? Damned if I know?

"No comparison, Mr. Taylor," I answer instead. "She owned Ben's heart. And now? She owns mine."

He nods slowly, over and over as he studies his coffee cup. "I guess that's all I can ask. You know," he hesitates. "I asked my Libby to marry me two weeks after I met her. Been married forty one years now."

"Congratulations."

He arches a brow as he looks up from his cup. "You gonna last that long?"

Sweet Jesus, if one more person makes a comment about my age, I'm going to head for Oscar's yard and start running the course just to prove myself. Well, in a couple of weeks anyway. Gotta get the stitches out, finish physical therapy, start working with weights again, and . . .

Pinching the bridge of my nose and taking a long deep breath, releasing it slowly, I finally state, "You could just ask, Mr. Taylor. I'll be forty in a month."

"That ain't what I asked, you dumbass," he snaps gruffly. "I asked if you were gonna last that long. Are you done going on missions? Are you done bein' shot up? You finished bein' a SEAL?"

I fight back a grin. The man holds nothing back. "I'm done with missions and hopefully done being shot up, Mr. Taylor." I dip my chin and answer honestly, "But I will always be a SEAL."

He scrunches his brow and narrows his eyes. "You gonna

give me grandbabies?"

"Didn't plan on making any today. We seem to have unexpected company." I grin cockily and wink. "But I promise, we'll get right on that."

He glares for only a moment. "You a born smartass, son?"

"Nope. Your daughter's been giving me lessons."

His sudden burst of laughter is unexpected but quite welcome as he waggles his finger. "I think I like you. Call me Tom."

The sliding door opens and out pops the villain with a mouth, the triumphant Cheshire cat with a shit eating grin so big I want to stuff it with puppy chow. Behind her walks a sheepish looking Brick with a thousand apologies written in his eyes. Rhea licks her index finger, swipes it in the air and whispers, "Check."

She flings out her arms and looks to Mr. Taylor. "Daddy T!"

"Well hello there, young lady," he returns as he stands and gives her a hug. "How are you? This surprise visit was the best idea you've had in a long time."

She looks past his chest at me and smirks. "You know it. Brains over brawn every single time."

"Oh hey, Brick." I look to my employee who stands with one hand in his pocket, the other arm still in a sling. "Wanted to let you know I need you in Georgia to oversee a project down there next week. You'll leave tomorrow, won't be back until next Sunday. Got them working six days a week."

"Wh - what?" He gasps, wide-eyed.

"What?!" Rhea shrieks. "A whole week?"

"Did I say week?" I scratch my head as if confused, my eyes set on Rhea. "I meant month." I have no intention of sending Brick anywhere, but she doesn't need to know that. Seeing her riled up, if only for the rest of the day, is enough. She really is a pain in my ass.

"A whole month?!" she screams, slack jawed.

I smile and pinch my finger and thumb together, moving them from one spot to another diagonally over the table. "Checkmate. You want to play in the big leagues, Rhea, better plan to win." I smirk and finish, "Wouldn't hurt to grow a few inches either."

# The End

Thank you for spending these precious hours with me. Please consider leaving a review on Amazon or Goodreads. It not only means a lot to your author, but gives you, the reader, a voice in the pages.

# Other Books By This Author

### <u>The Crew Series:</u>

<u>Run To Me</u>

<u>Wicked Lemonade</u>

<u>Find Another Hero: Just Make Sure He Can Dance</u>

<u>Tell Me Why, Jannie</u>

<u>The Fresh French Connection</u>

<u>Old Farts and Pop Tarts</u>

<u>Saari, Not Sorry</u>

<u>The Chauffeur: Phoenix Rising</u>

<u>Manipulation 101: Code of Ethics</u>

# About the Author

A diehard laughaholic who has learned to take everything with a grain of salt, Annie Mick loves to dish it out with a good dose of sarcasm.

If you can giggle while you wiggle, it's added exercise and spares you ten minutes on the treadmill.

It is true that if you can laugh while you cry, the tears are saltier and it makes the margaritas taste better.

If you can find your hero in one of her books, therein lies her success. If you can find a bit of yourself in one her characters, therein lies her joy.

Life is too short to not get lost in a fantasy; if only for a day, if only in a book, one page at a time.

Sweet dreams.

ANNIE MICK